The Bishop's Wife

DEREK TAYLOR BOOKS

THE BISHOP'S WIFE

Gillian Bence-Jones is a landowner, poet and writer living and farming in East Anglia. She is a great, great, great, great niece of Jane Austen. Her knowledge of history and love of nature is reflected in her work.

This is her first novel.

Search Amazon for selections of poems by Gillian Bence Jones and for WINSTON, her acclaimed verse biography of WW11 leader Winston Churchill

The Bishop's Wife

Gillian Bence Jones

A Derek Taylor Book

ISBN: 978-1-326-41385-9

A CIP catalogue record for this book is available from The British Library

Derek Taylor Books
207 The Metropole
The Leas
Folkestone Kent CT20 2 LU
UK

All enquiries to: books@derektaylor.org
www.derektaylor.org
+44 (0)1303 760546

Acknowledgements

I would like to thank Derek Taylor for laboriously typing up the notebooks in which this novel was first started. I would particularly like to thank my editor Ian Grant for his perseverance and painstaking work in editing the typescript created by Derek Taylor. I would like to thank Vicki Davis for her professional appraisal of the first draft. And last but by no means least, I would like to thank Jack Bainbridge for painstakingly copy-editing and proof reading the final manuscript.

Without these people this book would not exist.

I would also like to thank Philippa Bramson for her cover design, Neil Ford for his IT support and John Norris for his dust jacket photograph.

CHAPTER ONE

Number 10 Downing Street

A young man sat reading Quintillus in a comfortable room in 10 Downing Street. Every now and then he smiled which made his regular but rather severe features look much more agreeable. He was wearing a clerical collar. A fire burbled in the fine mantelpiece and a glass of wine stood on an occasional table beside him. The door opened and another even younger man came in. His high colour and snub nose made him look like a schoolboy, but he was in fact in his early twenties.

'George!' Pitt said, 'you made good speed and I'm glad of it. I badly need someone intelligent to talk things over with.'

'I trust I qualify?' asked George Pretyman. 'The senior wrangler doubts his powers? Did they feed you?'

'They offered, but I preferred to wait. Lord Shelburne's government totters?' replied Pitt.

'I had rather described it as being in mid-air, and likely to shatter on landing, and all for the want of a little courtesy,' the young Pretyman continued. 'His Lordship disregards his colleagues?'

'Disregards them, cold shoulders them, and treats them like gardeners. Never mind why. God knows I share his incapacity to suffer fools, but he carries it too high,' said Pitt, pulling a bell cord. 'I confess I am much to blame, I have relished being Lord Chancellor and learned, as I think, something of finance. But even to keep my post I cannot stomach Lord North. Would an omelette and some toasted cheese answer?'

'Admirably, I thank you. I never have banquets at late hours,' said Pretyman.

A servant appeared and took the order.

'How is my mother?' asked the young man.

'Excellent, well, and vastly busy. The neighbours attend her. She walks in the shrubberies and reads, "The Journal of the Plague Year", a gloomy study, I'll be bound. She gambles too. How is Miss Maltby?' Pitt asked.

'She enjoys good health and a good gallop. We agree very well and had I but a steady salary I would make her an offer. I wish now I had kept my Fellowship at Pembroke.'

'You could not marry then?' Pitt enquired.

'No, but I could have saved up and sought a suitable parish,' replied Pretyman.

'We must find you something. I trust I feel the blessing of peace as much as a Christian should, but this American amity grieves me,' Pitt described.

'You grieve for the loss of America?' asked Pretyman.

'Aye. Together we could have done much and amended much. I grieve for the Indians, who we tried to protect and who now will be slaughtered, and I grieve for the blacks who will be enslaved for a hundred years although we tried to free them, and I grieve for the Canadians who will be incessantly assailed and perhaps overrun, for Boston has a rabid hatred of all Catholics and never forgave us for not exterminating them.'

Pretyman pointed out, 'It is perhaps easier to be tolerant of Catholics and Indians when they are not scalping your family.'

'Doubtless it is, but the Indians' record of keeping treaties is better than that of the Americans and in 1783 I would like to think we are grown too civilised to slaughter the rightful inhabitants of a land to then steal it.'

Later, as they ate their omelettes in a dark dining room, George Pretyman inquired, 'Do you not find this massive house somewhat lonely?'

'I do indeed,' agreed William Pitt. 'I am often described as a schoolboy in the House, and in 10 Downing Street I often feel like one. A schoolboy who, owing to a sudden illness, has been left alone at Christmas in an empty school.'

'Can you not invite Lord Mahon, or Mr Eliot, or Mr Wilberforce?' replied Pretyman.

'I can. I do, and they come, bless them, but there are still too many empty evenings. I dearly love to see my friends but I fear I am not a very sociable man,' Pitt said.

'Nor I. Were you with Lord Shelburne this evening?'

'No. I went to see Charles James Fox. We need him. I had a hard task to persuade Lord Shelburne to let me go, and a harder one to persuade the King, and all for nothing.'

'He wouldn't agree to join your government?' Pretyman enquired.

'I rather think he would have me join his government. I informed him straightly, "I didn't come here to betray Lord Shelburne". As I wished not to waste much time I asked but one question: "Were there any terms on which he would come in?" He replied "None, while Lord Shelburne remains". I had hoped he would have some requirements, as I have, and we might work together. He is fire to my ice, but fire can melt ice, and ice can moderate fire,' Pitt expressed philosophically.

'What are your requirements?' asked George, helping himself to some more toasted cheese.

'Well, as you know, I desire moderate Parliamentary reform and have worked for it. We must try to broaden the electorate. Like my father, I wish to retain the connection with America, with less coercion and more partnership. That cause is lost and the world will be the more dangerous for it. But, above all, I am desirous to benefit the destitute. That our countrymen should be hungry, cold, ill-housed, and ignorant, seems to me as unnecessary as it is undesirable in a rich Christian country,' Pitt expressed passionately.

'True, very true, but how to prevent it?' Pretyman replied.

'It would have to be well thought-out on a parish basis. The Church might assist. If each poor worthy family was provided with a heifer calf… but you must be tired after your long journey. Have they shown you your room?'

'Yes. I thank you and I confess my bed begins to sing a siren song, but I can abide another half hour or so. 'Tis a rare pleasure to talk politics and policy with the Chancellor. Have you considered that Fox might now combine with North?' Pretyman proposed.

Pitt retorted, 'Not for an instant. 'Tis little likely after Fox has entertained the house with North's failings these last five years. No, if Lord Shelburne only holds his nerve we shall do very well. He is somewhat prone to sudden glooms and a conviction that the King is betraying him.'

'Why should he?' asked Pretyman.

'Why, indeed! His Majesty cannot abide Fox, and he has found North a frail tool, but what put that into your head? Are you a better politician than all of us?' asked Pitt.

'I know nothing of politics, though you make it all very clear and diverting, but my father, God bless him, though only a poor merchant in Bury, hard put to send us to Cambridge, the younger son of a younger son, was a keen student of human nature. "Consider the men you are dealing with!" he would say. It seems to me, from yours and your father's accounts, both Fox and North have much ambition and little principle. Such men often combine suddenly if it suits their interest. It does not last. 'Tis not soundly based. Both sides are looking around for a better bargain but for a time they work together to shut out their rivals,' Pretyman answered.

'You may just possibly be right. I must warn his Lordship. You had better be my secretary. I have one already, a Mr Bellingham, an army friend of my brother's. He has no duty but that of receiving about four hundred a year, and no ability but that of looking like a lobster in his scarlet coat, but you, with your knowledge of human nature, will be invaluable. I will give you five hundred a year,' said Pitt expectantly.

'I will not take it.'

'Why ever not?' queried Pitt.

'I think it improper in a churchman, and likely to strike such patrons of livings as I must discover it to, as showing I am no serious shepherd of souls. Informally, however, I shall be honoured to help you. Your interest in assisting the poor and my interest in mathematics might complement each other,' explained Pretyman.

'They are made for each other! We will drink to a free donkey for all drunks.'

CHAPTER TWO
Germains

A lady and a gentleman rode side by side through a country lane. On either side were the flags of high summer; great banks of rosebay willow herb, clumps of deep blue wild geraniums, fields of buttercups, and ripening corn decorated with poppies. Another older man, a groom by his dress, was riding a discreet distance behind them.

The lady, who rode side-saddle, was young, and if she was not beautiful, which the gentleman might have disputed, she was certainly very pretty with dark brown hair which glittered of gold in the sun, for she wore no hat. Her eyes were blue with a greenish tinge and small brown flecks. She was tall and well-rounded, without being in the least fat.

The gentleman was George Pretyman. 'It was a lucky strike,' he was saying, 'no more, but Mr Pitt declared himself much impressed by my gift of prophesy.'

'Is it true that he might have the government whenever he chooses?' asked the lady.

'Quite true. The King asked him first in March. The King dislikes Fox and North, but Mr Pitt judges he would not have enough support in the Commons,' explained Pretyman.

In response the lady said, 'Might that not alter?'

'It might indeed,' agreed George, 'a useful man named Robinson, Jack Robinson, brings the numbers to Mr Pitt every month, and last month, June, his probable supporters were near as numerous as his opponents, but those who are doubtful, or who will only support us if they are offered a place or a sinecure outnumber both the other parties.'

'How exciting it must be to live and work in the very centre of things and to hear the very latest political gossip and speculation,' said the lady with excitement.

'I suppose it is,' Pretyman went on, 'but I fear for Mr Pitt often. He is not robust. A fool of a doctor prescribed port when he was but a child and the habit has grown excessively and above all his manner. With mere acquaintances it is not ingratiating, which has made him too many enemies for a sensitive young man to be confident of public understanding and approval.'

'But is public understanding and approval good for the character?' queried the lady.

'It might be deleterious if it caused conceit, but that is a fault from which Mr Pitt is singularly free,' explained Pretyman.

As they rode the scent of elder blossom came in great drifts. Pigeons were cooing insistently.

'Pitt is, at present, in France,' declared George. 'He has long proposed to tour the Continent. Mr Elliot and Mr Wilberforce go with him. They were so good as to invite me to travel with them but I preferred to go to your house, to Germains.'

'We are gratified,' said Miss Elizabeth Maltby, but he feared she said it ironically.

He'd thought it would be easy when they were out riding together, every morning like this. He'd lead up to it gradually; it would happen naturally. But this was the last morning of his ten-day visit and he hadn't led up to it gradually, and it certainly hadn't happened naturally.

They talked politics. She was very interested in politics and quite knowledgeable. They talked history. She was very interested in history and fond of speculating about doubtful points. They talked about the birds they had seen and the trees they passed. She loved birds and trees and had taught him quite a lot, but they never got much further.

He had not thought of himself as a shy man, like Billy Pitt, but there was something about Elizabeth; she was quick, so clever, so…

They came to a gate. It was heavy and it took him some time to get it open. Was she thinking how clumsy he was?

'I'll shut it for you, sir,' said the groom coming up.

They had come on to the common that was full of butterflies and sunshine.

'Let's go a bit faster,' said Elizabeth, and her trot soon became a canter, and her canter a gallop.

Whoosh! Whoosh went the wind in George's ears. He was determined to keep up, but unlike Elizabeth he felt no exhilaration, only endurance, and he'd have greatly preferred a more decorous, pleasant, canter.

They were passing some gorse bushes and out of them suddenly appeared a large, black fawn-like animal with horns bounding straight for them.

When it nearly crashed into Elizabeth's horse and leg it swerved violently and vanished from their sight. But by then the horses had swerved even more violently and her horse had crashed into George's mare, knocking it into some high, green bracken.

What happened next George was never quite sure. The horse somehow disappeared under him, somersaulted round, and he was pitched off with great suddenness, hitting the ground with immense violence.

He heard himself making the most appalling, undignified whooping noise, and then he was fighting for breath. He couldn't breathe, everything was getting misty, colourless. Then, slowly, he could breathe again. He began taking in great gasps of air. The relief was immense. His chest hurt, but at least he could breathe.

'Are you all right?' Elizabeth was asking urgently.

'Yes I, think so. What happened?' George asked.

'Silk put her foot in a hole and you went flying,' Elizabeth replied.

'You were winded,' said the groom bringing back the mare.

'Likely got a cracked rib or two beside,' Elizabeth added.

'But why did that stag attack us?' George asked.

'Didn't! A buck, not a stag, lying up in them old bushes. When you come along helter-skelter, as Miss Elizabeth will do, that woke up sudden, and up and out to get away, right into y'.'

'I'd 've been off, too, if I hadn't been riding side-saddle,' said Elizabeth.

'You'd a been dead too if your hoss had been th' one to put its foot 'n a hole,' said the groom.

George got up. It hurt terribly. 'What's the cure for cracked ribs?' he asked.

'Ain't none. Y' can strap that. Hurt a bit less then; but heals slower,' said the groom.

'I'm so glad you aren't badly hurt,' said Elizabeth.

'Thank you,' said George, touched but very aware he had looked ridiculous.

'I'll gi' y' a leg-up,' said the groom, 'you'll need it.'

Even so, mounting was agonising and a gasp escaped him; at least it wasn't a groan, he thought, not quite.

'We'll walk all the way home?' asked Elizabeth.

'You'll have a long walk,' the groom informed them.

It was a long walk and while if he kept still George's ribs didn't hurt at all it was nonetheless difficult to keep still on a moving horse. He discovered it was unwise to take a deep breath, or laugh, or cough, or turn around.

'How long does a cracked rib take to heal?' he asked Elizabeth.

'I don't know I'm sure. Goodchild, how long does a cracked rib take to heal?' Elizabeth asked the groom.

'Couple o' weeks, so be y' young. One day tha's bad as ever. Next day you wake without it,' said the servant.

'Happy day,' said George feelingly.

He so wanted to show advantage. He'd always considered himself quite a good rider. He hoped she didn't think he was making a fuss.

At last, or it seemed so to George, Germains came into sight ahead of them, a pretty, pink house that seemed to have grown there as much as the trees around it. It was a medieval hall, a Queen Anne front, with a certain number of recent "improvements".

'I'll go 'n open th' side gate for y',' said Goodchild, trotting past them. 'It sticks!'

There was something reassuring, reflected George, about an outspoken old servant. You knew where you were with them. His father had just such a head groom in Bury.

He pulled himself back to Buckinghamshire with a jerk as he suddenly realised this might be his last chance to speak alone with Elizabeth. He wouldn't be able to ride anymore and they wouldn't be alone in the house, with three other people staying.

It wasn't at all how he'd hoped to continue things. There wasn't time to lead up to it gradually, however.

'Are you a coward?' he thought to himself, and then turned to Elizabeth saying, 'Will you marry me?'

'It looks as if I'll have to,' she said resignedly.

He wasn't sure if that was good or bad.

'Are your parents constraining you?' he said doubtfully.

'No such thing. My Papa always says he does not know how he will support losing me. No, it's just that we seem to belong together. Or don't you feel that too?' enquired Elizabeth.

The horses obediently walked slower and slower and then stopped.

'Indeed I do, but I hardly dared hope you felt it too,' responded George animatedly.

'I felt it, but until today I really thought I could not bear to leave everything and go and live in London, but when I saw you lying there and thought you were badly hurt I thought, "I suppose I must love him,"' said Elizabeth with a smile.

'A terrible fate,' said George smiling back.

'It is if you want to stay at home. My mother warned me I could not go on being a girl forever, but I thought, "A few more years" and then "only if he finds a living near here".'

Goodchild was still holding the gate open. They walked through.

'You come to an understanding?' asked Goodchild, as one being patient with children.

'Yes,' answered Elizabeth. 'We're going to be married but don't tell anyone yet.'

'I ain't no gabster. I seen it coming. Wish y' happy I'm sure,' was Goodchild's jubilant response.

They thanked him. George was truly happy already, despite considerable apprehension that dismounting would hurt terribly.

CHAPTER THREE

Wilberforce Villa, Wimbledon

'Are you sure you're wise?' asked William Wilberforce, his usually lively, cheerful face solemn with concern.

'No, but I am sure I am unwise,' answered his friend Billy Pitt. 'I foresee nothing but trouble, late nights, angry voices, contempt, and turmoil. Yet, if I missed this chance I know I should regret it and doubt my courage and my loyalty.'

They were breakfasting late in Wilberforce's villa in Wimbledon, and George Pretyman was with them, as Mr Pitt's Secretary. He was needed, for Mr Pitt was forming a government.

'At least we've got Temple,' said Wilberforce, 'and Dundas. Has so young a Prime Minister ever been known?'

'Never, I am persuaded,' answered George, 'and it seems unlikely there ever will be again.'

'It has advantages,' said Mr Pitt. 'I annoyed no-one in '65 and contradicted no-one in '70.'

'Are you going to call an election?' asked Wilberforce.

'No that needs careful preparation. In the spring perhaps, if all goes reasonably well,' replied Pitt.

'Why on earth did you send Pepper Arden to announce you're taking the Government to the House? No wonder they laughed. He's enough to make a cat laugh. That mincing, tittuping way of walking; his reedy, pernickety voice,' jibed Wilberforce.

'Cheap at the price,' replied Mr Pitt.

Wilberforce whistled, 'So that was his price. Typical dunderheaded thing to want.'

A footman came in looking worried. He announced, 'Sirs, there's a gentleman. He wouldn't wait.'

The gentleman strode in. He was tall; his strong face and thick eyebrows contrasted a pretty, almost girlish mouth. He wore a tie wig as most people did but his was lopsided, summing up his rage and haste. It was Henry Dundas.

'Here's a pretty kettle o' fish!' he announced. 'Here's a right calhappit strummer. Damned dolterheaded coward! Undischarged blunderbuss! The King'll ne'er forgive him and I canna blame him. I ne'er heard the like! Gormless Gowk!' spluttered the Scottish statesman.

'I feel you know,' Mr Pitt soothed, 'that it would help us to comment appropriately if you were to tell us to whom you refer.'

'Why Temple o' cos; your coot of a cousin. He's resigned. Ha' y' no heard?'

'I must confess I have not yet opened my post. I must also confess I am not altogether astonished,' replied Pitt.

'Won't you sit down and have some chocolate?' inquired Mr Wilberforce conscientiously.

'Chocolate!' barked Mr Dundas with infinite contempt for the innocuous beverage. 'Breakfast! I've been up six hours. If ye'd haver less and hear more, ye'd have a wee chance o' running th' country.'

'Mr Pitt I think works sufficiently hard,' said George, 'and his rare hours of recreation are most necessary to him.'

'But why?' asked Wilberforce.

'Aye, why indeed. Ye may well say why. There's no' a soul has th' answer. There's some say th' King refused him a dukedom. There's others have it he didn'ae like th' way they spoke o' him but y' didn'ae need t'ask why a Grenville gets out of it. They're as wambly as a whaup,' Mr Dundas continued.

'My cousin,' said Mr Pitt, 'is of a nervous temperament, and it is possible he relies too much on other people's opinions, but if he has no stomach for the fight I would prefer not to have him in my cabinet.'

'Weel said, by Bothwell!' expressed Mr Dundas, sitting down at last. 'But ye've no' so many men of experience, particularly i' th' Commons.'

'I have here a tentative list,' revealed Pitt.

They began to confer.

:

Parliament went back after Christmas on January twelfth. Fox attacked Pitt ferociously, continually, and with contempt. He appeared in full court dress to signify that, although the King had dismissed him, he was the House's choice and the rightful minister. He made a great play about the "Honourable Schoolboy" and soon there was a rhyme about it:

> 'A sight to make surrounding nations stare. A
> kingdom trusted to a schoolboy's care.'

Pitt's Government was frequently defeated in the lobbies and he was often urged to resign, but Parliamentary usage did not insist on it. Shrewd people noticed that Pitt was winning, his votes were going up, and very shrewd people noticed that it all depended on him. If he was away for one night his government must fall. In the middle of February 1784, there was a movement to include Fox in the Government. It came to nothing and was never likely to come to anything. But it persuaded some of the many undecided MPs that Pitt was a reasonable, flexible man.

Mr Pitt moved back into 10 Downing Street, and George Pretyman was with him, though George was looking around for a house of his own due to his forthcoming wedding, planned for May.

On the evening of February the twenty-eighth Mr Pitt, with his brother Lord Chatham and his cousin Lord Mahon, went to receive the Freedom of the City. George had thought at first that Lord Chatham was a bad copy of his younger brother, William Pitt. Now he thought he saw the likeness, with the same quick grasp of things. He showed the same coldness and indifference to most of the world, and the same warmth and interest to his friends. However, he did not possess the same energy. He was referred to as "The late Lord Chatham" because he was always late for everything. After a long, lethargic courtship he had married a Miss Townsend. He was a soldier, which seemed to suit him, despite showing little interest in his profession.

Lord Mahon was a slight, shy, schoolboy, and Pitt took him because he knew he'd enjoy the ceremony. They were coming back, attended by a large, generally friendly crowd, when, in The Strand, it insisted on taking the horses out of the shafts and pulling the carriage. It was not unusual but when the politicians heard the cheers turn to jeers and hissing they were shocked.

'What is it?' asked Mahon nervously.

'Carlton House,' said Lord Chatham smiling, 'they're hissing the Prince of Wales for not supporting you. Serve him right.'

There was plenty of hissing but no more movement.

'We will be here all night,' said Lord Chatham, as he opened the window, stuck his head out and shouted, 'Take us on friends. Mr Pitt has to get back.'

They were soon moving again but this didn't please Lord Chatham either. 'No! No!' he yelled, 'Not that way, stupids. Not up St James' Place! Take us on up St James' St. Mr Pitt.'

His loud voice was drowned out by even louder voices, which seemed to be arguing. But the polite, surprised, indignant, tradesmen's voices were soon overcome by rough jeering shouts. One man with a particularly loud and ugly bark kept yelling, 'Down with Pitt! Fox forever!'

There were scuffles just outside the coach, oaths, and a smack as someone was hurt.

'On! On!' shouted his Lordship half-out of the window. 'Take us on! Keep going! Dear God, we're just outside Brooks's and they're coming.'

'Who's coming?' enquired his brother.

'Chairmen with their chair poles and bludgeons. Waiters! Some gentlemen. I see Mr Hare and Lord Crewe. He's… God, I can't hold the door!'

He vanished head-first and they heard a crash, and then the hoarse voice that had yelled 'Fox not Pitt' then uttered, 'Stand aside, soldier boy, we got no quarrel with you,' followed by a series of yelps and shouts of protest.

'He's drawn his sword,' said Mr Pitt thoughtfully, 'I only hope he doesn't kill anyone. It would haunt him.'

'Surely… surely he'd be quite justified,' said Mahon, very white and clinging to his cousin.

'Justified perhaps but—' Mr Pitt started but he was interrupted by his brother who was outside.

'You'd better come out and we'll try and get in a house. The coach is not going anywhere now.'

'Come along!' said Mr Pitt calmly, detaching himself from Lord Mahon gently. 'I'll go first.'

Violent blows began to crash on the sides of the coach. The glass in the door that was open was broken and poured in on them. It crunched under Mr Pitt's feet as he went to the door.

When Lord Mahon scrambled down it seemed he'd descended into some sort of hell.

It was dark after the lit coach. Windows from the houses gave them a little light and showed wild figures pounding on the coach with sticks and cudgels. Their rage at the coach was so great they ignored him.

There was a street light not far away, but it only threw a minor pool of light over a number of men who were standing and watching. Lord Chatham, frantically trying to protect his brother with his drawn sword, which occasionally flashed in the light, produced a yelp and an oath. Mr Pitt was pulling jerkily on an iron bell rope under a torchère to the right of a step below a shallow porch and a smart front door.

He heard the bell pealing inside and then a man's voice shouted, 'Who's there?'

'Mr Pitt, Lord Chatham and Lord Mahon. We need shelter,' shouted back William Pitt.

Lord Mahon tried to fight his way over to where the others were. People were clustered around and he couldn't get through. It was like a nightmare. He tried to push between two of them but one, a tall man, immediately moved closer to the other and looked down at him contemptuously. 'Oo yer shovin' nan boy?' he enquired.

His cousin Billy saw his predicament and plunged down the steps back into the crowd.

'Billy! Come back!' shouted Chatham.

'By your leave, by your leave,' bellowed Mr Pitt, burrowing through the crowd with surprising strength and grabbing his cousin by the arm.

As they struggled back Mahon's coat got torn as someone tried to pull it off. Someone else shoved a stave in front of them which Mr Pitt grasped with his left hand and jerked sideways, still pulling the semi-paralysed Mahon along with his right hand.

As they stumbled up the steps the great black front door swung open, and light poured out, dazzling them. A deep voice said, 'Come on in then! Quick!'

They stepped in to the brilliantly peaceful hall which seemed like paradise after hell, in spite of the fact that a large bald elderly man was confronting them with a pistol. The door slammed behind them, propelled by a footman in full fine plum and gold livery, who then bolted and locked it.

There was a roar of rage from outside.

'It *is* Mr Pitt!' said the elderly man. 'Well, well. Somebody does not enjoy your eloquence.'

'Perhaps. 'Hardly regular attendees in the Strangers' Gallery,' suggested Mr Pitt. He went on, 'We are very much obliged to you.'

The elderly man replied, 'Think nothing of it. You will, I trust—'

'Can I come out?' called a woman's voice from nearby.

'Oh. By all means, Elinor. The coast is clear. The door is stout,' the elderly man said confidently.

There was furious knocking on the door but it hardly moved. The bell pealed.

'Not at home,' the elderly man informed the mob.

Mahon sank trembling into a chair. 'My best coat!' he thought sadly to himself.

'Oh what a deliverance!' said Elinor. 'I'm so glad; really, they are like wild beasts. Drunk, I am persuaded. You are not hurt, I trust?'

'A little bruised,' said Mr Pitt, 'but nothing too significant, thanks to your resolution.'

'If anyone had got in after you he was a dead man,' said the householder. They believed him. 'You'll stay to dinner?'

'No, I thank you. I must get to the House,' Pitt replied politely.

'Assuredly. Or that cad Fox'll be back. Best get into White's by the back ways and their porters will clear the roads and get you a Hackney coach,' the householder helpfully identified.

'It was a trap!' said Lord Chatham, 'I am convinced it was a trap. Had we gone up St James' Place we'd have been exposed amongst enemies. Fox planned this.'

'It would be wiser not to say so,' counselled his brother.

'Why? Why should he get away with it? I shall say so all I want. I'll bring a case against him. I saw his creature Lord Crewe working the mob. It's intolerable!'

'If you keep quiet it will do me good. If you make a childish fuss, it will backfire, but now I must get to the House.'

They thanked their host and hostess as they led them to the back door.

CHAPTER FOUR
London

Elizabeth was nervous; excited but nervous. She was going to meet the great Mr Pitt for the first time. She looked at the smart tall houses with their iron railings as they trundled past in their hired coach. They were much the same as their house in Brook Street. All the houses in this part of London seemed much the same, handsome but dirty, and with far too many stairs. It was very hot in July 1784, and she hated that too. You couldn't sleep. You could hardly breathe.

The battle in the Commons last winter had gradually swayed Mr Pitt's way. In March he called an election and in April he won by a large majority. So many of Fox's followers amongst the MPs were defeated. They were known as "Fox's Martyrs".

Elizabeth had hoped and expected to be home long before this, but the House was sitting into August over Mr Pitt's India Bill, and Elizabeth didn't want to leave George. She could have been home where you could breathe, galloping on the common, swimming in the old decoy, but, much as she hated the smells, noises, and heat of London, she didn't hate being married. It was comfortable. It was exciting. It was marvellous having a house to furnish, though they were buying the minimum of furniture. Luckily they both liked solid dark furniture from the last age which was cheap now. For George wouldn't take her money. She and her sister Emily were co-heiresses to her father's large fortune, and he made her a generous allowance, but George wouldn't take any of it, even to pay the rent or the servants. He believed a man should provide and he wouldn't take Mr Pitt's salary. He had become Dean of St Paul's, where he worked quite hard, and preached there every Sunday.

'You are sure it is only a small party?' she enquired.

'Mr Pitt said so. You are looking very well. I'm sure they will all admire you,' said George.

She wasn't sure. She was wearing the wrong clothes and she knew it – a pretty dress of thin muslin embroidered with clumps of violets by a woman in Midhurst who was famous for miles around. She looked like a slender white pillar. It was not really an evening dress but she liked it. George liked it and above all, it was cool, cool, cool. Kate Goodchild, the servant's wife, had piled up her hair in a becoming fashion, talking all the while with great giggles of the London prostitutes she'd seen and where they waited.

There was a sudden but prolonged and frantic outburst of yelling, some distance away.

'The Westminster election,' explained George, 'Fox and his friends are exciting themselves.'

'Katy says the Duchess of Devonshire is kissing all the tradesmen,' said Elizabeth.

'I fear it is all too true, a form of bribery previously unknown. Here we are,' proclaimed George.

Before the coachman could work the knocker, the doors were flung open by two footmen in livery. The coachman let down the step. George got out first, assisted his wife down, and together they entered Number 10. They followed the butler to a big drawing room, which seemed full of people. A pretty girl came forward.

She began to speak, 'I'm so very glad to meet you at last,' she said to Elizabeth. 'I have been hearing your praise this age. I'm Harriot and I'm playing hostess insofar as a sad, forgetful scatterbrain can do so. This is Lady Sefton and this is Lord Sefton, this is Edward Eliot, and this is Mr Wilberforce. "The Reverend and Mrs Pretyman". Two more to come and then we can have our dinner. I get so hungry. I am not used to these late hours.'

'Nor am I,' agreed Elizabeth.

'That is not an evening dress, child,' said Lady Sefton, her small form appearing to bristle like a cross cat.

'It is so pretty, though,' said Harriot, 'and just the thing for this stifling weather.'

Lady Sefton was about to say more, much more, but luckily the Dundases were announced.

Elizabeth found herself, as was correct for a bride, on Mr Pitt's right. He was looking at her in a worried way so she asked him, 'How does your India Bill differ from Fox's?'

'Very little, I think, but at least we listened to the East India Board,' said Pitt.

'It is a strange romantic chance to own land and employ natives where all is alien,' said Elizabeth.

'Indeed but it becomes a matter of some difficulty to discover the local customs and laws and whether they have been contravened,' explained Pitt.

'Yes. So is Warren Hastings a hero or a villain, or a bit of both, like most men?' asked Elizabeth.

'Undoubtedly the latter, but the matter is a delicate one, and as yet I do not have sufficient knowledge to judge it. He was certainly very hard-pressed but it would not entirely excuse injustice,' Pitt elaborated.

'No,' agreed Elizabeth, thinking about it. In the slight pause Lady Sefton addressed a remark to Mr Pitt from his other side.

Elizabeth sat in silence for a little while, sorry not to be talking to Mr Pitt any more. She had found him easy and friendly, and it was flattering and fascinating to be so close to the source of power. How bright the lights were! There must be a hundred candles in this room.

'How do you like London?' asked Mr Wilberforce from her other side.

'Not very well. I always used to be busy. I helped run our village school, and our cottage hospital, and the alms-houses, and we had a scheme to procure allotments. Here I am not unhappy, but I am often at a loose end and I feel very useless,' Elizabeth explained rather pessimistically.

'You sound exactly what I am looking for, a good Christian to help and advise us. Some gentlemen and I are running a small soup kitchen in Wandsworth. At first it seemed popular and the need is great but I don't know how, it doesn't operate as it should,' Wilberforce went on.

'I should be glad to try and assist,' Elizabeth replied thoughtfully.

'So should I,' said Harriot Pitt from over the table. 'We spoilt women should do more for the unfortunate. We'll go together shall we? Tomorrow? Botheration! No, I can't, there's a rout and a concert. The next day? Wednesday?'

Elizabeth agreed and they arranged a time and place.

:

After dinner Mr Dundas told her, ''Tis mighty agreeable to me to see the good parson happy. 'Twas a wee bit over conscientious laddy, but ye've shaped him to a right-forward manny. I ne'er seen such an alteration. Ye've made him human.'

Elizabeth could not but be flattered and was very pleased with her evening in spite of Lady Sefton's rudeness which, on the way home, George assured her was legendary .

She had made the good beginning she hoped with Mr Pitt, who was, after all, her husband's pupil and benefactor. Above all, she had made friends, by a most fortunate chance, with his sister. As they were thanking Mr Pitt for a most pleasant evening, she told him how delightful she found Harriot.

He smiled. 'Her friendliness, I think, must please, and do you know it is infectious; even a dry stick like me finds himself easy when she is by,' Pitt explained.

'My husband told me you were stiff in strange company but the most enchanting person amongst friends,' said Elizabeth.

'Well, I am shy but, despite that, I love to laugh and frolic, and you need not fear to find me stiff for I think we are friends already,' Pitt replied with a smile.

CHAPTER FIVE

Wandsworth

On Wednesday, Elizabeth and Harriot set off in good time in a chaise. Goodchild was driving and they had picked up Harriot at Number 10. Normally Elizabeth would have insisted on driving herself, for she was aware that she drove well, but today she wanted to talk to her fascinating new friend. It was hotter than ever, so the moving air was delightful, but the smells they passed through were less pleasant.

'I have never been to Wandsworth,' said Elizabeth.

'And you wanted to keep it that way,' muttered Goodchild.

Harriot smiled, 'Nor have I. We think too little of the rookeries and visit them too seldom. They shame us and so we avoid them and our shame grows worse.'

They passed Westminster Abbey and Elizabeth exclaimed, 'I have never been inside.'

'I will take you one day. We'll have to take William Wilberforce and Edward, too. I never can remember dates,' replied Harriot.

'A verger would tell us,' suggested Elizabeth.

'A verger would tell us much too much,' agreed Harriot.

When they arrived at a rather dingy looking house in a filthy, crowded street they were met by William Wilberforce, small, trim, and friendly as ever, and a plump, smiling little man who Wilberforce introduced as Mr Porter.

'Very welcome,' said Mr Porter, 'very welcome I'm sure. Beautiful ladies. Visiting the poor out of the goodness of their hearts can only inspire us to help the helpless.'

'We shall soon be a resort of fashion,' said William Wilberforce smiling.

'Where do we put th'osses?' asked Goodchild.

'Well now,' answered Porter, 'you'll find plenty of room in Astley's over th' way. Very obliging is Mr Astley. "Porter" says he to me, "use my stabling whenever you want". He's in Liverpool this summer so you'll find plenty o' room.'

Goodchild took the horses away.

'Come back in two hours,' Elizabeth said to him.

Elizabeth and Harriot saw the soup being made and the trestle tables and benches in a big room where it was served. Harriot seemed impressed, but Elizabeth noticed that nothing was very clean. Things were hard to keep clean in London. Mr Porter assured them the soup kitchen had made the whole difference to the district. 'There is not a widow or an orphan,' he told them, 'as goes to their humble hovel but what they blesses the gentry.'

Mr Wilberforce soon had to go to an anti-slavery meeting. Elizabeth and Harriot helped to carry the soup to the poor. They did seem to be grateful and appreciative. One worn woman said to Elizabeth, 'Fust bite of sup I 'ad this week.' That seemed odd. If things were that bad, why hadn't she come yesterday and the day before?

People were still coming, waiting in orderly lines, when the soup and bread ran out. The late-comers were turned away, and one or two of them groaned.

'Always the same!' said Mr Porter, 'Always the same! Much as we do, it's never enough. The need's so great. Mr Sharp talks of buying the next house.'

It soon seemed to be nearly time for Goodchild to come for them.

Porter took his leave. 'I hope you'll come and brighten our day again,' he said, 'an' that soon. An I thank y'er for your kind contribution but now I got to leave y'er, an go an buy th' very best meat fer tomorrow's soup. No end to this job but I don't grudge it. I'm a humble instrument of comfort to too many people. So if you'll excuse me.' And he vanished with surprising speed for one of his bulk.

'I enjoyed it,' said Harriot as they went out into the seedy, smelly street. 'It was very interesting. It seemed useful but…'

'Yes,' agreed Elizabeth, 'but I see exactly what Mr Wilberforce means and I think it's Porter. He doesn't ring true.'

'Oh do you think so? I did not altogether warm to him but he seemed a confident, able sort of a man,' said Harriot in partial agreement.

'Well, we will soon know more. I've—'

She broke off for three men were bearing down on them. They were the usual men you saw around there. Small, ragged, badly shaven, scrawny, and pasty, but there was something about their sudden appearance and intense gaze that was frightening.

'We'd better go back in,' said Elizabeth.

They scuttled up the few steps back to the door but found it locked. Elizabeth took off her shoe and started to beat on it.

'Shut out in the cold,' said a mocking voice, 'poor little darling. Don't fret we'll warm ya.'

'I'll have those bags,' said a more purposeful and chilling voice ''And 'em over an' y' can keep y' pretty glad rags.'

Elizabeth beat harder on the door and hung on tight to her reticule.

'Naw! Naw!' said the hateful, mocking voice. But to her immense relief Elizabeth could hear horses' hooves and the rumble of wheels behind it.

'You wanter play ball with us, you do?' went on the voice. 'We're flash coves, we are, but we gets a bit snarky when stuck up morts won't play with us.'

The wheels were close now, coming fast, and the mocking voice ended in a yelp. All three men were running, and Goodchild's whip was whistling through the air again and again. The men seemed to dive into an alley, and the carriage was around the corner and out of sight. Elizabeth didn't worry. She knew he'd soon come back.

'My goodness!' said Harriot, 'Your groom to the rescue. Coming up in the nick of time, just as a knight in shining armour should.'

'Nasty natty dips!' said an elderly woman, emerging from her little cupboard of a shop. 'Your groom fairly served 'em to rights. I 'aven't 'ad such a laugh since Bartholomew Fair. Them lot's more trouble than th' rats 'n' just as nasty.'

Goodchild reappeared and handed them in to the coach. He was still very angry but triumphant all the same. 'Told you so!' he said, 'You never listens to me. You knows best, you do, an' see what you gets for it. You was lucky I was afore my time.'

'We were indeed!' agreed Harriot. 'You were wonderful. Thank you so much.'

'Tha's what I'm paid for. To look after Miss Elizabeth 'n' her friends. But it ain't easy when she goes off queening it in a back slum.'

Elizabeth found she was shivering and pouring with sweat. The passing air was delicious. 'What's a natty dip?' she asked.

'I dunno what "natty" mean. I don't talk cant and no more shouldn't you, but a "dip's" a pickpocket. Next time you takes a fancy to go slumming it, I'm bringing Tom to guard y'.'

Tom was his eldest son, a well-grown youth; reliable, if rather bashful.

They were passing the Abbey again and the familiar cries and stink of London were somehow reassuring:

'Sweet lavender!'

Horse manure, stagnant water, cheap scent, lime blossom, urine, and coal smoke.

'Cherry ripe!'

'Fresh fish! Fish still swimming, fresh fish!'

'What did you find out?' asked Elizabeth.

Goodchild responded. 'That Porter's a right wrong 'un but I could'a told you that th' moment I clapped eyes on 'im. 'E set you up I reckon. Got them rapscallions to frighten you off. 'E's sellin' th' stuff. 'E's got boys all over, an' if they see one th' committee coming they run 'n' tell and then they brews up. Hardly cooks one day in ten. Th' head groom did think o' givin' me a hint but that Porter's a bad enemy.'

'What can we do about it?' asked Elizabeth, confident that Goodchild would, as ever, have the answer.

'You needs a man, 'n' a good man too. If not several. Mathew might come. 'Is old woman's on at him to give up coaching,' answered Goodchild.

Mathew was Goodchild's cousin who was a coachman.

'That would be admirable. Mathew's so reliable,' said Elizabeth.

'Not much admirable about them slums. Porter's in with every villain for miles,' explained Goodchild.

'Are you all right?' Elizabeth asked Harriot, who was looking a bit pale.

'Never better. I am not such a Lent Lily, I hope, that I faint for a few insults. I was lost in admiration as you and your groom rearranged Wandsworth,' she replied.

'Take more 'n me,' Goodchild told her, 'you needs a regiment o' soldiers to guard you if you tries to help that lot.'

CHAPTER SIX

Wandsworth/Germains

Two years later and twenty degrees colder, Harriot and Elizabeth were again coming back from Wandsworth, only this time they were in a coach with Edward Eliot and William Wilberforce.

Several other things were different. Harriot had married Edward Eliot the year before and was having a baby. She laughed at all the anxious questions, and declared she'd never felt so well and energetic in all her life. Elizabeth could not but help remembering, with a pang of worry, the village women saying that if you had an easy pregnancy you would have a difficult birth. She couldn't help feeling a little jealous too. She was two years married, still very much in love, but no sign of a child. Her mother told her she was fortunate. 'The women who have a child a year usually die of the twelfth,' she'd said last summer. 'You're like me, slow to conceive. I'd been married five years before I started you and then it was another two years before Robin came along.'

Mr Pitt had carried his India Bill but been defeated on closer links and more favourable trade for Ireland. Goodchild's cousin Mathew had come and run the soup kitchen. His wife was relieved and delighted. 'Coachmen never live long,' she kept saying. She and her husband didn't live long in London either, for the house caught fire. Mathew dropped his wife out of the window and then jumped. She sprained an ankle. He broke his leg. Porter was suspected, but nothing could be proved. Another house was taken and the place seemed to be flourishing, but in spite of all the Bow Street runners who were protecting them, they all feared more trouble.

Yet a lot of Wandsworth was on their side now. They met with more and more friendliness and gratitude. Mathew was confident that Porter was a spent force. The new house was a large one, and they allowed young men to board there cheaply, which should be some protection thought Elizabeth, or would it be an added danger?

'How is the Infallible?' asked Harriot.

She had acquired a great admiration for Goodchild and called him "The Infallible".

'He's well, but grumbling about how hard it is to keep the horses fit with all this traffic,' answered Elizabeth.

'How does he solve it?' Harriot asked.

'By exercising them very early. Perhaps that is why he is so grumpy,' suggested Elizabeth.

'We are all pining for the kind countryside,' said Wilberforce, 'even me, who has what should be a sufficiency of greenery.'

'And I shall be going there soon,' thought Elizabeth, with pity for Harriot, who could not leave her doctor and midwife. 'At least it is not oppressively hot.'

'The division is so wide,' said Harriot.

'It becomes less,' Edward told her. 'The country is becoming more prosperous, thanks to your brother's measures.'

'I hope so, but it is likely to be but a poor harvest,' Harriot replied.

'Still, farming is improving too,' said her cheerful husband. 'Coke is doing great things in Norfolk. There is "Turnip" Townsend, Arthur Young. Even the King is vastly busy about it and writes letters to the farming journals under the name of Robinson.'

'So like him!' beamed Harriot. 'But for all your improvements too many still go to bed hungry. How they must hate us.'

'Perhaps by feeding some of them and helping others to become richer we are protecting ourselves and our children. Christianity is oftentimes our only hope, though we do it for the love of God and not for love of the vulgar,' theorised Wilberforce.

'There is not so much poverty in the country,' declared Harriot. 'Nothing that could not be put right. Billy's so hoping to put it right, but the towns are terrifying.'

'And people are flooding out of the country and into the towns,' professed Wilberforce, 'perforce very often thanks to all these appalling enclosures.'

'And yet they say enclosures increase the yield of corn,' pointed out Eliot.

'My sister tells me there is a poet in Wandsworth,' said Harriot. 'When the tedious babe is born I mean to go and visit him. Mathew speaks highly of him. He is an engraver too, and so perhaps I could buy an engraving. My sister met a painter in Shoreham who is a great admirer of this poet.'

'One would hardly suspect a poet in Wandsworth or a painter in Shoreham,' said Wilberforce. 'Have they got names?'

'The poet is called William Blake and the painter is Samuel Palmer. My sister bought some of his paintings and I mean to as well next time I venture into Kent. We cannot see them but the Muses are abroad now, and they are not snobs like us. They tap a ploughman on the shoulder and whisper in the ear of an ostler, and behold, we have a painting ploughman and a poetic ostler.'

'I feel that too!' said Elizabeth. 'I had not marked it 'til you explained but I felt it. There's something in the air. Perchance 'tis having a young dutiful man at the helm. Perchance to more and more acquiring a smattering of education.'

'I shall become a patron of the arts,' proclaimed Harriot, 'and Billy will have to enlarge Number 10 to encase my library and gallery.'

:

A few days after this conversation Elizabeth, George, and their household went down to Germains for August.

The weather improved. It was a difficult harvest even so as the corn was very late, but it was a heavy crop and most of it was saved. Elizabeth corresponded with Harriot who said she continued very well. Someone had made another attempt to burn down their house in Wandsworth, but one of the lodgers woke and they put out the fire in the nick of time.

Elizabeth galloped, swam, and ate peaches and nectarines; she had a lovely time. George read, preached, fished, and enjoyed himself too. He seldom rode with Elizabeth now as she liked to ride before breakfast and only unrequited love could get him up early.

The day before they left to go back to London, George got a letter from Mr Pitt. It said, 'I rejoice to tell you my sister has presented us with a girl. Both she and the babe are as well as possible.'

They were both delighted to hear it and their journey south was brightened by it. They'd decided to stay in a hotel from fear of being a nuisance at such a time. They hurried south because George had promised to help Rose with the budget for next year. Pitt liked the mathematics reduced to a simple formula before he started tinkering with the figures. Rose's knowledge of mathematics was limited, so George was a great help to him.

It was a hot day in September when they arrived. London seemed very stuffy and smelly after the countryside, and they washed and dined before George opened his post.

'Alack!' he exclaimed, being given to old fashioned words.

'What is it?' asked Elizabeth, dunking tea and watching a fine coach with a coat of arms on the door rumble past.

George passed her Pitt's note.

> *I am grieved to inform you that Harriot has a high fever. The doctors seem powerless to assist her. We are distracted and despairing.*
> *Your devoted friend,*
> *William Pitt*

'Heavens!' she said. 'We must go there. Goodchild will say the horses are too tired. We'd best get a Hackney.'

'And take Goodchild for we may have to stay late,' added George.

When they arrived and rang the bell, nothing happened. There was straw down in the street.

'Dozy lot,' said Goodchild, ringing the bell for the third time. 'Always was.' He pulled off his shoe and hammered on the door. Dusk was falling and, in spite of the sound of wheels and shouts nearby, it looked like the end of the world, Elizabeth thought.

The door opened suddenly and there was a familiar footman in the livery, but his buttons were done up all wrong and his eyes were glassy.

'You can't come in,' he said. 'She's dead and they are drunk.'

'So 're you,' Goodchild said and pushed past him, holding the door open for Elizabeth.

'I shaid you can't come,' the footman uttered. 'They're, they're. Not at home.'

Goodchild clicked his tongue impatiently, pushed the footman out of the way and closed the door. Another footman came into the hall and recognised George.

'Thank God you are here, my Lord,' he said. We're in such a state! Can't get any orders. They won't eat any food and the cook has given notice. Mains and I are at our wits' end.' Mains was the butler. The bell rang again and Goodchild opened the door.

'Message for Mr Pitt!' announced the messenger. 'Express from Mr Dundas.'

'I'll see he gets it,' said George, taking it and closing the door.

'Where are they?' Elizabeth asked the sober footman

'In the library, Madam,' he answered.

They went to the library – usually a cheerful room, but it was cold and gloomy. No-one had lit the candles and the fire was out. Mr Pitt leapt to his feet and looked at them piteously. Then he put his finger to his lips and pointed to another easy chair where Edward Eliot was sprawled. All you could see were quantities of curly light brown hair. Edward never would wear a wig, except for very formal occasions, and Harriot used to say that he looked like an undertaker when he did wear one.

Mr Pitt led them out. 'I'm sure there are all sorts of things to do, but I cannot – I do not – function, all I can think of is...'

'Just so', said George. 'You will be better by-and-by and she is safe, laughing with your father in heaven.'

'Do you really think so?' asked Mr Pitt wonderingly. 'She did used to tease him.'

'Make up the fire very quietly,' Elizabeth told the footman, 'and then light a candle in the corner, well away from Mr Eliot.'

'Yes, Madam,' said the footman and went into the library quietly.

'How is the baby?' Elizabeth asked Mr Pitt.

'I know not. It was crying, but I do not hear it now. The doctor thinks she will not live. I asked my housekeeper to try and find a wet nurse, but I haven't asked if she achieved it,' stifled Mr Pitt.

'I will go and see,' Elizabeth told him. 'But another matter is that you must eat something. What would you dislike least?'

'A bowl of soup, I think. Yes a bowl of chicken soup and some bread and butter,' Pitt answered.

'That will suffice,' said Elizabeth, making for the back quarters.

'Elizabeth is always so...' said Mr Pitt. 'I was glad you said what you did about Harriot. I fear I cannot altogether believe it and yet I feel it may be true.'

'It is true,' George assured him. 'She will be waiting for you. Have you made arrangements for the funeral?'

'Not yet. I suppose...' muttered Pitt. 'I will arrange it, but we have to—'

Here Elizabeth reappeared. 'She found a good wet nurse,' she told them, 'and the baby's suckling and looking much better. It was the luckiest thing that one of the maids had a sister who'd just had a baby. Your soup's coming and then you must go to bed. You look very tired.'

'I must confess I am fatigued. We did not sleep and I was so glad to see Edward fall asleep,' said Pitt.

'I'll just peep in,' said Elizabeth, and vanished again.

George gave Pitt the note from Dundas saying, 'This came. I don't suppose it is of any urgency, but I judged you should glance at it.'

Mr Pitt looked at it. 'Only about the budget,' he told them, and put it in his pocket.

Elizabeth came back. 'Still deep asleep.'

'The better,' said Mr Pitt, 'though I apprehend he will be appalled when he wakes and remembers.'

'Dinner is served,' said the butler.

Elizabeth suspected it was the unseen hand, or perhaps tongue, of Goodchild that had produced it with such unusual speed. George and Elizabeth sat watching Mr Pitt drink his soup in the panelled dining room, talking gently of Lincolnshire and their journey down.

'Which reminds me,' said George pleasantly. 'You too have had a debilitating day, my love. You must go back to our hotel and sleep.' He rang the little handbell.

'You will stay?' said Mr Pitt eagerly. 'And Elizabeth would be very welcome and invaluable of course, but perhaps…'

'I shall stay,' said George, 'and Elizabeth will come back in the morning, but not too early sweetheart,' he finished, turning to Elizabeth.

'You rang, sir?' said the sober footman as he came in.

'Ask Mr Goodchild to come would you?' said George.

'Yessir,' replied the footman.

'I am irrepressibly grateful,' said Mr Pitt who had drunk his soup. 'I cannot tell you.'

'There is no need,' Elizabeth cooed. 'You must lean on George for a while. He will be very glad to support you, and I too shall do exactly as I'm told and hope to be fathoms deep in an hour.'

Goodchild came in. 'That's the ticket,' he told Mr Pitt. 'A little cold meat now perhaps? Or a junket, or some apple pie?'

'Do you know, I think I could eat some apple pie,' Pitt announced.

Goodchild responded, 'Cold or hot?'

'Cold, I think, but with a little cream,' asked Pitt.

'Spot on,' said Goodchild, and went to fetch it.

'We were so happy,' Mr Pitt told them. 'We four – Harriot was entrusted with the baby and it seemed to respond. We sat in her room and she made us think about having to buy new frocks, for the old ones would be too tight and the new too loose, as Edward said.'

Goodchild came back with the apple pie and cream, three plates, and spoons on a tray.

'I'd like you to get a Hackney and take Mrs Pretyman back to the hotel,' said George to Goodchild.

'Quite right,' said Goodchild. 'Had enough for one day. May I say, sir, how sorry I am,' consoled the coachman, and he was gone.

'She called him "the infallible",' said Mr Pitt, staring at the shut door.

When George and Elizabeth kissed each other goodbye in the hall, she said, 'See somebody looks in now and then in case Edward wakes.'

'I shall not fail to,' said George.

'Main's a trifle overwhelmed, but the housekeeper's quite good. Tell Mr Pitt to read if he cannot sleep, but to try and sleep every half an hour or so,' Elizabeth alluded.

'Admirable notion. I will do so,' George replied softly.

:

'A bad job,' said Goodchild as they drove back. 'A very bad job.'

'Yes,' said Elizabeth, as the tears poured down her cheeks and she struggled to get her handkerchief out of her reticule. 'I'm sorry. I was determined not to cry in front of Mr Pitt, but now—'

A sob took over her.

'You have a good cry,' advised Goodchild. 'I have seen tears in his eyes come to that.'

'He said Harriot was used to calling you "the infallible",' sobbed Elizabeth.

'Wish I was. I'd 've taken her ladyship to your parents. There's our Mrs Potts, never lost a mother,' explained Goodchild.

'I've heard she was good,' said Elizabeth, sobbing less now, 'but that's remarkable, is it not?'

'Shows she knows her job; that there man midwife, he let poor Lady Harriot die. Mrs Potts she say you want to be clean and you can't tell me you can be clean in this here town,' Goodchild exclaimed.

'If I ever start a baby, I shall fly to Mrs Potts,' promised Elizabeth.

CHAPTER SEVEN

London

'Was there ever such a flat, dull party?' thought Elizabeth whilst agreeing politely with her cousin Augustus that the music was vastly agreeable. It was eight months later in May 1787, and they were dining in a box at the Rotunda in Ranelagh Gardens. It was quite diverting watching the people circling the floor like a swarm of colourful insects moving about on marble. Her uncle Oliver had been apprenticed young to a wine merchant, whose daughter he had married, like Dick Whittington. Elizabeth's aunt, Amabel, was no Alice, however, but a garrulous, snobbish woman who had persuaded her son Augustus to propose to his cousin Elizabeth five years ago and had never forgiven Elizabeth for not accepting him. George and Elizabeth asked them to dinner about twice a year and they accepted about one in ten of their copious invitations.

''Tis a most sickly season,' said her uncle, rescuing Elizabeth from her tedious cousin, but with no very lively change of subject. 'Cholera in the rookeries, measles in Kensington, and I am told the Lord Bishop of Lincoln dropped dead of a stroke last week.'

'You'd think such a fine spring would be healthy,' replied Elizabeth.

'Far from it. Diseases always thrive in the heat, most particularly in large towns. I shall be glad when I can retire to the more wholesome country,' explained her uncle.

'I shall too. Mr Pitt hopes to find George a handsome living, but I always seem to dislike the few he found,' Elizabeth posited.

'My dear niece, you must not stand in the way of your husband's career. As Amabel so rightly says, amongst your many good qualities you have a tendency to wilfulness which may yet ruin all,' said Oliver.

Elizabeth did not, unlike him, think Amabel infallible, but she was fond of her stuffy uncle and replied patiently, 'We are very well as we are. George loves his job at St Paul's and is of the greatest help to Mr Pitt and therefore the country. We have enough to live on if we practise economy, and I desire no more.'

She repressed a sneaking feeling that it was going to be harder to practise economy soon though.

'Well, we must away,' said her uncle to her delight, 'the press increases later and my wife, whose nerves are sensitive, dislikes the mob. It is quite her aversion.'

As they walked back through the well-lit pleasure gardens, George, whose manners were always punctilious, walked in front with Amabel on his arm. Elizabeth followed with her uncle, who declared he was sure to catch something in this crush, and asked her if Pitt really hoped to alleviate the nation's debt.

A way to their left some fireworks were shooting out over the river like flowers in air and water. One of them looped up in the air and came whirring down on them. Elizabeth shouted a warning for she thought it was going to land on George. Instead, it landed on the back of Amabel's voluminous and not very becoming purple dress. Her uncle gasped, dropped her arm, and plunged forward. People were screaming and shouting. Amabel's dress was on fire. George was doing something with his hat. She saw no more for a sort of wave of screaming, fleeing people hit her and carried her for some way. She was running amongst other screaming people, but she was not moving as fast as some. People pushed past her roughly and twice she nearly fell. The pace slowed and she looked around. She'd never been in this part of the Gardens but she could see the Rotunda in the distance.

'What happened?' an elderly woman asked her.

'A rocket went astray and set alight to a woman's dress and then the crowd panicked,' Elizabeth explained.

'That they did! I was pushed over and trampled on. I'm black and blue and my dress is torn and I've lost my husband and our party.'

'So 've I. Shall we take a Hackney to our homes?' asked Elizabeth.

The elderly lady replied, 'I think I had best return to the Rotunda. I am acquainted with one of the officials there and he will assist me.'

They parted with mutual expressions of esteem, sympathy, and best wishes. Elizabeth was sorry. She'd felt much safer with a companion and considered going back with her, but she could see a gate not far away and she was tired. She'd be home sooner if—

'A damsel in distress,' said a rather common voice, 'just what I like. Come and have a wet, dear girl.'

A rather plump young man who kept licking his wet lips was between her and the gate.

'No thank you,' she said walking round him.

He slipped an arm round her neatly, giving her a squeeze.

'Now! Now! No tricks! You play fair with me and I'll play fair with you. But you can't get away from me, you know, and if you try that again I might turn nasty,' he uttered eerily.

During this speech Elizabeth longed to smack his face but instinct told her it wouldn't be wise. She looked frantically round for help. One moment a mob, and now no-one when she needed them. There was a tall young man coming up behind her perhaps he—

'Mrs Pretyman?' a gentle voice asked.

'Yes,' she gasped thankfully.

'Ah. Let go of the lady!' said the voice.

'No! Why should I? She's coming with me for a drink. She wants to,' whined the plump young man.

He sounded exactly like a small boy whose toy was being removed. The young man, whose name she couldn't remember, took hold of the plump man by the neck and squeezed. The man let go of Elizabeth and the tall young man, Harding that was his name, of course, offered her his arm.

'Was Mrs Maltby hurt?' she asked.

'A little scorched, I fear, but nothing dangerous. Your uncle took her home. We have been searching everywhere for you. Your husband is vastly concerned. We found my sister Elena quite soon, and your cousin Cordelia was having strong hysterics so loudly that it led me to her, but you were carried some distance in the press. I regret infinitely that I did not come up in time to save you from insult,' Harding explained.

'At least you came in time to save me from being affronted for very long. We are to meet George at the Rotunda?' Elizabeth enquired.

'The fountain in front of it,' he replied.

She was very tired. Of course, he was Septimus Harding and his father was a business partner of her uncle's. She always thought he was dull. But she'd been wrong.

'Elizabeth!'

George had seen her and came rushing over. She felt very safe in his arms.

Her cousin Augustus said, 'Thank heaven you were preserved. Do you think father ought to sue?'

George seemed to realise how tired she was. He ignored Augustus' pleas that they wait with him for his father's coach to return and he got her into a Hackney. They paused only to thank Septimus who was embarrassed and kept saying, 'No, no, nothing,' and 'Honour, I assure you.'

As they drove back through the dark streets Elizabeth thought how often she had ridden like this with Harriot and how much she missed her.

'If it's a boy what shall we call him?' she asked.

'Edward, after your father. Or William? William is a Pretyman name; or both, say, William Edward? I like the sound of it,' expressed George thoughtfully.

'And if it's a girl?' asked Elizabeth.

'Harriot. We couldn't call her anything but Harriot.'

CHAPTER EIGHT

Number 10 Downing Street

The next morning they arose late and were still breakfasting when a messenger arrived from Mr Pitt. The message explained that he had good news for them and, if it was not inconvenient, he hoped they would do him the honour of dining tonight. It would not be a dinner party but a small gathering.

'And we've got good news for him,' smiled Elizabeth crunching crisp bacon.

'I doubt if he will esteem it good news,' George said a little dryly.

'Now darling, I'm not having you, or Mr Pitt, or anyone else brooding over my tragic fate for the next six months. Harriot was very delicate and we knew it. We feared for her but I'm as strong as a horse,' Elizabeth proclaimed.

'Certainly, having recovered you safe last night, I should be an ingrate did I not endeavour to trust God will preserve you in March,' George expressed.

'God and Mother Potts,' Elizabeth replied.

When they arrived at Number 10 they met Mr Dundas in the hall.

'What is this good news?' asked Elizabeth.

'I mayna tell y'. He'd liefer tell y' his own self. I'm just hopin' ye'll conseeder it good tidings!' Dundas said gleefully.

'You suspect we may not?' asked George.

'Och ye weel, nae bother. It's yer missus I'm no verra sure of. She'll maybe take a scunner to it,' Dundas explained philosophically.

Mr Pitt appeared, looking pleased with himself. 'Good morrow, my Lord Bishop.'

'Me?' gasped George, shocked out of his customary urbanity.

'Yes, you. You're the new Bishop of Lincoln. Of course you've got to be enthroned, or anointed, or apostolically succeed, or whatever they do, but then we'll all curtsey and kiss your ring,' said Pitt with mirth.

Enough o' yer havers!' said Mr Dundas. 'Ye'd trouble enough to persuade th' King. Ye needna trouble to persuade th' manny. He kens enough to blow on his porridge.'

'I feel inadequate,' said George, adding, 'I am very sensible of your goodness though. I am unable to express…'

'And that's a snow white stag for y'! Georgie, unable to express! By Rob Roy McGregor, I ne'er thought to hear it. Come ye in, Mrs Pretyman, and take a stoup. Ye're host's over pleased with himself to offer, so I maun do it,' piped Dundas.

'Indeed I am being most remiss. I apologise but I am rather pleased with myself. The King said "Too young Pitt! Too young!" and when he starts repeating himself the matter is apt to be slammed shut, but I represented that I would not have been his Prime Minister but for you and the confidence you gave when I most needed it, and all of a sudden his Majesty said "He shall have it Pitt! He shall have it! So, now, we must celebrate",' Pitt explained.

'But how do you feel my love?' George asked Elizabeth. 'If you mislike it, I must of course decline the honour.'

'Oh please do not mislike it,' begged the powerful Prime Minister. 'It would break my heart.'

'I don't think I'll make a very good Bishop's wife, but at least I'm a good enough wife to want what would suit you so well,' Elizabeth said poignantly.

'It will, won't it,' agreed Mr Pitt. 'He is just the man to be a fine figurehead and a good giver.'

'Weel,' announced Mr Dundas, 'if ye're biding in the draughty hall 'til ye grow moss, I'm no...' and he vanished with his customary decisiveness.

'I'm glad he's gone,' Elizabeth told Mr Pitt, 'because I wanted to tell you. I know the timing's dreadful. I'm sorry but I'm having a baby.'

'Oh!' Pitt said, startled, horrified, but sympathetic. 'And you are rejoicing?'

'I am rejoicing,' confirmed Elizabeth.

'So was Harriot. Women are so brave. Where would we be without them? God knows but not here certainly,' Pitt expressed compassionately.

'I am to go home shortly where there is a wonderful midwife, so you are not to worry,' Elizabeth reassured Pitt.

'And I am not to worry,' stated George, 'an instruction I am finding far from easy.'

'I remember all too well how impossible it was,' agreed Mr Pitt. 'Come to the drawing room.'

Already, thought Elizabeth, Number10 was shabbier than usual. Not dirty exactly, but unkempt, unlived in. No flowers, no books, or parasols, or music scattered on tables. The drawing room seemed to be full of men. There was poor Edward Eliot, Mr

Dundas, of course, holding forth about "cocky leekie", whatever that might be, and two other men she didn't know.

'No women?' she asked Mr Pitt.

'Nor there is!' he answered, 'I had not remarked. You see we quite count you as a man, Elizabeth. You are so discreet and unlikely to interrupt.'

Edward Eliot came up and greeted her warmly, so she asked after the baby.

'She thrives,' he answered, 'and I am growing fond of her. At first, I confess, I regarded her with reservations and avoided her. But Billy pointed out how wrong that was, and once I became acquainted with her I soon succumbed to her charm and her determination to live in spite of the worst possible start in life.'

'I long to see her. May I come one morning?' asked Elizabeth.

'By all means. Come tomorrow, if you will. You are fond of infants?' asked Edward.

'I have no prejudice against them but I am not at present acquainted with any,' Elizabeth explained rather flatly.

:

Dinner was announced and Elizabeth found herself between the two strange men; Mr Pitt was engrossed in an animated conversation about Russia with Mr Dundas and so neglected to introduce anyone. She turned to her right and there was a middle-aged man, somewhat plump and unremarkable, but alert and intelligent-looking.

'I have long wanted to meet you,' he stated, 'I am Sir Joseph Banks.'

'The man who went to Australia?' queried Elizabeth.

'I might be so described, though I'm prouder of being President of the Royal Society,' he said with relish.

'What was Australia like?' asked Elizabeth inquisitively.

'A large question. It was different. Everything was entirely different and yet well-made. I often felt that wonder a man might well feel if he was walking on the moon,' Banks expressed passionately.

'Was it friendly?' came the next question from Elizabeth.

'Again, a large question. Do you know I really think it was different, and in many ways dangerous in some circumstances, but basically friendly, and perhaps offering a second chance to poor, fallen men. There was a sense of space, of freedom. I hope so indeed, for we are to send convicts there. I recall Captain Cook, with all his worries, remembering that he'd not had such a good holiday since he was a boy. Just to see those flowers and butterflies was worth all the hardship,' Banks answered in an illuminative way.

'I envy you. And seeing the natives?' Elizabeth continued.

'Strange. Very black and primitive but I judge well adapted to their land, and well-nourished and athletic. But I am being decoyed down primrose paths and neglecting my duty. Mr Pitt summoned me to tell you all about Lincolnshire, not Botany Bay,' Banks went on.

'Alas! I was very happy in your new world. Who should we cultivate in Lincolnshire, then?' Elizabeth said.

'You know the Rutlands?' Banks asked.

Elizabeth replied, 'Very slightly. I have met them here once or twice.'

'It is an admirable start. When you are well-settled I will come to Scrivelsby and give a small party for you. One becomes acquainted more rapidly in small gatherings. But Mrs Pretyman, may I say, you need have no fears. With your easy manners and lively intelligence you will charm all the locals,' praised Banks.

Elizabeth told him he was too kind, but she thought to herself, 'I'm interested in Australia. I shan't be in the least interested in turnips and gossip.'

CHAPTER NINE

Germains/Buckden Palace

'It won't be very much longer now,' said Mother Potts.

'I hope not,' gasped Elizabeth. 'It's getting pretty bad. One pain runs into another.'

'It does that at the end, but it is the end. Soon be over. You'll soon have a fine boy. The pain'll soon be gone,' Mother Potts tried to reassure her.

Elizabeth screamed.

Something had her in an iron grip. She was being torn apart. She was dying. But Mrs Pott was still there. She and her niece Maisie were still there: still calm, still soothing.

Time had passed. Later, everything was very peculiar, but better. Someone was crying and crying. It was not her, she wasn't in pain anymore.

'A fine, big boy,' Nan Potts said showing her. 'Over eight pounds! No wonder it took all night. We washed him and weighed him and James's gone to tell your husband. Rare taking he was in. Thirsty?'

She was terribly so.

'Yes,' she said in a gasp, and almost immediately there was lemonade made from real lemons. It was delicious, just right, the best thing there could be. She drank it all at once and was soon given another. She polished that off too, but more slowly. It was so sweet. Sweet was just what she wanted and needed.

'You'll drink a lot for a day or two,' said Mrs Potts. 'That's right and good. Meat broth I'll bring you presently. Lovely morning for his first.'

Sunlight fell on the baby as he slept in a cot beside her.

'Blue eyes?' she asked.

'Blue,' Nan confirmed. 'Mind you they all have at first. But his'll stay blue, I reckon. If you could just move over a bit I'll tidy up here.'

Sleep was pulling at her, but she was afraid of giving way to it. She didn't want to leave him and George. 'I'm not going to die am I?' she asked urgently.

'My word alive, no! Why ever should you? You come through remarkably well considering what a big boy he were, 'n' th' first, too. Never a tear. Afterbirth all out.

No, no, you'll be fine. Have a nice long sleep and you'll wake up good as new, or nearly,' Nan reassured her.

She went to sleep.

When she woke up she didn't feel good as new. There was the most awful noise. The baby was crying.

'What do I do?' she asked, muddled and worried.

'Feed him,' said Mrs Potts, who was strangely but blessedly still there. 'That's if you're still of a mind to. If you don't feel up to it yet, I'll take him down to my daughter's. They've goat's milk a'plenty.'

'No I'll feed him,' said Elizabeth, 'but you'll have to show me how.'

It was a success. William Edward suckled mightily and so, presumably, he got some sustenance, though there didn't seem to be much milk yet.

Into the heavenly silence Mrs Potts said, 'You'll get to know each other best this way. Grand ladies and them as wants to be grand won't do it, but I likes to see it. It means all's well to me, but you must drink, too, girl. You needs it as much as he does.'

She found there was a glass of milk, another of lemon, and a third of water beside her. She reached for the lemon. It tasted wonderful.

'Have you been here all along?' she asked.

'Gracious, no. You slep' for six hours. Small wonder the little un' was hungry. 'N' speaking of hungry, what d' you fancy?' Potts asked.

'Almost anything, now you mention it. Chicken broth. Steak and kidney pie, perhaps. Chocolate mousse,' replied Elizabeth enthusiastically.

Mrs Potts continued, 'I'll go 'n' see to it. And I'll tell your husband he can come in for a few minutes. Never seen a man in such a taking in all my born days and I've seen several all het up.'

'Yes, I'd like to show him the baby,' Elizabeth said.

'Not for long, mind. Nought so tiring as folks, 'n' you must eat first,' Potts reminded her.

When George tiptoed in half an hour later. He looked worried, overwhelmed, and hardly able to believe it. 'Are you all right?' he asked.

'Sore, but it's better. Nan says I had a very easy time really, considering he's a big boy and the first,' Elizabeth explained exhaustedly.

'Thank God, I prayed. He looks… red,' George gasped.

'He's had a tiring time. I think he looks like a William Edward, don't you? Reliable, sensible, and a little formal with strangers, like you,' Elizabeth said with a smile.

'How on earth can you tell all that? Do you think you should really be feeding him? How long will you have to?' said George with consternation.

'About a year. Why ever not? Great ladies don't, I know, but I'm hardly a great lady,' said Elizabeth truthfully.

'That's just it. A Bishop's wife *is* a great lady and people might think it odd,' George said.

'Let them! Really, darling, I shan't much like being a Bishop's wife if I've got to be stuffy, pompous, and unnatural,' Elizabeth groaned.

'I suppose you are right and must do what accords with your nature, but I have not always been as secure as you are. When I was young we were poor and in trade, and even my father's elder brother would not receive us. It seemed to matter so much whether good society would accept you or not,' explained the Bishop.

'I suppose it does, but why ever shouldn't they? Was your uncle the most terrible snob?' Elizabeth asked.

'I think he was just weak. He was adopted by his rich cousins in Bacton, and he was ashamed of having a brother in trade, but, as he drank, a lot of respectable people preferred my father to him,' George went on.

Elizabeth followed up, 'What a sad story. Why didn't—?'

'Beg pardon for interrupting you, but that's time, Mistress Pretyman needs to sleep again. She needs lots of sleep and then she'll soon be good as new,' said Mrs Potts, coming in to the room.

'I suppose I am rather sleepy, though we are having a fascinating conversation,' said a rather disappointed Elizabeth.

'Have it tomorrow,' reassured Potts.

:

There followed a heavenly fortnight. Mrs Potts encouraged her to get up after two days. The weather was unusually sunny and warm considering it was winter. The baby flourished and everyone admired him.

Elizabeth and George had a quarrel, really their first serious difference in four years. It was over where the baby should be christened. She, her parents, and the whole village badly wanted the baby to be christened in the village church. George badly wanted him christened in Lincoln Cathedral.

'We must remember that he is to be Mr Pitt's godson and I feel it would create a good impression and provide an optimum start to my ministry,' argued George.

'Pity I didn't have twins and then they'd have provided twice as good an impression,' said Elizabeth sourly.

'I fear you had best give way,' her mother told her. 'It means so much to him. If I were you I'd get a few concessions though.'

'What concessions?' asked Elizabeth.

'Whatever you want most. Being allowed to come back here for a month or two in summer. No, I'm being selfish. I want my Grandson back. Only ask for that if it's what you most desire. Another house? Singing lessons?' her mother enquired.

'I think I'd better prefer to have etiquette lessons. I am going to need them. Do you know, I really want nothing more now I've got Ned,' Elizabeth answered.

Her mother replied, 'You are fortunate.'

'I'm so fortunate it quite frightens me sometimes. Can it last, I wonder?' Elizabeth uttered.

Within a fortnight George went off to be installed. Elizabeth felt quite well enough to go with him, but everyone, even Mrs Potts, said it was too soon. The weather turned very wet and the roads were flooded. Elizabeth began to be rather bored. She read and walked but she was a bit jaded, and wondered that she should have been quite happy here only a few years ago. The baby continued to flourish. Nobody visited them. The roads were too appalling.

George wrote about twice a week and it was a struggle to answer as often. Elizabeth was not a very good letter writer and, besides, not much was happening here, whereas Lincoln, it appeared, was one endless reception for their new Bishop. All the same, George's letters were gratifyingly full of how much he missed her.

> *Elise, my dearest Elise, let us never be parted again, for without you I am a mere figurehead, imposing perhaps but lacking any real function or feelings.*

Elizabeth had very mixed feelings when it was time to leave in April. She longed to see her husband again but she hated leaving her parents. She longed to see her new imposing home, Buckden Palace, but she dreaded all smart functions and forms of worship.

CHAPTER TEN

Buckden Palace/Number 10

It wasn't nearly as bad as she'd expected and the reason was Mrs Mann. Mrs Mann was the housekeeper at Buckden Palace. She was a brisk, skinny woman of about fifty, and the 'Mrs' was her honorary title. She was a very competent, hard working woman, but what kept her going was her insatiable curiosity. She told Elizabeth all about the housemaids' love affairs and the tradesmen's inadequacies. She was a lively pithy talker.

Goodchild disapproved of her. 'Never could take bossy women,' he told Elizabeth when they were out riding one morning. 'An' you didn't ought to let her take you over the way she do. You wanta remember the dog as fetches also carries.'

Elizabeth took his meaning and knew she ought not to gossip so much with Mrs Mann. The truth was she was a bit lonely. George was so very busy. Sometimes she could help, and he always liked to talk things over with her, but he wasn't there most of the time. She spent hours playing with her baby and every day he grew more responsive. By ten months he was talking.

They gave parties and they were asked out quite a lot; she enjoyed it but it still left a lot of space.

Mrs Mann's father had been a clergyman but he was bad with money and when he died there was little left. The wife of the last bishop took her in as a companion and she was soon running everything. Their butler was a quiet, humorous man named Derry. He was terrified of Mrs Mann and admired Goodchild who wasn't afraid of her. They started a soup kitchen in Lincoln, and a lawyer called Mr Carter proved helpful when flattered and asked to smart parties. They gradually pulled down the dreadful houses and built better ones. It was wonderful to have money and to spend and be generous without worrying. Elizabeth still kept careful accounts though. She knew how easily rich people could slip into debt.

George went to London every two or three months to sit in the House of Lords. Elizabeth didn't go with him because of Ned, but her excuses wore thin, and she was very bored alone in the vast spooky palace. So in October 1788 she too travelled to London. They stayed in the Bishop's lodgings in Regent Street. They were very elegant, decorated with lots of gilt and satin stripes. George and Elizabeth were somewhat preoccupied as, on the last night of their many stays on the way south, George had received a letter from William Pitt. It said that the King had gone mad.

'If this lasts beyond a certain time it will produce the most difficult and delicate crisis imaginable in making provision for the Government to go on,' the letter said.

'The Prince will get rid of him?' Elizabeth asked.

'I fear so. The Prince of Wales has been a fervent Whig these many years. I am concerned lest His Majesty has no spiritual consolation. It has been my experience that if you can but bring the sufferer to a belief that Christ loves them you have the beginnings of a cure,' George uttered optimistically.

'But suppose the mischief is bodily, as a man might have in the throes of a high fever?' suggested Elizabeth.

''Tis possible. We know so little,' George forlornly admitted.

'At least we shall know more tomorrow,' said Elizabeth.

The short journey to Downing Street took longer than it should because it was raining hard and the streets were slippery. Goodchild took it carefully but they saw two horses that had slipped over. They had the usual warm welcome from Mr Pitt, and they dined together before he went to the House.

'It is a delicate situation. I feel it my duty to proceed with a Regency Bill but…'

'You are not hurrying,' put in Elizabeth.

'I had forgotten the speed of your wits. Just so. I am not hurrying. One of the doctors, and he is the best, swears he sees a very slow but consistent improvement in the King's condition. I think my greatest advantage is that I am a patient man and my opponent, Mr Fox, is not,' Pitt explained dutifully.

:

It was arranged that they should go to Westminster that evening and sit in the Strangers' Gallery. Mr Pitt enquired about his godson, William Edward, and told them that Harriot's child, rather to their surprise, had lived and was a lively, chatty little girl. She stayed with her grandmother, Lady Chatham, at Burton Pynsent. Edward adored her and went down there a lot. She was called Hester Harriot Pitt Eliot.

They all went in Pitt's coach to Westminster. There was a great crowd. Pitt found an usher he knew who said the Strangers' Gallery was packed but that there was a small gallery used by royalty.

'If any of them come you'll have to go,' the usher said, 'but I doubt they will. The Duke o' York's too busy nowadays. Clarence is at sea. The Prince Regent never comes, though you would think – today.'

'I expect the Prince's friends who are members tell him all,' suggested Elizabeth.

They were just in time to see Mr Pitt come in below them. There was a sort of stir amongst the MPs, like the stir in the sea when the tide turns. Most MPs turned to look at him and someone shouted 'Cave! Here comes the incorruptible prig.'

An MP was talking about India, which he managed to make rather boring. Sub-clauses proliferated. 'We are bound, by the nature of our calling, to provide prosperity and all its many blessings to the natives of that subcontinent, heathens perhaps but, like all mankind, capable of improvement,' he suggested.

He finished at last and Charles James Fox spoke. He spoke very well and clearly. He talked at length, but Elizabeth, watching that dark, lively face, sensed that the House was beginning to fidget. He stressed the dangers of their position and the need for haste. Fox kept it a bit vague, except for one impassioned plea: 'This Government has no validity, no title and no authority.' When he sat down Pitt whispered something to Wilberforce who was beside him. Wilberforce laughed, heartily but still quietly.

Pitt rose to talk. He spoke very well, paid tribute to the King, and said, 'It has been suggested to me that the affliction is bodily rather than mental, as a man might be out of his mind during the course of a high fever or after a blow to the head and yet be of perfectly sound mind for the rest of his long life. This may be the case here. Certainly the doctors are at a stand. The King may recover completely. I pray it will be so and virtue will resume its throne. Vinco veritas. We would, I feel, be foolish to do anything in haste or not in the correct form. I have been looking up the precedents and there are sufficient examples.'

He went on to say his cabinet relied on the sound counsel of the Attorney General, and Pitt proposed with all convenient celerity to bring in a Regency Bill.

The Members listened to him in attentive silence but Elizabeth noticed several of them nodding as they took in a point. 'From this room,' she thought, looking round the crowded, slightly shabby chamber, 'England is governed, and so is India and Canada and…' At this point, Mr Pitt brought his speech to a graceful, but grave end.

:

That night they had a small dinner party. Mr Dundas and his wife, the Duchess of Gordon, Edward Eliot, and William Wilberforce were guests. The Duchess was a very good looking woman in her forties; indeed she had been called the "Beautiful Duchess". She was a staunch supporter of Mr Pitt. Her husband spent most of his time in Scotland. She advanced on Elizabeth now and said, 'At last we meet! Mr Pitt sings your praises and declares you are the only female of his acquaintance as outspoken as myself.'

'Not nowadays,' answered Elizabeth. 'I am a bishop's wife and I say, "Good day!" to every goose.'

'Pooh! Pooh! I concede a duchess is as much in the public eye as any bishop's wife, but I do not let the circumstance make me mealy mouthed,' replied the Duchess.

'Should you have the misfortune to annoy a rich man it is no matter, but should I the poor will suffer for it,' answered Elizabeth philosophically.

'They're pulling down half of Lincoln,' Mr Pitt said to the Duchess, 'and building it up better.'

'We all have our charities,' she replied, 'but I sometimes wonder whether we should encourage the saucy poor to breed as we do. One of these days more of them will get the vote, and they'll vote in such taxes as will destroy us.'

'Ye're a lucky lassie,' Mr Dundas told her. 'Ye can flout yeer friends and talk-havers and all they think is how original ye are. There's no many in that position.'

'At least I do not talk like a kail cutter from Auchterlecty,' she snapped back.

Mr Pitt laughed happily. Mr Eliot, Mr Wilberforce, and the Bishop were listening too.

'Ah 'm no ashamed ah guddled trout and pu'd gowans wi' the bit laddies o' th' village, an I'll tell you one o' those bit laddies, a shepherd's get, is a doctor th' noo. Another's a factor. Ye'd no get that in England,' was Dundas' reply.

'A better education means more opportunities,' said Mr Pitt thoughtfully. 'Were it possible to make gifts to grammar schools, provided they took in ten worthy poor boys, it might do much.'

'Ten worthy poor boys!' exclaimed the Duchess. 'There is no such thing as a worthy poor girl?'

'You had best start a school for them,' replied Mr Pitt dryly. 'The main subject would be how to insult men.'

''Tis easy done,' declared the Duchess. 'Just hint they are not perfect.'

At dinner, Elizabeth was between Mr Wilberforce and Mr Dundas. She immediately asked William Wilberforce what Mr Pitt had said to him after Fox's speech.

'He said "I'll unwhig the gentleman for the rest of his days". It made me laugh immediately but this evening I was wondering…'

'Ashamed of you, I was,' added Mr Pitt. 'Giggling like a schoolgirl. 'M' inclination was to bid you leave the chamber, but I feared what the cartoonists might make of it.'

'They're over bold,' agreed Mr Dundas, 'nae respect for their betters! Nae decency! In Scotland we order the press better, they'd soon find themselves on th' stool o' repentance.'

'I'd like to see that,' declared Mr Pitt, 'but I apprehend the press is like a wasps nest, better left alone.'

'What did you wonder?' Elizabeth asked Mr Wilberforce.

'I wondered if it was prophetic,' said Wilberforce in reply. 'They say Chatham and his family made a visit to the Melbournes once, and later Melbourne said something disparaging about Billy, and Lady Melbourne observed, "That odd little boy will black our Charles James" career all his life long.'

'Mr Pitt is a political genius is he not?' Elizabeth added.

'Truly I think he is and yet he is so human, so unspoilt, so unaffected, so little changed from the boy of fourteen I knew first at Cambridge,' Wilberforce said wistfully.

'George told me he and Mr Pitt were so shy and polite to each other, at first there was no bearing it. Then one of the other undergraduates made a ludicrous mistake in his Latin and George repeated it to Mr Pitt who enjoyed it prodigiously, and all of a sudden they were friends,' Elizabeth said whilst smiling.

'And a good friend he has been to him,' agreed Wilberforce.

'Mr Pitt was after telling me,' said Mr Dundas on his other side, 'ye're away th' noo. Ye will 'ne bide w' us for Christmas and Hogmanay forbye. Ye're away to the wilds.'

As Elizabeth was explaining about Ned and how they had promised him they'd be home for Christmas she saw an earwig drop out of the flowers in the centre of the table and walk across the polished surface.

'An earwig,' she thought, 'in December? I suppose the flowers came from a greenhouse which may well be full of insects.'

Mr Pitt held out a silver spoon which the earwig obligingly walked on to. With a neat flip, Mr Pitt dropped it down the back of William Wilberforce's collar. Mr Wilberforce began to fidget. Mr Pitt, talking intelligently to the Duchess about Methodists, glanced at him from time to time.

Wilberforce put a hand up and scratched in the wrong place.

Elizabeth took pity on him. 'I fear a *farabutto* has put an earwig down the back of your neck.'

'Billy! The wretch! Here you! Alf! There's an earwig down my neck. Get it out, would you?' Wilberforce requested.

The man removed it deftly with a fork and walked carefully out of the room.

'Thanks! What would we do without servants?' professed Wilberforce.

'Very little, I fear,' said Mr Pitt.

:

They got back to Buckden two days before Christmas. Ned was ecstatic, overexcited, galvanised and sick. They had a peaceful, pleasant Christmas. Elizabeth gave a party in a church hall for the slum children living nearby. Sir Joseph Banks came for a few nights and brought a friend of his, a spare elderly man, Marmaduke Tomline, who lived in North Lincolnshire. Elizabeth hardly noticed him he was so shy and retiring. However, as they were coming back from visiting some new houses that one of the Housing Associations had built a large flock of geese flew over the coach singing a sort of question and answer song, and Elizabeth noticed that he was staring up at them with a wistful intensity.

'Are they greylags?' she asked him.

'Pinkfeet,' he answered. 'I have a partiality. I often watch birds.'

'We should pay more attention to natural history. I'm very fond of flowers myself. At home I have about a dozen sorts of flowers; I used to visit when they were in blossom. Some of the country people knew them all,' remarked Elizabeth.

'Have you perhaps read the Reverend White's worthy *History of Selbourne*?'

'Yes indeed,' Elizabeth replied. 'My father was very fond of it. He was much interested in where swallows go in the winter.'

'All ornithologists share his fascination,' Mr Tomline declared. 'Myself, I am persuaded they go overseas. I have conversed with a fisherman on the south coast who frequently sees an immense quantity of hirondelles passing over the Channel in autumn and returning in spring. He stated all the fishermen laugh at stories of swallows hibernating in ponds.'

'That is very interesting. I am always so glad to see them back. Here we are, home again.'

After that Elizabeth talked easily with Mr Tomline about birds and flowers. He seemed to admire George and was very interested to hear he had been a Fellow of Pembroke.

Mr Pitt sent news every few days. The King was still mad at the beginning of January, and the Regency Bill was drawn up and ready for debate. At the beginning of February there was still no change. Mr Pitt wrote that he would go back to the law. 'I need the money so it may be all for the best. Charles James will do very well now we are in a better financial position, though I do not like the look of France.'

'Why doesn't he like the look of France?' asked Elizabeth.

'There have been some disturbances and talk of reform. They intend calling the States General,' explained George. 'I had esteemed it an excellent thing, but Mr Pitt's political instincts are, of course, much better than mine, and he's been to France.'

In the middle of February, Mr Pitt wrote that the King was better. He had had lucid intervals before but now they were more frequent.

The next letter said that the King was quite recovered, the doctors had pronounced him convalescent, the Regency Bill had been postponed and quite likely no more would be heard of it.

'I am so glad,' said Elizabeth. 'The poor Queen. What an ordeal.'

'It is the Lord's doing,' said George, 'and it is marvellous in our eyes.'

CHAPTER ELEVEN

Lincoln

Elizabeth was riding. She ought not to have been for several reasons, but it was August and she hadn't been out for weeks. The willow herb was brilliant everywhere and butterflies made the air restless. There was a good breeze, which kept off the flies. Goodchild was with her, grumbling away about Mrs Mann, who had quarrelled with his wife about fish last week. Mrs Goodchild had said the fish wasn't fresh and would poison them all. The fishmonger turned out to be Mrs Mann's cousin and umbrage was taken. They were going up a long hill to gallop on the Wolds. Coming round a sharp corner of the road between high hedges they saw a fearsome sight. Cattle were pouring down the hill towards them. Shaggy chestnut cows with high horns.

'Back!' Goodchild shouted beside her. 'They've no business driving them Highland cattle without a man in front to warn folks. I see a farm half a mile back. We can get in there.'

'And we can go faster than them,' Elizabeth reassured herself.

But when they went round the corner there was a hay cart coming up. It filled the entire road and pieces of hay were catching in the brambles.

'Hell!' roared Goodchild, and then a second later, 'Hold th' hoss while I get this gate open.'

He slid down, threw her his reins, and started fighting with the gate which was an old bedstead, tied up with rope. The gate instantly fell over but he wrenched it up and out.

'Cattle coming!' Elizabeth shouted to the carter.

'Eh!' he said. He was old with a grey beard.

'There's cattle coming!' she repeated impatiently.

'What say?' he replied dully.

'Come on through for God's sake,' said Goodchild. 'If they're blind and deaf, you can't help them.'

Elizabeth obeyed, but as she went she saw the herd was pouring down the hill at, she guessed, ten miles per hour, while the hay cart was plodding up at what can only have been two miles per hour. The women on top of the load were shouting at the old man now, and he did try to hurry the horses, but the hill was steep and the load heavy and they couldn't trot.

'Go behind the hedge!' ordered Goodchild, as she went through the gate. Elizabeth obeyed him. Her horse, though its head was up, was quiet enough, but Goodchild's horse was thoroughly frightened and she could hardly hold it. A moment later the high shire horses plodded through the gate. Elizabeth was very glad to see them safe. The vast load of hay stuck in the hedges. A hullabaloo of screams, moos, and crashing burst out. A woman fell off the load in a whirl of dress and petticoats, and she thumped into the field. She just missed the shaft of the cart and soon got up. Another woman slithered off screaming into the thick hedge where she could be seen flailing about and could be heard screaming, even above the cattle bellowing. Elizabeth could see the other three women and two men were hanging on for dear life to the depths of the hay. The old driver kept saying something over and over in angered tones, but no one could decipher it. The air was full of hay.

'Hold still, maid!' shouted Goodchild to the girl in the hedge. 'I'll soon cut you free.'

She obeyed him, sobbing, and he started cutting the great briars with his sharp knife. The bellowing got further and further away. One of the men on top of the hay sat up and shouted after an unseen figure, 'You got no right to drive kine all over th' shop without no one else to check 'm.'

''Tis no my blame,' a voice floated back, 'I lost Dougal in Derby an th' Sassenach are o'er covetous. Ah canna thole their cost.'

It could now be heard what the old man was saying, over and over. 'I don't go much on that. I don't go much on that. That's not right. Kine all over th' shop. I don't go much on that.'

Goodchild had, by now, extracted the sobbing girl who was being comforted and mopped up by the woman who had fallen by the shaft. It was her mother.

'You'll need to back hosses out,' Goodchild told the driver.

'Eh?' was the rather dim response.

'I'd best come down,' a young man said from the top of the load. 'If Ephraham get down, that take ten men to get him up again. Hang you on!'

He slid deftly down and backed the horses out, saying as he did so, ''Tis my lucky day. I ain't seen so much leg since I got wed. Beautiful legs, too.'

'Cheek!' cried the girl. Blood was still running down her face but she'd stopped crying.

'You mind your tongue, Harry,' said her mother, 'a better man wouldn't a' looked.'

'I think we got off lightly, all things considered.' said Elizabeth.

'That's a true word,' said Harry, 'thanks to you. If your man hadn't got th' gate open… most generally take us half an hour to get that gate open.'

'We'd best be going,' said Goodchild, back on his horse, 'we're late enough.'

'My life, yes! And we've got Sir Joseph Banks and his friend coming to stay. Won't we catch up with the cattle, though?'

'See 'em ahead of us. Go the other way,' suggested Goodchild.

'You got far to go?' asked the mother.

'Far enough,' said Goodchild.

'Back to the palace,' said Elizabeth. 'I am the new Bishop's wife.'

There was a murmur of surprise and the mother said, 'Fancy that! Next time you ride out this way, look in on us and take a cup o' tea or a glass of ale. Warners' farm, anyone'll tell you.'

Elizabeth replied gratefully, 'I'll do that, but I can't often get away.'

:

They were late back and George, who'd been worried, was inclined to be cross.

Sir Joseph Banks was his usual soothing self. 'I informed your husband the English countryside is one long adventure nowadays. What with highwaymen and sheep, not to mention Highland cattle, one is always at a stand. Oh, this is Wordsworth, by the way. I told the Bishop I always held Goodchild would look after you.'

'He did. I must fly up and change or I shall be late for dinner too,' replied Elizabeth.

Some might have wondered why a distinguished man like Sir Joseph should travel with Wordsworth, a tongue-tied youth, who he obviously hardly knew, but the Pretymans were well aware of Sir Joseph's good nature and dislike of being alone, so they were not surprised.

At dinner they talked about flowers at first. The speechless youth became quite eloquent on that subject. Wordsworth was obviously observant about country things. Between his artless prattle about pasque flowers and bog pimpernel they learned quite a lot about him. He was an orphan, an undergraduate at St John's College in Cambridge, and particularly fond of his sister, who was at present living with a cousin in Penrith.

'We mean to go on a tramp together,' he said. 'Dorothy, my sister, is more observant than I, and we always admire the same wild prospects and fine trees.'

'But first you and I are to botanise at Scrivelsby,' said Sir Joseph. 'I am keen to show you a wood, thick with heliborine.'

'What is the talk in town about the disturbances in Paris?' enquired the Bishop.

'Most of the *ton* are delighted by it, and are persuaded the French are about to set up a government on the English model, a circumstance that seems to me unlikely,' answered Sir Joseph.

'I do not see why the Bastille was so important,' declared Elizabeth. 'Three coiners, two murderers, and a child molester: what is so wondrous about setting them free?'

'It is a symbol,' explained Sir Joseph, 'a symbol of the old ways. Autocracy, tyranny as they think. Moreover, there was some powder and shot there. They are persuaded everything will be different now, and so it will, but I fear after a few bursts of wild excitement it will be found to be even worse.'

'I mean to go and see myself,' said Mr Wordsworth. 'My friend Jones, he's a bit of a radical but he's good company. He means to go to France and I mean to accompany him.'

'It will be interesting,' said Sir Joseph. 'If I were ten years younger and unmarried I should come too, to see for oneself. Yes, yes, history in the making.'

'I am far from pleased,' said George, as if the success of the revolution depended on his approval. 'Mr Pitt always had doubts. Anything that disturbs the established order is undesirable, and now some English Liberals are forming corresponding societies and Lord knows what else. I cannot but feel the French have taken leave of their senses.'

'Let us hope it is not that bad,' said Sir Joseph. 'How does your slum clearance progress?'

George told him all about the prodigious price the owner was asking for a street of the worst slums; how their architect had quarrelled with their builder, and similar sad facts.

Meanwhile, Elizabeth got Wordsworth to talk about Cambridge. He said that much as he esteemed the classics he had found the curriculum rather narrow. He explained how he would have to make his own way when he left college, but that he was not drawn to any profession.

'What I should really like,' he added, his long bony face becoming lively at the thought, 'is to be a poet, but I do not suppose I shall ever be good enough.'

'You will if you practise and observe. I love poetry, not modern poetry. I find it rather flat, but old poetry and the ballads,' she described.

'You're in the right of it. Modern poetry is flat, all that smoothness and regularity, and the ballads are dramatic.'

'Like at night drinking the wine
Or early in the morning
They made a combat between them
To fight it in the dawning,'

'About the middle of the night she heard the bridles ring,
The lady was as glad at that
As any earthly thing,' riposted Elizabeth.

'Last night I dreamt an evil dream
Against the Isle of Skye
I saw a dead man win a fight
And I thought that man was I.'
'The second sister made his bed,
Jenifer, Gentle and Rosemary,
And put soft pillows under his head
As the dew flies over the mulberry tree.'

'How I love them,' finished Elizabeth. 'You must say me a whole long one after dinner. Do you read Walter Scott?'

'Yes, indeed, particularly the poetry. You know I was somewhat apprehensive. I thought a bishop and his wife would be…'

'…stiff and starchy?' Elizabeth finished for him. 'Well, we are younger than most bishops and their wives, you see. "Too young, Pitt. Too young, shan't have it!" the

King said. Then, alas, I am sadly informal. Perhaps I will come by the trick of it in time, but for the present I love to laugh, and gallop, and quote poetry, and I find people intriguing,' Elizabeth said enthusiastically.

'So they are, to be sure. "The proper study of mankind is men". I find them more congenial in the country. In the towns their souls are as congested as their bodies,' Wordsworth argued.

The youth was a little over serious and long-winded thought Elizabeth, however she could not but like him all the same.

'Have you got a poem of your own here that you could read to me?' she asked.

'Well, as it chances, the merest fragment. I hope to improve it,' explained Wordsworth.

'You must show me after dinner,' Elizabeth replied.

:

When Elizabeth and George were in bed, alone at last, George said, 'You certainly got that shy hobbledehoy to speak at last.'

'He wants to be a poet,' she revealed.

'He looks more like a sheep than a poet,' George said with mirth.

'He read me rather a good poem. Too wordy and gaudy and so I told him, but it had quite a rhythm, and he knows and enjoys a lot of poetry which is a good sign,' explained Elizabeth.

'Joseph will be bringing schoolboys next. Never was such a convivial man. I confess I am apprehensive of this French business. No good will come of it. Once the social contract is broken the devil takes a hand. All the news seems to be dispiriting,' said George.

'I have some news which I trust you will not find dispiriting. I am going to have another child in the New Year. January I think; about time is it not? I never wanted Ned to be an only child,' Elizabeth said pleasingly.

'My dear, I am inexpressibly gratified by this happy news. I shall of course be nervous on your behalf, but I think we may have confidence in Mrs Potts,' George said with glee.

'Yes indeed, thank God for Mrs Potts. I shall have to go home in September or October before the roads get too bad. You could perhaps come for Christmas?' she asked.

'We will have to talk it over and make arrangements. I so dislike being apart, but your health is of course paramount,' George stressed. He turned away from her and asked, 'In view of this should you have gone out riding?'

'I suppose not, but I so seldom get to ride now and I planned it when I was far from sure,' she replied.

'I beg of you, my love, have more of a care of your precious health,' George asked caringly.

'I hope it is a girl this time.' said Elizabeth.

CHAPTER TWELVE
Belvoir

'It's worse than last time,' gasped Elizabeth, 'is it going wrong?'

'No, no,' said Mrs Potts, 'that's going along a master, but that's quicker than last time, d' y' see, so that seem worse.'

'Thank God for that! If it went much longer I couldn't bear it,' Elizabeth huffed.

'You don't hev a lot of choice, m' love,' Potts mentioned.

Half an hour later she heard Mrs Potts saying through a haze of pain and exhaustion, 'I'm afraid this's another boy but he's got, yes, he's got red hair. Any red in your families?'

'Yes, my husband's father, or so I've heard!'

Mrs Potts responded with a smile, 'Your husband'll be right pleased then. Men like to see the family come again. Now when we've got you all cleaned up, you must have a good sleep. Four hours that took start to finish. If'n you hev another I'll hardly get here in time.'

George was indeed very pleased with the baby's red hair and full of information about his father when young. He also explained that a great aunt Dorothy had told him when she was young her hair was as red as a fire, three men came courting, and she took the poorest, Nelson from Norfolk, and was very happy.

The aunt had talked of a red haired uncle, called Henry, who had been at the siege of Colchester in the Civil War.

'He was a good 'un,' she had said. 'Everyone came to him for succour.'

:

Elizabeth recovered fast and soon was walking about to see the garden.

Ned viewed his little brother without favour and said, 'He is very red. I shall call him "lobster".'

'He got a bit red being born,' explained Elizabeth, 'and Papa says there is red hair in his family, but his eyes are blue, "just like yours". He will get less red presently.'

'Why did you want him?' Ned asked.

'It was so pleasant having a little boy I asked God to send me another and he finally did,' Elizabeth said caringly.

'Be better soon,' Ned declared, stroking his brother's red hair.

They followed the same pattern as last time except that where there had been occasional worries, because Ned was not very well, George was always in rude health. He did get a cold once at Belvoir, but it didn't seem to affect his appetite or his unusual capacity to sleep quietly.

Everywhere they went people were discussing the French Revolution. They were well informed but always placid, all their reliance on Mirabeau. He was apparently a miracle worker.

'I mean to say he has the measure of the mob,' the Duke of York told Elizabeth after dinner at Belvoir. 'Understands them d' y' see. Not many do. Even th' Jacobins listen to him. Long as he's there it'll peter out gradually without destroying trade. As for giving some of the land to the peasants, good idea, they farm it now. Farm it better when they don't pay rent. Their nobles are damn useless. Not allowed to do anything useful.'

'The mob has felt its power,' declared the Duke of Rutland, 'and it will require a great deal of blood or address to get the genie back in the bottle.'

'They murdered poor Lavoisier,' put in George. 'They announced that the Revolution did not require science or learning.'

'They mean well,' said the Duchess, 'surely they'll learn to do better in time.'

'The French Revolution is, of its nature, violent,' stated the Duke of Rutland. 'A strong man will take charge of it, as Cromwell did, but 'til then it will be chaos, murder, and hunger.'

'Darling, you will have us all sobbing into our syllabub,' avowed the Duchess. 'Let us talk of something cheerful! Who can think of something to make us laugh?'

'Bully Burke prosecuting the one old India hand who never took an anna or a saucepan,' said a tall dark man, whose name Elizabeth had forgotten.

'Lord something was it not?' she thought. 'But then everyone here had titles, but them.'

'I hardly see a cause for mirth there,' uttered the Duchess. 'I had rather call it tragedy. What possesses Mr Burke? I had even esteemed him one of the better sort of Whigs. What drives him?'

'He has been nobbled by that scub Francis,' the Duke of Rutland told them, his heavy, dependable face cold with contempt. 'Francis and Hastings fought a duel in India. Francis was badly wounded, he'll never forgive Hastings.'

'More than that to it,' said the Duke of York. 'Burke's Irish. He's sound enough as a rule, but when it comes to one race ruling another race he loses his head. Seen too much of it in Ireland I daresay.'

'The Indians,' said the tall, dark unknown man, 'are so far from resenting their treatment by Hastings that no less than seventeen of them have written to the King or the "Honourable Vizier" commending his actions and the simplicity and amiability of his nature.'

'That is impressive,' said their host.

'Prodigiously,' agreed their hostess. 'All London is divided on the inquiry. I scarcely dare mention it lest my friends come to fisticuffs. Dear Fanny Burney told me the King, of his courtesy, gave her two tickets. She took her brother William, home on leave from his ship. Burke spoke and spoke so well Fanny began to be persuaded against her better judgement, when her brother pulling at her sleeve desired to know, "When will he come to the point?"'

'Well, said the Navy!' exclaimed the dark man. 'There is no point. Nothing but a maze of demmed, demented rhetoric. The man's mad!'

It appeared on enquiry the tall, dark man was a soldier called Lord Moira.

:

The rest of the year seemed to pass in hardworking happy days of flowers, and sunlight, and babies. In the new year of 1791, Mirabeau died, and people were no longer so reassuring about the French Revolution.

Sir Joseph Banks came to stay and he brought his wife. Also so did Mr Dundas who was on his way to Scotland, a tall man called William Coke, pronounced Cook, who was going up to Brocklesby to advise Lord Yarborough on his sheep, and two boys they had picked up at an inn on their way north. George said that Mr Coke was a well thought-of farmer. He and his wife entertained hundreds of people at their sheep shearing. The two boys, Tom and Will, were painters. Tom never stopped talking, but Will seldom spoke. Elizabeth had difficulty in persuading them to stay. Tom begged to be allowed to go to a small inn, and he declared they had no 'slap up duds,' and that they were 'a brace of scruffs, only fit for an ale house, or sleeping under a hedge.'

'Mrs Pretyman cares nothing for that!' Sir Joseph assured them in the magnificent hall, which did little to confirm his assurances. 'She's no high in the instep, cock-lofty dame. It's open house here. All welcome. No flummery.'

'Well I hope so,' thought Elizabeth. 'To be sure,' she said, smiling at the good looking Tom. There was something rather taking about the little one, though he shouldn't exactly be good looking with that nose. 'We keep no great state as a rule, and if I should chance to give a grand party you may go to your ale house and escape the tedium.'

'That'll be the ticket,' Tom said, smiling back. 'For when all's said and done, it's the nobs as have the brass and taste to buy our pictures.'

'Is that what we're for?' asked Mr Coke. 'I had often wondered. I cannot but think though, employing men and providing them with decent houses has its uses too.'

'Of course,' agreed Tom. 'I meant no harm. I'm no radical. England would suit me well enough if bread was cheaper.'

George, sure enough, was plaintive about the boys. 'I do think Banks might have more consideration. That undergraduate he brought was at least more or less a gentleman, but these two are nought but low cockney louts. People will think it strange,' he said.

'They are painters which makes a difference, and if the Duke of Rutland, say, calls in unexpectedly he may well feel those boys are outside of enough, but he will also feel, depend on it, pleasure at finding Mr Coke here,' Elizabeth explained.

'I must admit that you are in the right of it there. Mr Coke has a sportive manner that must please, and his eminence in agriculture is much in the mode. Even the King participates and writes in farming journals under the name of Robinson,' George retorted.

'They call him "Coke of Norfolk". And then there is Mr Dundas, who, after all, is a cabinet minister. We have enough good company to excuse a slight lapse,' Elizabeth decreed.

:

It was a particularly fine May, so, while they had company, Elizabeth gave one of the fashionable outdoor meals, or as some called them, a 'picnic.'

She asked the Dean along, as well as his clever, bookish wife, Amabel, Sir Henry Fane from Fulbeck, and his wife and son. They met at the Warners' farm, where there was a bluebell wood above the river. Somewhat to George's annoyance Elizabeth had also brought Ned and his nursemaid Nell Potts. Nell was Mrs Pott's niece; a shy and quiet girl. Elizabeth thought, 'The country and running about in it was so good for him,' realising she also wanted to show off such a pretty, chatty child. The Warners had put out straw bales for chairs and tables and three of their best chairs for the ladies. Everyone had brought some food and Elizabeth had brought two footmen and four linen tablecloths; the simple dishes, some kept hot in a haybox, looked very elegant. The young men, having eaten an amazing amount in a short time, went away and were to be seen in the middle distance painting furiously.

'The younger one, Will,' Elizabeth told Sir Henry Fane, 'who is only sixteen has had a picture exhibited in the Royal Academy.'

'God bless my soul! At sixteen! Boy must be a genius,' he replied with astonishment.

'It makes me regret my wasted youth,' declared the younger Henry Fane who had been a cornet in a good cavalry regiment.

'He's a taking little tyke,' said Sir Joseph, 'somewhat diffident but dedicated to his art.'

'I like a braw picture, mesel',' said Mr Dundas. 'I've one o' a castle and, by Bothwell, ye can feel the chill.'

A nightingale sang in the wood and the scent of bluebells wafted over occasionally.

Ned, who had behaved beautifully for half an hour, only speaking when he was spoken to, began to fidget and climb on the straw bales. Nell took him away and they could be seen picking primroses by the river.

'Is it true what people say that you once danced with the unhappy Queen of France?' Sir Henry asked Mr Coke.

Mr Coke smiled, responding, 'Entirely true. More than once in fact. It was on my Grand Tour. She was the most enchanting creature, with the grace and attention span of a butterfly. I fear for her.'

'With reason,' said the old soldier grimly. 'I compliment you on your arrangements, Mrs Pretyman. All too often a picnic means squatting in a damp tussock whilst you try to stop your glass upsetting and eat slippery chicken, but here we're totally snug, and there's no lack of flat surfaces. I congratulate you! Wouldn't have come if m' wife hadn't wanted to but you have it all in hand, even the weather.'

'I am acquainted with the farmer,' explained Elizabeth.

'What's the name of that boy?' asked Mr Coke. 'The one who's a genius.'

'Turner,' answered Sir Joseph. 'Joseph William Turner. T'other one's called Tom Gurton. I sometimes think England's like a cherry tree that's just going to burst into flower, all covered in buds.'

'Let us hope so,' said Mr Coke. Then he announced, 'Kingfisher!'

The blue bird went smoothly and swiftly along the water below them and vanished round the bend.

'Such a deep colour,' said Elizabeth.

'Aye,' agreed Mr Dundas, 'but if ye saw it every day ye'd no regard it.'

A nightingale sang. A footman brought round more champagne.

'I feel I am living in Boccaccio,' said Amabel.

No one else felt inclined to join her with that poet.

'We do not pay enough attention to our water supply,' acknowledged Mr Coke. 'Some physicians are of the opinion water can harbour diseases.'

'What a lowering notion,' said Amabel. 'The children would always be at risk. Have you read *A Journal of the Plague Year*?'

A series of screams interrupted them. Tom and Will, who were nearer the screams, discarded their paintings and ran towards the noise. Elizabeth followed them. She was afraid Ned had fallen in. As she ran round the corner the screams stopped, and she soon met a sodden group.

'He ran on ahead,' said Nell.

'Lucky I can swim,' said Tom.

Ned clung on to his mother sobbing.

'He ran on ahead,' said Nell again, 'an' there was this stream full of crowsfoot. He go for to gather it an' tumble in, too. Tha's ever so deep an' cold, and muddy, but this gentleman pull him out and then pull me out.'

'I am very much obliged to you,' Elizabeth said to Tom, and then to Ned, 'you're quite safe now, darling.'

'I am glad I persuaded them to stay,' she thought to herself.

'I handed him to Will,' explained Tom, 'but the clumsy oaf near dropped him.'

'I did not! I near fell in with him. He's heavier than he looks.'

Elizabeth went back, meeting George who, rather belatedly, wanted news of Ned. The men were discussing the situation in France and George joined in. Amabel was sitting alone, so Elizabeth sat down by her and said, 'You look melancholy.'

'Not melancholy so much as afraid,' Amabel muttered.

'Oh? Why? You're not…?' Elizabeth replied inquisitively.

'I am, alas,' Amabel finished. 'For the tenth time in ten years I am having a child and Augustus is not one yet. Will it be an agonising, protracted birth, or an agonising, tragic miscarriage?'

'It needn't be either. As I have told you before, if you just come to my old home with me, Nell's mother is a genius who never lost a mother,' Elizabeth insisted reassuringly.

'But I can't leave John and the children. He's so impractical. Susan forgets to order food,' explained Amabel.

'Your health is more important. You could bring a couple of the older children,' encouraged Elizabeth.

Elizabeth made a mental note to talk to John.

Amabel continued, 'You're very kind, but I really do not feel… You're so lucky – a baby every three years – how do you arrange it all so adroitly?'

Elizabeth replied with a smile, 'It just happened, and I sometimes wish the boys were closer and could play together. Ned has such fun with your Jack.'

The nightingale was still singing.

CHAPTER THIRTEEN
Germains

Marmaduke Tomline invited himself to stay again in September. He was very little trouble and spent all his time stalking and sketching a pair of cranes that had taken up their abode five miles east of Lincoln. In October, Elizabeth and Amabel, two servants, and three children started on the long journey south. The coach was full and the children were restless. Amabel was not at all well and the journey seemed very long.

They stayed in various country houses and that was pleasant enough. The inns varied. Some were extremely comfortable, the food good, the service excellent and the beds soft. But others were just the opposite, particularly when the hostelry was full. One of the bad inns was noisy and Amabel could not sleep. The next day she looked very ill. It was a wet autumn, and on three occasions, one of which they were staying in a terrible, dirty, noisy inn, it rained so hard they could not travel. The roads got worse and worse, and countless times they got stuck and had to be pulled out by carthorses, which meant they only travelled few miles that day. Then, after they had travelled for only a few hours, the two small boys grew bored. Ned would whine incessantly and Jack would start to kick and climb about, opening the window and trying to hang out of it. Only little George was endlessly happy, ceaselessly entranced by everyone and everything. He seldom cried and when he did usually had good reason to. Perhaps Jack had kicked him again, or Ned had dropped a toy on him.

Elizabeth told stories until she was hoarse, and she nursed Ned, and handed out sweets until she was sticky. Always the jolting and swaying of the coach. The journey had seemed very long and tedious. Sometimes Elizabeth rode in the morning. It meant starting later than the cumbersome coach, and it was much pleasanter.

Goodchild was wonderful and so were Tom, Nell, and Kate, but the constant worry about Amabel was a strain. She did not seem able to sleep or eat much, and Elizabeth suspected she was going downhill, very slowly, but steadily. Nell loved the baby and the journey helped. She'd never been out of the village before and her mouth was often open at the smart houses and inns where they stayed. It was an immense relief when they rumbled into the sweep at Germains on a dark, rainy November evening. After Elizabeth had made sure Amabel was in bed, had greeted her parents, and had agreed George was adorable, she sent someone to fetch Mrs Potts. That someone, a footman called Charles, returned after an hour. Mrs Potts was with Mrs Hands at Pond Hall Farm, and could not come until morning. It was frustrating after travelling so far but Elizabeth was too tired to worry much about it. She came the next morning, taking a hopeful though far from complacent view of the patient.

Potts said, 'She be worn to a thread, fretting and planning and scraping to make ends meet, and all dead again her nature, I should reckon. Be her husband very thrifty?'

'No, not that I ever heard of or noticed. He has got six children to provide for and now another. They entertain well enough,' Elizabeth replied.

'People are mostly bound to make a show when they shouldn't, 'specially the middlin' sort. You done right to fetch her here 'n' none too soon. We got a month p'haps. I doubt she'll come to term,' Potts said ominously.

'What must we do?' Elizabeth enquired thoughtfully.

'Get her movin'. If she walks she'll soon eat 'n' sleep. Just a little at first 'n' then further,' Mrs Potts asserted confidently.

'I'll do my best, but she's so pleased with the library she will hardly come out of it and the weather is inclement,' Elizabeth explained.

'Tell her life depends on it,' went on Potts. 'That's no more 'n' the truth. She got to help herself. No one else can. She's gone all flabby 'n' if she don't walk she won't have the strength for labour. You t'gether kin afford to coddle y'selves but it don't do y' no good.'

To begin with it was a hard, depressing task. Amabel would be puffed at the smallest exertion and stumble at the smallest declivity. She got better though, and by December she was walking a mile in spite of her great bulk. She ate well and slept well, and she had some profound conversations with Elizabeth's father, who was a considerable reader, too.

:

One night in early December Elizabeth was woken from a deep sleep by Amabel. She was holding a candle and wearing a white night dress and crimson shawl, and looked like an immense tragedy queen.

'The hour has struck,' she announced.

'It's started?' Elizabeth said surprised.

'Aye, and worse than that. I know I'm going to die,' Amabel foretold morbidly.

'Don't say anything so silly. I didn't take all this trouble for you to do go doing that. I'll send Nell for her mother,' Elizabeth reassured Amabel.

She made up Amabel's fire, which, luckily, wasn't out yet, and prayed Mrs Potts wasn't out on a case. Mrs Potts came in no time but not before Amabel had given Elizabeth careful instructions for her funeral.

'Go on with you!' scoffed Mrs Potts. 'That's a christening you had ought to be a thinking on, not a funeral. Do you go back to your bed, m' dear Mrs Pretyman,' she said to Elizabeth, 'there's nothing you can do, 'n' if you hang about in that thin wrapper you'll catch your death.'

Elizabeth went thankfully back to bed, and was even more thankful when she found Nell had made up her own fire. In the morning Nell reported that all was well.

'Won't be much longer, Mother do reckon,' Nell informed Elizabeth.

But it was two o'clock before Mrs Potts herself appeared. 'She'll do now,' she told them. 'Healthy little girl 'n' she mean to call it Elizabeth. I had a job to check th' bleeding but she do now.'

'I am inexpressibly glad to hear it,' said Elizabeth's father. 'We are much obliged and grateful for your skilled attentions.'

'Tha's a pleasure to me to save a fam'ly. But she'd best not fall for another for a year or two. I'll talk to Mrs Pretyman about that later. I'm off now.'

'Surely,' said Elizabeth's mother, 'she's scarcely likely to start another child at her age. Elizabeth tells me she is thirty nine.'

'You'd be surprised,' remarked Mrs Potts, and she then plodded noisily out of the drawing room.

Amabel recovered rather slowly but steadily. 'It was bad but not nearly as bad as usual,' she said to Elizabeth one sunny, frosty morning when they were walking in the garden, 'and as I got my beloved babe from it I incline not to resent it.'

'Did you incline to blame the other babes?' enquired a shocked Elizabeth.

'No, truly I think not. I was just too shattered to observe them except with exhaustion. But thanks to your divine Mrs Potts, I love my little Eliza dearly. I so wish I could feed her,' Amabel eludicated.

'Jenny does that adequately,' Elizabeth added.

'Yes, indeed. I even grew attached to Jenny's Reuben, though he is somewhat given to bawling.'

'Mrs Potts tells me many of the poor give babies gin because the noise is unendurable in a small space,' Elizabeth noted.

'How terrible! Could we not…? No, I suppose not. How pleasantly the sun strikes today,' Amabel declared.

'Yes indeed, those little green needle points will be snowdrops. Fancy that! Alas, I shall not see them, and they do not come 'til March in Lincoln,' Elizabeth pronounced.

:

They spent Christmas quietly but happily, and soon afterwards George and the Dean arrived in the Pretyman coach, which Goodchild had taken back for them. How happy the reunion was between the Dean and Amabel, Elizabeth could not make out. The Dean was a cold fish. George, though, was simply passionately glad to see her again. 'Let us never part again,' he kept saying.

In January, the Andrews, their four children, and Nell all went back to Lincoln in the Pretyman coach. George and Elizabeth posted to London where they were to stay in Downing Street with Mr Pitt. He was unaffectedly glad to see them and full of questions about Lincoln. He even proposed to give a dinner party for them some time in the next week or two.

'There was much to be said for London in the winter,' thought Elizabeth six days later. They'd been to a play, two concerts, and a lecture on the properties of air, and now they were off to the Tower. They went by water, and George showed her the stone that Princess Elizabeth sat on when she refused to go into the Tower to be imprisoned during her sister's reign. It seemed unlikely to be the same stone, but Elizabeth still found the magnificent fortress and the busy river with salmon leaping among the wherries very impressive. A warder greeted them and offered to show them around. Elizabeth hoped he knew his history because George was well informed. The Warder had been carefully trained however, and, if what he told them was well-known, it was also accurate.

'Lady Jane Grey,' he said, 'no more wanted to be Queen than I wants to be a bishop like you, sir. She wasn't but sixteen, but her father-in-law, Northumberland, he wanted to keep on being th' top dog.'

'We must also remember,' replied George, 'that the dying King was much concerned for the continuance of the Protestant faith. He was acutely aware that his elder sister, Mary, was an implacable papist. The Lady Jane was as staunchly Protestant as he could wish, and he therefore thought her the only hope for a Protestant future.'

'Fancy that,' said the Warder. 'I never heard that. The poor young King, doin' his best for our Church. He had ought to 'a' known though the English would 'a' held by th' right succession. And it all turned out well in th' end. Don't that just show 'ee that the good Lord keep us safe?'

'It can hardly be said,' objected George, 'that it all turned out well for Cranmer, Latimer, and Ridley, to mention but three of the hundreds of who died in the flames.'

Elizabeth was barely listening to this exchange. She usually loved history and George's exact grasp of it, but she was gazing at the couple ahead of them trying to see if it really could be her sister. But then the couple and their guide paused to admire the White Tower and as they got closer she saw it was.

'Emily!' she called joyfully.

'Sister!' exclaimed the girl in the green dress whose tangerine pelisse lit up the dull winter's day.

The man with her was young, fair-haired, and very trim in naval uniform. The sisters were soon clasped in each other's arms.

'Give you good day, brother-in-law,' said the officer. 'This is just the place I might have looked for a don like you and blue stocking like Lizzie, but want-wits like us seldom visit improving places. Thing is, we wanted to see the lions.'

'However it happened, it is the greatest good fortune,' said Elizabeth. 'No one else,' she thought, 'called her Lizzie, thank heaven,' but her brother-in-law said it with such good humoured affection she could not resent it. She continued, 'We are in London for another s'en nights, and you?'

Elizabeth's brother-in-law retorted, 'We have inflicted ourselves on my cousin Cairns in Chelsea. You behold in me a gentleman of leisure, or, should you prefer, a poor wretch of a half-pay lieutenant. My cousin's house is none too spacious so we thought to remove to my parents next week. Emmie longs to go home after that but in the spring we might give the palace a try. And you have an address for us? Where do you lodge?'

'In Number 10 Downing Street. I fear we are an imposition but Mr Pitt would have it so and we are to go to hear Mrs Hastings on Tuesday,' Elizabeth answered.

'I wonder, you could bear to leave your dear little baby,' said her sister. 'If I had a dear little baby I am sure I should never leave it.'

'Elizabeth is the most devoted of mothers,' said George reprovingly, 'but George is weaned now and very well with his nurse. He is a most contented child. Ned will miss her more, but it is only for a few weeks.'

'I think it is just as well we've no children now; we are so very poor. Shall we repair to a cookhouse? All this history has made me hungry,' asked Emily.

'I had intended to visit the Church of St. John,' protested George.

'Another time, old cock. The wife of my bosom is sharp set and I must cherish her with chops. Can't say I blame her when my cousin's wife keeps a poor table,' explained the officer.

They tipped and thanked their Beefeaters and then went to find food.

Mr Pitt was very interested to hear of their encounter. 'A naval officer,' he said, sipping his tea. 'I trust he is bluff, cheery, and outspoken?'

'To a fault,' said Elizabeth, smiling.

'Just as it should be. I shall ask them to my dinner on Friday. I say dinner, but really it is likely to be more of a frost. But a naval officer will be a great resource and should stir up Grenville. He's really too flat. If he was a pond you could say he was stagnant,' Pitt proposed.

'Elizabeth's sister and her husband are young and impoverished,' pointed out George. 'They might perhaps be overwhelmed by your gracious invitation.'

'It takes a lot to overwhelm Emily,' her fond sister asserted.

'Let us hope they have no previous engagement, for I am keen to see a big wave smash into the pond,' Pitt expressed excitedly.

:

Elizabeth chanced to come down to breakfast early next morning. George was still shaving and Mr Pitt, having greeted her, hoping she had slept well, asked, 'How does George bear the bluffness?'

'Stoically, for my sake. He was not however, I fear, best pleased addressed as "old cock",' expressed a smiling Elizabeth.

'No. Would I had been there. We need more candour. Society now often talks of nothing much in measured periods. If only your brother-in-law will but call my cousin "old cock". It would do him the world of good. His fiancée too, another cousin, is altogether too stiff. The poker and the tongs, one each side of the hearth, they will be. She is an admirable woman and, was you to beg from her for your slum clearance in Lincoln, she would donate a neat terrace, but the last time she saw a joke was when I fell over into a cowpat. She was five and I was but four,' Pitt elaborated.

'He calls me Lizzie,' Elizabeth revealed, alluding to her brother-in-law.

'He would. I am sure if a true serving officer had but met Cleopatra he would have called her "Pattie"?'

:

Mr Pitt had got good seats for them in Westminster Hall at the trial of Warren Hastings, which all the *ton* in London were talking about. It was very crowded and the uproar sounded like a smart party, but when a lawyer called for silence it came so completely that footsteps sounded very loud. The legal arguments were tedious and seemed endless. Elizabeth was quite content at first, looking up at the marvellous roof and reflecting on its long history, but it was cold in the stone hall, in spite of the braziers, and she began to think of leaving. George was always considerate and would, if she told him how cold she was getting, certainly depart.

All the numerous spectators were clearly as bored as she was and began to chatter in spite of numerous, sonorous shouts of 'Silence in Court'.

'It is strange, but Mr Burke, so wrong-minded on the proceedings of poor Mr Hastings, is very sound on the French Revolution,' George said to her in a low voice.

Elizabeth whispered back, 'Indeed. Mr Pitt told me the King is forever saying about his book *Reflections on the French Revolution*, or some such title, "It is a very good book, sir, a very good book. Every gentleman should read it".'

George began to reply, 'This gentleman will read it but I can do that at Lincoln, whereas in Number 10 there are many profitable books that—'

He was interrupted by a powerful voice declaring, 'Call Edmond Burke.'

The high hall fell silent.

'Mr Burke had an interesting face,' thought Elizabeth, and missed the start of his speech. Not a handsome face, but lively. Not a large man, but the way he stood, the way he held out a hand, appealing, accusing, throwing things away, told of purpose and solid, implacable determination. He was saying, 'These women in India, helpless in a world of warriors, dependent for all means of sustenance and nurture on strangers they did not and could not understand and could not communicate with, suddenly reduced from affluence to beggary, may we not shed a tear for them? May we not feel they were betrayed?'

He went on for some time in the same strain. Elizabeth was baffled and uneasy. Could it be true? It would be appalling if it were, but how could we possibly tell? Come to that, how could Mr Burke possibly tell? He had never been in India, and someone had said one night in Belvoir Castle that he was being advised by a Mr Francis, who was Mr Hastings' long-standing, bitter enemy.

After what seemed a very long speech the Court was adjourned, and the Pretymans went, as Mr Pitt had advised them, to a nearby hotel, where they warmed up by a beautiful blazing fire and ate a simple but excellent luncheon of omelettes and syllabub. George agreed Burke's oratory had had a very odd effect.

'He makes it all sound so reasonable; one shares his apprehension that if the Indians are to be ruled by the British they must be ruled justly and with humanity. But, then, you cannot but reflect that his knowledge of India is only hearsay, whereas Mr Hastings has thirty years of the sub-continent,' George justified.

'I thought that, too. Mr Pitt says Burke could make a slaughterhouse sound delightful. I think he nets you in a web of clever words and then when you can scarce move you think, "but was it really like that?"' asked Elizabeth.

'We are not in a position to judge. However—'

Here the host broke into their talk by ringing a hand bell and then saying, 'Any ladies and gents as wants to go back to the bear pit is hereby given notice th' bear's afoot.'

'What can he mean?' wondered Elizabeth.

'Do you refer to Mr Hastings?' enquired George of the host.

'Course I mean Mr Hastings, and Billy Burke's a socking great mastiff as never lets go once he gits a hold,' the host replied enthusiastically.

'The insolence of the Londoners is without parallel,' muttered George indignantly as they walked back.

'I rather enjoy it. It is completely like bear baiting. I can scarce wait to view the bear,' Elizabeth answered gleefully.

It seemed colder than ever in the hall. The lawyers were arguing, the crowd was chattering, but the landlord was right. Hardly had the Pretymans sat down, pulling their shawls about them, then the usher bellowed, 'Call Mr Hastings.'

Mr Hastings, a small man, appeared. Elizabeth felt sorry for him at first. A little man standing there all alone in that vast space. Then she realised he was not small but very medium-sized, only very trim, filling the space with his composed presence.

A lawyer was asking him questions. They were complicated questions but his answers were meticulous.

One question went, 'Were you aware that your machinations had been the occasion of great hardships and perturbation to two helpless, aged women?'

'I was well aware they were bound to be infuriated and that they were not without influence,' replied Hastings.

'I refer not to their sentiments but to their sufferings,' explained the lawyer.

'I fear I am no judge of their sufferings. I was, however, aware of the hardship suffered by their stepson and step-grandson owing to their thefts,' Hastings answered.

'Are you implying that those harmless, sequestered women had by some arcane, nefarious method stolen specie from their all-powerful kinsmen?' the lawyer probed.

'I am indeed. The manoeuvrings of an Indian royal family are somehow complicated, and it is often hard to decide who is robbing whom. Nevertheless, their kinsman was undoubtedly inconvenienced by their having intercepted his father's wealth,' Hastings elaborated further.

Elizabeth began to shiver in spite of shawls.

'It grows cold,' whispered George. 'Had we not better repair to Mr Pitt's warm fires?' he proposed.

It was tempting. It was almost irresistible, yet Elizabeth was fascinated by the neat, indomitable figure, so close and talking about things that had happened far away.

'I have the greatest respect for Indian law,' Mr Hastings was saying, 'and I tried to administer it as I judged Akbar would have wished. I should say, perhaps for those who are familiar with Indian history, that Akbar was a previous Great Moghul. However, I regret to admit Indian law is now much influenced by bribery, to the detriment of poor men.'

'Why did you employ Indians rather than English to collect revenue, then?' asked the lawyer.

'I only employed those Indians whom I judged to be capable of honesty, as I only employed those British whom I judged to be capable of courtesy, for courtesy, you must know, is essential in India,' Hastings eloquently replied.

'Did you judge you had metamorphosed into the Great Moghul?' enquired the lawyer. 'You seem to have given little consideration to the wishes and revenues of the Company.'

'The Company's revenue was dependent upon its good name and ultimately on its power,' Hastings professed.

The cold seemed to be seeping into Elizabeth's bones, and she turned to George, who rose immediately and helped her up the steps.

'I feel I've learned a lot,' she said, as they rode back to Downing Street in a Hackney carriage, 'but I would like to learn more. More about Akbar, Indian law, and Indian families. Unless you know you can't really judge.'

'We are unbecomingly ignorant of our Indian responsibilities,' agreed George, 'but the men on the spot seem to become knowledgeable. I found Mr Hastings impressive.'

'Oh so did I. He did not try to cast spells on you like Burke. But he explained what happened, and you felt he was telling you the truth. How he manages without breaking down! Day after day in that horrid cold!' exclaimed Elizabeth.

Mr Pitt was discovered drinking tea with his friend and fellow politician, George Rose. As they thawed, inside and out, with hot tea and chortling fires, they poured out their impressions of the impeachment.

'It is a tragedy,' Mr Pitt uttered. 'Euripides, or perhaps Aeschylus. I gave him a hint but he scorned it.'

'He was unwise to lecture the House,' agreed Mr Rose. 'They never like it. They feel they are not schoolboys anymore and yet, alas, where Indian affairs are concerned they are schoolboys, or even infants.'

'My opinion of him has fluctuated,' said Mr Pitt. 'I had presumed he must be a man of parts to have won an empire, not that it is quite what we require. Canada, where we can grow wheat, is likely to be of more service, but I share the English instinct for tidying things up, and I thought Mr Hastings must be an exemplary personage. Then there were disclosures about Chait Singh. I signed to Mr Wilberforce to meet me behind the Speaker's Chair, as we do on occasion, and said, "Does not this look very ill to you," and he replied, "Very bad indeed," so I felt there was occasion for an inquiry.'

'Who was Chait Singh?' asked Elizabeth.

'An Indian prince whom Hastings had dealings with. He does indeed seem to have played him false, but Hastings fined him a disproportionate amount,' explained Pitt.

'The English cannot hope to understand India,' stated Mr Rose, 'unless they can speak with one who has lived there and has considerable power of eloquence.'

'I am persuaded you are in the right of it,' agreed George. 'My wife and I were both desirous of learning more, but so little is known, even now, of Hindustan.'

'Is it not unusual for a man to pass thirty-five years in that hot climate, as Mr Hastings has, and be in no way the worse for it?' enquired Elizabeth.

'An interesting conundrum,' commented Mr Rose. 'I am acquainted with a Mr Coote, a soldier from an Irish family, who was some time in India. I must ask his opinion. He is a prodigious admirer of Mr Hastings, and declares in his forthright, soldierly way that there were many men in India who should have been impeached, but Mr Hastings was not of their number.'

'Did they work together?' asked Elizabeth.

Rose went on, 'I believe Coote led a force which fought for Mr Hastings in some of the campaigns. He states, as an example of Mr Hastings' tenacity, that he waited ten years to be married.'

'How so?' asked Mr Pitt.

Rose began to explain. 'Amongst the other passengers on one of Mr Hastings' voyages to India there was an Austrian Baron and his wife. Blessed if I can remember the Baron's name – Imhoff, something of the sort. At all events the Baron seemed to have little use for his wife, so the other gentleman entertained her and Mr Hastings kept up the acquaintanceship in India. Some years later the Baron went back to wherever he came from – I'm almost sure it was Austria – but without his wife, who remained in India, properly chaperoned and received everywhere. A few years more and the Baron received a divorce, and Mr Hastings married the lady. Coote says they live very happily.'

'A little risqué, perhaps,' objected George. 'I am no friend to divorce.'

:

The next day was Mr Pitt's dinner party. Emily and her husband, Harry Meynell, were coming. Emily kept saying she had nothing to wear: 'I mean for a dinner party.' But it was obvious she was delighted. Harry said, 'You wouldn't think he'd want a simple cove like me but I met m' old Captain Collingwood in Bond Street and he said that was just where I was wrong. Mr Pitt's always been mad about the Navy.'

It seemed unlikely that Captain Collingwood had expressed himself in quite those terms, but George agreed Mr Pitt had always shown a great regard for the Senior Service. A lady, Anne Pitt, who was engaged to her cousin Mr Grenville, came in with him, she having arrived a minute early and he having arrived a minute late. She was a tall, gaunt, forbidding figure in a very plain grey silk dress which did not suit her. Her cousin and fiancé, William Grenville, would have been rather handsome if he had any expression in his face.

Mr Pitt greeted them vaguely.

'Are you not going to introduce us, Billy?' demanded Anne. 'These harum-scarum manners will not do, you know. You are no longer a boy in coats with your nose in a book.'

Mr Pitt introduced them meekly, but Elizabeth saw, not for the first time, that he was laughing in a straight face.

'Is the party complete?' enquired Anne of Elizabeth.

'My sister and her husband, who is a naval officer, are yet to come. I fear she is often sadly late. She dresses in good time and looks charmingly, insists her mantua does not really become her gown and, removing both, makes a fresh start,' Elizabeth revealed.

'The young are all too often quite without conduct,' Anne pronounced from the senility of her twenty-eight years.

'My brother is so often late they call him "the late Lord Chatham",' said Mr Pitt.

'It is what I have no patience with,' pronounced Anne. 'On several occasions I have started without him.'

They believed her. A footman handed around Ratafia and Madeira and they stood about awkwardly until Elizabeth, who was tired after their expedition, firmly sat down.

'You are fatigued?' enquired Anne, raising her eyebrows and looking like an outraged governess.

'Somewhat. We went to the impeachment of Mr Hastings in Westminster Hall and it was rather chilly,' Elizabeth clarified.

'You should have worn furs,' said Anne, sublimely unaware that most people could not afford them. 'It is Mr Burke who should be impeached, causing such a bother and listening to that scrub Francis.'

Elizabeth looked guiltily at the clock. Past six.

'How is your zealous friend?' Anne asked Mr Pitt. 'Still desirous of making us all evangelical?'

'I think he is even more desirous of turning you abolitionist,' Pitt suggested.

'You know perfectly well, Billy, I have been abolitionist this ten years. The cause is just, so pray, why do you not progress with it?' Anne argued.

'Wilberforce is to bring in a bill to abolish slavery as soon as may be,' answered Mr Pitt. 'At first to prevent the further importation of slaves. I shall give it my full support and I really believe it may prevail.'

Elizabeth glanced at the clock again. Six twenty. Oh dear!

'One must not forget,' said Mr Grenville, speaking for the first time in a deep, deliberate voice, 'the extreme prosperity of the sugar islands, largely, I fear, because of their free labour. Or, indeed, the ferocity of the revolting negroes in San Domingo.'

'If they seize power, they will naturally avenge their ill-treatment,' said George. 'One can hardly wonder at it. But if they are set free and guided to a better more Christian life they may soon prove to be exemplary, intelligent subjects.'

'I am quite of your mind,' said Anne, nodding at him approvingly. 'And, indeed, the only negro of my acquaintance, Dr. Johnson's old servant, Francis, was a regular communicant and a mild, benevolent man.'

'Why, then, when all intelligent men, such as we are, are of one mind, does your friend Dundas, Lord Melville I suppose I should now call him, oppose it?' asked George.

Elizabeth looked at the clock again. Six thirty. Could Emily have met with an accident?

'He is of the opinion,' Mr Pitt was saying, 'that it is unwise to interfere over-much in the colonies. We may endeavour to persuade them. We may stop the slave trade. We may, in time, be in a position to reimburse them for the value of their slaves, which should make them more amenable, but we may not, he feels—'

'Mr and Mrs Meynell,' announced the butler, and everyone breathed a relieved and hungry sigh.

'Terribly late,' said Harry truthfully. 'It came on to rain and I couldn't get a cab.'

'You should have hired a coach,' said Anne.

'I shouldn't,' said Harry, contradicting her cheerfully, 'or I'd soon be getting free transport to a debtor's prison.'

'We are just not rich enough,' agreed Emily. 'It is monstrous, provoking, and tedious, but most people have to be careful when they are young, so we make the best of it.'

'Dinner is served,' declared the butler.

Elizabeth found herself sitting on Mr Pitt's left, with Harry on her left. She asked Mr Pitt what he proposed to do in the next few years now that he had amended the country's finances.

'I would not go so far as to say that. They are in better shape, certainly, which is much. I hope to pay off the debts with my Sinking Fund in five or ten years. I wish to do something for the farm labourer. Free cow for each poor family, perhaps. There is slavery, as we were saying earlier, and above all I hope to do much for the Navy,' Pitt described.

'That's the ticket,' interrupted Harry from Elizabeth's other side. 'Rule Britannia! You want an island taken or a fleet sunk? We're the boys to do it.'

'I do not doubt it,' agreed Mr Pitt. 'Lord Halifax said in King William and Queen Mary's time, "The first article of an Englishman's political creed must ever be that he believeth on the sea".'

'I've never heard that before,' said Harry enthusiastically. 'That's good, that is! Say it again.'

Mr Pitt obliged smiling, and added, 'It went on if I do not mistake, "We are in an island, confined thereto by God almighty, not as a penance, but as a grace; that grace the greatest that be given to mankind".'

'That's a true word, as they say where I come from,' said Harry delightedly. 'Good stuff! Who was Halifax?'

Pitt started explaining, 'Lord Halifax was a politician around the end of the seventeenth century. They called him "The Trimmer" and he astutely wrote an essay entitled "On the Nature of a Trimmer". Would it not be convenient if the French were in England and we in France? Yet we still held the sea, so when they started slaughtering each other we simply shut them up in their house and the infection could not spread.'

'Vastly convenient,' admitted his cousin Anne, actually smiling at the thought.

'And if a Frenchman visited France which was then England, he would have to ring a bell and shout "Unclean! Unclean!"' suggested the Bishop.

'Of course,' agreed Mr Pitt, 'unless he had not caught the hypochondria, as we see with the aristocratic French, when we must give him tea and sympathy.'

'I never heard anyone talk like you,' said Emily. 'I suppose it's only right that the Prime Minister, who talks more sense in the House than anyone else, should talk more nonsense than anyone else in his own house.'

'You are in the right of it,' Mr Pitt assured her, 'but one day I shall forget and talk nonsense in the House.'

They all laughed.

'Fox might insinuate,' said Mr Grenville, 'that your speeches are already somewhat lacking in liberty, equality, and fraternity.'

'You will only have the first and the last if you avoid too much of the middle one,' said Mr Pitt.

CHAPTER FOURTEEN

Bacton

Mr Pitt's party was generally agreed to have been a success.

'Poor Anne was unfavourably impressed by the lateness of the Bishop's sister-in-law,' said Mr Grenville to Lord Chatham, 'and I could not blame her, for it is indeed prodigiously discourteous in the young. However, Billy's discourse was, as ever, diverting, and she ended by enjoying the evening.'

'You do have the most ill-assorted guests, Billy,' said Anne, 'and ill-organised dinner. But the warmth of your heart and the sportiveness of your disposition repairs all wants, and proves irresistible.'

'I am glad of it,' said Mr Pitt meekly.

'Mr Pitt surpassed himself,' said George. 'I do not know when I have laughed so much.'

'It was amusing,' agreed Elizabeth, 'and pretty to see him instructing Harry.'

'Mr Pitt's a great gun,' suggested Harry. 'Never know what he'll say next. He made things so clear. "It is the first article of an Englishman's creed that he believeth on the sea".'

'No one told me Billy Pitt was fun,' said Emily. 'I wouldn't have believed it. He was like a jolly, easy-going uncle. He was quite taken with you, darling. I wonder if he'll find you a ship?'

:

Two days later, Goodchild arrived with the coach to take the Pretymans back to Lincoln. Ned was very pleased to see them, and George smiled at them. Amabel was well and was not having another baby, and little Elizabeth was very well and growing fast.

In the summer, the Royal Family of France tried to escape but went too slowly and were captured just before the frontier. After that they were imprisoned, separated, and treated badly.

Harry was offered a ship, at last. First Lieutenant under Captain Alexander Hood on the *Hebe*. Whether Pitt spoke to Lord Melville, they never knew.

In April, 1792, Mr Wilberforce brought his bill to do away with slavery and Mr Pitt spoke superbly.

'How is this enormous evil ever to be eradicated, if every nation is thus prudentially to wait 'til the convenience of all the world shall have been obtained? There is no nation in Europe that has, on the one hand, plunged so deeply into the guilt as Britain, or that is so likely, on the other, to be looked upon as an example, if she should have the manliness to be the first in decidedly renouncing it.'

Later on in the speech he said, 'Why, might not some Roman Senator, reasoning on the principles of some honourable gentleman and, pointing to the British barbarians, have predicted with equal boldness, "There is a people that will never rise to civilisation. There is a people destined never to be free – a people without the understanding necessary for the attainment of the useful arts, depressed by the hand of nature below the level of the human species, and created to form a supply of slaves for the rest of the world"?'

At dawn as the first rays of light broke shining through the windows above him, he chose two lines from Virgil's *Aeneid* to illustrate the coming of dawn in Africa:

> Nosque ubi primis equis ouiens adflavit anhelis;
> Illus sera rubens accendit illuma Vesper
>
> (And when the rising sun has first breathed on us
> with his panting horses / Over the red evening star
> lighting his late lamps)

Yet the House voted against abolition and instead for a clause Dundas put in that slavery be abolished 'gradually'.

In August 1792, the King made Pitt Warden of the Cinque Ports. This meant £3,000 a year and the right to live in Walmer Castle.

'I am so bent on this I shall be seriously offended at any attempt to decline,' the King wrote, knowing Pitt had declined a lot of the money and honours he'd been offered, including the Garter.

Pitt didn't go much to Walmer at first as he was very happy, and was busy planning and planting at his other home in Kent, Holwood. His friends often found themselves digging holes for trees in company with the hard-digging Prime Minister. Lord Grenville didn't take to it at all.

Austria, under the Duke of Brunswick, proposed to attack revolutionary France.

'Mr Pitt feels that what the French do, though unwise, is their own affair,' George told the Dean, as he and their wives walked back after Evensong on a fine late summer evening.

'Long may it remain so,' replied Reverend Andrews, 'but I read in the paper that the Tuileries has been stormed, the Swiss Guards slaughtered, the King imprisoned, and the Monarchy suspended. Such infamy is likely to prove infectious.'

'I could wish Austria would hold their hands,' said Amabel. 'It is but natural that they should fear for Marie Antoinette who was their princess, but it is always wiser not to stir up a hornets' nest.'

'You are mistaken,' said her husband. 'I am persuaded the Austrian army will have little difficulty in dealing with a rabble of "sans-culottes".'

'I am in hopes you are right,' said Elizabeth, 'but I am far from certain. We are in uncharted waters here and there are prodigious quantities of Frenchmen.'

At this point they reached the Deanery, and John Andrews said, 'Here we are. Will you not step in for a moment and partake of a glass of wine with us?'

'You are very kind,' replied Elizabeth, 'and tempting, but I promised the boys I would be back for their bedtime.'

'I will see you on Friday, then,' said Amabel.

'Yes, indeed,' replied Elizabeth.

After they had parted Elizabeth said, 'I must tell you that I rather think I am to have another child.'

'Oh! You…are…pleased?' George said with astonishment.

'Very much so. I have, as you know, always wanted four. Four is a nice round number, but time is going on and I am thirty already,' Elizabeth said philosophically.

'I should like a daughter,' George replied.

'And so should I, so it is bound to be another boy! But the timing is awkward. I do not wish to be away from you for six months, yet to travel after October is to ask for trouble,' Elizabeth made clear.

'We must consider. We might perhaps take a house in London and then you could, even in winter, visit your parents and I could return here,' George suggested.

'But could we afford it?' enquired Elizabeth.

'I think so, yes, but we will discuss this further later, for I see you are stayed for.'

Ned, who was five now, came running down the drive calling out, 'Mamma! Mamma, you're so late! Why're you so late?' pursued by Nell, who didn't run as fast as him nowadays.

:

On Friday, Elizabeth and Amabel went, as their habit was, to see if all was well in the two new little terraced houses they had built and let in a mean backstreet. In the first house all seemed well, except there was pitifully little furniture. The husband was out working and the wife and her two children were speechless with awe at the presence of such fine ladies. The wife and the little girl curtseyed very prettily, while the little boy bowed, but their answers to all questions were muttered and therefore virtually inaudible.

The next little house was very different. The wife was nothing if not chatty. 'Good day, your Reverences,' she greeted them. 'I'd just like to say thank'ee. I never dreamt o' having such a place. We hardly knows ourselves. Think we dropped in'ter heaven by accident. An' it's that easy t'run. I ain't had so much free time since I was knee high. I'm knittin' my Tommy a nice wool jersey again th' winter.'

Everything was very spick and span. There was a pair of black cow-creamers with gold stars on the mantelpiece. Elizabeth admired them.

'My mistress guv me those. "Ellen," she says, "you never broke a thing all th' years you worked here, so I know you'll take care o' them". And I hev.'

Amabel asked if there was anything they required.

'No, indeed. We'd be right ungrateful if we wasn't satisfied. A bakehouse, an' all. I bakes once a week now and you should see the childer scoff them cakes.'

They parted with many expressions of mutual esteem, the two ladies declining a cup of tea on the grounds that the Dean must not be kept waiting for his dinner.

'Mine's just the same. Steps in and says, "Is dinner ready?" Thinks I can cook it when I see him coming and have it ready by the time he's come.'

As they were walking back Elizabeth told Amabel about the baby.

'No!' said her friend. 'Every three years! How do you do it? It's too provoking! And I keep…' she checked herself.

'You've not started another?' Elizabeth asked.

'Well, I hope not. Twice before I feared and they were false alarms. It might well be the change of life, too. And anyway, it's eighteen months since Elizabeth's birth, and Mrs Potts said not for a year. Think what fun they will have playing together, should it be so,' explained Amabel.

Elizabeth was more inclined to think of haemorrhages.

'I suppose you leave in October and return to your parents, and the proficient Mrs Potts,' asked Amabel.

'October, yes, but we plan to go south in slow stages, staying in Belvoir, then Holkham, and then my husband's parent's in Suffolk. They complain they see little of their grandsons. If you are with child, you must come in good time,' asked Elizabeth.

'I will, to be sure. You are hoping for a girl, I collect?' Amabel suggested.

'Yes, but not so much as before you gave me a small share in your delightful Elisa,' Elizabeth said smiling.

'She is delightful, is she not? Even her father, who has no patience with children as a rule, is quite won over,' Amabel replied.

:

The journey went well, through perfect October weather that mocked the wet summer, and then a wet November that reflected the summer. They arrived in Bacton, near Stowmarket, in late November, full of the glories of Holkham. Bacton was a handsome red-brick manor house in the middle of the village. It had walls around it, except on the front, where it was open to the village street, for you liked to see your neighbours when in the countryside. The house had been built by George's great grandfather in 1710. On the whole, Elizabeth liked it there and readily agreed to stay for Christmas.

George's father was a tall, thin man, a little deaf now but still very active. He was a source of local and family knowledge, which Elizabeth found fascinating and meant to try and pass on to her sons. Mrs Pretyman was plumper and of medium size. She had been a Hubbard, a small family of local gentry. She was a capable housewife who prided herself on doing a lot of things. Some of her remarks seemed very wise and some very silly.

The boys loved it there. The animals were plentiful, and Ned was soon riding quite well and adoring it, though he couldn't yet prevent his shaggy pony grazing whenever it wished, which was often. George was equally enchanted with his grandparents' five dogs: two pointers, a spaniel, a good ratting terrier and a strange, sandy mongrel George's father had found starving in Bury. George used to trot off and climb confidently into the spaniel's basket where he was given a good lick over, which made him giggle.

'They are such good boys,' said their fond grandmother. 'I have heard George cry but once, and then he'd grazed his knee.'

'Ned is apt to be a bit lazy,' said his fond mother.

'So was my John but your George loved his books,' replied Grandmother.

'Bad news from Europe,' said her husband, who had ridden over to Bury and come into the drawing room at that moment.

'There always is,' responded his wife resignedly. 'Being papists makes them irrational.'

'The mischief is more that the French are not papists anymore. But they've won a great victory at a place called Valmy and the Duke of Brunswick is scuttling back to Austria,' her husband explained.

'Surely not,' said his wife. 'Everyone said—'

'Everyone was wrong. They often are, but the worst of it is the French go on into Holland. Our treaties mean we must needs go to war for it,' George's father expressed with dismay.

'Grandpa!' exclaimed Ned, running in. 'I rode all the way to Wetherden, and Rodwell says I shall soon be off leather for London.'

'You should 'a seen this room twenty years ago when we first came into it,' her mother-in-law said to Elizabeth the next day.

They were sitting by a blazing fire in a panelled room and peeling chestnuts, a rather fiddly job.

'Did you never come here when your brother-in-law lived here?' asked Elizabeth.

'Not once. We were not near grand enough for them. We were in trade and low. Mind you, there was 'a plenty ask us to their parties as would never 'a asked my brother-in-law and his uncle. Drunken lot they were. Hardly made sense half th' time, by what I hear. They were all right 'til Baron's wife died. That's Baron in th' picture there, riding past this house with a spaniel ahead o' him. He was called Baron because his grandmother was a Baron, th' last o' a Huguenot family. They say he never got over not having children, so he took in my George's brother 'n' ruined him,' her mother-in-law replied.

'He was spoilt?' Elizabeth queried inquisitively.

'Spoilt rotten. Tried to marry every good looking girl 'round about as had a good dowry but they'd more sense than to take him,' her mother-in-law confirmed.

'It is a sad story,' said Elizabeth, dropping a chestnut into the small bowl.

'It is a sad story,' agreed her mother-in-law. 'There was my poor husband, scrimping and saving, and working away for very little an' it done him no harm. His brother was living easy and it ruined him. Well now that's done. I'd best go and see how th' hens have laid.'

In early December, George's father came back from a meeting of the "Association for Liberty and Property against Republicans and Levellers" with the news that the French had taken Brussels and were trying their king.

'Why should they suppose murdering people will make things better?' enquired George's mother.

'Ah there's a question,' her husband alluded, as he pulled off his riding boots with the elaborate jack that stood in the hall.

'They have lost God,' George answered her, 'and the people who have become alienated from their Maker are with no long interval under the authority of the devil.'

'They had been very badly treated,' pointed out Elizabeth, 'and perhaps it has driven them mad.'

'Grandpa!' called Ned, running from the regions. 'Did you remember my top?'

'Gwanpa,' called little George, talking resolutely after his brother.

'Master Ned! Master George!' called Nell, faint but pursuing. 'How often have I told you not to go botherin' the grownups?'

'Oh, let them be,' said their doting grandfather. 'I have the top here, and I think, yes, I seem to remember, there's another present in the packet.'

A letter arrived from Amabel. She was having another baby. In April. Elizabeth sighed and told George who was working on the next Sunday's sermon, the Rector of Bacton being delighted to have acquired a bishop.

'Doubtless the estimable Mrs Potts will be equal to the emergency,' George said soothingly.

'Amabel, forty-one, and it's her eleventh,' Elizabeth replied with amazement.

'The gloomy Dean will have his quiver full,' joked George.

'Yes, drat him!' Elizabeth announced.

Christmas was celebrated with all due ceremony, and Ned was sick. Soon afterwards some neighbours came to dine and meet the Pretyman's distinguished son, whose fame had spread as far as Woolpit. There were two couples; the Rector, Theophilus Harding, and his wife, Louisa, and Major Humphrey Tollemache with his wife. The Major seemed very well, a small, informed, foxy man.

George's mother, her four maids, two gardeners, henwife, and back'us boy all worked very hard, and on the night a country banquet was in the ovens. The evening was pleasant but predictable 'til the Major, who had made himself so useful to so many people he'd ended his career as a military attaché to Lord Auckland, announced, 'The French, it appears, have annexed the world.'

'How so?' asked George's father.

'They passed one of their estimable decrees on the sixteenth December that all the land they conquer should straight become French, republican, and godless,' the Major explained.

'I recollect the Duke of Rutland saying the revolution would go on getting worse 'til a strong man took charge of it,' declared Elizabeth.

'His Grace is in the right of it,' agreed Major Tollemache, 'but the strong man may prove to be even more troublesome than the revolution.'

'Will they come here?' asked the senior Mrs Pretyman, suddenly frightened in the middle of her roast goose and shining silver.

'The Navy forfend,' replied the Major. 'I am informed the Chinese have a curse: "May you live in exciting times", and we seem fated to live in exciting times.'

'It is all new,' said Major Tollemache's pretty, young wife unexpectedly. 'I am Dutch, so I do not vant the French guillotining my Stadholder, but I see vy the young excite themselves. It sounds fairer. The French have halted slavery. They give people chances. You vill no longer be stuck in dull town. You vill no longer be stuck in dull marriage. You can go anywhere, do anything.'

Six pairs of eyes contemplated her without favour in spite of her pink, white, blue, and silver–yellow prettiness. The seventh pair of eyes, Elizabeth's, contemplated her with interest.

'I see what you mean,' said Elizabeth. 'Do you think it will take?'

'It will take the vorld by storm,' said Mrs Tollemache. 'The old people, the people over forty, they vill say, "No! I do not vant it! Take it avay!". But the young, who are more, they vill say, "Now I can go and be a soldier. Now I can be a politician and change the vorld. Now I can run off vith my lover".'

'Do not religion and morality count for anything?' enquired the appalled Bishop.

'For some they vill, but if you are much in love, very poor, very bored, it seems change must be good,' Mrs Tollemarche said in reply.

The discussion ended with the young lady's six elders explaining to her how undesirable and reprehensible this attitude was.

'In England we are mostly Christians and I think that will hold,' said Elizabeth, 'but I see what you mean for the Continent and, besides, if you were French and didn't really like the Revolution, you would still have to pretend you loved it and work for it, because it would be so dangerous otherwise.'

CHAPTER FIFTEEN
London

Three days later the younger Pretymans set off on their journey to London. The start of 1793 had been very cold, with swans sitting indignantly on the ice, but in the middle of January it suddenly thawed and George thought it would be wise to continue. His mother was very disappointed. She had been counting on a hard winter and was looking for midwives.

They spent two nights very comfortably with a business associate of George's, and one night rather uncomfortably at an inn near Brentwood. Goodchild was full of praise for the industry of the Suffolk labourer. 'They're slow like them Punches, but, like them, they get there. They know what they're doin' 'n' they git it done. Called our horses "them hackneys".'

To be back at Downing Street was almost like coming home. Elizabeth was a bit nervous that Ned's roaming, inquisitive ways would annoy Mr Pitt; Ned did walk into a meeting, but merely amused Mr Pitt, who asked him what he thought about an expedition to Holland.

'I should like to go with it,' replied Ned enthusiastically.

They had arrived on January twenty-third, 1793, and the news had just come of the French King's execution.

'Poor devil,' said Mr Pitt, as they ate their first breakfast at Downing Street. 'A harmless, well-meaning man. He was greatly given to industrious watch-making, and he abhorred the notion of a civil war so greatly he would not let his followers fight, and now the French will have twenty years of ceaseless civil war.'

'The poor Queen,' said Elizabeth.

'Unfortunate, indeed,' replied Pitt. 'And those unprotected children. They were so near to their salvation. I should perhaps warn you I am expecting a call this morning. A young man of some parts, but I fear the debate will be political, so I will not resent it if you flee the house or take refuge in the morning room. How is my young friend Harry?'

'Heaven knows. He is no correspondent and my sister is even worse. The last we heard was a short note written in Jamaica but posted in Portsmouth, doubtless by a friend. He sounded happy and informed us that the bananas were first rate,' Elizabeth stated.

'I rejoice to hear it. Ah, here is Mr Canning, dead on time,' Pitt expressed with pleasure.

A young man came in quickly. 'At last I meet the erudite Bishop and his irresistible wife. Mr Pitt speaks of you so often and so highly,' the man said.

'Tea?' offered Mr Pitt. 'Coffee? Chocolate?'

'None of those, I thank you. I breakfasted long since. I trust you have made it quite plain, if they invade Holland, we join Austria,' the young man announced.

'To be sure we have, but I am in doubt that they will pay the least attention, if, indeed, they have not already invaded. Their decrees, intentions and Foreign Ministers alter so often, it is like trying to negotiate with a blue tit,' Pitt uttered.

'Yes. A blue tit may be brought to feed regularly. Have you tried bribery?' the younger man enquired.

'It is hard to determine who to bribe. Pray, sit down. You hover over us like an assassin about to strike,' Pitt replied.

The young man, Mr Canning, pulled out a chair, fell into it, and elaborated. 'They say the Duke of Brunswick was bribed with the Queen's jewels to lose the Battle of Valmy.'

'Even if they say true, I hardly think Monsieur Danton or Her Majesty would agree to the transaction,' Pitt returned wittily.

'One would do anything to avoid war,' Mr Canning added.

'Indeed and indeed,' agreed Elizabeth, thinking of her sons and her unborn baby.

'Yes, but if one party had determined on war,' declared the Bishop, 'no concession or sanction will be sufficient.'

'That is the case, I fear. So, while praying and working for peace, I am devoting some thought to preparing for war. I extremely distrust any ideas of my own on military subjects. My father had a feel for it; I have none. I had so much rather spend our hard-won money on fruitful improvement than weaponry and recruits,' Pitt explained.

Canning sprang up and went to lounge against the side of the bright fireplace, his hands in his pockets. 'The Navy is ready,' he stated.

'It is of inestimable reassurance to me. Our safety depends on Harry and Tom Bowling,' Pitt replied.

'I was totally at a loss to comprehend the uncanny attraction of the French madness,' said the Bishop, 'but both Elizabeth and I felt a chance-met Dutch woman, married to a Tollemache, threw some light on it.'

'Tell me, I beg,' said Mr Pitt, pouring himself another cup of coffee, 'for I am totally at a loss, too.'

'You could perhaps express it more exactly, my love, being both young and female,' George asked his wife tenderly.

'Not very young anymore, but certainly all too female. She said…'

Elizabeth gave a clear summary of Mrs Tollemache's views.

'Interesting,' said Mr Canning, flinging away from the fireplace and going to sit on the window seat. 'Explains a lot. Take a trifle of stopping. Fox said the King's execution stained the noblest cause that ever was.'

'It is unhappily characteristic of Mr Fox to consider the extinction of religion noble,' said the Bishop.

'But the best of it is,' replied Mr Pitt, 'that we can now make common cause with our late enemies, the Catholics. Our tragic estrangement from our fellow Christians is surely at an end.'

:

The next day, Elizabeth came early to breakfast and told Mr Pitt they must be going before long. It was February already, the baby was due at the end of March, and the Bishop was beginning to worry.

'You must, of course, go whenever you judge it wise, but if it will bear another week or two, I should be grateful. Having you both here is the greatest resource to me at this critical juncture,' Pitt articulated.

Goodchild, when consulted, was of the opinion he could get them to Mrs Potts in a couple of days, the weather being rather cold but dry.

The eighth of February was a fine sunny day, so they agreed to go for a stroll in Hyde Park. Elizabeth felt Mr Pitt wasn't exercising and needed relaxation.

'This is vastly agreeable,' said Mr Pitt, as they strolled along in the sunshine, admiring the ducks and patches of snowdrops. 'I should never have thought of it for myself. It takes Elizabeth to recall us to the simple, invaluable resources.'

'Walking is good for me now,' said Elizabeth.

A man that Elizabeth had been watching wistfully pulled out of the concourse of riders, trotted over, and pulled up beside them. 'I say, Billy, shall we have a war?' he asked Pitt.

'The Lord preserve us from it, for I do not think I can. This is my mannerless brother, Lord Chatham,' Pitt clarified. 'The Bishop of Lincoln and Mrs Pretyman,' said Pitt, introducing the pair to his brother.

'How do,' said his Lordship, nodding to them. 'If you don't want war, why did you boot out the ambassador?'

'I judged the murder of their innocent monarch was intolerable,' Pitt answered.

'Bit of a bloomer, to be sure, but it don't do to be innocent in France. You need quick wits and no morals,' Chatham returned.

'A republic devoted to its master, the devil,' proclaimed the Bishop.

'I daresay, but devils from hell take a trifle of baulking and so you'll find. Wish I was still a soldier,' yearned Lord Chatham.

All three of his listeners thought fleetingly that it was just as well he wasn't.

'Hear they're going to send York,' Chatham announced.

'Surely he is too young!' exclaimed Elizabeth.

'That's what they said about Billy here, but he soon proved them wrong. York's twenty-eight. It will prove a young man's war. I mustn't get this quad cold. He's a barb,' Chatham went on.

He was gone, trotting, then cantering away from them.

'A horseman has an automatic advantage,' said Mr Pitt. 'I could wish to turn my brother's mind to something besides society and gossip, for he has some ability, if little application, but my sister-in-law naturally has more influence than I.'

Back home they were told there was a messenger and Mr Pitt was off to hear him. He came back before long. 'It has come,' he said.

'A declaration of war?' asked George, who was reading the paper.

'Yes, on the first of February. They have declared war on England and Holland without one dissenting voice,' Mr Pitt illuminated.

'Dissenting voices could soon be silenced,' pointed out Elizabeth.

'True. They rule by fear and we by consent. Time will prove which is best, but oh the waste! You can go home now, for I am sure I shall be too busy to be able to attend to you. I must recall Parliament and issue five notes and I know not what,' Pitt groaned.

'If we could be of the least use,' said the Bishop.

'You cannot, but you have been of great use keeping me company during the waiting. I do not know when I have spent a pleasanter morning or when I shall spend such another,' Pitt confirmed.

:

The following journey was uneventful, except that Goodchild told them while his son was driving the coach that Mr Pitt had a pack of slovenly servants. 'I never met such a crew,' he said, 'Waste! Dirt! Things disappearing! If I had the ordering of it, I'd soon put half a dozen in prison, turn the rest off without a characuture and start afresh. When you get one or two bad apples in a barrel you soon got a bad barrel.'

'Oh dear!' said Elizabeth. 'Should I write and tell Mr Pitt?'

'Better not. He's got enough on his plate. It'd take a good man to sort that lot out. I've thought of a couple down our way, but the mischief is I doubt they'll want to live in town,' Goodchild replied.

'And meanwhile,' said George sombrely, 'his debts multiply.'

Elizabeth's parents were delighted to see them after all the delays. Mrs Potts said all was going well but puffed out her lips when asked if it was a girl.

'Reckon not. You're carrying high. I bin wrong afore now but I reckon not. Take what the Lord sends and, if it's healthy, bless Him.'

Amabel wrote that the Dean was bringing her and little Elizabeth in a hired coach, which would then take him back sometime in mid-March.

The Austrians won several victories in France, and the French were thrown out of Belgium. There was a financial panic, some small banks failed, but Mr Pitt's arrangements and new five pound notes calmed things down.

Mrs Potts was gloomy and resigned about the advent of a pregnant Amabel.

'Better April than October,' she said.

'Why?' asked Elizabeth.

'Count of, if it come to that, your father'll let me have some ice out've his ice house. Only thing I know staunch th' bleeding when all else fails,' Potts explained.

'Won't she catch pneumonia?' Elizabeth replied worriedly.

'She may but she's mostly bound to bleed to death without ice. Let's hope it won't come to that,' Potts explained forebodingly.

Elizabeth, her husband, and parents were drinking tea in front of a blazing fire after dinner one night when they heard the doorbell.

'Who can it be?' asked Elizabeth's mother.

'Mrs Harte begging for her orphanage again?' suggested her father.

'At this hour? It is nearly dark and there's no moon. Surely…'

Emily hustled through the door, preceded by a vast stomach, and talking as she came.

'Oh, father, could you pay the coachman. He asked such a lot and I'm short again. Mother, I'm so sorry I didn't write. I kept meaning to but there was so much to do and pack. Well, sister, you see we're in the same case. Harry says we're not to get them muddled up. Oh, I'm so tired and cold and hungry!'

Not until she had been fed, warmed, and fussed over did her shocked mother enquire whether she'd really come all that way without so much as a maid.

'Oh, well, she didn't want to come. Her family, as they all live in Portsmouth, you see. And after all, there's plenty here. I'm a married woman, so it doesn't signify,' Emily rationalised.

The next day, Mrs Potts shook her head over Emily's fecklessness. Not to Emily's face, but to her parents and Elizabeth afterwards. 'No more idea of when it's due than a cat has! Eating for twenty and lolling about! No clothes for baby! You do set me some puzzles, you t'gether.'

They excused Emily as best they could, and Elizabeth dragged her out whenever the weather permitted, but she was full of reasons why she couldn't walk that day. Amabel wrote from an inn at Cambridge that the journey had gone well so far, and they were spending a week with her favourite brother, who was a Don at Trinity. She sounded to be in her element but wrote more of Plato than that of the coming baby.

Mr Pitt wrote that his government had raised some more troops and sent them to the Low Countries where the Duke of York was advancing on Dunkirk.

One morning in March the rain was beating on the window and Emily said happily, 'Not even you can want to go out in this. Let's trim a bonnet. I've got several that are sadly drab now and mother's box of scraps and felt flowers and bobbles and broken jewellery will be just the thing.'

They got Kate to light a fire in the old schoolroom and before long were happily at work. Emily was very good with her needle when she could be persuaded to pick one up.

Emily began, 'There, that's done. For this one I'm going to have one big sunflower like this and then… why did you insist on coming up here? What was wrong with the dining room table? Those stairs have given me a backache.'

'The sunflower looks charmingly,' said Elizabeth, who had insisted on the schoolroom so Emily should at least climb the stairs. 'But I suspect anything else would be a bit much.'

'Yes, perhaps. Oh, it hurts! It hurts terribly! I'm dying!' Emily moaned in pain. She was bent over and gasping.

'It is the baby coming! I'll send for Mrs Potts,' Elizabeth consoled her.

By the time she'd done so Emily was all right again but very frightened. 'Will it hurt like that again?' she asked.

'Now and again, I'm afraid, but you're lucky to have started. I quite envy you, I'm sure. I've got another week to go and I'm always a few days late. We had better remove to your bedroom,' Elizabeth comforted her.

'You don't really mean it. You couldn't. You're just saying that,' Emily tried to argue.

'No, I'm not. The sooner it begins, the sooner it is over. Come along,' Elizabeth replied caringly.

'I hardly dare breathe, let alone move, for fear of starting it off again,' answered Emily.

'I do not think it signifies. It will return in its own good time and regardless of how you move,' Elizabeth described to her sister.

'Oh, very well, then. Oh, Nell, tell my mother I need her. It's started and it's very bad and I want her,' Emily asked.

'Very good, Mum,' Nell answered obediently.

Their mother, a messenger, and the next pain all arrived together. Emily was groaning and throwing herself about. Mrs Maltby was patting her, only she often missed, and was shouting commiserations. The messenger, a young housemaid, was telling them something, yet no one but Elizabeth was listening. The girl said that Mrs

Potts had been out at Rose Cottage, where a babe had been born yesterday. 'So I ran on there and she's coming, only she don't run as fast as I do,' the young housemaid mentioned.

She stood about, watching Emily as if the baby might appear at any moment. Kate came in and asked if they wanted hot water yet and Mr Maltby came in looking for his wife. So when Mrs Potts appeared three minutes later she found six people in Emily's little room.

'Out!' she bellowed immediately. 'Out! Out! Her mother and sister can stay for a bit if she do want, but the rest of you clear off! Begging you pardon, sir, but we'll need the room.'

'Not at all, Mrs Potts, you are mistress here. I will go to the church and pray,' replied Emily's father.

'You couldn't do better. Now, madam, how long between pains?' Mrs Potts asked.

'I don't know. Not long. It was even worse than before. As if I was being squeezed so tight, I couldn't breathe,' Emily gasped.

'Ah, so you have got some muscles, then. I must admit I wondered. I couldn't see much sign of them. Anyone with her?' Mrs Potts enquired.

'Yes,' said Elizabeth. 'I was. I didn't look at a clock but I would say about ten minutes between her first two pains.'

'Good. Good. Glad somebody's got a head on her. Sounds like it's go'n to be short and sweet,' Mrs Potts said thankfully.

'Sweet!' protested Emily. 'It was horrid, dreadful, beastly. Isn't there any way to make it stop?'

'Sometimes you can find a position which eases it,' said Mrs Potts. 'Listen to what your body's tellin' y', an' I got'ta drink here as takes th' worst off.'

'Give it to me, then,' demanded Emily eagerly.

Mrs Potts did so and Emily complained of its nasty taste.

'Think of the dear little baby you will have soon,' her mother suggested.

Emily looked rather blank and very cross. A few minutes later another pain took her and she gave a yelp and clutched at her mother's hand.

'Don't do that!' said Mrs Potts, prising her away, 'or she won't have the use of them for weeks. Clutch the bar o' the bed, if you want. Six minutes. I think you best be going, madam. Yer husband'll be back and looking for you to give him company at dinner. You, too, Mrs Pretyman. You can't do no more good here. Send Nell up with some hot water.'

'No,' said Emily, panting so and moving convulsively. 'Don't leave! I need you. Oh! Oh! Am I dying?'

'No such thing,' Mrs Potts told her. 'Off you go, madam.'

Their mother went, hurriedly and gratefully.

'I'll go and fetch the hot water and I'll come back,' said Elizabeth. 'It was awful to watch,' she thought, 'your little sister in such pain, particularly when you knew you were going to go through it yourself soon. Still, I must behave as if it was all nothing much and perhaps it won't be.'

When she got back Emily was out of pain again and asking if she might lie down on her bed.

'Cos',' answered Mrs Potts. 'Lie, walk, crouch, whatever you feel like. Some women sleep for a bit between pains and it does 'em good. It's a tiring old business, y'know.'

'It is tiring,' agreed Emily. 'I'm sure I don't know why but it's very tiring.'

She lay down on the bed and went instantly to sleep. Mrs Potts beckoned Elizabeth out of the door and closed it gently. 'Do you go and have your dinner and then a good rest,' she advised. 'You're carrying, too. If she ask for you, I'll send, but I reckon she'll be too took up with herself.'

Elizabeth, George, and her parents were dining peacefully a little later.

'It's pleasant to have daylight at dinner again,' said Mrs Maltby.

'Indeed,' agreed her husband. 'I cannot see to read much by candlelight nowadays. The Rector was telling me of a new patent lamp that is much brighter.'

'We must obtain one,' said his wife. 'I need it, too.'

'It's odd to think,' said Elizabeth, 'that Emily's and my children will both be born into a country at war.'

'It is a sobering thought,' George admitted.

'But at least,' said Mrs Maltby, 'even if they are all boys, the war will be over long before they are old enough to want to fight in it.'

'You cannot be sure,' Mr Maltby told her. 'As Elizabeth explained, this is a new sort of war. Colonel Lane was telling me the French think of decreeing a "levée en masse". Meaning that every young man who hasn't got an excellent excuse must go and be a soldier.'

'But can they do that?' asked her mother.

'Who is to prevent them? The guillotine silences all dissent. The people govern, as they proclaim, but "the people" who govern are of the worst Paris mobile,' said George.

'And they intend to impose that on other countries?' asked Elizabeth.

'They intend to, certainly, but…' A distant scream interrupted him. 'You never screamed,' George said to Elizabeth.

'I did at the end and Mrs Potts did say I was fortunate,' Elizabeth replied.

'Anyone will scream if the pain is bad enough,' Mrs Maltby told her husband. 'I well remember how terrible it was with Robin.' Another scream came. 'Oh dear!' she added.

'I do hope the children can't hear. Ned would be… I'd rather go and see,' Elizabeth said.

She got up but before she got to the door it opened and the housekeeper came in.

'Mrs Potts said to tell you she got Kate to take the young gentlemen for a walk,' she said. 'And that baby is just now born, a lovely little girl, and both well.'

CHAPTER SIXTEEN

Lincoln

Much to everyone's relief and somewhat to most people's surprise, Emily took to her daughter, saying that Harry had wanted a girl. She thought of exotic names that might suit and Elizabeth had to keep a list. Esmeralda was the first name and fairly typical of the rest. She insisted on feeding her daughter herself. 'If Elizabeth can, so can I,' she would say.

Everyone started asking Elizabeth how she felt and she began answering: 'Deplorably well.' On the night of March the twenty-fifth she was woken by a strong pain. She lit the candle and looked at the clock. 2 A.M. 'I hope the baby isn't going to be as tiresome as this all its life long,' she thought wryly.

George woke rather noisily, grunting, and then coughing. 'Has it started at last?' he asked thoughtfully.

'Yes. If you could call Kate, she'll fetch Mrs Potts. Tell her there's no hurry and to wrap up warm,' replied Elizabeth.

Just as the sun rose on a perfect morning Elizabeth's third son was born. She could not help being a bit disappointed. At thirty-eight she probably wouldn't have another, but the baby was healthy and that consoled her. Ten days later the family was disturbed again by the pealing of a bell as they dined.

'What now?' asked Mr Maltby. 'It cannot be the Andrews already, can it?'

'They were to arrive about the tenth of April,' said George, 'and it is only the fifth now. Perhaps, if they had a remarkable journey.'

Harry burst in. 'Where's Emily?' he demanded.

'She still goes back to bed for dinner,' said Elizabeth. 'I'll take you.'

In the hall she told the worried footman who'd opened the door, 'It's Miss Emily's husband.' Of Harry she asked, 'Have you eaten?'

'Not since noon and precious little then, but a chop would answer, or some scrambled eggs,' he replied.

'Ask them to send some dinner up to Miss Emily's room. Something quick and simple, but lots of it,' she said to the footman.

'You always say the right thing straight off,' remarked Harry. 'Wish I could. How is she?'

'Perfectly well again, but inclined to be lazy. You'll have to get her out,' Elizabeth stated.

'You bet! And the child?' asked Harry.

'You must stop her calling it Cleopatra, or Theodosia, or most of the other names she's thought of,' Elizabeth commented.

'I will, but how is she?' he replied.

'Splendid. Growing. Rather pretty, as babies go,' Elizabeth answered happily.

They arrived in Emily's room. 'Look who's blown in,' Elizabeth said to her.

'Harry!' exclaimed Emily, lying back on her bed and looking frail and tragic but still very pretty.

Elizabeth left them to it.

It transpired that Harry's ship had had a battle with a French first rate. There were other ships involved and the account was far from clear, except to Harry and his messmates, but they'd lost their main mast somewhere towards the end of the fight and struggled home to Portsmouth without it.

'As First Lieutenant, I had to see repairs in hand,' he told them, 'but I held out for a clear month after that and got it. So here I am.'

'Most welcome,' said Mr Maltby a little dubiously. He found his younger son-in-law a little overpowering.

'Very welcome indeed,' said Mr Maltby's wife, who doted on her bluff son-in-law. 'I could wish it were longer.'

'So could I. Whose was that jolly young 'un?' he asked, pointing to a picture.

'That was our son Robin, who came between Elizabeth and Emily and died of the morbid sore throat when he was only seven,' Mrs Maltby replied.

'Oh, I'm sorry. I had not asked if I'd known. Emily never spoke of him,' Harry returned solemnly.

'She never knew him. He died before she was born, but he and Elizabeth used to play together so prettily and ride together, too. He loved to ride,' Mrs Maltby recalled.

:

Harry towed his wife firmly round the garden later and even round the countryside on every fine day. Emily complained but came along nonetheless. Harry often carried his daughter, who he thought the most beautiful baby that ever was seen. He selected the name Camilla from out of the long list, most of which had many more syllables. He also tactfully selected his mother's and his mother-in-law's Christian names for his daughter's second and third names.

The Dean and his wife arrived in a hired carriage and Amabel took refuge in the library. George, whose conscience was often troublesome, had decided he had been away too long and proposed to return to Lincoln with the Dean. Elizabeth wanted to go with him and said so. Mrs Potts made no objection. 'You keep y'self fit, you do, so you soon get over things like.'

But Amabel begged her to stay. George promised to send Goodchild and the coach back for her at the end of April. 'Perhaps it is for the best,' he said. 'Six of us and three children would have been somewhat congested in a moderately-sized coach.'

Before George and the Dean left they held a double christening for Richard Henry Pretyman and Camilla Amelia Mary Meynell. George was godfather to Camilla, and Elizabeth and a rich local widow called Lady Hall were godmothers. Harry and the Dean, who stood in for the Duke of Rutland, were Richard's godfathers, and Mrs Potts was his godmother. Mrs Potts was gratified. 'I got fifty-three godchildren all told,' she said, 'and plenty more as is over twenty-one and don't count no more. But tha's th' first time I bin godmother to a young gentleman, and as for being god-sister to a duke. Well, who'd 'a thought it? I can't but wish the Duke would 'a come.'

Harry made the party go by flirting with all the ladies and assuring all the men that the Navy would keep off the French.

'You've got a baby shipyard here, sir,' he told his father-in-law at the tea party after the christening. 'Two first rates launched and one on the stocks.'

'That is a very nautical way of putting it,' said Amabel. 'The Bible tells us they are arrows in the hands of a giant. Arrows going into the nineteenth century.'

'I like to think of my Camilla as a first rate sailing out on a long, prosperous voyage,' said Harry.

'What nonsense you do talk,' replied Emily. 'But she's going to be a smasher, you can see that, and I shall have to go through it all again, because I must have a son.'

'I wouldn't mind one bit if we only had daughters,' insisted Harry, 'as the old rhyme says – girls are much nicer.'

'But boys are most necessary to carry on the name and fight the foe,' pointed out Lady Hall.

Mrs Potts found Emily the perfect nurse girl. She was fourteen and the eldest of twelve, so she was good with babies and glad to get away.

Everyone disappeared, or so it seemed, after George and the Dean departed in a northerly direction, and Emily, Harry, Camilla, and the nurse girl went back to Plymouth. When he met Elizabeth in an upstairs passage on the morning he was leaving, holding his daughter as usual, and shadowed by a redundant nursemaid, Harry said, 'I expect you think I'm soppy about this baby, but th' case is, y'see, we waited eleven years for her.'

'No, I think it greatly to your credit you are so pleased with a girl. Some men only want boys,' highlighted Elizabeth in reply.

'Silly asses,' said Mr Meynell contemptuously. 'Want to thank you, Lizzie, for all you done for Emily. She grows quite sensible.'

'About time,' thought Elizabeth, but she said, 'I like her candour.'

'Every time,' agreed Harry. 'Can't stand cunning girls.'

:

It was a superb spring, in spite of the cold east winds, and Elizabeth and Amabel walked about happily, seeing a new flower every day. Amabel seemed well but when Elizabeth met Mrs Potts and her portmanteau in a narrow lane one morning she asked, 'Do you think Mrs Andrews may need a caesarean?'

'Better not. Even more risky than birth for her. She bleed so easy. At least she's much less flabby and low than last time. I fixed up th' ice with your Dad, though I'm hoping we won't need it,' Mrs Potts responded.

'Do you think it will start soon?' Elizabeth asked.

'Any day now. She never carry to term and tha's a blessing,' Potts replied again.

'I do hope she won't have any more,' Elizabeth said in a worried manner.

'So do I. Tha's getting less likely, she's well into the change. I could wish, God forgive me, that husband of hers would get himself a mistress,' Mrs Potts implied.

'Mrs Potts!' said Elizabeth, laughing and throwing up her hands. 'You shock me! To speak so, of a clergyman, too.'

'Well, Madam, you may make a mock o' me, but it's my job to keep women alive and you start thinking how it could be done,' Mrs Potts replied more seriously.

'You never lost a mother or a child,' Elizabeth stated.

'Tha's a true word, but I wish folk wouldn't say it. Tha's temptin' fate, fare to me,' Mrs Potts said stoically.

Amabel started labour the next day, soon after breakfast. Elizabeth sat and talked with her for most of the morning. They discussed Dr. Johnson, and Fanny Burney, and their writings. The afternoon being fine and Nell helping her mother, Elizabeth took the two elder boys to the lake to feed the ducks. It was an occupation that delighted them, particularly Ned, who could identify all the different species with a precision that would have pleased Mr Tomline. When she'd got back and fed Richard she peeped into Amabel's room to be greeted enthusiastically.

'We bin talkin' about books,' said Mrs Potts. 'You might think I don't know nothin' about books 'n' you wouldn't be far out, but the Good Book I do know. Father used to read to us together from it. And the Prayer Book I know pretty well. And my grandfather had an old copy o' Th' Pilgrim's Progress. M' sister didn't make much o' it, but I relished it. There was a man sweepin' th' straw on th' floor into fancy shapes 'n' all the sweeping an angel was offerin' him a shining crown, but he wouldn't hev it. He was too took up with his silly old shapes.'

'And as he went down into the river the trumpets sounded for him on the other side,' said Amabel.

'Tha's it,' said Mrs Potts excitedly. 'Tha's it! You say it so clear, too. That bring out th' sound o' it.'

'There's some good poetry in…' started Amabel, but then gasped and doubled up as a pain took her.

'Tha's right,' said Mrs Potts, 'coming thick an' fast now. Won't be long.'

'Shall I go away?' asked Elizabeth, but Amabel shook her head furiously, gasping with pain.

'Them as is fond o' books,' said Mrs Potts, 'they do fare to be a great comfort to 'em. Same as drink t' some folks and music t' others. Time I can't do 's much I hope to buy some books.'

'As I was saying, there's some very fine poetry in the Prayer Book,' persisted Amabel. 'Take the prayer for All Sorts of Conditions of Men: that all those who profess and call themselves Christians may be led into the way of truth. O-oh!' Another pain gripped her.

'Oughtn't she to lie down?' asked Nell.

'Tha's just as she's a mind. Sit, lie, walk. However that take her,' answered Potts.

'That's one of the ways your mother's so much better than an ordinary midwife,' Elizabeth told Nell. 'I believe they expect you to lie tidily in bed.'

'So they do,' agreed Mrs Potts, 'and won't let the body help itself.'

She signalled to Elizabeth that it was time for her to go.

After dinner they waited tensely in the library. Kate came in now and then to relay what Nell had told her about how things were getting on. 'All well,' she kept saying, 'just a little slow.'

About eight o'clock there was a commotion upstairs and heavy feet could be heard trampling up the stairs.

'What can that be?' asked Mrs Maltby.

'The ice,' thought Elizabeth and her father.

'Perhaps the child is born and they are getting it washed,' suggested Elizabeth.

'Should I go up and see?' asked Mrs Maltby.

'Better not,' said Elizabeth. 'We'll only get in the way. Mrs Potts is very clever and reassuring.'

'So she naturally acts as a magnet to ladies in an interesting condition,' said Mr Maltby. 'I fear I shall have to become a man-midwife to be able to follow your conversation.'

Kate came in. 'Th' babe's born,' she said. 'It's a boy and doin' well. It were an easy enough birth but we had to put Mrs Andrews on ice to slow the bleeding. Mrs Potts seems to think she'll do now but she's proper poorly.'

CHAPTER SEVENTEEN

Lincoln

Amabel recovered very slowly. She just slept at first, but everyone who found her awake quickly ordered broth. This was because Mrs Potts insisted on it. Luckily, Amabel drank it eagerly and soon began to eat eagerly, too.

'I never would have believed I'd eat much meat or even liver,' she told Elizabeth one evening. 'I have always abhorred liver since my governess made me finish it up, but now it tastes delicious, just right.'

'That's because you need it,' Elizabeth said smiling.

The baby flourished, so Amabel decided not to have him christened 'til they got back to Lincoln and his father. The Dean had left instructions that he was to be called Benjamin.

'It may be a case of wishful thinking, but at least one must grant him biblical knowledge,' said Mrs Maltby.

'Why?' enquired Elizabeth.

'It means "the last one",' Mr Maltby explained.

'Amen to that,' said his wife.

'Amen, indeed,' agreed Elizabeth. 'Mrs Potts and I have been stressing the desirability of that.'

:

They had quite a good journey and arrived back in Lincoln at the beginning of May when even the North Country was admitting it was spring. In July, a letter from Mr Pitt arrived. The high-minded but half-witted government of France had come out from arranging a better world to find itself confronted by a worse world in the form of one hundred and fifty cannon pointing at them. A lot of them were arrested and soon sent to a better world, for we feel almost anything must be better than Jacobins.

'They have decreed I am an "Enemy of the People",' wrote Mr Pitt. 'I hope I am indeed an enemy of such people but a strong friend to ploughmen.'

'How does he mean "a strong friend to ploughmen"?' asked Elizabeth, as she was reading it.

'He may be speaking sportively,' replied George, 'but he does not often write sportively, and I think he meant it literally. In our walks he often spoke to such countrymen as we might meet, listening to them with respect and admiration. It was ever his hope to do something for the rural poor.'

'A worthy ambition, but with this war?' enquired Elizabeth.

'Aye, there will be no money now for ought else,' George retorted.

In August, the Duke of York besieged Dunkirk, but the Prussians wouldn't come as they had promised because they feared the Austrians were doing too well, and he was soon greatly outnumbered by the French. There was a muddle in the Admiralty and the essential guns arrived just in time to be captured by the French.

George went to London in September for a debate in the House of Lords and came with the latest news, a French tutor – a man known as the Marquis of Chavaise, and an invitation to Windsor Castle. The news was expected, the tutor hoped for, but the invitation was a complete shock.

'A courtier came up to me in the House,' explained George at their first dinner after his return, 'and said His Majesty was giving a little party in October and hoped we would come. A card is to follow.'

'And I suppose "little" means about fifty people,' said Elizabeth crossly. 'We shall have to stop in London so I can get some fashionable clothes and they're always so uncomfortable.'

'We say "Il faut souffrir poor être beau",' said the Marquis. 'I went on occasion to Versailles and I did not wish to live there, but for a short stay for a boy it was magical.'

'I fear you will find us very dull,' said Elizabeth.

'It is all I ask,' said the Marquis with conviction. 'I have had sufficient adventures for one lifetime. But I fear your sons will not like me.'

'Oh, I think they will. Ned is studious and anxious for information, and George, though so young, is always curious,' replied Elizabeth.

'They executed the French Queen last week,' George told Elizabeth.

'Poor lady. She's well out of it, but those children haunt me,' Elizabeth stated.

'Me also,' agreed the Marquis. 'They have apprenticed the little King to a cobbler. But I assure you it is not only the "ci-devants" who suffer. I worked among the poor after my father told me I must escape, and they live in fear. A man has a good English wool coat, a woman a pretty brooch, someone will inform on them, repeat or invent something said that shows they are not true patriots, then they will be guillotined and the informer will be given the warm coat and the pretty brooch.'

'And they have forbidden all religion,' said George.

'It is true, though brave priests may still sometimes be found. The Abbé Edgeworth was with the King on the scaffold and he said, "Fils de St Louis montez au ciel," and then after he walked into the crowd and they parted and let him through. They say the crowd were people from the slum parish where he had been a much loved curé. And when the soldiers chased him the crowd would not let them through,' the Marquis elaborated.

'What a heartening story,' said Elizabeth, 'but how did you escape?'

The Marquis began to explain. 'My father was one of the Girondins. I happened to be in Paris, a rare occurrence, when they arrested him. I went to see him in prison. It was rash, I knew it, but a son's feelings were too strong. He said to me, "Things we teased you about will prove useful now," and when we embraced on parting he said quietly in my ear "Go!" I told him I would always honour and obey him. You must know my family have always teased me over two matters. The first was my fondness for the English; the second was my preference for looking after my own horses when time permitted. They called me the "groom". There was a good man from our estate who kept a small livery stable in Paris. I went to him and passed as his nephew from Provence. I speak the patois well enough. When opportunity served to take a customer's second horse to Calais I rode it. There was an English merchant ship in the harbour and the captain, from the goodness of his heart who would take no money, took me to Dover. They gave me some of their clothes and said I was one of the crew. I had to walk to London. No great hardship in fine weather, but in London I had friends and one of them, Sir Joseph Banks, recommended me to you, and so you see me.'

'And the rest of your family?' asked Elizabeth.

The Marquis' lively face became tragic. 'I do not know. My father was guillotined when I was yet in Paris. My mother is dead, fortunately. My elder brother is on our estates. We thought he would be safe there, but now I do not know. Perhaps he will disguise himself as I did, though… One sister is quite safe. She is married to a diplomat and they are in Spain. I have written to her. My other two sisters, I do not know. I fear for them and their children.'

'You seem to have used great address and resolution,' George told him.

'I was fortunate. I am told there is an Englishman who travels to France to rescue his friends,' the Marquis queried.

'So I am informed. He is called Massingberd, and he lives at Gunby, not so far from here. Being vastly fond of yachting he went often to France, so he is well-known and welcome in many harbours. But now, with the war, it may become impossible,' George illustrated.

'I honour him,' said the Marquis, 'and should wish to meet him.'

'So should I,' agreed Elizabeth, 'and we have some acquaintance with the Turners of Stoke Rochford, who are, I believe, his cousins. Next time we meet I will ask if they would not visit and ask him, too. We are here, I should imagine, half-way between Gunby and Stoke Rochford.'

'Hardly,' said George. 'They are both further east.'

'Near enough. If you will forgive me, I think I shall go to bed. I rode some way this afternoon and, in spite of the fascination at your stories, I can hardly keep my eyes open,' Elizabeth expressed.

'I, too, find myself tired,' said the Marquis. 'To travel in England, that was one of my ambitions, nor did it disappoint. Yet, I cannot convey, it was as if someone had put me on the moon.'

'It must seem so,' said Elizabeth. 'Yet little by little I think you will come to life again, and this is your chance to teach us benighted, bucolic English to appreciate France.'

'I see little to appreciate at present,' the Marquis suggested.

'One would have to be a saint to appreciate Robespierre,' agreed George, 'but the peasants sound to be reservoirs of piety and integrity. A considerable extent of France is in a condition of counter-revolution.'

'It is true,' said the Marquis, 'but they have no arms.'

'Mr Pitt writes that Lord Grenville and the Duke of Richmond are distinctly in favour of neglecting all else to convey arms to them; also, to convey a few good regiments to liaise with them and advance on Paris,' George revealed.

'It would be the best chance if one of the King's brothers went, but I keep you up. We have happily many days to discuss matters,' the Marquis added.

The Marquis was a great success. He was a good mimic, and Ned loved him and made him act out over and over again what the miller said when the old lady accused him of cheating her; and what the cook said when the kitchen maid dropped the eggs. George preferred the Marquis' animal and bird noises, but both of them learned quite a bit of French during bouts of delighted giggles.

The Marquis thought he should be plain Mr Blanchard, as a beggarly marquis was ludicrous, but Elizabeth pointed out to him that this would grieve George, who was very happy to employ a marquis, and one should go down with all flags flying; if one flag was still flying when the rest of the ship was underwater, so much the better.

Everyone approved of the Marquis except Mrs Mann, who said he made the children too noisy, and she always noticed foreigners were smarmy but let you down in the end. Amabel, who was well again, was delighted with him and sent Jack to share Ned's lessons. The Dean was happy about that but refused to pay. Amabel paid the small sum out of her pin money that she and Elizabeth thought right. The Marquis accepted it reluctantly.

'I am already well paid, but some of my friends are in need. Not all are as fortunate as I have been,' he said.

The Duke of York and his army were retreating. One of the many risings in France was at Toulon, and they asked the English to come and help. There were few men to spare but some were sent.

The Marquis had a letter from his sister in Spain. Their brother was dead. Many people begged him to run away or disguise himself, but he would not, and had been guillotined. Another sister and her husband and three children had escaped into Spain and were now safe, though their fourth and youngest child had died of cold when they were crossing the Pyrenees.

Richard and Benjamin both grew rapidly. Elizabeth began weaning Richard, as she could not take him to Windsor.

Goodchild approved of the Marquis. 'Ain't much he don't know about 'osses,' he told Elizabeth. 'An' a well-spoken gent, too. It ain't th' folk as is grand who freeze you out, it's the folk as wanter be.'

:

In London, Mr Pitt was worried about Ireland. This was nothing new but was caused, in this instance, by his persuading most of the Whigs to join him. Charles

James Fox was no longer a danger, being no longer a leader. This made Parliament much easier for Pitt to control, but the King much more difficult to manage, as the King no longer had to agree for fear of getting his bête noire as Prime Minister.

One of the newly acquired Whigs was Lord Fitzwilliam and, as Mr Dundas said, he was "a right popinjay, away with the little people, and ah'm after wishing he'd no but bide there".

'He feels himself to be the saviour of the Irish nation,' explained Mr Pitt. 'And the Irish nation feels he will remove them to a castle in Spain. I am far from sanguine as to the results of these unusual proceedings, but that was the calling price of his joining us.'

'And, although we did not want him, we had to have him,' explained Mr Rose, 'or the other Whigs, out of somewhat misplaced loyalty, would have refused to join.'

They were having an impromptu luncheon at the time. Although Elizabeth entirely agreed with Goodchild about the rapacity of Mr Pitt's servants, she had to admit the cook was good, and resourceful to cope with the quantity of politicians who wandered in to confer and stayed to consume.

'Ah, aye, tell 't y' 'twas nae for good,' said Mr Dundas. 'By th' Lord o' the Isles he's louse of th' Isles.'

'Mr Pitt has been fishing for Whigs these two years,' said Mr Canning, who was standing on a chair to look at a high picture. 'You can hardly expect him to throw them back now he's landed them.'

'The advantages outweigh the drawbacks,' said a tall man who'd been introduced as Lord Castlereagh.

'What distresses me,' disclosed Mr Pitt, 'is Fitzwilliam's disinclination to work with Mr Beresford, who is the only man I ever met who can explain the Irish.'

'He doesn't work with anyone,' said Mr Canning, leaping off the chair, snatching up a chicken leg, and conveying it to the window. 'He merely muddles them.'

'It'll end in a strumacher,' warned Mr Dundas.

'It's raining again,' said Mr Canning.

Indeed the rain could be heard tapping on the window.

'We must give Lord Fitzwilliam credit for a laudable desire to benefit the Catholics,' pointed out Mr Pitt, 'but if he goes about in such a way that he infuriates the Protestants he will scarce benefit the Catholics much in the long run.'

'Mr Burke,' announced a footman, and that personage was with them, talking.

'You must do more about Toulon. The men are outnumbered and they rely on you. I met a Navy man who told me the French have sent one of their best officers, a Corsican gunner called Napoleon Bonaparte, and they were aware of his talent immediately. He presses them hard. When are the reinforcements likely to come up?'

'It is hoped next month,' Mr Pitt told him.

'Too late. You should have sent them sooner, but if the wind serves… how many?' replied Burke.

'We think two thousand men,' said Pitt.

'What is the use of that?' asked Mr Burke.

Pitt returned, 'You may be sure the French are pouring them in. It cannot be easy. It is an opportunity unlikely to recur.'

'We were discussing Lord Fitzwilliam's imminent descent on your countrymen,' Mr Rose told him.

'Oh that! Why send a tactless fool to govern the most sensitive, wronged race in Europe? But, about Toulon?' Burke exclaimed.

'Do you not find discussions such as we had this afternoon trouble your digestion?' Elizabeth asked Mr Pitt when all the visitors had gone and they were supping peacefully alone.

Pitt replied to her, 'I do indeed. It often gives me gout in the stomach. Yet nothing could be more clarifying than clever men debating affairs informally.'

'You must take care of your health,' said George.

'You sound deplorably like my dear old nurse. Bear in mind that the King is easy and natural but the Queen's German dresser, who rules all, is stiff and unnatural,' Pitt eludicated.

'I have the needle already,' said Elizabeth.

'There is 'n occasion for it. The King approves George because George disapproves of Catholics; the Queen approves George because she is a blue light Queen. They will both approve you because you have a way with you,' replied Mr Pitt.

CHAPTER EIGHTEEN

Windsor Castle

The impressive bulk of Windsor Castle loomed up in front of them, the round tower particularly marvellous, Elizabeth thought. 'I wonder who will be there,' she supposed in trepidation.

When they arrived a pompous comptroller, with a staff of office, told them they were expected, and showed them to a large, magnificent suite of rooms looking out over the Thames. Elizabeth asked the comptroller if there were many people staying, but he replied formally and unhelpfully, 'No more than is customary.' He then announced, 'The King will dine at five,' and left them.

Their luggage appeared, carried in by a variety of footmen and maids. The maids bobbed a curtsey and some even smiled, but the footmen were impassive.

'Will the Queen wear a crown?' Kate asked, as she helped Elizabeth dress.

'No, that's only for special occasions, I think. It must be most uncomfortable, nearly as bad as corsets,' Elizabeth proposed.

She spoke with feeling, for after eighteen months of bearing and nursing a child, having to sometimes wear her fairly comfortable old corsets was bad enough; having to wear these tight new corsets was a depressing prospect.

'But she will wear jewels?' asked Kate again.

'I expect so,' Elizabeth muttered.

A middle-aged woman came in, curtseyed, and then said, 'I'm to look after you, Ma'am. I'm that sorry I was late. One of the ladies kept me. My name is Susan. Is there anything you'd like? A bath perhaps?'

'Not tonight,' answered Elizabeth, 'there isn't time. Tomorrow, let us hope. If you'd just show my maid, Kate, where everything is, I'll start on putting up my hair.'

Elizabeth saw to it they were soon ready to go down. Susan, who seemed a very pleasant, obliging woman, offered to guide them as far as the top of the stairs. They had arrived at that eminence and were descending when a cheerful voiced hailed them. 'Bishop. Mrs Pretyman, you look vastly elegant. I declare, I was quite in awe of that fine lady 'til I saw it was you. My wife's gone on ahead. She would not miss a minute of our apotheosis, but I had letters to write.'

It was Sir Joseph Banks.

'It is a great comfort to meet someone we know,' said Elizabeth.

'You are in luck; it's quite a small party. Much cosier, do you not think? This way. Know anything about landscape gardening?' asked Sir Joseph Banks.

'Not a thing,' answered Elizabeth, 'but George and Mr Pitt are grown devoted to it. They make improvements and…'

Before she could finish they had crossed the huge hall and Sir Joseph had turned towards a door. Two of the loitering footman in livery opened one leaf each and they were suddenly in a large room full of elegant furniture and people. A man came over to them, a medium-sized man, with a high collar and short, white wig. He looked like most of the other men present, but there could be no doubt this was the King.

'Here you are!' he said. 'Good! Good! Now we can have a bite. Have a good journey?'

'Excellent, I thank you, Your Majesty,' answered Elizabeth, curtseying.

'Bishop Pretyman, here's just the man you've been looking for,' said Sir Joseph. 'He knows everything about landscape gardening.'

'What? What? D'ye really? Thing is, we've bought Frogmore and we want to brush it up a bit. I'll just show you the plans after dinner. Just a rough sketch I made,' said the King.

'I would hardly claim to know everything,' said George, 'but Mr Pitt and I have both given some time to the subject and endeavoured to improve our respective properties. There is a man called Humphrey Repton, whom we approve, who holds you must full use the lie of the land, altering it as little as possible, to provide vistas, focal points, and water features.'

'Well, y' ha' no difficulty wi' th' water feature,' said a good looking man. 'Whole blinking river forbye.'

'The river's windings were most striking from our windows,' said Elizabeth.

'That's it,' said the King. 'Sort of thing. Got to look right. Here comes the Queen.'

She did indeed, wearing a gold dress with huge sleeves, a choker of pearls, and a pearl bracelet on each wrist. She was much the same height as the King, tall for a woman. Not beautiful, but with a striking face.

'I have been quite neglecting you,' she said, with just a trace of a soft, charming accent. 'But believe me, I have been much looking forward to your visit. I do not suppose His Majesty has told you who anyone is, and there may not now be time before dinner, but I will make a start. Here we have our son, the Duke of Kent. This is the Bishop of Lincoln and Mrs Pretyman, Edward. The gentleman in red is Sir John Scott. That is his wife in the green dress. I believe he will be your neighbour. The tall man is Mr Price. The lady in grey he is talking to is Lady Banks. The lady in silvery-blue is in waiting at present. You are to go into dinner with Sir Joseph, Mrs Pretyman. He told me you were friends and so I thought it would be easier for you. The Bishop is to take me in. I look forward to discussing the Catholic schools now setting up in England.'

'Trouble is,' the King was saying, 'trees take such a deuced long time to grow. M'gardener says you can transplant quite big trees if you...'

'Dinner is served,' said the black-suited butler with his chain of office.

'I saw that boy again the other day,' Sir Joseph told Elizabeth, as he led her into dinner.

'The painter?' she asked.

'That's the one. Young Turner. Always thought he was a Jew with that nose of his, but he said not. Anyway, he's getting along. Drawing for some magazines. *The Pocket Magazine* was one. You sit here.' He pulled out a chair for her.

'The one I often wonder about is the poet. What was his name?' Elizabeth remembered.

'William Wordsworth? Yes, I never heard any more of him but I'll say we will one day. D' y' read Crabbe?' Sir Joseph asked.

'I have done, though not recently. Rather affecting stories, some of them. I met him once at Belvoir,' Elizabeth revealed.

Banks replied, 'Burke's his patron and a good one, too. Crabbe says he just wants to tell th' truth. Not easy done, but if you can it makes a good story. Sticks in people's heads somehow.'

'Yes, indeed. Would it be the ring of truth?' Elizabeth wondered.

'Might be. Might be, just he transports you, so you observe what he has observed. I congratulate you, Mrs Pretyman. Most people are somewhat overcome by royalty but you're quite unaffected,' complimented Sir Joseph.

'I always find it best to simply be myself. Do you think for every poet who acquires Burke as his patron and so does well, there are a dozen, as good in their way, who have no such good fortune and so are never known?' Elizabeth supposed.

'An interesting conundrum. I must ponder on it, and then tell you of my opinion. But now I must speak with Mrs Scott,' Sir Banks rounded off.

Elizabeth sat happily for a bit gazing round the high room. There were some fantastic pictures. She recognized Charles I on a horse, and Elizabeth I. There were several she didn't recognize. She thought she must ask about them if she got the chance.

'Ye're the Bishop's wife, are ye not?' asked the good-looking man on her left.

'For my sins,' she said, smiling.

'And I'm a lawyer forbye, for their sins. Th' names Scott, Sir John Scott. M' old dad is of the opinion we're kin to Bucleugh, but I ha' me doots. Will yer old man preach for aye?'

'No, he's not too bad now. I've forbidden him to go on for longer than half an hour,' Elizabeth responded cheerfully.

Sir John Scott began telling an old story. 'Bonny lassie! Cutty Sark! If they dinna mind ye th' first time, they will'na th' thirty-first. There was a bit preacher in King Charles' time, old Rowley, they callit him after a horse, and a preacher was long, long, an' th' Lordling right under his nose snorin' away. "My Lord, my Lord," callit th' preacher, "Y' snore so loud you will wake the King!"'

Elizabeth laughed.

Sir John laughed. 'Ah'm one for th' tales. Y' kin hear old folk talkin' in them. Hae ye bairns?'

'Three boys. The last one's not a year old yet. We were in hopes he'd be a girl,' Elizabeth told him smiling.

'I've a lassie and she's m' springtime, but she's a wambly forbye and I'm aye frettin' on her. An I've three young rascals a' laddies. Ah need na' fret about their health, and yet y'ken, it's a chancy world,' explained Sir John Scott.

Elizabeth enjoyed her dinner. So did George. His conversation was less light-hearted and more religious, but he engaged in it just as much. The Queen turned out to be well informed about the latest religious ideas.

:

The next day George looked at the King's ideas for improving Frogmore with Mr Price, who was also knowledgeable, and then headed for the library. Elizabeth went for a ride with the Queen and Lady Banks. The Queen drove them.

'So nice to be able to say what you wish,' she said.

The day was sunny, though rather cold, and they drove through Windsor Great Park where the leaves were falling and the deer were roaming.

'It is to be hoped they do not take the pony for a stag,' said Lady Banks.

'Indeed,' agreed the Queen. 'It takes me back to the forests of my youth, but the stags were heavier there and you might see a boar, or even wolves.'

'Were you very homesick at first?' asked Mrs Banks.

The Queen replied, 'I suppose I was. I fancied the English were quite without proper etiquette or sentiments. The King was kind and I found him handsome, but I missed my family and found the English language very abrupt, and impossible to ascertain what they meant.'

'Not much, usually,' said Lady Banks.

'How old were you?' asked Elizabeth.

'I was in my seventeenth year, but I had lived retired. The clothes and jewels pleased me at first and to find myself in a position of eminence, but within a week I found the worry of the jewels and the responsibility of place greater than their worth,' revealed the Queen.

'Did you find some friends?' asked Elizabeth.

'By the grace of God, I did, not least that God of grace,' she confirmed.

'We might be in the middle of the New Forest!' exclaimed Lady Banks.

The Queen replied, 'Indeed! It is a pleasure to leave civilization for a time and return to the primeval world, but now, if you will forgive me, we must go back to the modern world. I promised our youngest, Amelia, that she should come for an airing when she'd finished her lessons. The two little boys that were just older than her died, you see, so she is a bit solitary.'

'But, of course,' said Lady Banks, 'I always enjoy meeting Amelia; such a taking child, with hair like ripe barley. But all your children are too beautiful.'

Elizabeth looked with awe at this serene woman who had lost two children, whose son was in Flanders, and whose husband had once been mad for months.

The princess was waiting with her governess. She was, as Lady Banks had said, a very pretty child with long fair curls.

'I thought you were never coming, Mama,' she said. 'I thought you had forgotten.'

'Your Mama always keeps her word,' the governess said.

'Curtsey to Lady Banks and Mrs Pretyman,' said the Queen.

The child did so very prettily and then scrambled into the little cart and sat in front beside her mother.

'Can we go to the lake?' she asked. 'Oh, let's go to the lake!'

'You always want to go to the lake,' said her mother.

'You can see duck and geese and moorhens, and sometimes a kingfisher or a fish jumping.'

'When I was young I loved water, too,' added Elizabeth. 'When I could swim my father got the village carpenter to make a little boat and I spent hours paddling about on the river. I sometimes saw otters.'

'I wish I had a boat. Did you ever upset your boat?' questioned the girl.

Elizabeth responded, 'Often, but it only mattered once. I could readily right it and tip out the water, but once my little sister overturned the boat, grabbing at water crowfoot. She couldn't swim, so she sank. I should never have taken her, of course. I grabbed her hair as she went down for the second time and I towed her to the bank. She cried and said I'd hurt her terribly; we were both wet and cold, and my mother and her nurse were very cross.'

'But you saved her, so they shouldn't have been. How old were you?' the little girl asked.

'Fourteen and she was five,' replied Elizabeth.

The little girl's face was full of excitement. 'Oh, I should like a boat. Can I have a boat, Mama?'

'You heard Mrs Pretyman say her father would not give her a boat until she could swim. When you can swim we'll see,' the Queen said back to her.

'I'll learn next summer. What else did you do when you were young, Mrs Pretyman?' the little girl probed again.

Elizabeth began a small story. 'I rode a lot. Once I got run away with. The pony must've been stung by a bee or a wasp, they thought. I was all alone because I'd slipped out and saddled the pony, without even a groom. We went faster and faster, and everything flew past and the wind blustered. And then I wasn't secure, because I was riding astride, which I'd been told not to do, so when the pony turned sharp right into our drive I fell off, hit my head, and was unconscious for two hours and in bed for a week.'

'How old were you?' the little girl enquired.

'Ten, but my brother had just died, so my parents made more of it perhaps than they would have done otherwise,' revealed Elizabeth.

'I'm ten and my brothers died,' the little girl said more solemnly.

'When I was a child,' said Lady Banks, 'my brother and I used to turn over a table and put a blanket across it and say it was our flying coach, and then we'd say we would go to the moon in it, over even Mars or Venus, and when we got there we found lots of queer moon beasts and then we shot some of them dead, because they attacked us.'

'What sport,' said the Princess, clapping her hands. 'Next time my friend Meliora comes to tea we will play that game. Oh, Mama, can we stop so I can paddle?'

They were drawing alongside the shore of Virginia Water, which shone brightly and lapped gently below them.

'I fear not,' replied the Queen. 'I must get back and attend to my guests. Lady Scott will be awake by now and wishful to talk about balls and routs. Sir John Scott will be on fire to tell me some of his diverting anecdotes. Sir Joseph will want to talk sensibly about Corresponding Societies and the King will wish to show me his new plans for Frogmore.'

'Only my George,' said Elizabeth smiling, 'will be happy as a sandboy in the library and need no entertaining.'

'The perfect guest,' said the Queen. 'You English have such harum scarum country childhoods. Mine was a bit more formal, but we were out and about quite a bit, too, and at Christmas we went tobogganing, and there was a Christmas tree with candles on it.'

'We have one here, too,' said the Princess. 'It's so pretty. I put fir cones dipped in silver and gold on it.'

'The King always gets a tree for me,' said the Queen.

The Pretymans stayed for a week and found their worries were needless. The King and the Queen were both easy and friendly. The Princess had taken a fancy to Elizabeth and wanted endless stories about hers and Emily's childhood. George preached a sermon on "the sword of the Lord and of Gideon" in St. George's Chapel for half an hour, and was more complimented on his brevity than on his holiness or eloquence.

On their last evening, the King took Elizabeth into dinner and, once they were seated, asked in his abrupt way, 'What d'y' think about enclosures?'

She answered, 'They are an excellent thing if compassionately done, but a disaster if the cottagers' grazing and firing is taken away from them.'

'That's what I say. That's just what I say. We must have more corn, not a doubt about it, but there is no occasion to take all th' commons. Folk do better if they can keep a cow, perhaps a pig or two. I do not like to hear of my people going hungry. I don't indeed. But how're we to feed them in these monstrous towns? Tell me that,' the King wondered.

'It is a puzzle, Sir. If there's but enough employment… Mr Pitt was in hopes that he could do something for the poor, but with this expensive war, I fear it will not be practicable,' Elizabeth replied politely.

The King replied graciously, 'No, no, you are in the right of it. The French have run mad. And how is Mr Pitt? He works too hard – works too hard. You might think he was the only man that could decide anything the way they plague him.'

'His clarity of mind is naturally much in demand, but I think he bears up pretty well,' stated Elizabeth.

Later, Sir John Scott talked to Elizabeth about the Civil War.

'In the Royalist news-sheets there are some verra droll pieces. There was a report Sir Jacob Astley had been killed, and in the Mercurius it said, "Sir Jacob Astley desires to know if he was slain by a pike or a musket ball?"'

Elizabeth laughed. 'You'll have to talk to my George. He loves reading old documents, too. In the library here he's discovered some letters from a Norfolk family in the Middle Ages called Paston. He is so taken with them the King has finally lent him a great pile of them.'

The next morning they parted, amongst many expressions of gratitude. The Queen said they must come again.

'Never been in such a ramshackle old place in all my days,' Goodchild told them in the coach. 'Th' stables are well enough. Th' head groom know what wants doin' an' he see that's done, but th' castle! The front part's all glass 'n' gold, but the back's plain dirty, some of it. And same as Downing Street, there's forever o' waste. Don't think many o' them are on th' take exactly, but no one seems to be in charge in some places, so they waste half their time. An' that old woman the Queen brought with her spends more money on knick-knacks than the Queen does.'

CHAPTER NINETEEN

Number 10 Downing Street

Back in 10 Downing Street it soon seemed as if they'd never been away. They only stayed two nights this time, being anxious to get home. But on the second day Mr Pitt told them at breakfast that Mr Wilberforce was coming to dinner and was bringing his pastor.

'One Newton,' said Mr Pitt. 'Used to be a slaver and then the Lord spoke to him in a storm. The Lord does choose the oddest places for a chat. He's the parson in some London church now and people rush to hear him preach. I'd be more inclined to rush away. Those evangelists preach so well there's no holding them. If he discovers I've about as much religion as Monsieur Robespierre, he'll be very grieved.'

'How can you speak so?' said the Bishop.' Your faith is soundly based, though somewhat inarticulate, like that of so many English Christians.'

'We leave preaching to the parsons and the raving to the revolutionaries. I'm told there's a French senator who walks about naked to show his republican simplicity,' retorted Pitt.

'He must show all sorts of things,' said Elizabeth gravely.

'This lack of ladylike delicacy puts me to the blush. We must try and avoid lewd discourse when we have an apostle in our midst. He writes hymns,' Pitt added.

'Good hymns?' asked Elizabeth.

'I am no judge. Wilberforce says one of them would be good, if only someone would put a good tune to it. Something about smiting at all your foes. I could do with it,' said Mr Pitt.

Mr Newton was a small man; or perhaps he gave that impression because he was rather bent. There was something soothing and serene about him, and even Mr Pitt when with him didn't produce his usual icy politeness with strangers.

:

At dinner they talked about John Wesley.

'It was the greatest tragedy,' said Wilberforce, 'we could not keep him in the Church of England. He wished to stay, but there was a want of tact, of foresight.'

'Perchance, Methodism needed to develop in its own way,' suggested Mr Newton.

'John Wesley declared he had not thought it possible,' said Mr Pitt, 'still less, desirable, that a man could be converted except in a church.'

'And the good Lord taught him better,' said Mr Newton, 'and sent him where he was needed.'

'Coalmines. But what I find curious', said Mr Pitt, 'is that he has resurrected the phenomenon of speaking with tongues, discontinued seventeen centuries ago.'

'I do not think it ever was discontinued, you know,' Mr Newton told him, 'merely driven underground by the hardness of our hearts. I heard of several cases in America and I have experienced two myself.'

'What were they?' asked Wilberforce eagerly.

'The first was a parishioner of mine who confessed to a grave sin from which I was eventually able to absolve him. He reacted with tears and rapture, and some words in an unknown tongue. He could not account for it, nor could I. It sounded a little like one of the American-Indian languages. The other time I was asked to exorcise a house where there had been disturbances, and to my simple prayer I heard myself add a sentence in a language I did not know, although I was aware the sentence meant "go back where you belong". It was strange, very strange, as if another was speaking through my voice. Yet I felt no fear, rather relief and gratitude. The words echoed in my mind and I had every intention of recording them, but by the time I reached home I was exhausted and repaired to my bed. Next morning I had no recollection whatever of the words, except the impression there was some affinity with Greek.'

'Did the disturbances stop?' asked Elizabeth.

'Oh yes, yes. The family was most grateful. They have faithfully attended my church ever since,' replied Newton.

'Did they hear you speaking in an unknown tongue?' asked Wilberforce.

'Indeed, but, being simple souls, they took it for Latin,' explained Newton.

'It is an edifying and arresting account,' said Mr Pitt. 'What purple lives you priests lead. Did you ever meet any evil spirits, Bishop?'

The Bishop piped up. 'I am thankful to say I did not. I do not feel my bent lies that way, but should the occasion arise I would, as ever, call upon my Saviour for assistance.'

'You could not do better,' said Mr Newton.

'I sometimes wonder,' stated Mr Wilberforce, 'if, now France is given up to the devil, the angels are gathering in England to assist us.'

'I will have Michael, if they please,' said Mr Pitt. 'I understand he is an astute general.'

'But perhaps,' said Mr Newton, 'he is already with a young major in Flanders who is to be our salvation.'

'Surely he could advise two people, or even twenty? I should not have thought that presented any difficulty to an archangel. You apprehend it will be a long war, then?' remarked Mr Newton.

'I do, God help us! This is a new thing, a perilous thing. I have wrestled with the Lord in prayer for the victims and even more for the murderers and, if I understand my Maker aright, there will be an improvement 'ere long in Paris, but peace – peace is to be for our children,' commented Mr Wilberforce.

Mr Pitt, George, and Elizabeth all agreed during their hurried early breakfast that Mr Newton was vastly impressive.

'That complete simplicity and serenity was delightful,' said Mr Pitt. 'I had thought Will exaggerated on the subject of his mentor's merits but he did not.'

'I felt like one,' said George, 'who is laboriously, though contently, climbing a great mountain and, of a sudden, encounters a pilgrim who has visited the peak on several occasions.'

'Perhaps you will be a saint like him by the time you are an old man,' offered Mr Pitt.

'It is strange how you recognise a saint,' commented Elizabeth. 'I have only met with them among the country people 'til now.'

'You must come back with George soon, Elizabeth,' her host urged her. 'Your candour lights up my gloomy life. Bring all three boys, if you will, and their tutor, too, but come, I beg of you.'

:

'We're getting on well,' said George in the coach that afternoon, 'and should…'

There was the sound of plunging hooves, frantic, louder, and then shouts and a crash, and everything was tilting and toppling. Elizabeth was on the wall of the coach with Goodchild's son, Tom, on top of her. She couldn't breathe; Kate screamed.

'I'm, sorry, Madam,' said Tom Goodchild, pulling himself into the corner, 'we're over, I think.'

His father could be heard shouting outside.

'Are you all right, Elizabeth?' asked George.

'Fine, and you?'

'I am uninjured, too,' responded George.

'I've hurt my arm,' said Kate.

The coach door opened above them and Goodchild was peering down, shutting out most of the light. 'Are you all right?'

'Yes,' Elizabeth said, 'at least, Kate's hurt her arm, but otherwise we are.'

'Blasted maniac! Put Mrs Pretyman's foot in your hands, Tom, and hoist while I pull,' said Goodchild.

She was yanked out like a cork from a bottle and lowered carefully by strong hands. There was a tall countryman holding a shire horse, which was attached to a huge log on a trailer. Their four horses had been cut loose and were grazing.

'You all right, Mum?' asked the countryman.

Elizabeth replied, 'Yes, thank goodness, but—'

Kate screamed again.

'Lift her out, Tom,' said Goodchild. 'I can only pull on the good arm. That's it.'

'I never see nothing like it,' said the countryman. 'He come along hell for leather for London.'

'Who did?' asked Elizabeth.

'This here madman, drivin' a chaise.'

'Is there a good inn nearby?' Elizabeth enquired further.

The countryman scratched his head, 'Well now, not as you might say good, being quality, but the White Harte is about a mile back way. I'm a' goin' an' you're more'n welcome to ride with me. Though I only got room for one or p'haps two at a squeeze.'

Goodchild had extracted Kate by now.

'What happened?' she asked, clutching her left shoulder, in obvious pain.

'Crazy gent'lman in a chaise try to overtake me 'n' crash inter your coach,' informed the countryman. 'Let me hev a look at that shoulder. I'm a bonesetter, as that chance. I reckon that's out.' He felt very gently with skilful fingers. 'Yes, that's out. Hang on a minute. Take hold of my hand. Now.'

He gave a quick wrench and Kate screamed for a third time.

'That's back. You'll do now.'

George, having been extracted from the coach, came over.

'Has Kate broken her arm?' he asked.

'Dislocated it,' answered Elizabeth.

'That's about th' sum of it, but I put that back,' said the woodsman.

'It feels sore,' said Kate, 'but not terrible anymore. I'm much obliged to you.'

''Tis a blessing I was by, certainly. Th' longer tha's out th' worse that git,' the country gentleman described.

A carriage came, going away from London. It stopped and a man poked his head out of the window. 'I see you've met with that madman. He nearly had us over, too. Can I give you a lift?'

'How far is the next village that way?' Elizabeth asked the woodsman, meaning onwards.

'Matter o' a couple o' miles,' he pointed out.

'Is the inn there any better?' Elizabeth supposed.

'No, miss. 'Least th' White Harte's clean,' he replied.

Turning to the man in the coach she said, 'I think we'd better go back to the White Harte, then, but thank you for offering.'

The coach went on. It began very gently to rain.

'We'd better go with this gentleman, Kate and me. You can walk with the horse. It's only a mile… Oh.'

Another carriage was coming along. Rather a shabby one. It stopped and the coachman said, 'You won't get out of that th' night.'

The window opened and an elderly head poked out in a black bonnet. 'You have met with a mishap? May I be of service? What happened?'

'A blithering idiot called Lord Barrymore, drunk as a wheelbarrow, banged into us. I got in a good one with m' whip. He's got a weal now, an' don't I wish th' whip had gone round his silly neck. I do, no error!' said Goodchild with optimism.

'Oh! Can I give some of you a lift to the White Harte?'

'That would be very kind,' said Elizabeth. 'Just three of us, please. The groom'll have to bring the horses. Give him some money.'

This last was to George, and she nodded to the woodsman. George produced a sovereign.

'I don't need no money. I ain't done much, an' I didn't 'spect y' t' pay me. Are y' sure y' can spare it?'

'Take it, Josh,' ordered the old lady. 'And send Peter to school.'

'Well, I was thinking. Thank y' kindly, sir. That's a year's schooling for my lad, an' he's mad to learn, same 's I was.'

'Thank you for curing Kate's shoulder.'

Goodchild helped open the door for them. Elizabeth was glad to get out of the rain which was falling quite heavily now. 'Are you all right, Goodchild?' she called belatedly.

'I've a fine bruise but I feel middling.'

CHAPTER TWENTY
Belvoir

By the time they reached the White Harte a mile or so back they knew that the lady in the carriage was Mrs Sharpe, that she had been a widow for ten years, and that her only son was in Flanders with his regiment. When she discovered she was entertaining a bishop unawares she was enthralled, and asked them to dinner tomorrow night.

'We were hoping to get off tomorrow, perhaps not early, but…' Elizabeth began.

'Oh, my dear, I'm afraid you mustn't be in hopes of that. Even I could see your coach was in bad way. We have an excellent wheelwright in the village but even so you must resign yourselves to staying with us for a se'night. But we shall all enjoy having you. A great honour, I'm sure, and if only Philip was here, he'd say so too,' Mrs Sharpe said.

'You don't know,' thought Elizabeth, yet she said, 'You are too kind and the honour is all ours.'

The White Harte was, as advertised, simple but clean. Its proprietor, one Clodpole, bustled about when Mrs Sharpe told him to. His wife, however, started describing the things they had not got.

'No meat,' she said. 'We had a joint last week but there's none left. No port. The gentry has to have port but I dunno where we can get any. No feather beds, we…'

'Ought we to sue Lord Barrymore?' George asked suddenly.

'Better not,' answered Elizabeth, and asked the innkeeper's wife to show them to their rooms.

In spite of Goodchild's efforts and the excellence of the carpenter, it took two days to mend the coach. Elizabeth enjoyed Mrs Sharpe's party, a pleasant, friendly, ordinary gathering such as she had been used to ten years ago. George was bored but concealed it manfully.

There was the local parson and his wife, both rather overwhelmed; there was the squire of the parish and his wife; there was a retired soldier, a widower, and an Alderman of the City, also retired now, and his chatty wife.

The parson ceased to be overwhelmed when he got on to his favourite subject of butterflies. Unfortunately, everyone but Elizabeth clearly felt butterflies were much like bluebottles and about as interesting. Elizabeth luckily had always liked them and could offer Purple Emperors for Fritillaries.

The parson's wife was very taken up with the church school, which the woodsman's son was now about to join.

The squire appeared to think of little but his land. Elizabeth had much the same conversation with him as she had had with King George last week. The squire was delighted when she told him so, and even more delighted when she told him they knew Mr Coke quite well. The squire's wife was less delighted with her when they talked after dinner, and it was discovered that, in spite of having just had the felicity of a stay in London, she knew very little about the latest fashions.

Elizabeth had no speech with the retired soldier but he sounded to be a quiet, sensible sort of a man. The retired Alderman looked a worried man because he had been a wine merchant, and he didn't see how they were going to get any wine. His wife was that dreaded woman, a complainer about servants. Elizabeth was thankful to have had no speech with her, but was aware, all the same, that the Alderman's wife's cook was extravagant, and her butler drank.

:

They continued on their journey and, as usual, stopped off at Belvoir. Much as they always enjoyed staying there, they were very glad to get home.

Ned said, 'You won't go away anymore?'

Elizabeth couldn't promise that but she said she'd try and take him next time she went away. Young George had done some flowers for her room. They consisted of some hips, some yarrow, and a dandelion, but it seemed a rather generous effort for a three year old. The second night they were back the Marquis asked if he might speak with them.

'I hope you will not think me presumptuous,' he said, 'but I wish to marry Jane.'

Jane was the Andrews' second daughter, a cheerful tomboy of twenty.

'And she wishes to marry you?' asked Elizabeth.

'She says so. I think it is a little like Othello and Ophelia, but I hope it will end happier,' expressed the Marquis.

'But where did you meet her?' asked Elizabeth. 'Where did you get a chance to converse?'

'You were so obliging as to say I could exercise your horses. Jane is a good little rider. I would often meet her, with a groom of course as escort, and sometimes her sister, Letitia,' explained the Marquis.

'Have you asked her Papa?' enquired George.

'Yes, indeed. I expected him to send me away with a flea in my ear. Who should blame him? A penniless Catholic of unknown origins? But he was extremely kind and sympathetic. I think also Jane is his favourite daughter, except perhaps for little Elizabeth, and Jane had already pleaded our cause. He says that, if you do not object, we can rent a small cottage or terraced house and set up our establishment with a bonne à tout faire. I do not know the English – ah – yes – the same: "maid of all work".'

'No need for all that,' Elizabeth told him. 'There's plenty of room here.'

'You are all that is amiable, Mrs Pretyman, and make a poor refugee feel quite at home. Jane is a little chatterbox. She makes me laugh, which is a pleasure after so much sorrow. But for a scholar such as your husband it might perhaps be an aggravation?' suggested the Marquis.

'We will have to talk and think about it. I must see what Mrs Mann feels, and the cook. The Goodchilds like you, luckily,' Elizabeth clarified.

'And what about religion?' asked George.

'The Dean was surprisingly moderate in his views. I was astonished. I am a Catholic and shall always be one. The worst of Catholics and quite without any conviction that it is the only true religion, but still a Catholic. I am the last of my line and it may be that I shall have to go and fight in France. I hope to have a son and should wish him to be Catholic too. But the daughters, if there are any, shall be Protestants. My Church will not like this arrangement, but it seems to me just, and I admire the Anglican Church too much to think it will object,' the Marquis went on to Elizabeth.

'The arrangement seems to me just, too', said Elizabeth, 'and so I must congratulate you. I've always liked Jane. She's like a lively puppy, all bounce and enjoyment of life, quite unquenchable and well-informed, too.'

Mr Pitt wrote that he was having great difficulty in finding more troops for Toulon but that the Whigs who had joined him were now more and more amenable.

'They see that their titles and possessions are in danger,' he wrote, 'and they think their best chance for preserving them is by supporting the Government and joining me.'

The Duke of York had failed to take Dunkirk and was retreating. Some very necessary guns were delayed by the Ministry and came up just in time to be captured by the French.

When it came to the Marquis and Jane, Mrs Mann took a poor view of having a young couple living in the Palace. 'This is not a lodging house. Them foreigners. I warned you! Never satisfied! Always on the take. They'll be turning your husband out next.'

The cook was more indulgent. 'I call that ever so romantic. Poor young gentleman. They say he lost his brother. 'Course we can spare a kitchen maid.'

The couple celebrated Christmas very happily, though it was cold and slippery with a sprinkling of snow. With Goodchild's supervision they made a little kitchen and suite in the west-wing and planned the wedding for March, in the Cathedral. Amabel, who was very excited by her daughter's romance, confided that the Marquis and Jane would slip off the day before and be married by a Catholic priest who visited Lincoln from time to time, but this was to be kept very secret.

:

In the new year of 1794 there seemed to be nothing but bad news. The English, outnumbered and out-generalled, lost Toulon. The Duke of York, overwhelmed and let down by the Austrians, had to retreat in Flanders. Lord Fitzwilliam sacked John Beresford and encouraged the Irish to think he would give the Catholics equal rights tomorrow, so they could take over the country the day after tomorrow, which annoyed the Protestants so much so that he had to be recalled, leaving chaos for his unlucky successor.

The Marquis wrote off to an old friend of his father, Général d'Arblay, who had escaped and married an English woman, Dr Johnson's old friend, the writer Fanny Burney. The Général agreed to come and be best man.

The winter continued to be very cold, and the soup kitchen Elizabeth and Amabel ran had more patrons than ever before. The price of bread was high too. In February, it thawed and, although it was wet, raw, and windy, it was no longer slippery, so Elizabeth, Jane, and the Marquis could ride quite often.

Général d'Arblay arrived at the beginning of March and delighted everyone. He had been a moderate reformer, like the Marquis' father, and was a friend of Lafayette.

'We did not realise we were dealing with gunpowder,' he said when he was out riding with Elizabeth, Jane, and the Marquis one bright, cold morning. 'In our ignorance we thought we were dealing with clay we could mould to a better shape and then bake. We tried to bake it but it blew up and blasted us to England.'

'I am very content with England,' said the Marquis, 'for I have found in Mrs Pretyman a gracious patron, and Jane for a sweetheart.'

'You'd better lose me again, quick and sharp,' said Jane. 'I won't make much of a Marquise.'

'Oh, the contrary, you will make a very good Marquise,' said the Général. 'A lot of our sufferings are owing to the icy formality of our nobles. Naturalness and kindness, such as you so often find in England, might have prevented this disaster.'

'Not all the English are natural and kind,' pointed out Elizabeth, 'and the French have wonderful taste.'

'So wonderful they chose Robespierre,' joked Jane.

'The man was the usual pettifogging, liberal lawyer with a grievance by all accounts,' said the Général, 'but now, I think, he is mad.'

'Goodness, the wind strikes cold!' said Elizabeth. 'Where are we going?'

'Over to that wood,' answered the Marquis. 'When we put it between us and the wind it will be much warmer.'

'Let's canter, then,' suggested Elizabeth.

Behind the wood they were out of the battering wind, and it felt more like June than March.

'That's better,' said the Général, 'delightful, in fact. How are your sisters taking your engagement, Antoine?'

'Elodie is taking it like an angel,' replied Jane for him. 'She wrote me such a kind welcoming letter. And Marie-Claire is taking it like a devil.'

'Come now!' remonstrated the Marquis. 'You go too far. My sister Marie-Claire is distressed at my marrying a Protestant. She is very devout and I fear her stay in Spain has made her fanatical. She feels I am betraying the Catholic faith.'

'Pooh! Pooh! Pooh!' puffed the Général impatiently. 'It is time we forgot those old quarrels and united against the common enemy. For my part, if there is no Catholic Church nearby, I go happily to the Anglican Church and have often found holiness.'

'I also,' agreed the Marquis. 'And Father Peter, who has told Jane a little about our faith, says we are growing less intolerant, most of us, and God is saying "about time too".' The Marquis pronounced, 'We will turn back here,' for they had reached the end of the long wood. 'Then we shall have shelter again some of the way back.'

'Shall you have eleven children like your mother?' Elizabeth asked Jane.

'Not if I can help it. I think four would be about right. How many do you want, Antony?' as they had begun to call him.

'I, too, think four would be about right. Two of each. I need sons but I love little girls,' he agreed.

Two days later Jane and the Marquis were married. Twice. Once in a shabby room. And once in the Cathedral, with four of her sisters for bridesmaids, Ned and Jack for pages, and a large congregation. George and Elizabeth promised to take them for a honeymoon next time George went to the House of Lords, so that Jane could see London and Antony could see his émigré friends. He hoped still to hear news of his missing sister. They had planned to go to a small hotel but Mr Pitt wrote that they would be very welcome in Downing Street.

Jane settled in happily. For Elizabeth it was almost like living with Emily again, but a brighter, riding, outdoor Emily. The daffodils came, and then the swallows, but warmth was largely absent 'til well into May. The wedding journey had to be postponed, because by May Jane was going to have a baby and she was very bad with morning sickness. She made light of it and Nell made up a mixture that her mother recommended, which did seem to help, but she was not fit to travel.

They planned to go, two coaches full, to Elizabeth's parents for Christmas so Jane would have Mrs Potts for the birth. After a slow start it was a good summer. George's parents came for a long visit, complaining bitterly of most of the inns on their way.

Elizabeth enjoyed their stay. They were a sensible, cheerful couple, and full of praise for her housekeeping and charities.

On the first of June, 1794, Lord Howe's squadron met a French convoy bringing grain from America and scattered it, taking six ships. There was immense rejoicing, and the King, the Queen, Mr Pitt, and Mrs Dundas all went to Portsmouth to welcome the fleet and give thanks in the local church. The only trouble was the ships carrying the grain got through and so there was no famine in France which might have started a counter-revolution.

Harry wrote at the end of June, a curious mixture of formal dutiful writing and informal forceful language. He had been wounded in the battle and was enjoying six months' leave. It was only his arm and it was near sound again:

> *So we thought we'd pay you a visit, sadly overdue, and shall be with you, if all prospers, in the third week of July. We must needs make haste slowly as Emily is awaiting a happy event in December. Should the appearance of four gypsies, for we shall not part from Camilla and her nurse, cause you the least inconvenience, pray send to Portsmouth as we can very well remove to Emily's parents and the prodigious Mrs Potts a little earlier. We desired however, by your leave, to present our humble duty, and renew the esteemed acquaintance and watch George topping it the nob*

Elizabeth wrote back saying how delighted they were to have a visit at last, and asking him to remind the idle Emily she had a sister, who had written to her four times in the last year without a single answer.

The news from France, more rumour than news at first as was usual nowadays, but confirmed later, was that various leading Jacobins, realising that their turn must come soon now everyone of any note was being guillotined, turned the tables by guillotining Robespierre. Now living in France, if not exactly safe, was certainly much safer.

Harry, Emily, Camilla, and the nurse arrived in August, and the Palace ceased to be an ecclesiastical centre and became a topsail schooner on a pleasure cruise. Harry still had his right arm in a sling but he assured them it was 'right as rain now. The sawbones said, "keep it in a sling for a month or two", so Emily keeps sending me for the sling. But the last sawbones she made me see in Stamford took out the stitches, said it was good as new, and, sure enough, I have to catch up Camilla before I feel a thing now.'

Emily confirmed to them she was 'worn to flinders with all the worry about Harry, and then Camilla got a dreadful cold, and we had such a tiring journey.' And now this new baby. But she looked very well.

Camilla was a pretty and taking child, but her parents' conviction that she was an infant angel met with no agreement from anyone else, as she was very spoilt. Fortunately, she did seem to mind her nurse, provided her parents were not by.

Harry was enraptured by their charities. He visited the new houses and mended a shutter. He entertained the old people in the workhouse and the children in the ragged school with a lively account of his recent battle. He gave money to all these causes. 'For we're in funds now with my prize money,' he'd say. He bought fruit, sweets, and biscuits, and distributed them in the hospital. He also made fireworks for bonfire night.

He was less enraptured, though, by the local clergy. 'Whenever I go to church, or church comes to me aboard, we have that bit about making your chosen people joyful, but it seems to be more than God can manage round here. George is jolly enough in his bookwormly way, but that Dean is a dumb animal, th' Archdeacon's worse and, as for that chaplain of yours, all he does is apologise.'

'Mr Morris is new here and very conscious that he owes the post solely to his aunt's eminence,' said Elizabeth. 'On further acquaintance he may prove to be sparkling company.'

'And you and Antony do not help by gazing at him with surprise and disdain,' pointed out Jane. 'You were thrown into deep water and found you could swim, but we can hardly send all boys to sea, or threaten them with the guillotine to give them more confidence.'

'I wouldn't want to treat anyone like the Froggies do,' retorted Harry, 'but I can think of several gentlemen who might have been tolerable had they been midshipmen.'

The disturbances over the price of food became so bad Mr Pitt had suspended habeas corpus and kept a number of protesters in prison.

In November 1794, Elizabeth, Emily, Harry, Camilla, Antony, Jane, and Ned all started south in two coaches. George had gone on ahead by way of London to sit in the House of Lords. The journey went well, except for an awful incident at Cambridge when Camilla stole Ned's knight on horseback and he pulled her hair so as to recover it.

The weather was almost all sunny and cold. It froze at night and only thawed a bit in the early afternoon, but that meant the roads were unusually good, though it got very cold in the coach in spite of foot warmers, hand warmers, and sheepskin coats.

Ned was easily amused but Camilla, who was a restless, peevish toddler, was a great nuisance. Her father sang to her, said nursery rhymes to her, told her stories, cuddled her for hours, but even he couldn't keep her happy for long.

They stopped every two or three hours, and if the inn they stopped at in the afternoon was good, they stayed the night there, but it still seemed a very long journey. It was bliss to arrive and have a warm welcome: Camilla removed, hot baths enjoyed, or a good sleep, if you preferred. Kate, Goodchild, and Tom Goodchild, of course, had a lot to do yet, but everyone else subsided into lazy enjoyment.

:

'I shall have to acquire a sign with a screaming baby portrayed on it,' Elizabeth's father announced at dinner, 'to acquaint the populace that we are now a lying-in hospital.'

'If you've got Mrs Potts, you're going to get babies,' declared Harry. 'If you put out jam, you'd get wasps.'

'The metaphor is very just,' sighed Mr Maltby. 'How is your wasp?' he asked Emily.

'If you mean Camilla—' she began crossly.

But Elizabeth, fearing a family argument, interrupted, 'I have now read *Reflections on a French Revolution*. It really is an extraordinarily prophetic book. Do you think it will all happen just as he said?'

'Mr Burke has a feel for that history in the making which we call politics,' answered Mr Maltby, diverted as she'd expected, by literature. 'A Mr Dillon, whom I met at an assembly, pointed out that the English Tom Paine has convinced most of the Irish with his *Rights of Man,* whereas the Irish Mr Burke has convinced most of the English.'

'The English appreciate reason and the Irish appreciate rhetoric,' said Antony.

'You have read both books?' asked Elizabeth.

Antony replied happily, 'Indeed. I delight in the Bishop's library. And, being French, I am naturally concerned. Mr Paine writes well but he takes too benevolent a view of human nature. The English may be in general content, because their circumstances are improving overall, but this, alas, was not the case in France.'

'The English are getting uncommon rich in the north country,' said Harry. 'They all seem to be digging and spinning and making things go round and round. Speaking of going round, is there a good sound mathematician about here, Father-in-law? I look to have my own ship soon and should wish to know where I was. The Navy taught me some maths with a rope's end but I had no taste for them then, and now I've acquired one all the clever coves are too busy being bright to attend to me.'

Mr Maltby replied, 'Mr Mathers, the priest at Long Bocking, is said to be a tiger at trigonometry. Having private means, he has built an observatory in his garden. I sit on the bench with him and we endeavour to moderate the severity of most of the other magistrates. I will ask him to dine next week when there is a moon to see by. His wife is a chatterer but a good natured, charitable woman.'

'I should wish to join the class, if he permits,' added Antony. 'When I was a soldier I thought of little but horses, but, hearing the Bishop instructing Ned, I begin to see the fascination in figures.'

'I'd like to learn too,' said Emily piping up, and then, seeing people's astonishment, adding, 'Well, not trigonometry exactly, but I'd like to know where Harry is. He often writes but I never know where Batavia is.'

'Did your governess, who promised to instruct you in the uses of globes, fail to do so?' enquired Mr Maltby.

'I daresay she tried but I was always thinking about balls then, you know,' answered Emily.

'And what, pray, do you always think about now?' Maltby went on.

'Harry and Camilla, and our son, who'll soon be here, and our house in Portsmouth, and fish,' Emily replied.

'Fish?'

'Harry is very fond of fish,' Emily explained.

They settled in happily. Mrs Potts was optimistic about Emily, but not so pleased with Jane.

‘She’s no notion when she’s due,’ said Mrs Potts of Emily. ‘Same's last time, but she had no trouble to speak of then and she’ll have no trouble now. I ain’t so happy about that Marquise. She’s a good age but she’s pulled down by all them months she couldn’t eat, and it may be she bleed easy like her mother. Her mother ha'n't started another?’

‘No, thank goodness,’ replied Elizabeth.

‘Amen to that. I’ve only once or twice known such a touch-and-goer. You keep'n well?’

‘Too well. I want a daughter,’ Elizabeth replied.

‘Time enough. But I dunno, you don’t fall for babies easy and you’re getting on. I shall have to find you a new nurse, I reckon; Kate tells me Nell’s giving in to Tom Goodchild.’

‘Oh, I’m glad. He loves her so. He asked me to try and persuade her but I couldn’t,’ cooed Elizabeth.

‘She won’t be in no hurry, bein' happy with you. But if a girl don’t marry she mostly bound to be a spinster and that’s wuss,’ argued Potts.

Elizabeth continued, ‘And Nell’s twenty-five now. She shouldn’t have more than four children, or six, if she wants, with a little luck and care, but oh dear, I shall miss her. She’s just the sensible, laughing girl I like to look after my boys. Where will you find such another?’

‘She won’t be far away. Nell don’t want to marry 'til May,’ Potts explained to Elizabeth. ‘That want thinking about and talking over with a right forward mother, but I don’t despair of it.’

:

Parson Mathers proved to be a good teacher, and he was delighted with the progress of both Harry and Antony. Emily, however, was another matter.

‘I learn more than she does,’ he complained, as he, Elizabeth, and Harry rode over to his rectory for dinner after a morning’s work. ‘I learn all about the price of whelks and why scarlet ribbons look better with a dark green dress than crimson, and how Harry’s captain’s wife never asks her to parties, but whether she learns anything, I am far from sure.’

It was a lovely day and Elizabeth soaked up the sun. You never appreciated the sun so much as when you were going to lose it, or had just got it back.

'Em is a sad shatterbrain and chatterbox,' admitted Harry, 'but you know our house in Portsmouth is as snug as a dormouse in its winter quarters, the grub's good, the cook doesn't complain much, th' maid's always grinning, th' nurse doesn't complain, and not all my shipmates could say th' same.'

Some plovers were wheeling and wailing in a big grass field beside them.

'All the world waits willingly on Emily,' said her sister. 'That's her technique, helpless and slaphappy, 'til they set her right.'

A white butterfly floated past them.

'Say goodbye to butterflies,' said Antony poetically. 'I knew, of course, an English naval officer was heroic and proficient, but I was not aware they could also be cheerful and unaffected.'

'Well, I've got a lot to be cheerful about right now,' pointed out Harry. 'You should meet me in the doldrums. Mumchance ain't in it.'

'A man who is good at his trade and enjoys it is commonly found to be of sanguine temperament,' said the Rector. 'Good day to you, Rose! Have you filled your basket?'

This last was to a little girl who, after picking up sweet chestnuts in the road, had curtseyed and shrilled out, 'Ar'ternoon, Mr Mathers! Yeth! So I get two baskets full now and Mum'll be pleased.'

'The eldest of six,' explained the parson. 'The two next eldest, boys, are in our school. I have endeavoured, and so has my wife, to get Rose for our school. It is, after all, not full. Her father would be willing, but her mother is not. She declares it will make Rose discontented with her lot, but I think Rose is too useful.'

'I think poor women have every reason to be discontented with their lot,' declared Elizabeth. 'They work and work. They lose child after child and they die young from sheer exhaustion.'

Mr Mathers began, 'Come now, it is not always as bad as that. Round here most of the men give their wages straight to their wives and the wives manage very well. Or they were managing very well before the price of bread went up. It is, I grant you, more difficult now. As for children dying, except for families where there is consumption, we scarce lose one child in twenty. And many a woman lives to be eighty, though for that, I grant, we have to thank Mrs Potts. Here we are and I am glad of it, being sharp set.'

Emily started the baby on the first of December when Mr Mathers was giving her a geography lesson. Mr Mathers, horrified, wanted her to go away, go to bed, but she declined.

'It'll be ages and ages before anything much happens,' she assured him. 'And I sent for Mrs Potts. We might just as well go on. Have I got it in the right place?'

'Er, no, not really,' answered Mr Mathers, eyeing her as if she were a live explosive of some sort. 'The equator doesn't really run through Spain. It's further south, through Africa.'

'Draw it for me and then I'll remember,' said Emily.

Mr Mathers obeyed, still very nervous. 'I recall vividly when our Cressida was born and I'm persuaded my wife went to bed. Is not that "which brought to bed" implies?'

'Oh, yes, later, you know. There, is that better?' Emily replied impatiently.

'Certainly better, in fact, tolerably accurate in Africa… a little too far south in America. Are you sure…?'

Mrs Potts came in still wearing a coat and hood, and stood there looking at them.

'Ah, Mrs Potts,' said the Rector thankfully. 'Ought she not to go to bed?'

'That all depends, sir. How long ago was your last pain,' she asked, addressing Emily.

Emily responded enthusiastically, 'About five minutes, I think. Ten, perhaps. We're doing geography. Now draw Asia and I'll see if I can remember where the equator goes there.'

Mr Mathers obeyed unhappily.

'And that were your first pain?' Mrs Potts went on.

'Yes,' Emily retorted.

'Do sit down, Mrs Potts,' implored Mr Mathers. 'Your profession must be so tiring. We are all indebted to you. It is a great comfort that the women are safe in your hands.'

'Thankee, sir. I do get a mite tired now I'm in my fifties, but the child's going to be a good considerate daytime child, I do believe.'

'There!' said Emily triumphantly. 'How's that?'

'A little too far north,' said Mr Mathers, 'but a good effort, all the same. I will draw it in red ink where it does go.'

'This here equator now. It's just a pretend line, is that right?' asked Mrs Potts.

'Quite correct. We draw imaginary lines on the map to help us grasp the dimensions of the world and so navigate our journey,' Mathers explained considerately.

'That's ever so interesting, sir. I shall have to show my grandchildren. My son as is the smith has got a little enamel globe, and I reckon that'll mark th' equator,' Potts said gleefully.

'Now, let's do longitude again,' demanded Emily. 'Let's… ooh!'

She doubled-up.

'I really think I'd better be going,' said Mr Mathers, starting to gather up his things.

'Not at all, sir. Don't you hurry,' advised Mrs Potts. 'Anything that take her mind off it is all to the good.'

'Heavens above, it's like being hugged by a bear,' Emily told them, 'only the bear's inside you. I always seem to start in the schoolroom. With Camilla we were trimming hats. It's dead punctual, isn't it?'

'Difficult to say,' Mrs Potts answered.

'Draw a globe and then show us how us how the lines go,' Emily went on.

The lesson and poor Mr Mathers' apprehension continued, but at his usual time he left hurriedly, and at midday Emily's son was born.

'Two hours, start to finish,' said Mrs Potts. 'That's what I like to see. No waiting about. Now what would you fancy for dinner?'

'Chicken and bread sauce, and roast potatoes, and bacon and sausages.'

CHAPTER TWENTY-ONE

Lincoln/London

Jane's baby was a girl, and took much longer than Emily. They decided to call her Elodie after Antony's friendly sister. This was Jane's idea. Antony doubted the English would pronounce it well and was told by Jane they'd learn.

Emily, being deflected with difficulty from Theophilus and Marmaduke, called her son Phineas. Harry was glad to settle for that.

They had a very happy Christmas. Mrs Potts warned them Jane must be sent to bed when she got tired, but it often proved difficult to persuade her.

'I feel I have failed fifty generations of Chavaises,' she said, 'and they are all glaring at me and making French noises. Br br br… she shoe shoe! Pooh pooh pooh! Jamais de la vie! And then they all shrug their shoulders together.'

'You mock my ancestors and imply they did not like ladies,' answered Antony. 'It was quite otherwise, I assure you. And if blame there must be, surely I am quite as much to blame as you are.'

Jane was quick to respond, 'Oh, no. No one ever blames men. We'd better swap babies quickly, Harry. You like girls and there're masses of Meynells. We need a Marquis.'

'You might be able to persuade me,' Harry told her, 'but you'll never persuade Emily. She's got what she ordered and she's no end chuffed. Poor Camilla's quite neglected.'

It was hardly true. "Poor Camilla's" father was as doting as ever, but it was true insomuch that Emily could now be brought to see Camilla's screams were not what they needed in the drawing room.

After the long labour Jane didn't have much milk, so Emily, who had masses, fed Elodie, too.

In early January, Harry, Emily, the two children and their nurse left for Portsmouth. The children were christened the day before by the long-suffering Mr Mathers, who had disliked Emily feeding her baby in front of him almost as much as having Emily in labour in front of him.

It seemed very quiet and dull without the forthright Harry, the ingenuous Emily, and the frenetic Camilla.

Emily's very competent nurse had been looking after Elodie, too, though Jane, as soon as she was well enough, insisted on doing quite a lot herself, saying that with eight younger brothers and sisters she was all too experienced with babies. Mrs Potts recommended a woman called Molly Andrews, whose husband had been killed in Flanders.

'She's got his little boy o' seven but he'll mix with Master Ned, I reckon. She had another younger, but he died o' th' cholera. That was what make her husband restless, I fancy. Mr Mathers told him straight that it was his duty to bide with his wife and child, but he would have it that was more money. So it was while it lasted and, to do him justice, he sent that him regular, but when that stop she had to give up the cottage. Her parents took her in, but they got six left at home already, so that ain't a mucher. She's good with children.'

Elizabeth liked the woman when she met her, and she thought Ned, a rather solitary little boy, except for his friendship with Amabel's Jack, would benefit from the company of Molly's son, John. George was less enthusiastic. 'Do you not suspect the child, when older, may prove troublesome or acquire ideas above his station?' he said once.

'I'm sure I hope he will. The poor are not nearly ambitious enough all too often, and he will have excellent opportunities with you and Antony teaching him,' Elizabeth commented.

George, who had no intention of teaching him, was too good a husband and too flattered to object anymore. He wrote to Mr Pitt that they were numerous, and in some cases juvenile, and would go to a hotel. But Mr Pitt answered that had he had a vast, empty barracks at Number 10, and would welcome hearing a baby howl again.

Mr Mathers lent them his carriage and coachman as they were really rather too many for one coach. They arrived one afternoon in late January, 1795. Mr Pitt was said by his secretary, 'to be in conference over the Irish troubles, you know, but hoped to join them for dinner.'

'I'm scared,' said Jane, as they waited in the drawing room.

'I also,' added Antony. 'Refugees do not belong in these august settings. We live like rats in dirty, poky rooms.'

'Try not to be so childish,' advised Elizabeth. 'Mr Pitt is shy, and you'll make him worse. He's perfectly human, and easy and conversable, only he's shy. Talk about something solid and cheerful and interesting. Say you find the farming's much more advanced in England than in France. Ask when he thinks slavery will be abolished, or, if it's easier, just smile and leave it to George and me 'til you feel you want to join in.'

Mr Pitt came in rapidly, followed by Mr Dundas.

'George! What a joy to see you! Elizabeth, you look blooming. I regret infinitely my lateness but Lord Fitzwilliam is presenting us with endless difficulties,' Pitt alluded.

'I ken verra well he was no but a hoggit,' stated Mr Dundas. 'Wolly and wambling. But I didna ken he'd keep bleating blethers 'til a' the protestants were up in arms and a' the papists were dancing jigs.'

'This is the Marquis and Marquise Chavaise,' Elizabeth told them. 'The Marquis has been teaching our boys the most beautiful French.'

'By Hogg, they'll likely need it in a French prison camp, which is what we'll be in by the time they're bit laddies,' remarked Dundas

'Do you feel there is any hope from these risings in France?' Mr Pitt asked Antony.

Antony replied, 'None. They are brave and angry but their leaders are not soldiers, and they have no guns. If you were to send about twelve good regiments under, say, Cornwallis, it might well be quite different. The French peasants then would make excellent scouts and auxiliaries.'

'He has a head on him, forbye,' declared Mr Dundas, 'but, hoots, toots, we canna find one good regiment, nor spare Cornwallis.'

'Are you adamant you will not stay to dinner and continue this illuminating conversation?' Pitt asked Dundas.

'I canna. I'd best face m' wife early rather than late. If you'd but think to ask her y'd hae me, too. Gie you goo' day,' said Dundas, and he left rapidly.

'Dinner is served,' announced the butler.

Mr Pitt put Jane on his right and Elizabeth on his left. Antony was next to Elizabeth and George to Jane.

'Before I forget,' said Mr Pitt to Antony. 'There is a letter come for you. Would you wish to have it now or later?'

Antony replied, 'After dinner, perhaps.'

'Pray, remind me, then. I grow shockingly forgetful. I hear I have to congratulate you on a healthy daughter,' Pitt enquired.

'Yes,' said Jane. 'We needed a son but she will do for now. It is to be hoped she does not bawl you out of house and home. It would look as if the war was going badly.'

'Or the corresponding societies were becoming dangerous. I suspect if I resigned my head would be off in six months. But Mr Fox would very much regret the necessity,' Pitt expressed.

'And you ought to very much regret keeping him out of office,' said Elizabeth. 'He's not without ability; perhaps he would not drink and gamble so much if he had something better to do.'

'And I have lured away half his playmates, though he is more than welcome to regain Lord Fitzwilliam,' Pitt returned.

'You speak as if it were a game,' Jane told him.

'To some extent it is a game and therefore the players understand each other better than others can ever do. And most of us play fair, though misunderstandings are apt to arise,' Pitt explained to her.

'I hear Wilberforce wanted peace,' said George.

'I was grieved and so was he, but I will not long hold it against him. It is only right, to be sure, for a Christian to desire peace and were I but persuaded it was possible on terms that were likely to last, I would desire it as passionately as he could wish,' Pitt wished.

'What did Wilberforce do?' asked Jane.

'Moved a resolution to treat with the French,' George told her. 'He did not warn you?'

Pitt replied quickly, 'No, perhaps wisely. I should have endeavoured to persuade him and he to persuade me.'

'How is Lady Chatham?' enquired George.

'Well, I thank you, save only for rheumatics in her left knee, which comes and goes.'

'And little Hester?' asked Elizabeth.

'Also well. She writes the most charming letters to her Papa, which he often shows me, full of cousin Hester galloping, and processions to burn a Tom Paine in effigy, and suchlike rural jollities, and they end with great solemnity "your affectionate daughter, Hester Harriot Pitt Eliot".'

'Her mother, Mr Pitt's sister, was one of my closest friends,' Elizabeth told Antony, 'but she died in childbirth.'

'I can't believe I am sitting here and talking to the Prime Minister,' Jane told Mr Pitt.

'You could always pretend you were a seal and I a walrus,' he suggested. 'Then you could bark at me and I could cough at you.'

Jane barked briskly and explosively, somewhat to the surprise of the others.

'I feel,' she said (Mr Pitt coughed), 'more like a mouse and you look more like an otter. So I squeak at you and you vanish with a string of bubbles.'

'I should adore to be able, on occasion, to have the skill to jump into the Thames from the terrace and vanish with a string of bubbles,' Pitt said in response.

After dinner Antony asked for his letter and went into a corner to read it. After a bit Jane joined him there. Mr Pitt and the others were discussing the latest news from the West Indies.

'Bad news?' Jane asked Antony quietly.

'Yes, though I had anticipated it. My sister is dead. So are her husband and three sons, but the girls were saved by a strange chance and we may yet be reunited. The letter is from Général d'Arblay. A man came to him, a Frenchman, who had escaped from Toulon and had been told d'Arblay was a friend of my family. He is willing to speak to me, but he has acquired a post with a merchant, and his duties have taken him to Bristol. Do you want to read the letter?'

'No thanks. You know my French is wanting. Give me a short account of it,' Jane replied honestly.

'This man was present when my sister and her family were brought to the main square in Marseilles to be guillotined, along with many others, you understand. They murdered my sister, her husband, and the three boys. The youngest was just six years old. Then there were the girls. The man who worked the guillotine, such scum have power and great prestige, said to the crowd, "It seems a pity to cut off such pretty heads. If they are ci-devants, we cannot let them live. But suppose, just suppose, my friends, there were two good citizens here who would be willing to marry them, they would then become good citizenesses and we could let them live."'

Antony paused and twisted his signet ring. 'Many men came forward. The girls were, they are, beautiful. The man, Boucher, who interviewed d'Arblay, came forward. The authorities allowed them to talk a little. Boucher says my elder niece asked him if he would let her be a Catholic; he promised he would, but she chose a young doctor, and her sister chose a timber merchant.'

'What an extraordinary story. It is scarce believable. Do you want to go to church and pray?' Jane asked.

'Tomorrow, perhaps,' Antony replied.

'Do you want to tell them?' Jane whispered, referring to the others.

'I could not bear it at present. I shall just say my sister is dead. But you may speak of it as you will. It is no secret.'

'Would you like to go straight to bed? I am sure Mr Pitt will understand,' Jane said caringly.

'No, I thank you. I shall be better with good conversation for distraction. Let us join them and explain,' Antony suggested.

They went over to the others and Antony said, 'As I had suspected, my sister and most of her family are dead.'

'I am very sorry,' said Mr Pitt. 'Just when we think the world grows less cruel there is another bad outbreak.'

'I am very sorry, too,' said Elizabeth. 'At least you have a daughter.'

'She is the greatest comfort to me,' agreed Antony. 'One of my own blood who I can see and touch.'

'You will need all the consolations of religion,' said George. 'In the absence of kind Father Peter perhaps you would do well to speak with a saint. Mr Wilberforce brought one last time we were here. His name is Newton and he is the priest of some church in London, I misremember which. He would, I am persuaded, make you realise the wall of death is not very thick or lasting.'

'To speak with a saint,' said Antony thoughtfully. 'If the Abbé Edgeworth were in England – but I do not think he is… Your saint would be too busy, it is likely, to speak with me.'

'Saints are never too busy,' declared Elizabeth. 'They ask God to make time for this need and He does.'

'I also misremember which church John Newton has,' said Mr Pitt, 'but I should be glad for my own reasons to send to Wilberforce tomorrow, and request him to arrange with Mr Newton for an interview. I conjecture, for his own reasons, he will be very willing to comply.'

The next day Antony went early for a ride in Hyde Park. Then he walked to a small, discreet Catholic church where he lit five candles, heard mass, and arranged for some masses to be said for his sister and her family. Then he went to the d'Arblays and stayed for breakfast while the Général told him more, and Fanny, his wife, exclaimed and consoled and confided.

Meanwhile Jane, also at breakfast, was telling Mr Pitt and the Pretymans the whole story. They were spellbound, appalled, and fascinated.

'What a play it would make in the hands of a good dramatist,' said Mr Pitt. 'Of the moderns, only Goldsmith, I apprehend, could have handled it and he is too drunk now to handle anything. He would drop it.'

'How would it feel to be married to a doctor you'd never set eyes on before?' enquired Jane.

'Somewhat embarrassing,' answered Elizabeth, 'and the doctor would not be able to practise much because every man is equal, and cobblers and carters are just as good at amputating a leg as surgeons are. So the doctor and Antony's niece are almost certainly impoverished.'

'Let us hope that circumstance is out of date,' said Mr Pitt. 'The Directoire seem to be venal but sane.'

'Who can know?' demanded Jane. 'France is like China now: a mysterious, terrifying country.'

'And, like China,' added Mr Pitt, 'it has a lofty contempt for all other nations, and intends to make them wear pigtails presently.'

Mr Newton asked Antony and Jane to visit him that evening.

Antony came back comforted. 'He is an amazing man,' he told them. 'So simple and close to God. He made me believe they are truly happy now in paradise. Well, I should hope I believed it already, but Mr Newton had the power to make me almost see it.'

:

A week later they all went back to Lincoln. Ned had enjoyed his London season and said so as they rumbled northwards. 'I liked the soldiers, and the lions, and the fireworks, and when Mr Pitt played the spillikins with me and Mama and Molly and John.'

Molly was proving a success. She made everything easy, and both Ned and the baby clearly felt happy and safe with her. Her son was a quiet, observant child, but he and Ned were soon friends, and as he became less overwhelmed by all these grand people he began to giggle, and even talk.

Goodchild was displeased by his stay. He grumbled about the rapacity of Mr Pitt's servants 'til Elizabeth told him he'd better be quiet 'til he could find someone to order things better.

Elizabeth and Antony rode for an hour or two most days, leaving more room in the coach, and enabling them to get to an inn before the coach.

They had three wet days after which the roads were so bad they stayed two nights in one place. Antony told them there were plans for a royalist expedition to France and that if it came to anything he would have to go.

'Could you not argue your first duty is to an old family?' Elizabeth asked. 'And so you cannot risk your life until you have a son?'

'I do not think so. It is extremely tempting, but all my surviving friends are going. The Général purposed to go and he is well into his forties. He is, however, subject to sciatica and Fanny swears she will not let him go if he is suffering.'

Luckily for them Elodie was a contented baby who cried very little and could always be pacified by her mother.

It was good to be home. Little George had done some flowers again for his mother, though they consisted of two not quite out snowdrops and a pink dead nettle. Amabel was delighted with her first grandchild, who was only two years younger than Benjamin. Nell and Molly, who had been to Mr Mathers' charity school together, were enchanted to be reunited, and soon George, and even Richard, was as happy with Molly as Ned already was.

:

Spring always comes, though sometimes, particularly in Lincolnshire, it seems an intolerably long time in coming. This spring brought news of the Prince of Wales' forced marriage. The Government and the King paid his debts yet again if he would marry Caroline of Brunswick. The marriage, by such gossip as Elizabeth heard mostly at Belvoir, was not a success, but, all the same, there was soon an heir to the throne on the way. Elizabeth wished she could ask Mr Pitt, who was always well-informed, though charitable, whether he thought it was really true that the Prince had been already married to the Catholic, and therefore quite impossible, Mrs Fitzherbert.

In April, Tom Goodchild and Nell Potts got married and set-up house in a pretty cottage near the Palace.

'Quite time you married, too,' Elizabeth told Kate, who was washing Elizabeth's hair one fine morning.

'I don't fancy it. I'm very well as I am. Good company. Good pay. Good lodgings. Allus something going on.'

'Don't you want children?' asked Elizabeth indistinctly from the wash basin.

'Wouldn't mind a couple if I didn't have to mind them.'

'Perhaps Jane will have another and Molly can mind yours with hers,' Elizabeth wondered.

'I have had offers, good offers, but I was only tempted th' once.'

'Who was that?' enquired Elizabeth.

'Rolly. He was that helpless when his wife died, being a charity boy. We all bore a hand and he ask me. I'm quite partial to Ellie and you could make somethin' o' that cottage, but, as I told y', when you're in th' spud field stay there, as th' pig said. There, that's done. I'll just snip a bit off,' Kate replied.

'You'll end up like Mrs Mann, bossy and barracking,' Elizabeth joked.

'Don't talk to me about that woman. Know what she say? She say, as if you hadn't got enough bothersome boys, you had to go and find another.'

'Poor John. I wouldn't call him bothersome,' Elizabeth said.

'No more wouldn't I. Dear little mite. She'll grumble about paradise, if she get there, which I doubt.'

In May, a summons came from the Général; the émigré expedition was to go to France. Antony and Jane borrowed two horses and rode south. Jane confided to Elizabeth before they went that she rather thought she might be with child again. 'It's too soon, I know, and Mrs Potts will be cross with me, but what could we do?'

'Ought you to ride if you're with child?' Elizabeth asked.

'Well, it's very early days. I'm far from sure, and what makes me think I'm just a bit late is that I don't feel in th' least sick. Not like last time,' Jane described to her.

'They do say some women feel sick with a girl and not with a boy and some are the other way about,' Elizabeth implied.

'I hope so. Look after Elodie for me. I'm afraid she will miss me,' asked Jane.

'I promise, and so will your mother,' Elizabeth confirmed.

'When not reading or writing. Say half an hour a day,' Jane insisted.

Mr Pitt again insisted on their staying with him. George had already been there for some weeks, visiting the House of Lords. The first night they were there Mr Pitt was in the House, but next day he dined with them and so did his cousin and Foreign Secretary, Lord Grenville, who was all for the expedition to France. 'Dundas is pessimistic as to your prospects,' he said, 'but, then, Dundas is seldom sanguine.'

'Had he been with us on that unfortunate occasion at your house he would have howled, rather than barked,' declared Mr Pitt.

'Was you playing tigers?' asked Jane.

'Not exactly. There was a bird in the room, so Billy here, who's partial to birds when he's not shooting them, opened all the windows and would have us make noises to drive it out,' Grenville said.

'You brayed to the manor born,' remembered Mr Pitt.

'You hissed like a particularly malevolent serpent,' retorted his cousin.

'Did the bird go?' asked Jane.

'Eventually. I think it was somewhat overcome, and it flitted about from perch to perch for some time. I do not know how it is I behave with decorum suitable to a Foreign Minister in general, but when Billy is by I may end up braying like a donkey,' Grenville answered.

'Lord Mornington was there, too,' said Mr Pitt, 'and he meowed very plaintively, but his rutting stag near scared us up the chimney, bird and all.'

'The Prime Minister of England, the Foreign Secretary of England, and a grand lord,' said Antony thoughtfully.

'Dreadful, is it not?' asked Mr Pitt. 'It must be said we were all somewhat disguised but does that make it better or worse?'

'Worse,' said Jane. 'You should not drink so much.'

'Very true, alas, though a doctor recommended it when I was but a child. I was beginning to drink much less before the war, but now I seem unable to do without it,' Pitt explained.

The next day Antony took Jane to stay with Elizabeth's parents, and they rode on to the meeting place. Germains was reasonably handy for news from France and very convenient for Mrs Potts.

Mrs Potts confirmed that Jane was having a baby and agreed that her complete freedom from sickness might mean it was a boy this time. Elizabeth's parents and the Mathers were delighted to have her back, but it all seemed rather flat without Antony, and Jane missed her daughter, too, though her mother and Elizabeth both wrote regularly.

Antony had found a French woman to continue Ned and George's French lessons in his absence and if he didn't come back. She was called Madame Lebrun, a widow of a French admiral, and she was living in poverty in London, giving French lessons, and selling a little fine embroidery. If she was needed in time she was to travel with George and his parents, who were visiting London to see their other son.

It was July 1795 before there was any news and then it took an unexpected form. Harry walked in one day when they were dining, looking uncharacteristically serious. Jane got up and raised her hands as to ward off a blow. 'He is dead?' she asked.

'Yes,' said Harry. 'They shot him. They shot all of them. I met a man who got away. He threw them money and they scrabbled for it and he got away. He said they all surrendered on the French Général's promise of mercy, which he kept, 'til their friends in Paris told him to shoot them. My ship was there under Admiral Warren, so I saw quite a lot of Tony. He was very hopeful. I told him to skedaddle and wave his shirt and I'd send a boat, but this man who escaped said they needed him to the last riding errands.'

'You must be hungry,' said Jane. 'Sit down and eat.'

Harry obeyed. Mrs Maltby muttered to the footman who brought him food. Jane sat down, too, but did not eat anymore.

'I am sorry,' said Mrs Maltby. 'I was much struck by his heroic qualities.'

'Yes,' said Jane, 'but he didn't want to be a hero. He just wanted…' Her face crumpled.

'You'd better go to bed, dear,' said Mrs Mathers. 'And have a good cry and then a good sleep and you'll feel better.'

'She had better do whatever she prefers,' Mrs Maltby declared.

'I should like to wait 'til Harry has finished eating and then go for a walk with him and hear some more.'

'That is what you shall do. Phineas had a cold, so the doctor was seeing a lot of him. Camilla remembered me,' said Mrs Maltby.

Harry explained later that the landing had been joined by a good number of Chouans, or Breton guerrillas, but they did not push on into friendly territory. They were outnumbered by the French army under Général Hoche. There were twice as many of them. Antony always said it was hopeless.

Harry could not stay long. His ship, a frigate called *Cassiopea*, was waiting for him.

The Dean wrote a dignified letter of sympathy suggesting his daughter came home. Amabel wrote an undignified, heart-broken letter advising her daughter on no account to come home yet, as she was much safer with Mrs Potts.

Mr Maltby said he trusted she would stay for a prolonged visit as he and his wife were bereft nowadays without a bawling baby. Mrs Maltby said she did hope Jane would, because, really, under the circumstances, it was all so terrible. And now their chick was flown it was nice to have someone young about again.

Mr Pitt wrote a polite, polished letter of condolence and gave it to George to send on. He also offered through George to be godfather.

:

The wet autumn blew itself into a cold winter and soon it was 1796. Jane's son was born in the middle of January. He didn't take as long as Elodie had, though he was a bigger baby. Antony had asked that he should be called Joseph after his elder brother, it having been a common name in his family.

'I've never had a Marquis afore,' said Mrs Potts, pronouncing it in the English manner. 'I shall be too big for my boots soon. Midwife to the nobility! That's me. Who'd a thought it?'

The snow was six inches deep and, as it was sunny, it thawed in the middle of the day and froze at night, making everything very slippery, and life was hard. They had a job keeping the baby warm and Jane moved into Emily's room, which had only one window and a good fireplace.

In the middle of February, they woke up one morning and the snow had all gone. There were floods instead, of course, for it was raining and, what with that and the melting snow, the roads were impassable for a week; it wasn't cold anymore. They felt delivered and Jane felt Joseph was safe now.

There were rumours spreading slowly up from the coast, through the snowdrifts, that all the Parisians had been shot. It seemed improbable, even by French revolutionary standards, and, sure enough, before long it was modified: thousands had been shot by the Directoire when the Paris mob had rioted. An even more sober version arrived with the newspaper from London, a week and two days late, because of the floods: Barras had employed a young gunner named Napoleon Bonaparte to fire on the crowd and about five hundred people had been killed.

Elizabeth wrote that they still had snow but that as soon as it went they would come and fetch Jane and Joseph. Jane rode out every day, now sometimes with Mr Maltby, often with the groom. One fine day in March, Mr Maltby and Jane rode over to dine with the Mathers. All the birds were singing and they heard a chiff-chaff, which, as Mr Maltby remarked, was often the first of the summer birds.

The Mathers had their son staying, who was a lawyer, with his pretty young wife and their three children, who were kept out of sight. The pretty young wife was rather overshadowed by the rich, landowning Mr Maltby at first, and quite overwhelmed by the titled Jane. But Jane got her on to the children and she soon relaxed.

'What would be your estimate, based on observing the contemporary scene with a somewhat cynical eye, for the duration of the war?' Parson Mathers asked Mr Maltby.

'Twenty years,' replied Mr Maltby.

'Oh, surely not,' said Mrs Mathers. 'We can't go on like this for years and years. The people are getting hungry, and the armies never do any good, and the French get worse and worse.'

'Worse they may be, but wise they are,' said Mr Maltby. 'Their method of making war cheaply, to steal everything from everyone, could hardly be improved upon. It also precludes bankruptcy. As for the armies never doing any good, the British Expeditionary Forces are frequently referred to as "Back Every Fortnight", I admit, but we have accumulated India and Malta, the latter of which may yet prove useful.'

'Need we fear that the thieving French will beat the honest English in the long run?' asked Jane.

'In the long run honesty may indeed be the best policy,' replied Mr Maltby, 'if it is combined with efficiency, but I see little sign of that at present.'

'I must be going,' said Jane. 'I'm still feeding Joseph.'

'I will accompany you,' offered Mr Maltby, 'though I confess I had rather accompany that admirable apple turnover for a bit longer.'

'Do, then! What harm will I take riding four miles on a quiet horse and a fine day?' said Jane.

'Get a groom to come with you, dear,' advised Mrs Mathers. 'It looks better and you never know.'

Jane smiled and thanked her for dinner.

:

In April 1796, George and Elizabeth arrived in their coach and stayed for a month. They left Elodie behind as she seemed entirely happy with Molly. Jane agreed to take a local girl to London, as it would be difficult to look after the baby and join in society at Number 10, but refused to take her on to Lincoln.

'I'm going to need to be very mean,' she said, 'and really I rather like looking after babies, except when they wake me up.'

'Has Antony left you very badly off?' asked Mrs Maltby.

'No-o,' said Jane doubtfully. 'He left quite a bit of money. Amazing he'd saved so much. But I don't think I'd make much of a governess, do you? So there won't be anything coming in for years, and Papa has ten more children, though Letitia is engaged to a rich man.'

Mr Pitt had started to show signs of strain, but he greeted them warmly and was, he said, particularly pleased to see his godson.

'This French Général Napoleon Bonaparte has captured all northern Italy,' he told them at dinner. 'How the French do it I cannot tell for they are virtually bankrupt.'

'Elizabeth's father said they do it by stealing everything from everyone,' Jane told him.

'There is all too much truth in that, but it cannot be good for trade. We are trying for peace again but I fear they are wedded to war,' Pitt explained.

Jane went to see Mr Newton as her husband had before her. She, too, found him very comforting. She went to visit the d'Arblays, taking Joseph with her. They had a son of their own by now and Fanny had written a new book.

The Général told her she must take great care of the Compte de Chavaise. 'He is the future of France. If France is to have a future that is something else besides greed and cruelty, it will be by men like him, who have, let us hope, French flair and English kindness.'

They only stayed a week for they were all three eager to get back to their children. They arrived back home at midsummer, and young George had arranged roses and ox-eyed daisies for his mother.

Everything seemed to be in flower and you could go about freely in the thinnest clothes. Madame Lebrun was installed and exuberant. The boys liked her, though Ned confided to his mother he did not like her as much as the Marquis, who 'had made you laugh so much you didn't realise you were learning.'

Ned went with Jack to a local school now, and they were pleased with his French and Latin. No one was pleased with Jack, who was clever enough, but too heedless, active, and naughty to learn much.

Elodie had forgotten her mother. Molly was upset by this. 'I kept talking about you, Madame, and she often says, "Mama," but she didn't have no picture of you like.'

'Of course not,' said Jane, 'let alone a baby brother. She'll soon get used to me.'

Amabel wanted Jane and her children to come home, but Jane said she was better off in the Palace. 'There's fewer screaming children.'

Madame Lebrun professed herself enchanted with her position. 'To live like a civilised being again. You cannot imagine the relief, the refreshment to my spirits. Dear Antony told me I would be happy here, and I regret only contentment comes to me from his death.'

She painted flowers in a delightful, delicate way, and told them she had taken lessons from Redonté, who was one of the late King's painters. She, too, had lost a son at Quiberon Bay, and another was fighting with the Austrians.

Amabel was getting up a play to raise money for their hospital. It was *Romeo and Juliet* and she played the nurse. The third daughter, Lucasta, a very pretty girl of sixteen, was Juliet, and Mr Morris, the curate, who was getting over shyness, was Romeo.

'Mama and Papa named us alternately,' Jane told them one lunchtime. 'I was lucky. It was Papa's turn, so was Mary. Titty and Cassy got blighted by Mama. Elizabeth was different, because Mrs Potts saved Mama. They both wanted to call the baby after you. 'Twas fortunate Ben was a boy, for had he not been, nothing would have stopped her saddling the poor mite with "Cleopatra".'

Jane, Elizabeth, and Amabel took Joseph to be christened as a Catholic when Father Peter visited in July. Elizabeth and Amabel decided not tell their husbands.

CHAPTER TWENTY-TWO

Belvoir

'Sir Joseph is coming again,' said Elizabeth in September, as she opened a letter at breakfast. 'Who will he bring?'

'A crossing sweeper or a leading Jacobin member of a corresponding society, very probably,' said George.

'What fun!' exclaimed Jane. 'I was in the schoolroom when he brought the poet and the painters, but Mama told us all about it, and that one of the painters was a tiny little cockney but amazingly skilful.'

Sure enough an express reached them from Grantham with the information 'I am bringing a friend'. The 'friend' was a large, plain north countryman called Arkwright, who was very diffident about his sudden appearance. 'Say the word and I'm off to an inn. Sir Joseph would have it you'd want me, but why ever should you, after all – a complete stranger?'

'Nonsense, Arkwright. Of course they want you,' Sir Joseph assured him. 'Open house here. All welcome. I won't ask are you well, Mrs Pretyman, because I see you're blooming, as usual. Always a bit rum to have a young pretty bishop's wife.'

'I was but thirty when I first became a bishop's wife. You are very welcome, sir. My husband is most interested in the North Country and its manufacturers. He says they will provide employment for the poor, who are so greatly increasing,' Elizabeth replied.

'He shows unusual good judgement in that. Most people in the South just consider us a plague of dirt and stinks,' Arkwright stated.

:

Over dinner Sir Joseph told them more. 'Arkwright here had a father who invented things – looms and carding machines, that sort of thing. Invented the whole damn factory system, didn't he?'

Arkwright confirmed, 'Indeed, he was a remarkable man, the youngest of thirteen children. Born poor, too, and knighted by the King. For my part, I am thankful to say I declined to expand further, and concentrated instead on the welfare of the hands. So now, while the bigger firms are all bankrupt, we are still making a small profit.'

'I collect that trade is falling off?' supposed Elizabeth.

Arkwright answered, 'Exports are. The Continent buys little nowadays, though there is still America, and the home market holds up well.'

'How many people do you employ in your factory, sir?' asked Jane.

'Just over a thousand, counting both women and children, though I will not employ children under ten. I do not think it right. Their fingers may be deft but the long hours are too fatiguing,' Arkwright answered.

'You could always employ them for just five hours a day,' suggested Sir Joseph.

'Why so I do when they are turned ten. It is all agriculture round here, I suppose,' Arkwright retorted.

'We produce the wool for you to spin,' Elizabeth told him. 'Yet Lincoln prospers and I think there are few or none without work. Can you say as much?'

Arkwright responded, 'That I can't, and more's th' pity. Th' worst of manufacturing is most firms turn away their hands in bad times, the way you might lay aside a thick coat in warm weather. It makes for great hardship.'

'It would do,' said George. 'This new money is giving too much power to people who are not responsible.'

'M' old foreman say when you were turned out of your cottage by the enclosures or a bankruptcy almost any employment was better than none,' Arkwright asserted.

'Has your friend Pitt told you he's getting hitched at long last?' asked Sir Joseph.

'No,' replied George. 'Not a word. I had a letter last week, all about fighting in Italy.'

'Who is it?' asked Elizabeth.

'Eleanor Eden. Auckland's daughter. They live near that house of his and they're just the sort of funny, romping family he favours. Mind, I don't say there's anything fixed yet, but the *on dit* is that it's going on nicely. The Aucklands are no end chuffed.'

There was a startled, baffled silence. 'This "Loyalty Loan" is proving a great success,' went on Sir Joseph. 'They raised five million in the first day alone. The Duke of Bedford gave a hundred thousand, Smith gave forty thousand. Suppose I ought to call him "Lord Carrington" now. They both took eighteen million. But we need every penny. Damned expensive things, wars.'

'Have some more goose, Mr Arkwright,' offered Elizabeth, passing the crisp brown slices.

'Thank you, I will. It's uncommon good. As long as we hold the sea we're safe enough, but to ever get any peace we'll need to hold some land, too.'

'Let's not talk about the war. I'm tired of it,' said Jane.

'What would you prefer?' asked George.

'New South Wales,' said Jane firmly. 'Are we going to colonise it?'

'There have been some proposals,' said Sir Joseph. 'I fear the Government will only put up money for a penal settlement, which is not what I would wish. Some call it "Australia" now – the unknown land. One seaman, a farmer's son, was persuaded there was some good grazing there.'

'The unknown land,' said Jane, 'I wish I could see it. What are the animals like?'

'Different. Quite different. There is one about the size of a large sheep that sits up and hops. Kangaroo, the natives call it, and they eat it with relish. Then there is a little squirrel thing, but more like a small grey bear, in the trees. The trees are very rum, too,' Banks informed her.

'I should love to see it, too,' said Elizabeth. 'Perhaps Ned will, or his son. Shall we leave you? Or is the party too small to separate, do you think?'

'Much too small,' said Mr Arkwright. 'I never loved drinking port and listening to men talking about money for half the night. Let us all go back to your pretty withdrawing room.'

They all enjoyed Mr Arkwright's stay and pressed him to come again on his way north and south.

:

Nell, who was married now and living with Tom in one of the houses in the yard, was going to have baby.

After Christmas it turned cold, and on New Year's Day they woke up to snow and life got difficult, as we know it does. Blazing fires, good ovens, and braziers kept the Palace and its stables fairly warm, but the price of coals and wood was soaring, and Elizabeth and the curate, Mr Morris, had to start a fund and a store to provide the poor with subsidised and, in some cases, free fuel.

They waited to hear of Mr Pitt's engagement, but the papers were silent on the subject, and the knowledgeable gentry had heard nothing and didn't believe it.

Amabel's play was well done but poorly attended. It chose to snow again that night and not many people turned out. The pit, who lived in the slums nearby, came and enjoyed themselves. They were a bit noisy and apt to suck oranges and crunch pork crackling, but they were enthusiastic and cheered and clapped in all the right places, as well as some of the wrong ones. The stalls, however, were thinly inhabited by Elizabeth, George, Mr Andrews and his fortunately numerous family, a few tradesmen and their wives who lived nearby, and the Warners, who had come by daylight behind two shire horses and were, they explained, staying in a hotel.

Amabel was good and thoroughly enjoyed herself. Lucasta was quite well. She was reserved at first, which worked well enough, but when she got going she was more convincing and much more audible. But the Reverend Augustus Morris was excellent, producing a dashing, fervent character that was all too absent from his usual behaviour. Augustus Morris was the Duchess of Rutland's nephew.

They made nearly fifty pounds for the hospital, and were very pleased with themselves. So was Elizabeth, who'd had rather a job to persuade George that amateur acting for charity was quite different from disreputable play-acting.

George was inclined to be hurt by Mr Pitt's failure to confide in him, but Elizabeth told him everyone was rather shy about their love affairs, and Mr Pitt was sure to be even shyer. 'If she has refused him he would not wish to talk about it. If he has decided he is too poor to marry, still less will he want to talk about it.'

'You comfort me, as so frequently, my love. I shall no doubt find out more when I go to London.' George said to her.

'Why do you say that?' wondered Elizabeth.

'The situation grows ever more menacing and I have three sons. You must not attempt to travel in this weather. Goodchild says a gentleman's coach got stuck, and when his coachman got back with a plough horse, he found his master dead.'

'An elderly gentleman, doubtless, with a weak heart,' Elizabeth wondered.

George wanted Elizabeth to come with him, but she didn't want to leave the children or travel in this weather.

News reached them that the French had sent a big naval expedition to Ireland. The horrible weather that had brought snow to the Midlands defeated them. The English ships had missed them both coming and going. Several big ships lay in Bantry Bay for a fortnight waiting for better weather, which never came. Pellew, in his *Indefatigable,* managed to drive a big French first rate, *Droits de l'Homme*, on to the rocks off Britanny and most of her huge crew were drowned.

At the end of January, there was a slow, cold thaw, and George set off on his slow, cold journey. At Belvoir, the Duchess explained that Mr Pitt's romance had come to nothing. 'I flatter myself I apprehended as much as any, but even I do not know the secret. I suspect none will ever do so. I favour his financial circumstances, but my husband thinks it was his declining health. Mr Canning, I am informed, thinks he is just too cumbered with affairs of state, and Mr Dundas, they say, suspects it was delicacy, and wagered five hundred pounds that Pitt never touched a woman.'

'It might well be to some extent all those things,' said the Duke, 'but you have, my love, as so often, told the tale backwards and the Bishop is pardonably at a loss. Pitt wrote to Lord Auckland renouncing "that happiness I had ventured to think might be mine" – something of the sort. Auckland has been showing off about it, and allowing half his acquaintance a peep. But I only have it at third hand. I shall hear more when I next go to town.'

'Funny thing is,' grunted the Duke of York, 'all th' women think it's a shame and they nearly lived happily ever after. Th' men mostly think it's a narrow escape and it would never have done. Marriage is a great gamble, but th' winners are set up for life. What's this I hear about th' French and Spanish ships being out?'

The company debated it. No one knew anything for certain, so they were free to speculate. In London, Mr Pitt was more worried about money. There were rumours of another invasion, in Devon this time. It was said to have landed and done a lot of damage. It was also said to have landed in Bristol and burnt it. No one knew really, but there was a run on the banks.

One evening, Mr Pitt and George were dining alone. 'Some feel we must not be materially diverted from the war,' said Mr Pitt, 'but I feel that with reform you disarm the Jacobite. You remove their most dangerous weapon.'

'I am persuaded it must be so,' agreed George, watching the firelight reflected on the windows, for no one had drawn the curtains, and the candles glinted off the polished tables. 'I was particularly impressed by the Parochial Fund for Old Age Pensions. Our workhouses are overwhelmed by those too weak to feed themselves, who could yet make shift well enough on a pound a week.'

'And the cost of maintaining them in a workhouse must doubtless be greater than that sum. Wilberforce made the same point. But the response is, in general, unfavourable, to my great regret,' Pitt replied.

'I apprehend it is somewhat in advance of the public sympathies. When the security and peace of many an independent nation has been violently interrupted men most naturally fear all alterations. Do you not recall when we spoke back in the eighties of relieving the poor?' George reminded Pitt.

'Vividly,' Pitt replied animatedly. 'How young we were! Jeremy Bentham is implacably opposed to my poor remedies. The rascally deprived will sell their free cow, the children will learn at Schools of Industry how to pick pockets and break houses, and those given a shilling a week to support each child will but support ale houses, he opines.'

'It is rarely Christian or justified by experience to suppose none of your fellow countrymen has as good a heart and as cool judgement as you have. As it is, the Bill has been withdrawn for amendment, and amid the fury of war and fear of penury, I doubt it will ever be heard of any more.'

Pitt, besieged by worried people, persuaded the banks to print more paper money. He and George spent some time doing the sums, and with the bank printing £1 and £5 notes the queues at the banks dispersed.

It may also have been because the French invasion was soon rounded up by Lord Cawdor and his Castlemartin Militia in Wales. The French consisted of a dubious Irishman, who called himself Colonel Tate, and the contents of several French prisons. They described themselves as the Black Legion and decided the *Dublin Packet* was a man-o'-war, and some Welsh women, peering at them from a hilltop in their red cloaks, were the Grenadier Guards.

Soon after this in early March, 1797, there came news of a sea battle off the Cape of St. Vincent. It was a considerable relief. There had been so many rumours. The French and Spanish fleets were coming. They were going to escort the French army over the Channel. The last danger was clearly the greatest but now it was gone. Sir John Jervis had scattered the huge fleet and Nelson had taken two ships, one larger and the other much larger than his. They called it 'Nelson's Patent Bridge' for boarding first rates.

:

George went home in early April and got a warm welcome. The weather was suddenly warmer and the blackthorn was out. Ned, who was ten now, had been going since September as a day boy to a small local school. He liked it and had made some friends, but he was very shocked by the French master's appalling accent.

There was an account in the papers in April that the Navy had mutinied at the Nore. Lord Howe, who was a very popular officer, and Lord Spencer had been to hear their grievances. This was followed by a letter from Harry. His ship had mutinied and he wanted to bring Emily and the children to stay with them. Elizabeth wrote back saying she'd be delighted, though in fact her delight was modified by knowing Camilla and George were better apart. She wondered why Harry hadn't just taken his family to Germains, which was so much nearer.

Jane was pleased. 'Camilla will terrify the nursery,' she admitted, 'but I quite dote on your sister. She makes you laugh and tells you what's going on.'

Elizabeth replied, 'My father always complained she was a perfect goose, gobbling away about bonnets, as geese most likely gobble away about grass.'

'She is not interested in a lot of your father's concerns, it is true, but where she is interested she's very sharp.'

They arrived at the end of April 1797. Harry would only stay for a couple of nights. 'Old Howey finds me handy,' he told them at dinner, 'just as a dogsbody of course. He's got the gout and can't run about. They settled it all in no time. Lord Spencer came down and he's a good egg. Pitt loves the Navy. Pitt'll see us right.'

'You do not feel the mutiny is the one thing that might let the French in?' asked Jane.

'Not I? The men keep saying they'll come back to their duty directly the French are ever out. They're perfectly orderly and respectful. It's only they've been so badly treated. We've never had a rise since old Rowley's time, Charles II. They want some help for wounded men and quite right, too. This mutiny is not just trouble-making. I think it's a capital notion.'

'And do most sea captains think it's a capital notion?' enquired Jane.

'Oh well, some do and some don't, you know. But the ones who've talked to the men, like me, are all for it.'

'However much one may sympathise with their aims and their wrongs, one must deplore disobedience,' pointed out George.

'Yes, there might be better ways all right, but they've tried those. One of them told me they wrote to old Howey last year and he agreed when I asked him. Lots of letters, good letters, and he passed them on to the Admiralty and egged them to do something, but they just sat on the letters, so what were the men supposed to do?'

'I must say, they seemed quite harmless,' agreed Emily, 'as if they were taking a holiday. I hated Spithead and so did the children – horrid and cramped lodgings. But everyone agreed that while it was a dead bore, it wasn't the men's fault.'

'Let us hope it'll be settled without any more trouble,' said Elizabeth.

In the long run it was. Yet in the short term there were more and worse mutinies.

Elizabeth and Jane took the children to the Warners' haymaking one fine day. There were seats for the ladies in the shade of the trees. George and Camilla made a sort of hay nest for Elodie, Phineas, and Richard. Jane, yielding to her daughter's shrieking demands, strolled over to inspect it.

The roses were out in the hedges. The birds still sang. There was a refreshing breeze. The haymakers sang like the birds and drank like camels.

'Will she or won't she?' enquired Emily.

'Will who do what?' asked Elizabeth, rather sleepily breathing in the smell of fresh hay.

'Jane, of course. Will she marry Gussie Morris?'

'Does he want her to?'

'Of course. Haven't you noticed? You are blind! She could not 'til it was a year but I think she'd be mad not to,' Emily explained.

'I suppose he is rich.'

'Vastly, and well connected, too. And not every man could want someone else's children, but he dotes on them,' agreed Emily.

'Did Jane tell you?'

'Not she. Clams ain't in it with our Jane. Gussie, course.'

'She keeps refusing him?'

'Twice a week. Oh dear, here comes Phineas.'

He did, bellowing. He had some thistle pins in his finger and they had to be extracted. Elizabeth stopped the uproar with shortbread and Phineas rushed back to the rest.

'The tiresome thing is,' assured Emily, 'I think I'm having another.'

'What's tiresome about that?' enquired her sister enviously.

'Everything. They're so troublesome and expensive and I didn't want anymore. I've got Phineas.'

'I would have liked six. Four girls and two boys. But I only had one every three years. Amabel was so jealous of me,' Elizabeth clarified.

'Well she might be! But that's it, you see. I don't want to be old and fat and tired like Amabel.'

'She's not! Anyway, three is scarcely eleven. You no sooner stop fretting because you don't have any, than you start fretting because you have too many,' Elizabeth added.

:

Next day was Sunday. Ned, who was allowed to come to some of their dinners now he was ten, asked to get down and then returned after half an hour looking worried.

'Whisper, then,' said Elizabeth, knowing he'd been taught not to interrupt and the company was unlikely to stop talking about the war.

'They're on the roof,' he whispered, 'and George nearly fell off. I pulled him back.'

She started up and flew out of the room followed by Jane and Ned.

'What is it?' asked Jane.

'Some of the children are on the roof. God knows… oh, Tom, some of the children are on the roof. Could you come, go and get them down. Ned will show you. Hurry!'

'Yes, madam,' said Tom Goodchild as he ran upstairs, followed by Ned and more slowly, because of their skirts, by Jane and Elizabeth.

'Camilla wouldn't take Elodie or Phineas,' said Jane. 'She always leaves them behind and says they're too young.'

'That's some comfort,' Elizabeth agreed as they arrived at an attic where she'd never been before. It was full of curious objects, mostly broken and filthy. There was also a ladder and an open trapdoor.

They peered up and heard voices.

One was Camilla's, shrill with anger. 'Ned's a dirt sneak!'

Tom's mumbled reply was inaudible but effective. Camilla's pantalets appeared as she climbed down the ladder, followed by George, Richard, and then Tom.

'I'm afraid I'm to blame, madam,' said Tom unhappily. 'Mrs Harding took me and Father up there once. I told Miss Camilla when she was helping me brush out the coach, but it never crossed my mind she'd take the young gentlemen up there.'

It appeared upon inquiry that George had not been dangling from the parapet, as his poor mother had imagined; he had merely slipped off a ridge. And, although it was true he might have tobogganed down the slope and gone smash through the aged parapet, it was unlikely with his weight.

'Camilla is what you might call a loose cannon,' said Madame Lebrun to Elizabeth two days later.

'She is indeed,' agreed Elizabeth with feeling. Camilla had driven away the fishmonger's cart this morning while he was delivering Dover sole. The fishmonger, who fortunately was only middle-aged, but was unfortunately fat, had had to chase them up the drive. Yesterday, she had stolen Mrs Mann's tinder box and set alight to the nursery.

Madame Lebrun was completing an exquisite picture of the 'magnolia grandifleures' that grew up the side of the Palace. Elizabeth was weeding her little wildflower garden. She had blue geraniums, poppies, ox-eyed daisies, frumenty, hardheads, corn marigolds, cornflowers, pheasant's eye, and evening primroses. The only trouble was you had to pull the grass out by hand before it stifled everything.

''Er mother, having spoilt her, now prefers the boy,' went on Madame Lebrun. 'It is bad that. And a pretty, clever little girl who is disturbed is difficult. 'Er father, 'e's a good wit 'er, but 'e's always away.'

'My parents won't have them there anymore,' confided Elizabeth. 'My mother's not very well and my father won't have her bothered.'

'One day I must try and paint some of your wild flowers. Dey are so pretty and delicate. Ve are foolish to disregard them, and you 'ave opened my eyes to dem.'

'I'm glad. What can I do about Camilla?'

'Try to be 'er friend. For now you will find it difficult, but you say you vanted a daughter. For a bit she vould draw-draw and paint. She 'as talent but she vill do no more. Leettle George 'as not as much talent but 'e vork 'ard and voila! 'e began to paint!'

'His work is lively certainly. I must go and wash. We've someone coming to dine.'

:

George was off to London again in late June, and Elizabeth yielded to his pleas and went, too. She did not like leaving the country in summer but she wanted to see her parents. Emily and the children came, too. Now the mutinies were over at last, Harry was meeting them in London and taking them back to Portsmouth, where his new ship, a captured French frigate, would be waiting.

At Baldock, one evening there was a tap on the door and a constable appeared, followed by an elderly gentleman, trailed by a subdued Camilla. 'Is this your girl, M'am?' enquired the constable.

Elizabeth replied, 'No, she's my sister's little girl.'

'Well, perhaps you'd better fetch her mother. She bin telling this gentleman as she was really a princess,' the constable admitted sternly.

'She came into my private parlour and told me she was a "princess of Milan",' said the gentleman, 'stolen away by the French and that she'd escaped by stealing a horse and riding here. Didn't believe a word of it, of course, but, as she wouldn't tell me where she belonged and the innkeeper didn't know, I thought I'd better take her to the constable.'

'One of the waiters told me she was with you,' explained the constable.

'That's right,' said Elizabeth. 'I am very sorry she gave you so much trouble. My sister's in bed with a headache and we were confident Camilla was in bed, too, fast asleep.'

'Apologise this instant!' said George, glaring at Camilla.

'Oh, no need, no need. These imaginative children tell these tales,' said the old gentleman. 'They hardly know they're lying because they believe it themselves. My sister was just such a one. Told my uncle she'd been stolen by gypsies and that her parents had to pay ten thousand pounds to get her back. Not a word of truth in it! Well, now she's safe, I'll be off to bed. I've an early start. Thank you, constable. You soon cleared it up.'

The affair ended with mutual thanks and apologies.

'Taking Camilla into 10 Downing Street will be precious, like taking a bull into a china shop,' said Elizabeth to George when they were in bed.

'I fear so. I am in hopes her father will arrive before us, for she is another child while he is by. But, if that fails, we can only be thankful for Mr Pitt's pronounced sense of humour.'

They found the usual turmoil. Harry was there, and he and his daughter had a touching reunion. But Edward Eliot was there, too, and so was Mr Dundas, Mr Canning, and Mr Rose, who all came and went with bewildering rapidity. They were greatly concerned about the peace negotiations that Malmesbury was carrying out in Paris. They were going well apparently and everyone was hopeful, particularly Mr Pitt, whose disposition was always optimistic.

Mr Pitt remembered Harry and was touched to hear him recite the passage from Lord Halifax. He was always delighted to see George. Camilla did nothing terrible, unless it was to tell Mr Pitt that her papa was very disappointed not to have been at the Battle of Cape St. Vincent. They discussed naval tactics very gravely for some minutes and, when the Meynells had left, Mr Pitt told Elizabeth her niece was a very pretty mannered, taking child.

When they were all assembled in the drawing room before dinner, Mr Canning, who no longer climbed on the furniture, but was still somewhat impetuous, told George and Elizabeth, 'We think of putting Mr Addison in Mr Pitt's place.'

'It will be for the best,' said Mr Rose.

'Addison!' exclaimed Elizabeth. 'Are you all mad?'

'Addison will do very well for a time,' Edward Eliot told her, 'under Mr Pitt's direction. It would not do forever, but Mr Pitt will be the better for a rest.'

'And what rest will he have watching that clown slipping and slopping?' demanded Mr Dundas. 'As for the notion th' French'll prefer him the French'll ne'er ken his name, and small blame to them. He's a wraithe of a man.'

'Mr Addison has made a perfectly adequate Speaker,' said Mr Pitt reprovingly, 'and would, I doubt not, make a perfectly adequate First Lord. If he finds you a bit overpowering, you must recollect a lot of English had the same sensation when a wild highlander loomed up out of the mist waving a claymore and screeching.'

'Havers!' said Mr Dundas, but the rest of the company laughed.

Mr Addison was the son of Lord Chatham's family doctor, so he and Pitt had known each other all their lives, and Pitt was fond of him. He was an agreeable man, devoted to his wife and seven children. Elizabeth felt, though, he had not the strength of mind to stand up to the French.

The next day, George and Elizabeth removed to her parents where they were able to compare horror stories of Camilla's behaviour.

Elizabeth's father seemed quite unchanged, but her mother's rheumatics had grown worse. She walked with a stick and found the stairs difficult, so they were making a downstairs bedroom for her. Elizabeth volunteered to have Camilla for the winter so that Emily and the angelic Phineas could come to her parents', who thought it a marvellous idea. George did not.

Mr Pitt's hopes were disappointed yet again. Just as peace seemed more or less agreed, the more bellicose members of the Directoire got rid of the more humane members and demanded impossible terms. Lord Malmesbury came home.

:

They went north in August, through endless hot harvest fields and dirty roads. Little George had an arrangement of poppies and purple loosestrife waiting for his mother in her bedroom. The poppies didn't last long but it was very pretty.

When Elizabeth paid attention she saw Mr Morris was indeed in love with Jane. Sometimes Elizabeth thought Jane was getting quite fond of him, sometimes she thought she found his persistence irritating; it was hard to tell.

In September a sad letter arrived from Mr Pitt. Edward Eliot had died suddenly. 'He can't have!' exclaimed Elizabeth when George read out the news at breakfast. 'He was perfectly well when we were in London. If it had been Mr Wilberforce now – but Edward was hale and hearty.'

'A sudden seizure,' read out George, 'without any degree of warning, a circumstance we can only be thankful for on his behalf. Mr Pitt is indubitably much affected.'

'Small wonder!' declared Elizabeth. 'And the poor little Hester is entirely an orphan now. She and her father were so close. She must be in her teens. Her grandmother, Lady Chatham, won't last forever, though someone was saying she was still excellent company. Who was it? Oh yes, Mr Canning. He'd gone to stay at Burton Pynsent. Mr Pitt's first reaction to all disasters is to write a reassuring letter to his mother.'

'What a good son he is,' said George. 'Won't Harriot be pleased to see Edward again, though all authorities assure us that time passes painlessly in heaven. "And there they dwell in such delight/Such pleasure and much play/That unto them a thousand years/Does seem but as a day".'

'Very true, I make no doubt,' said Elizabeth, 'but it seems sad that there is no marrying in heaven. Edward and Harriot had such a short time. Are we not fortunate?'

'Vastly so my love, and therefore we should give thanks and endeavour to be worthy of it.'

'You could start by being a bit more amused and less irritated by little Camilla,' Elizabeth chided him.

'Well, well! I will try but she disgraces us so. I am sure I should want to be a good uncle and I have a great regard for Harry, but she wastes so much precious time. I realise the young cannot always be expected to… but I see her upset you and that upsets me.'

'She only frustrates me at the time. Afterwards, I laugh, and so must you.'

:

In December, they took the boys to London for Christmas. Snow had fallen at the end of November and it was bitterly cold. They had a hard journey, often stopping for several nights along the way. Richard, who was easily amused by songs and stories, bore it well. Little George, who had a fine treble voice, often sang, so all the others all joined in, except for Ned, who couldn't sing.

Mr Pitt had pressed them all to stay with him but, tempting as it was, Elizabeth thought it was wiser not to. One child for a few days was likely to be a success, but six children for a month was likely to involve trouble, especially when one of the children was Camilla. And poor Mr Pitt had troubles enough. Besides, little George was so curious, and Richard was often noisy. So they took a fine house in Piccadilly for a month. Elizabeth hired seven servants, and Goodchild fired two of them within several days; one, because he drank, and the other, because she was a most accomplished thief. They would never have proved it, except that John and Camilla hid behind a screen and saw her taking Mr Canning's gold-topped cane. They ran after her shouting 'Stop! Thief!' and Goodchild and Molly came running. The woman threw the cane back down the stairs and swore most convincingly that Camilla had taken it, but, luckily, Goodchild had seen her slip it through the banisters. Nevertheless, they had spent a most uncomfortable few days suspecting everyone.

Mr Pitt asked George to preach a sermon at St. Paul's, giving thanks for their naval victories and pointing out in dignified and theological language that God helps those who help themselves. It was a great success and very much talked about; many people told George they had wished he had gone on longer, which, as Elizabeth pointed out, was a sure sign he stopped just in time.

It was rather a worry living in such a magnificent house with a pack of lively children. Ned and George broke a window playing battledore. George brought back a starving puppy he'd found in Hyde Park and it made messes everywhere at first so that the butler gave notice.

Little George and Phineas turned over a gold table which was, for them, Nelson's ship the *Captain,* and from which they climbed on to a sofa which was the *San Nicolas* at the Battle of St. Vincent. From the sofa they climbed on to a high chest which was the *San Josef* and took the surrender of the sword, an umbrella, off the Spanish captain, who was Phineas. Of course, one of the gold swags got broken, and it was very troublesome and expensive to arrange for it to be replaced.

Camilla and George disappeared for three hours. Luckily, Phineas remembered Camilla talking about the Tower, and there they were eventually found, enjoying the horrors.

Emily was getting rather large and sorry for herself, declaring her daughter was killing her, so Elizabeth asked Camilla if she'd like to come back to Buckden with them, 'For I have too many boys and not enough girls.'

Camilla nodded solemnly. 'There are too many boys, though George is nice, and Elodie is too young to be any use.'

'So will you come for a bit and cheer us up.'

'Grandpa doesn't want me anymore?'

'He doesn't want Grandmama bothered, but I want you.'

'I'll come, then. I like Magwamp.'

Magwamp was little George's pony.

CHAPTER TWENTY-THREE
Lincoln

Harry arrived on Christmas Eve. His frigate, the *Panther*, had been damaged in a battle with the Danes at Camperdown, and he had been persuading and bribing the shipyard at the Nore to repair her.

The whole tobogganing atmosphere became happier. Elizabeth had thought they were happy enough, except for Camilla's and (occasionally) little George's exploits. But now everything was easier, merrier, and the children never got bored. The servants found nothing of any trouble, partly because Harry had brought his coxswain, a most capable man called Baker, and even Emily cheered up and stopped moaning.

Harry had also brought presents for them. A fine piece of watered silk each for Emily and Elizabeth; there was a very pretty bonnet for Emily; George received a handsome chronometer, which he seemed vastly pleased with; Camilla, a very elegant emerald pendant. There was a picture book for the studious Phineas, hoops for all the boys, including John, and one for Camilla, so she shouldn't feel left out of the game. On Boxing Day, Mr Pitt and his niece, Lady Hester Stanhope, came to dine. He told them he would've like to dine on Christmas Day but he thought they ought to go to his brother, Lord Chatham, though it was likely to be very stiff and dull.

Mr Pitt did not look well Elizabeth thought, observing that he was thinner and ate very little. His niece was a fine, bold girl, attractive rather than pretty, friendly and confiding, but with an element of dash about her that made Emily describe her later as "that dreadful fast girl" and Harry to describe her as "a bit of a goer".

Mr Pitt begged that the children should be allowed to come. Richard was too young Elizabeth felt, and Camilla might easily set him off whistling or singing or hollering. John, who was still shy, would be happier with his mother, but the others were there. Harry was delighted to meet Mr Pitt again. 'You told me that piece out of Lord Halifax about believing on the sea,' Harry said. 'I often tell that to the other chaps, they dote on it. It's good to know you're needed.'

Mr Pitt replied, 'I assure you, you are needed as never before. There are stories that the French are planning an expedition from Toulon. No one knows where it is bound. The Austrians are pressing me to send a fleet to the Mediterranean again. We cannot really spare it but…'

'Nelson?' asked Harry.

'He would be the best, I imagine.'

'Much the best. He'll find them, if anyone can. He'll need frigates, though,' Harry alluded.

'And we are very short of them. We are about to build more, but then all too often money is needed elsewhere.'

'I say send Nelson,' declared Lady Hester. 'I've heard you say your father used to quote Montrose:

He either fears his fate too much
Or his desserts are small
Who will not put it to the touch
To win or lose it all

'I do feel that,' agreed Mr Pitt, 'but it will leave our back gate unguarded.'

'Ireland?' asked George.

'Ireland,' agreed Mr Pitt. 'Wolfe Tone is trying to unite Catholics and Protestants in the French interest.'

'Terrible to think that his godfather was a Wolfe,' said the Lady Hester, 'and the same family who took Canada had a tenant's son who was a traitor.'

'I imagine if you were a kind, clever youth in Ireland you could progress from pitying the poor to becoming a traitor by imperceptible stages,' pronounced Mr Pitt.

'Not if you were a Christian,' declared George firmly.

'Christianity saves us from a multitude of errors,' agreed Mr Pitt.

'For my part, I'm never sure if I am a Christian,' said Lady Hester.

Everyone looked at her in amazement and some of them in disapproval.

'Are you a witch?' asked Camilla.

'Camilla!' gasped her mother.

'Never mind! Never mind! When I was small I asked such questions. Perhaps I am a white witch. I admire Christ, of course, but he doesn't speak to me as Voltaire and Rousseau and Shakespeare do,' Lady Hester described.

'I'm even worse,' said Harry. 'Christ speaks to me but I don't do a thing about it. Say the odd prayer, give away some money, cheer people up sometimes, but that's all I seem to have time for.'

'You are leading a Christian life,' pronounced George, 'as not many do. Our duty to be cheerful and therefore agreeable is all too often neglected.'

'But where are the French going?' asked Harry.

'Ah!' said Pitt, 'that is the question. I think Ireland, though only because I fear it. Hester thinks Istanbul, when they will become Turks. and take over the East, and so on to India. Canning thinks they will, like the invincible Armada before them, come up the Channel and shepherd over the French veterans of Italy from Calais.'

'Let's hope so,' said Harry, grinning.

'We need a diviner,' said Mr Pitt. 'I shall go and ask a fortune teller at the fair.'

'But where will you find one in January?' enquired Ned.

'Ah, that is the problem. I asked a talking parrot belonging to the Duchess of Richmond last week, but all it said was "take a damper, cully".'

'What a rude parrot!' said Phineas.

'Totally mannerless,' said Mr Pitt, shaking his head sadly. 'It also remarked "take a wet!" and "shut it scuttlebutt!" I fear it has been keeping low company.'

'Duchesses ain't low,' Camilla told him.

'Not as a rule, but where did she get the parrot? That is what I ask myself. I fear it may have been from a seafarer,' Pitt wondered.

'We're a low lot,' said Harry.

No you're not,' his daughter said, 'you just don't waste time boring and leaving cards.'

'If only he did,' said Emily, 'he would be a Post Captain by now.'

'We shall have to wait and see where the French go,' said Mr Pitt. 'Meanwhile, we could do worse than eat plum pudding. Shall we play blind man's buff after?'

There was an enthusiastic chorus of assent. Soon after this the party broke up. The Meynells went to Emily's parents', and the Pretymans and Camilla went back to Lincoln.

:

It was a dreary journey. Snow and cold got deeper as they went north, and Elizabeth found it very depressing, really almost frightening, mostly on behalf of Goodchild, or Tom, up on the box, and the poor people they passed.

They stayed a week in Cambridge, which was a blessed break, though it meant the journey took nearly a month. Camilla behaved beautifully as she had promised her father she would. Richard fidgeted and chattered and shouted whenever he saw anything that excited him.

It was heaven to be home, though still cold, and you couldn't heat the whole Palace. Jane had given in and was to be married to Gussie in May. Amabel was complaining, 'My girls seem to marry such well-connected men. It is so expensive and troublesome,'

'You sound like my sister, who doesn't want a third child because it would be too costly,' Elizabeth joked.

They were helping in the soup kitchen, which was busy in this cold winter, drying up the soup bowls.

'Lot of ladies would give their eye-teeth to marry their girls as well as you are doing,' said Mrs Egerton, who was the sensible, capable widow of an archdeacon.

'Oh, I know, and the best of it is I haven't had to do a thing about it, it just happens. I was rather worried about Jane, all by herself with hardly any money and two small children. But the case is I don't mind entertaining now. I even quite like it, but not when it comes to Dukes and Duchesses,' Amabel replied.

'The Duchess is cosy,' Elizabeth told her, 'and easy, and no trouble at all. The Duke's a bit overpowering, I grant you. Clever, but he'll talk tithes, enclosures, and statutes with my George happily enough. What is more, you've only got to entertain him for a few hours. I've got to amuse him for a few a se'nights.'

'There, that's done!' said Mrs Egerton. 'Let's hope the weather and trade improve soon or my hands will still be red at the wedding.'

The weather did improve, though not 'til April, and the wedding passed off well enough. Gussie was clearly in a daze of happiness, while Jane was obviously rather bored by it all. Camilla and Elodie and Jane's sister, Fedora, and little Elizabeth made very pretty bridesmaids. Richard and Benjamin were rather naughty pages and went up a tree at the reception. The happy couple went off to spend their honeymoon at Belvoir.

In early June Elizabeth received a letter from Mr Canning describing how Mr Pitt had fought a duel with one Tierney, who felt the mantle of Fox had fallen upon him, and it had held up proceedings in the Commons. Pitt managed to imply Tierney was being unpatriotic and Tierney sent a challenge, which Pitt accepted. They fought in the usual manner at Putney, but Tierney was a bad shot, and Pitt wasn't aiming for him, so no harm was done. The wits said Pitt's slim form should've been chalked on Tierney's fat figure and all shots outside the chalk lines shouldn't count.

Wilberforce was grieved. He disapproved of duels. He was particularly upset that Pitt's duel had desecrated the Sabbath and so brought in a Bill to make duelling illegal. Pitt told him privately that if Wilberforce persisted with his Bill he would resign, so Wilberforce withdrew it.

'Knowing you share my love of the Muse,' wrote George Canning, 'I venture to include a short ode I wrote for the occasion. Mr Pitt was gracious enough to approve it, but requests I show it sparingly, as he prefers a veil to be drawn over the scandalous circumstances.'

The ode went:

Was ever a touch and goer seen?
Our legislators have been
Trying to kill each other
But one way and another
They failed, and the pastime paled

After the episode, Pitt was ill again and confessed to George, who'd gone south again, that, 'My exertions have been greater than my real strength.'

The French fleet had vanished. No one knew where they were, least of all Nelson, who hunted round the Mediterranean looking for them, lamenting his 'want of frigates'.

In Naples, Alexander Hamilton, the British ambassador, told him the French had gone to Malta and stolen the Knights' fabulous treasure. Napoleon had thrown the revered hand of St. John in to a corner after removing the beautiful diamond ring it wore, which he said would look better on his own hand. No sooner had they removed anything of value than they sailed off south–eastwards to Egypt. Nelson sailed after them.

Meanwhile, there was a rebellion in Ireland. The country was infested with informers, so the authorities were aware of the coming trouble and arrested its ringleader, Lord Edward Fitzgerald. Fitzgerald received a wound that killed him. He was a charming, kind young man who'd been persuaded by his tutor to accept most of the ideas of Jean Jacques Rousseau. He'd been in France for most of the Revolution and had apparently found it very edifying. It was probable that he was one of the 'glorious golden' school of thought. The endless executions were very regrettable, of course, but they were necessary to protect the 'glorious, golden future', when the people of France, even the poorest, would be free and prosperous.

The revolution in Ireland was not a success. The French never came but English troops did, and, as Mr Pitt had prophesied, the desperately needed frigates had to be cancelled to pay for the English troops that were sent to Ireland.

Nelson finally found the French ships anchored in Aboukir Bay. Nelson's ships navigated between the French ships and the shore. One of the English ships went aground but the others were devastating. After hours of noisy battle, the French admiral's flagship *L'Orient* blew up and there was complete silence. All the Knights of Malta's treasure ended up at the bottom of Aboukir Bay.

The news was slow to reach London but, when it did, George wrote to Elizabeth, 'Mr Pitt has returned from his house at Holwood in the highest possible spirits. He considers Napoleon is destroyed. Oh, my love, what joy!'

Elizabeth's father wrote:

> *Your new niece is to be burdened with the name Arethusa. Had Harry but been here, I am confident I could have prevented it, but as he is blockading Brest... Your sister is far from satisfied with her and the child's blooming health, and her rapid and easy delivery. She considers the child should have been a boy. She feels her figure should have returned to normal now. She declares the Lord Lieutenant should abandon such trivial amusements as repelling the French and entertain her*

The hot heavenly summer soon passed because it didn't start 'til the end of June, and it was over by the end of July.

Gussie Morris, on returning from his honeymoon, purchased a large house in Lincoln. Jane didn't want to live in Lincoln, but he assured her it was a mere temporary expedient as his aunt, the Duchess, was looking out for a good living for him near Belvoir where Jane could ride and hunt, and he could act and sing.

George came back in August, and they decided to give a garden party soon afterwards. It was a good way of entertaining all sorts of people without too much trouble or expense, though if it rained they'd have to come inside and then the squash would be considerable.

Elizabeth, Jane, and Madame Lebrun were arranging flowers before this festivity. Elizabeth was good with flowers, Madame Lebrun was exceptional with flowers, but Jane was simply terrible at arranging flowers, and Elizabeth knew she would have to redo them when Jane had gone.

Madame Lebrun was working in the morning room. Elizabeth and Jane were working in the drawing room and gossiping as they went.

'You were quite right for telling Mama there was no need to be afraid of the Duchess,' said Jane, ramming in a large bunch of flowers. 'She's a good sort. I thought the Duke was a cold fish at first, now I just think he's shy.'

'A lot of great men are,' answered Elizabeth. 'They make people nervous and that makes them nervous, and unless you find something that interests them, things get stiffer and stiffer.' She pulled out a rose and tried it on the other side. 'How's the Marquis?'

'Snivelling. His Uncle Jack gave him a stinking cold. There, that's done. I'll go and get some more,' Jane answered.

'She does six to my one,' thought Elizabeth, 'but they'll all have to be redone. I'll get Kate to help. She's got the knack.'

A wailing noise grew nearer and the noise eventually turned into Richard. 'Camilla and George have gone up that oak tree again,' he complained. 'I can't get up and they won't help me.'

'Well, go and find Molly and John, then. John will play with you,' Elizabeth replied.

'Camilla's more fun,' wailed Richard as he went. Elizabeth thanked heaven, not for the first time, for John's unfailing good nature.

Two minutes later, Madame Lebrun moved gracefully through the open French windows; she was holding trails of jasmine and a bunch of phlox and red roses.

'I have to thank you for some good advice about Camilla,' Elizabeth told her. 'I think we're becoming friends.'

'She needed only a little love and attention. She imagines much and sometimes she overcomes 'erself,' Lebrun replied.

'Yes, I see that now. She asked me where we would hide if the French came and if we would all become cripples like my mother. And it's so good she's painting again.'

'She begins to learn how to see things and what to put in and what to leave out. I think it will be a great joy and recourse to her. A rich woman who has no occupation is a sad creature.'

'Yes, I often see that,' agreed Elizabeth, thinking of Emily. 'I dare say I ought to see it in myself.'

'No, you occupy yourself with the poor, which is as God vishes. And you have a gift for easing people. I must continue.'

A few minutes later, Jane clattered back with an armful of ragwort and rosebay willowherb. Elizabeth often used wild flowers but this was ridiculous she thought. Willowherb wouldn't last an hour.

'You don't seem to get much further,' said Jane.

'People keep interrupting.'

'They do. You can't get anything done in your own house for interruptions. You can't go anywhere in your own house without seeing something that needs doing. Mama just ignores it. Gussie even keeps trying his sermons out on me,' Jane said.

'Are they very bad?' asked Elizabeth inquisitively.

'No-o, but they're much too in alt for the audience, and they'd go on forever if I didn't tell him most women have dinner to cook and a lot of men have beasts to feed and water.'

'George was the same at first,' Elizabeth alluded.

'There, that's finished. Want any more?' Jane piped.

Elizabeth answered, 'No, I thank you. I'll soon be done in here.'

'I'm an even worse wife for a parson than I was for a marquis. At least I can get him to leave his Latin and build better houses. I'll go, then. Joseph will be wanting me.'

:

The next day didn't dawn so much as get lighter, so you could see the rain as well as hear it. George was inclined to be glum.

'If only we'd had this yesterday,' he grumbled.

'There's room really and people entertain each other. Perhaps it'll stop. Rain before seven, clear before eleven.'

Everyone was saying this to one another but they were wrong. It was one of those days when sometimes it poured but it never stopped. Most people came and the squash inside was considerable, but nearly all of them knew how to enjoy themselves, and the flowers were admired.

Harry, who had leave, came to fetch Camilla. He was full of Navy gossip. Napoleon was besieging a town called Acre, and a naval captain called Sidney Smith was assisting the Turks. 'Smith's a bit apt to top it the knob,' said Harry, 'but he's plenty of bottom. Boney won't shift him in a hurry. The Frogs shut him up in a dirty great prison called the Bastille. Out bounces Smith like a Jack in the box. I was shipmate with one of his officers once, French cove called Philippeau, so we called him "Filthy Po". Loved playing about with gun powder. The French'll find themselves flying about in the sky with him there.'

'The Navy gets around,' said Elizabeth.

'Certainly does, top hole beef you get there. When you've been starved for months you don't half gobble up your grub,' Harry said happily.

'You must get a good drawing master for Camilla,' Elizabeth told him. 'Madame Lebrun says she has a gift for it.'

'Eet es so,' confirmed Lebrun. 'She must continue.'

'Will do,' said Harry. 'Now you've tamed her I'm looking forward to showing her off at Belvoir and Hatfield. Think they'll let her come to meals when I tell them we don't have much time together.'

Mr Pitt, judging from the letters, and the newspapers, was trying to get together another coalition against the French. Austria was keen, the Kingdoms of Naples and Sicily were keen, Russia was keen, but Prussia changed its mind daily: one day it was eager to help, the next it wasn't.

Camilla cried the morning she and her father left, but Elizabeth promised that she should come again.

:

In early 1799, George went off to London again to find Mr Pitt and all his friends talking about Ireland. It was natural enough after the rebellion of the year before but, unfortunately, not everyone could discuss Ireland without quarrelling. Mr Pitt wanted to unite the heavily Protestant Dublin parliament with moderate Protestant Westminster, and to bring the moderate Catholics into government. Mr Canning, as usual, quite agreed with him. The King, however, most certainly did not. The King had taken a coronation oath to keep the Pope out of Britain, and he wanted to do just that.

Dundas agreed about parliaments, but not about relieving and trusting the Catholics. He said, 'They're aye th' same and they dunna want y' to believe God's truth.'

Lord Grenville, too, had reservations about the Pope. He felt, however, a need for change. 'We can't go on like this,' he added.

Mr Rose felt that the Catholics could now, in general, be trusted, and that what Ireland needed was more trade, more capital, and more good farming, but he doubted whether destroying Dublin's Parliament would help. Wilberforce felt there was more religious tolerance nowadays which would solve the Irish problem before very long, but it was unimportant compared with the problem of slavery. His Bill for freeing slaves passed in the Commons, but failed in the Lords. Général d'Arblay, who George met at a smart party, thought the English would never satisfy the Irish; they were too different. It was unfortunate, it was even tragic, but so it was.

An Irishman called Hutchinson wrote to Mr Pitt, and the end of his letter summed up the situation tersely. 'I firmly believe there is no thought so dear to my countrymen as that of murdering each other. The Catholics like to kill in the name of the Pope, the Protestants prefer to kill in the name of the Law. But both sides think of their country only as an extended field of battle.'

Mr Pitt, so scrupulous in his own dealings they called him 'Honest Billy', didn't mind using bribes for politics. Poor Cornwallis, who was now the Viceroy of Ireland, wrote, 'It has been the wish of my life to avoid all this dirty business, and now I am involved in it beyond all bearing. How I long to kick those of whom my public duty obliges me to court!'

Meanwhile, at Lincoln, Amabel played Lady Macbeth to Gussie's Macbeth. This time the weather did nothing terrible and the audience and takings were large. Soon afterwards, Gussie, Jane, and her children moved to the village of Woolsthorpe in the Belvoir Vale where Gussie was the new parson. Before Jane could decide whether she liked the place and the rectory, she found she was expecting another baby, and disliked everything because she was so sick.

'That means it's a girl,' Amabel told Elizabeth as they dined in Amabel's house after a doctor's meeting. 'She was never in the least sick with Joseph. Gussie won't mind. He loves little girls. He's too sweet with Elodie, just like Harry and Camilla. They say Boney's back.'

'I fear it is all too true,' said the Archdeacon. 'He has escaped, leaving his unfortunate men to perish, and dodging the Navy with the devil's own luck, and arriving to what was apparently a warm welcome.'

'He is an odious, ruthless man, but a good Général,' pointed out Amabel. 'And as the French want to conquer the world they value those qualities.'

There was confused distant shouting from the street outside, and closer shouting from upstairs.

'Will it not be odd being in the nineteenth century?' asked Amabel. 'I cannot quite believe it. I am sure I shall get stuck mentally in the eighteenth, where I really belong.'

'I look forward to it,' said her daughter, Lucasta. 'People will become less stuffy and stupid, and women will be able to vote and become doctors, and people will realise actors and actresses are quite proper and important.'

'I doubt if the world will change that much,' said her father disapprovingly. 'It is to be hoped, however, that the nineteenth century will be less bloodthirsty and Godless.'

The summer had been wet and the winter was cold so the price of bread rose again. Ned went to London with his father, who then took him down to Eton. His letters were scrappy and not very informative, but he didn't sound unhappy or homesick. He came back for Christmas, bringing glowing reports. Only his mathematics, unlike his father's, was not very good.

Napoleon managed to take over France and soon went to war again in Italy. They had a good Christmas, for all that. Ned ate enormously, saying the food wasn't very good or plentiful at his tutor's. Elizabeth sent him back with a hamper.

The new century came in with warmer weather, though wet. Kate confided in Elizabeth one bright morning in January when the sun was just rising as Elizabeth was getting up. 'I reckon I better marry Roly,' she said it as if she had decided to go and consult a doctor, resigned and resolute. 'I always told you I want to have some children. I'm thirty-five now and, with luck, I'll only have one or two. I tell him if I have a child I'm off to Germains directly. I don't fancy the stories you hear about dirty old midwives.'

'Quite right. I'm sure Mrs Potts saved Amabel's life. Not once, but twice. When shall you marry then?' Elizabeth enquired.

Kate answered, 'I ain't in a hurry, I can tell you, and I wants to be married at home, so my ol' Nana can come. We all think th' world of our Nana. Father said you was going home to Germains in Maytime.'

'Yes, by way of London,' Elizabeth added.

Kate went on, 'Well, Roly say he could take th' stage down if you was to give him a week's leave. I say to him I'm not marrying you 'til you got a tap in th' scullery an' a toilet in th' cottage. He's got his own cottage and that took them five years. Him an' the children, but they done it.'

Roland Barber was one of the gardeners at Buckden whose wife had died having her fourth baby. He was a tall man, with a rugged, attractive face and a quiet, friendly manner. Elizabeth often consulted him about flowers.

'Of course, if you wants a fancy London dresser, that's your business, but if I was you, I'd take Sue Collins from out th' kitchen. She talk too much but she's handy and she's got gumption. An' I could teach her a lot 'fore I marry,' Kate said.

'I'll certainly see her. Won't the cook be cross?' Elizabeth wondered.

'She'll miss her, no denying, but it won't hurt to give someone else a chance, an' there's plenty of girls wanter come to a good house like this,' Kate explained.

They stayed with Jane and Gussie on the way south. Jane was still feeling very sick and could eat little, but she refused to go to Mrs Potts, saying the Duchess had found her a perfectly adequate midwife in Long Clawson, which was an adjacent village.

The two children were delightful. Gussie always spoke in French when they were alone at meals, so they should not forget their father's language. His French was good but Jane's was terrible, and she hated the practice.

Both Gussie and Jane were appalled by the poverty around them in Woolsthorpe. 'I had thought all was well in the country,' declared Jane, as they sat at dinner. 'It was in general round Lincoln and Germains, but it is not here. The copyholders are all right but there aren't many of them. The farmers grow rich, but they often don't look after their hands who are starving and housed in leaking pigsties.'

'My dear wife exaggerates somewhat,' said Gussie. 'But the poverty is indeed such as one cannot condone. No school. No hospital nearer than Melton. The workhouse is very unsatisfactory.'

'All the more opportunity for a rich man like you to do a lot of good,' said Elizabeth.

'I am, I hope, very sensible of the opportunity, but really it is hard to know where to start,' Gussie added.

'I should advise a small church school for their piety and improvement,' said George, 'and a soup kitchen for their bodies.'

'You could send it out cold to outlying cottages,' suggested Elizabeth, 'and, as for a cottage hospital, it would be best to consult the local doctor first.'

'He's always drunk and says there's nothing to be done,' Jane stated.

'The Duke's agent could perhaps find you an honest and assiduous overseer for the workhouse?' suggested George. 'How is the Duke, by the by?'

The conversation became a little more genteel.

:

Mr Pitt was, as always, touchingly pleased to see them, but he was also, as usual, besieged with politics and politicians. The coalition was quarrelling, and Ireland was worrying.

'Trouble is, we all hope for too much,' Mr Pitt explained at breakfast on their last day. 'The Catholics hope for relief and opportunity, and the Protestants hope the Catholics won't receive any.'

'And you?' enquired Elizabeth.

'I hope everyone will be reasonable. The vainest, saddest desire of all,' answered Pitt.

'I would be prepared to offer the Papists relief, or opportunity, or anything they required,' stated George, 'would they but offer the Reformed Religious and, indeed, the Jews, and followers of Mohamet, an equal indulgence in their own Papist territory.'

'But shouldn't we, as good Anglicans, and above all, as good Christians, be trying to set an example?' asked Elizabeth.

'We should,' agreed Mr Pitt. 'And so much as there is, and always must be, a contest between sects, it is by example and justice that we will prevail, or indeed hold our own in these changing times.'

Elizabeth's mother grew worse. She had a lot of pain and could only walk with crutches. She was taking laudanum and willow bark. The doctor would have preferred her to stick to a willow bark infusion, but she found the drugs were more effective after a rest, and took them alternately, one month willow and one poppy.

'You have done wonders with that brat,' her father said, referring to Camilla. 'She was obviously possessed of a devil, but you seem to have cast it out.'

'Poor little girl, she was just bored really. Harry's bringing her to Downing Street next week and we're taking her back for a nice long visit. I quite look forward to it and so does Madame Lebrun, who thinks highly of her painting,' Elizabeth said.

'How do you find Mr Pitt?' asked Elizabeth's father.

'The same unaffected, responsive, intelligent man as ever he was,' replied George. 'But Mr Rose wrote to me he fears Mr Pitt is far from well. He needs a rest.'

'And we need him. He has done wonders raising money. If we could but spend it to better purpose. He is very concerned about the scarcity of bread,' Elizabeth asserted.

'Well he might be,' said Elizabeth's mother. 'The servants tell me the most terrible stories. It is not too bad round here, but there are people starving in the towns.'

A letter arrived from Gussie saying Jane had had a daughter who they were calling Sophie. They were both well and Gussie was clearly delighted.

Kate's wedding went well, too. Elizabeth's parents put up the bridegroom and his three children. Young Sue Collins took over and, much as Elizabeth missed Kate after so long, she found Sue satisfactory and often rather funny.

:

They went back to London by way of Eton and picked up Ned and his luggage for the summer holiday of 1800. He was well, though hungry, and his reports were excellent, though it was clear he found mathematics and science dull.

Mr Pitt was still engrossed in getting the Irish Union through in both Dublin and Westminster. Getting it through Dublin meant a lot of bribery and creating new peers; getting it through Westminster meant lots of persuasive speeches, both in and out of the House.

'Surely, it is better if people have their own parliament?' said Harry at dinner.

'It would appear so,' answered Mr Pitt, 'but the Irish Parliament in general is obdurately prejudiced against their fellow Catholic countrymen. England, too, shares this unpleasant and unjust prejudice, so by dissolving the Irish Parliament we relieve the Irish peasants and their oppressors. And by transferring the Irish MPs to Westminster we remove the fear that the Catholics could outvote the Protestants.'

'It sounds all right,' said Harry doubtfully, 'but not everyone thinks straight like you, and people who hardly think at all and believe all sorts of nonsense are still fond of their country and their faith.'

'Nae doot,' agreed Mr Dundas. ''Tis aye "what o' Ireland?" Dunna fash y'self. Ye canna cure Ireland. Leave 'em bide 'n' wham 'em doon when they join the Frogs. What's all this about Lord Nelson taking up with a ladybird?'

'I hope it may be a storm in a teacup,' said Harry. 'Collingwood swears he is devoted to his wife. I think there can be little doubt he was committed to his wife and declared her nursing saved his life after his wounds, but there are cases with boy and girl marriages where the girl grows up, becomes dull, plain, tired, while the boy is as impetuous, and affectionate as ever. Then there must be a risk – and Lady Hamilton, as the British Ambassador's wife in Naples, is certainly of the greatest use to Nelson and to Britons. She is very close to the Queen, who rules all.'

'I dislike all such gossip,' declared George.

'Oh, so do I!' agreed Mr Pitt. 'I am persuaded the Princess of Wales is a modest violet, and Queen Jezebel spent all her time at prayer.'

'Why, what did they really do?' asked Camilla when the laughter had died down.

'I fear,' answered her father, 'they may have kissed a man who was not their husband.'

'Mr Canning has written a new poem,' Elizabeth told them, 'about the building block houses beside the Thames. It's rather good. It goes:

If blocks can a nation deliver,
Two places are safe from the French.
The one is the mouth of the river,
The other the Treasury bench

'Mr Canning has missed his vocation,' declared Mr Pitt. 'Did he not waste too much of his time playing the popular game of politics, he had become another Milton. You,' he gazed at the doubtful Mr Dundas, 'had been another Scott. Harry in course, did he not confound the King's enemies, would have been another Homer beguiling us with battles, voyages, and sirens. The Bishop, without doubt, had been another Bunyan. But you, Elizabeth, did you not run palaces and town houses, what would have written?'

Elizabeth answered, 'Perhaps another Burney of an innocent maid's misadventures among the *ton*.'

'Or another *Pastoral,*' suggested George. 'For she deals well with shepherds and milkmaids.'

'I'll write another *Gulliver's Travels*,' announced Camilla, 'only in India.'

'I'd write about something that really happened,' declared Ned. 'Another *Journal of the Plague Year,* or perhaps about the invincible Armada.'

'May you both do just that,' said Mr Pitt, 'in peacetime.'

CHAPTER TWENTY-FOUR

Woolsthorpe

The journey back was pleasant enough, as travelling slowly through England in summertime usually was. Everything seemed to be pink, green, white. and red: roses and elder blossom, flowering grass and poppies, the wind in the barley, the little partridges following their parents.

Camilla informed them as they lurched along, 'It will be wonderful to do something. Mama and her friends never do anything but talk and play cards. On occasion they go and look at a fine prospect, but what's the use of prospects when you're not allowed to climb the trees and hills, or paddle in the rivers and lakes, or ride the horses?'

'You certainly did lots of things last time you stayed,' declared Ned. 'Most of them mad.'

'I was a bit mad when I was small,' agreed Camilla. 'I got so bored you see. He just reads and reads.'

Gussie and their children came for a visit in September while travel was still pleasant. It was pretty to see how pleased Elodie and Joseph were with their little sister. Elizabeth gathered that Woolsthorpe, having felt the sweet breeze of Gussie's benevolence, was now exposed to the gale of a healthy Jane. They had opened a soup kitchen and a school, and were building twelve cottages and a small hospital.

Mr Pitt had got his Union with the Irish Parliament, and was now negotiating with his Cabinet to bring in relief for the Irish Catholics.

Gussie and Jane found a school for Camilla which she enjoyed, though she didn't seem to make any friends there, and it sounded as if the other girls thought her gauche and odd. She did, however, become friends with Amabel's daughter, Eliza, whose good nature made her everyone's acquaintance.

Elizabeth and Amabel took a pack of children to pick sweet chestnuts in the park one fine Sunday afternoon in October. George and Camilla were soon high in a nearby tree. John threw sticks to knock down more chestnuts and dutifully stamped out the nuts for Richard, Eliza, and Benjamin.

‘I hear they’ve got measles in the slums,’ said Elizabeth, sitting herself on a comfortable log beside Amabel.

‘They’ve always got some ghastly disease in the slums,’ answered Amabel. ‘I had thought we would clear them before now, but it’s so dear building houses, and more people keep coming in because, with the price of corn, the work-houses are so full.’

‘Look, Mama, at the great big one I found!’ said Richard.

‘Mine’s bigger,’ said Benjamin.

‘Whose is biggest?’ demanded Richard.

‘Yours, but Benjamin’s is a very fine chestnut, too. Big as a conker.’

The weather turned colder, and Ned wrote that they were only allowed a scuttleful of coal, so he and his friends went wooding.

George went off to London to sit in the Upper House and to then fetch Ned for Christmas.

‘One of the girls from my school has got measles,’ announced Camilla, as they were eating tea one day at the beginning of December.

‘I hear dat eet es a sort de most virulent,’ said Madame Lebrun. ‘How many of you 'ave 'ad eet?’

There was a silence.

‘I have,’ answered Elizabeth, ‘I remember because my head ached so much. And all three boys have had chicken pox. Ned got mumps, too.’

‘I’ve had chicken pox,’ offered Camilla, ‘and whooping cough when I was six. I was quite bad. Before Daddy often called me Miss Bulger, and after he called me Skinny Liz.’

‘Do you think I should send the children to Jane, and ask her to keep Ned when he and George stop there?’ asked Elizabeth.

‘Et is up to you. In general I say let dem get it young and get it over wit. But dis, perhaps not. I 'ear many 'ave died. In France, in de seventies, dere vas much diphtheria. My husband vould let no one into the château and so ve escaped.’

‘I think I’ll send tomorrow,’ said Elizabeth.

The following day, there were seven more cases at Camilla’s school and the Headmistress decided to close early. Little George disclosed to Molly, who told Elizabeth, there were several cases in his and Richard’s school, too.

Jane wrote, proffering her complete willingness to have the four children from the Palace, and four of her younger brothers and sisters, also to keep Ned when he arrived.

'It's lucky Woolsthorpe Rectory is so large,' said Elizabeth, as they were packing up.

But, next morning, George and Camilla were both ill with streaming colds, sore throats, and lurid blotches. Amabel sent a message that Jack, Benjamin, and Eliza had it, too. Elizabeth was in two minds whether to send Richard, Molly, and John, but Molly was against it. 'Them two have got it already, most likely,' she said, 'and I'd rather stay. I'm goin' t'be needed.'

The doctor, a middle-aged man called Jackson, was sensible, if scarcely reassuring. 'Keep them warm, try and see they drink a lot. Here's something which should help to keep their temperatures down. I'll try and look in tomorrow, but I am run off my feet, so it may be Wednesday. Send round if you're worried and even if I can't come, my young partner will. E's very sound and he needs less sleep than I do.'

The next day, Richard got it, too, and the day after, John suddenly fainted, having felt rather hot and peculiar all day. He'd not mentioned it for fear of being a nuisance. George arrived. He and his brother had had the measles years ago and had considered it a welcome rest from school, where they were working very hard and willingly.

Ned had great fun hunting with Jane in the Belvoir Vale.

Dr Jackson and his partner, Dr Hewitson, came every day. When little George and Camilla were burning up Elizabeth suggested ice and told Jackson how it had saved Amabel.

'I'm afraid not in these cases, Madam,' Dr Jackson stated. 'The lungs are too congested. You could try putting a little ice in the cold water you sponge them with, but they must not be chilled for any length of time.'

'Every day they seem to be worse,' said Elizabeth despondently.

'I'm afraid it is a nasty disease and it takes its time,' Dr Jackson explained.

'How are the Archdeacon's children?' asked Elizabeth.

'Benjamin and Eliza show signs of amendment, but I am worried about Jack. The elder girl has only just taken it,' Dr Jackson said with concern.

They seemed to live in a haze of worry and fear. When the day was fine, or even just tolerable, George and Elizabeth had a short walk or ride, but she hated being away and rushed back expecting the worst. And indeed she did, for Nell's infant daughter had died.

One of the young housemaids caught it and was a fifth who needed careful nursing. Nell helped, too, and said it took her mind off her loss.

'The girl will live,' said Dr Hewitson triumphantly one cold dreary morning.

'Her temperature does seem to be down a bit,' said Elizabeth tiredly, for she had not been able to sleep much. 'What about George?'

'It might go either way,' the Doctor replied.

On Christmas Eve, Jack died. On Christmas Day, little George slept longer than usual, and Elizabeth tiptoeing in noticed he was pouring with sweat. They had to change his bedclothes. Dr Jackson, coming in just then, was delighted. 'That'll bring the temperature right down,' he said. 'I was anxious as to know how much more his heart could stand, but he'll do now. A very healthy boy fortunately.'

Richard was still desperately ill. Camilla was better, but she had grown bored and very upset about Jack's death. Madame Lebrun got her sketching and then painting for short periods.

Just as they thought Richard was a little better John began to burn up.

Elizabeth sent Tom Goodchild to tell the housemaid's parents that their daughter was ill but not very ill, and they were taking good care of her. Tom came back two hours later. He had found the housemaid's mother and seven young children in a bitter, cold house.

'The mother'd had it young,' Tom told Elizabeth, 'and that was a mercy, but she was tired out nursing. They couldn't afford th' husband stopping at home and they couldn't afford the fuel day 'n' night. I made so bold as to go over to your fuel charity 'n' bring back some wood and a little coal. Th' room was warmin' up when I left. That'll give the children a better chance, though one of them's dyin', I reckon. Looked for all th' world like my poor Rose.'

'I must pay for the fuel and we must send one of the doctors and a nurse. Write down the address, would you,' Elizabeth replied to him.

The next day, Richard was obviously better, though John's temperature would not stay down. Young George disappeared and was found in Camilla's room, re-enacting the Battle of the Nile.

Mrs Mann got the disease, and so did the cook and one of the grooms.

Mr Pitt wrote that almost everyone was very keen on relief for the Catholics. Lord Castlereagh was convinced it would reconcile the Irish to losing their Parliament. Lord Cornwallis, the present Viceroy of Ireland, wrote, 'If Mr Pitt is firm he will meet with no difficulty.'

Jane wrote that the hunting was very good. Slowly, Richard and John got better, though unlike Camilla and little George, they were very weak, thin, and listless. The cook, the housemaid, and the groom slowly recovered, but Mrs Mann died. Elizabeth knew she would miss her very much. 'That efficiency! That thoroughness!' But she also knew all the other servants were delighted. No more grumbling, unnecessary work, and complaining about their labour.

George and Elizabeth went to Jack's funeral. Elizabeth couldn't think what she was going to say to poor Amabel, but in the event there was no need to say anything. They just hugged each other. Amabel had lost at least two stone and looked twenty years older. The Archdeacon looked much older and grimmer, too.

Four of the housemaids' younger brothers and sisters died. Dr Hewitson told Elizabeth he heard over a thousand people, mostly children, had died in and around Lincoln. 'When I was in Manchester,' he said, 'there was a cholera epidemic and thousands died. I think it was that which really made me want to be a doctor.'

'Could I be a doctor?' asked John.

'Don't see why not. Is he bright enough?' The Doctor asked Elizabeth.

'Oh yes, I think so. His teachers speak highly of him. Do you mislike the sight of blood, John?' Elizabeth said, turning to John.

John responded, 'Not particularly, Madam, though it frightened me when Tom cut himself with a scythe, but then Mr Goodchild tied that up tight.'

'Well, I shall have to take you round with me in a few years' time and see if you like it,' the Doctor replied.

Later that day, Molly and Elizabeth were conferring about John and Richard's finicky appetites, when the reserved, polite Molly exclaimed, 'Aren't we lucky, Madam! Oh, aren't we lucky!'

'Incredibly lucky,' agreed Elizabeth, thinking of Amabel and Nell, and that housemaid's poor mother.

CHAPTER TWENTY-FIVE

London/Buckden Palace

Elizabeth and George went to stay with Jane in mid-January, 1801. Elizabeth wanted to see her eldest son for a few days before he went back to Eton with his father. Gussie offered to send him back to Buckden in his coach. Jane wanted to go, too, but Gussie was very against the idea in case she got measles.

Mr Pitt and George were sitting in Number 10 drinking port on the evening of January twenty-eighth, when a distracted Dundas burst in on them. 'He's on t' us,' he announced.

'If, as I apprehended, you mean that Napoleon Bonaparte is hidden in the loft and listening to our discourse I beg leave to doubt it,' declared Mr Pitt. 'Have some port.'

'Not Bonaparte, the King. Aye, th' King came up to me at his levee. "What is the question you are all about to force on me?" quoth he. "What is the Catholic Emancipation which this young Lord, this Irish Secretary has brought over, that you are going to throw at my head? I tell you I will look on every man as my enemy who proposes that question to me. I hope my friends will not desert me".'

'Who can have betrayed us?' asked Mr Pitt, putting his glass down.

'Loughborough, for a million. He, aye, betrays his friends, the cahoopit cockle picker. By Weir o' Harrison, he's a scurvy scut! I warned y'. There may be more forbye. Yon Canning is overapt to yap yap, and he's likely yapped at the Princess of Wales. He's in with her. An' yer cousin Grenville's close enough, but his wife's likely told it to th' Court she was free'n the slaves and emancipating the Catholics an' feeding th' fleas.'

'It will prove impossible now to persuade the King,' said Mr Pitt. 'I will write to him but… without some measure of emancipation it will prove impossible to persuade the Irish. What is this fatality about Ireland that all the most promising measures go awry, and all efforts fail?'

'Hatred,' said George. 'As Mr Hutchinson pointed out, they indulge in hatred to an amazing extent, not without provocation and hardship, so they attract evil and join with whatever malice is contemporary.'

Mr Pitt wrote his letter. It was a good message but it failed to persuade the King, who answered the next day, offering to keep quiet about the issues, if only Pitt would, too.

'Hardly of great utility to the Irish,' commented Mr Pitt, 'or the Lords Cornwallis and Castlereagh. He will not even listen to us. I fear I must resign.'

George found it difficult to advise him. It was terrifying to think of the war without Mr Pitt to direct it. On the other hand, as Edward Eliot had said four years before, Mr Pitt would be the better of a rest.

:

On the fifth of February, 1801, Mr Pitt sent his resignation to the King. It was instantly accepted. Mr Pitt, by defeating or winning over the Whigs, had made himself dispensable to the King. Mr Addington agreed to become Prime Minister. Like the King, he thought it would be dangerous to allow the Catholics to become more powerful.

Mr Pitt had to move out of Number 10, after twenty years of tenancy. Most of his money would go with his job, and he was deeply in debt. George found a house for him in Park Place near St. James's Street and helped Mr Pitt move there, taking particular care packing up his large library. Many books were in Greek or Latin, but recent purchases were in French: Corneille and Boileau in green leather, with gold lines, and the Pitt crest, a crane, in gold. When the move was completed George left Mr Pitt and went back to Lincoln. George's old pupil seemed in excellent spirits and so he wanted to get back to his wife, who had been sadly pulled down by worry and nursing when he left. Letters from Mr Pitt followed him north after arriving at a country house or inn before he did.

The first one was still cheerful and had a postscript saying, 'Rose, I believe, will write to you, and very likely in a tone of despondency, which I am sure the case does not call for.' The next letter was full of the King's kindness at his levee on the eleventh of February. He had told Pitt, 'You have behaved like yourself throughout this business. Nothing could possibly be more honourable. I do not care who hears me.' He then took Pitt into his closet for a further half hour's friendly talk.

However, a letter waiting for George when he got home was less cheery. The King had gone mad again. Pitt couldn't hand over the Seals of Office, because people differed so on who he should hand them to.

All the problems of 1788 were back again – Regency, term of Regency, time of Regency – in the middle of handing over power, fighting a war, producing a budget, and negotiating for peace.

George found Elizabeth looking much better. Richard and John were recovering, too, though slowly. Little George and Camilla were out skating. When the children went back to their schools they found them tragically empty. Most children had lost a brother or a sister.

In March, Mr Pitt wrote that the King had made one of his sudden and total recoveries. He had said, 'I am better now, but who made me ill?' Mr Pitt was all too aware of what had made the King ill and so hurriedly agreed never to mention Catholic relief again when the King asked him to.

Most of Mr Pitt's colleagues resigned with him – Mr Dundas, Lord Grenville, Canning; not so Lord Loughborough, however, who turned up happily at the first Cabinet meeting, and had to be told he was not wanted. Addington might not be a very clever man but he was full of common sense and good will, and he could work out that a man who'd betrayed one master would soon betray another. He asked for Scott instead, the man who had told Elizabeth droll stories at Windsor. Some people found Addington as Prime Minister an improvement on Pitt. He was approachable, jovial, and facetious. Most people, however, found him slow to understand things, likely to forget a lot, and discursive. Canning made up one of his rhymes about it:

Pitt is to Addington,
As London to Paddington

Mr Pitt was not pleased when this rhyme got back to him, and he made Mr Canning write to apologise. He tried to make Mr Canning join Addington's government, too, but that turned out to be impossible.

Rose told George that Mr Pitt had 'drawn up a grand plan of finance which he has sent to Mr Addington but I fear the latter will hardly be brought to understand it.'

The people who Mr Pitt owed money to grew very demanding, and it was obvious something would have to be done. He considered going back to the bar, but Dundas pointed out that he was not well enough. At last, his richer friends persuaded him to accept some money from them. George gave a thousand pounds and so did several others, including Dundas, Carrington, Rose and Lord Bathurst. Wilberforce and Pitt's secretary, Joseph Smith, gave five hundred pounds each. With this, which came to eleven thousand seven hundred pounds, and the sale of Pitt's beloved Holwood, enough money was raised to pay his main debts. He felt the loss of Holwood, but luckily he was getting increasingly fond of Walmer Castle, which was his as the Warden of Cinque Ports.

Harry wrote in June, saying he had been at Nelson's victory at Copenhagen where he put the telescope to his blind eye and ignored his Admiral's order to break off the action. 'Lucky we had Nelson,' he wrote, 'but it was a bit like shooting tiger cubs. No one could deny the necessity but no one wanted to. All the Danish prisoners I talked to hated the French and gave sad accounts of their beastly thieving.'

He hoped to get leave and come to London soon, 'where the bouncing Bishop could perhaps escort my delectable daughter, but it is alas still somewhat uncertain. If I can get leave, I will send an express, and Camilla and I will spend an idyllic summer boating, swimming, sketching, and playing badminton. But if I cannot get leave, Camilla will be happier with you than at her mother's parties.'

There was a letter for Camilla, which she carried about and showed to nobody but little George.

No express followed but presently a regretful letter. Harry was off to Egypt 'to ferry our friends the French about the Mediterranean', and to take home the French prisoners Napoleon had abandoned. 'It is a sad disappointment,' he wrote, 'and I am in hopes you will console and divert my daughter as best you may. But, for all my regret, I need the employment for now your sister has grown monstrous fashionable, she has also grown monstrous expensive.'

'When did Emmie become so fashionable?' Elizabeth asked George in bed that night. 'She never used to be. She came into the cottages with me and was a great favourite, and when she and Harry first married and they were very poor; she didn't complain much and wisely made all sorts of peculiar friends. Papa declared he could scarce wait to see who she would bring home next, rat catchers or debt collectors. Mama, I fear, found most of them heavy going.'

'It is scarcely unusual for a middle-aged woman to become absorbed in her social circle. You, my love, are the rarity – a middle-aged woman who is yet lively, frank, and observant,' George complimented her.

'It may be because I see something of the appalling needs and sufferings of the poor,' Elizabeth alluded.

'It may indeed. I fear it is all too common for the rich to ignore the poor,' George agreed.

:

The preliminary articles of peace with France were signed in October, 1801. France kept most of what she'd stolen, Britain scarcely anything. Pitt's former Cabinet colleagues were appalled, but Pitt continued to support Addington. In November, he said in the Commons, 'If we had retained all our conquests it would not have made any difference to us in point of security. They would only give a little more wealth, but a little more wealth would be badly purchased by a little more war.'

Mr Pitt was to dine at Trinity College, Cambridge in December, and he promised to come and stay with Elizabeth and the Bishop at Buckden. This visit, so often proposed, sometimes accepted, but always falling through, was eagerly awaited.

Once it was safe, the English rushed over to France. They were received with reserve, but their money was received with enthusiasm. Général d'Arblay, his wife, and little son proposed to go in spring, and asked Gussie and Jane to go with them. Gussie declined; he was very happy and busy with his parish, and a great favourite with all the ladies up at the castle, but Jane felt she ought to go and take Elodie and Joseph, for Antony's sake. Gussie, who was a very unselfish man, agreed to this but said wistfully, 'You will not be so very long away, I suppose.'

'Not I. A month will have to suffice, for I am sure I shall be mad to be home again. I asked Antony if I should not learn French, but he held there was no point unless I wished, for I should never need it. You can come with us as far as London.'

Mr Pitt duly came to Buckden Palace. George was sure he would not want a large party, but the Duke and Duchess of Rutland came over, and Harry, coming to fetch his daughter at last, happily coincided with Mr Pitt. Harry had returned from the Mediterranean to have his ship paid off because of the peace. 'A year's leave and half-pay will suit very well,' he told them. 'After that we'll have to make some savings and, given our inability in that, at the end of the second year we shall have to remove to some convenient workhouse.'

'Could you not find some temporary employment?' asked Elizabeth.

'I do not despair of it, but for a few months I mean to work hard at being a father,' said Harry.

He and Camilla were inseparable; he went to her school and listened to the brisk but not very enthusiastic remarks of the Headmistress, and the almost enthusiasm of the drawing master. Madame Lebrun thought Camilla should go to one of two artists in London, both French.

Jane and Gussie came over, too, and stayed with Jane's parents.

They arranged for Mr Pitt to go partridge shooting on Mr Warners' farm with Henry Thorold, who lived nearby and brought his pointers. In spite of the cold, they had a good morning's shooting. Mr Pitt very much enjoyed it, and also his dinner with Mr Thorold afterwards. Luckily, there was a moon, so he could drive back without difficulty that evening.

'Mr Thorold told me he had quadrupled the amount of corn he commonly grew since enclosing,' remarked Mr Pitt at dinner next day.

'It's a common cry,' said Jane, 'and true enough, but he probably quadrupled the number of destitute cottagers.'

'I enquired as to that and he was of the opinion there might have been some slight loss of independence, but none of prosperity or employment,' Pitt clarified.

'He is, by all accounts, a good employer,' admitted Elizabeth. 'Yet if a family cannot keep a cow anymore both their health and their choices will deteriorate.'

'He said he had left the common and *panage* as they have immemorially been.'

'They can at least keep pigs if they have *panage* and can feed them in the woods sometimes,' admitted Jane.

'It may be, too, that lower taxes, now that we have peace, will cause prosperity,' said Mr Pitt.

'Hard on you,' said Harry. 'The moment you're out peace and good harvest fall into Mr Addington's lap.'

'It is to be hoped he likes a lap peace and by carefully scratching its tummy will induce it to linger,' said Pitt.

'Is peace a cat or a dog?' said Elizabeth.

'I envisage it as a golden cocker spaniel,' said Mr Pitt, 'silky, and very affectionate, but nervous and apt to vanish in case of unpleasantness.'

'And war is a wolf that comes suddenly and swallows the spaniel,' offered young George.

'Certainly,' agreed Mr Pitt. 'One must beware of wolves and keep the spaniel safe.'

'The Spanish have a saying: "the countryside is for the wolves",' declared the Duke of Rutland. 'Implying that all politics and culture resides in the cities. The English gentry have not, as a rule, noticed it.'

'I, too, have dwelt in Arcady,' said Mr Pitt. 'It was a bit muddy but full of coveys.'

'There is the more time for study, prayers, and contemplation in the country,' said Amabel.

'Many country parsons have produced works of natural history, as with Mr White, or poetry, as with Mr Herrick and Mr Crabbe,' remarked Elizabeth.

'True,' agreed Mr Pitt. 'There was Horace, too, on that point. No parson but yet a farmer and a countryman.'

He quoted a long passage in Latin. When he had finished, the Archdeacon produced an even longer passage, also in Latin, while Gussie, not to be outdone, burst out in Greek.

'We had best talk about flounces,' said the Duchess, 'or what you will, for we shall not understand a word for an age.'

'I will join you then in discussing flounces,' said Harry, 'for my knowledge of them is greater than my knowledge of Horace.'

'What flounce would you like to see with an orange, tawny taffeta gown?' the Duchess asked him.

'Oh, gold lamé without a doubt, unless perchance sky blue might answer,' Harry replied.

'You had better tell us things about sky sails and moon sails, Papa,' Camilla ordered him, 'because you don't really know anything about flounces.'

'Nor do I, to be sure,' said Amabel. 'It is a subject, as with ribbons and lace, I have always carefully avoided. But I think we are allowed to talk about our children, too.'

'You don't know any more about your children than you do about lace,' Jane told Amabel. 'Nor do I about mine. I can only hope they will thrive on benign neglect.'

'I think they will,' said Camilla. 'Because Elodie is always happy and Joseph is always noticing things.'

'I am an ingrate and worse still a noddycock!' cried Mr Pitt. 'Here I am dining with six beautiful ladies and I can find nothing better to do than conjure up the shade of an antique philosopher.'

'Who is the sixth beautiful lady?' asked young George.

'Camilla, of course,' said her father.

'Lots of people have said I was a pretty child but no one ever said I was beautiful. I think George is beautiful,' Camilla piped.

The company surveyed them: Camilla with her curly brown hair and her dark eyes, and George with his shining chestnut hair and his blue-green eyes.

'We tend to call men and boys handsome rather than beautiful,' said Gussie. 'The Greeks, however, often saw boys as beautiful.'

'Beautiful George,' said Ned hoarsely, and laughed.

'You can't get away from the Greeks,' said Harry, 'but Mr Pitt's quite right, as usual – Camilla is beautiful.'

'I hear you are building a new town in the Vale,' said Mr Pitt to Jane. 'What shall you call it? Clodhoppian? Or Tally Ho? Or perhaps just Cheese?'

Jane responded, 'We call it Rutland Gardens. They need good, big gardens for their good, big families. I am glad to see you have jumped off the terrace and vanished in a stream of bubbles.'

'So is Mr Addington. And I am glad to hear you are still squeaking and looking very sleek,' Pitt said in response.

Next day, being again sunny, though cold, George and Mr Pitt went for a stroll. Everything was furred with silver frost and shining in the sun.

'Madame Lebrun is engaged in painting a silver birch seen from the breakfast room window,' said George. 'I am persuaded it is a demanding task.'

Mr Pitt said, 'I had thought it impossible and await the results with great interest. She is vastly talented, and she declared that both Camilla and young George show promise.'

'I hope it may be so. Are you satisfied with Addington's government?' asked George.

'Tolerably so,' Pitt said contentedly. 'He has but little grasp of finance, but he is encouraging manufactory and, above all, as Harry pointed out, has a peace dividend.'

'I am apprehensive that too much unquestioning support may turn out to be a betrayal of our country. Pains have been taken, which indeed still continue, to lower you in the estimation of the public. Your present conduct is just what your enemies wish for, and your friends cannot approve,' George added.

Pitt began to explain, 'Mr Canning is entirely of your opinion but my position is delicate. Addington is an old family friend. I asked him to take on this task. His power is established for this reign at least, and the safety of the country would be hazarded by any attempt to shake him. How well the Palace looks over the lake. I was here once with my father, back in the seventies, and it was a gloomy, ramshackle old place then. Elizabeth has made it so homely.'

'Has she not?' George said in agreement. 'She has a gift for neat, unostentatious comfort; not perhaps of the most orderly, but one can only give one's approbation to what must please visitors, clergy, and family.'

'The air of homeliness amongst antique splendour is augmented by the flowers. How do you achieve that in the winter?' asked Pitt.

'I will show you as we return, but I could wish you had visited us in a kindlier season when the grounds and garden are at their best. We had, I think, better turn back, if we are to be in time for our dinner,' George announced wisely.

'I would not miss one of Elizabeth's marvellous meals for anything. I am a schoolboy again, all appetite. How does my godson at Eton?' asked Pitt.

'His Latin, Greek, and French instructors are pleased with him. His mathematical beak says he lacks both ability and application. I fear he takes after Elizabeth's family in that respect. His tutor says he plays a thoughtful, though lively, part in their debates,' George replied.

'Doubtless, the next Prime Minister but three. I hope I live to see him presiding over half the world, and arrange free schooling for the poor in this country,' remarked Mr Pitt.

The frost had fallen off the trees as the sun grew more powerful. Mr Pitt hoped Madame Lebrun had finished her picture. They went through a gate into the kitchen garden where there were orderly rows of cabbages and cauliflowers. George led Mr Pitt into a large glasshouse where the temperature was very different. Roly Turner was watering. Azaleas, narcissi, daffodils, and plum blossom were just about to come out in large earthenware pots.

'This is Mr Turner, our head gardener, and this Mr Pitt, our Prime Minister,' said George.

Pitt added gently, 'No longer. I was much struck by the flowers in the Palace at this season and enquired as to their appearance. The Bishop kindly offered to show me.'

'Well, sir, December is difficult, an' no mistake, but we had quite a bit o' sun this autumn, and when you got a cold house like this 'n', that's all you need,' Roly replied.

'They call it a cold house,' explained George. 'There is a stove for the nights but on a day like this you rely on the sun.'

'You are to be congratulated. The Palace has become a bower in May,' Pitt said.

'If you get bloom, you get summer,' said Roly. 'That there French lady, she get 'em on canvas beautiful. She give me one o' some tulips and that look right well in our parlour. Everyone remark on it.'

'The Bishop says she is trying to paint the effect of frost on a birch tree. I am eager to see it,' Pitt announced.

'That were pretty early, sir. I wuz right glad I come out last thing and fill up th' stove,' Roly replied.

'I fear we must return,' said George. 'It lacks but a quarter of an hour till dinner.'

CHAPTER TWENTY-SIX
Walmer Castle/France

It seemed rather flat after Mr Pitt had gone, but Elizabeth remembered the tension and exhaustion of this time last year, and was thankful for tedium. Harry took Camilla to Portsmouth for Christmas but promised to bring her back in January. Jane and Gussie came again for Christmas and brought the children. Sophie was very sweet, but she would not sleep and her nurse looked exhausted. Molly was able to help advise and, when all else failed, took a turn walking about with the child.

Elizabeth gave a small dance for the young. Amabel's daughter, Eliza, obligingly asked five of her girlfriends, so they stood up: seven couples. Madame Lebrun gave the Pretyman boys, Joseph, and Elodie dancing lessons, exclaiming over Elodie's grace and the boys' clumsiness. The party, though, passed off well, and so did Christmas.

Mr Canning wrote in the New Year about Pitt's continuing support for Addington's government; 'bland obedience and self-abasement… yet this is the mind that governed the world.'

In April, 1802, Addington produced his first budget. Among other things, it abolished income tax.

'Are you satisfied with Mr Addington's budget?' George asked Mr Pitt when he and others were dining at Walmer Castle.

'Sufficiently, for I devised most of it. The wells are dry and we must let them fill up before we can do more.'

'I fear I cannot follow you,' said Mr Rose, who was also present. 'The long war and high taxes consequent have quite emptied our coffers.'

'I am sure we are all quite penniless,' agreed Mrs Rose. 'There is never enough money, and silk grows dear.'

'I have been penniless for an age,' said Lady Hester, another guest. 'It saves one from buying things you don't really need that may prove encumbrances.'

'The wells are dry,' repeated Mr Pitt. 'Not only of money, but, above all, of gold, and without gold we have but little influence on the Continent.'

Mr Pitt, George, and Lady Hester looked out over the grey sea to the sinister, dark, grey land.

'O' pray heaven, there will never be another war!' exclaimed Mrs Rose, shivering. 'I could not bear it. Wars are so lowering. We always lose.'

'Not at sea,' said Mr Pitt, looking out over that wondrous element supporting a frigate that was running towards the German Ocean, or North Sea, as some called it.

'No, not at sea, I grant you,' said Mrs Rose, 'and I suppose it keeps us safe. But it does nothing to stop that tyrant rampaging about.'

'We are fortunate that it affects us but little,' said Lady Hester, 'and General Moore here will soon put a stop on his rampages, will you not?'

General Moore, a good looking, not very young man who was stationed nearby, replied composedly, 'The English soldier, if properly trained, led, fed, and equipped, will prove to be the equal of any in the world.'

'Well, but where are you going to find those who can do all that?' enquired Mrs Rose. 'Most of the officers I know are amiable idiots.'

'I must admit the purchase system does not commonly result in earnest, hardworking, young officers, but I do not require them. I find most of the young subalterns, who Mrs Rose so accurately describes, will make reliable officers, if they are sufficiently coaxed and cursed for a few years.'

'But is anybody doing all that?' persisted Mrs Rose doubtfully.

'In a good regiment everyone is doing that, and there are many good regiments. Moreover, we have the advantage of some splendid men, tradesmen's sons, for the most part, often Methodists, who make admirable sergeants,' General Moore said.

'You reassure me,' said Mr Pitt. 'In what proportion of regiments is this improvement in force?'

'Perhaps half. There are many zealous young officers who have studied the campaigns of Napoleon, and the Archduke Charles, and will profit from them,' General Moore answered.

'You do not expect a long peace, then?' enquired Lady Hester.

'I hope for it, but I do not expect it. The insatiable nature of Napoleon Bonaparte makes me judge he will never be satisfied and must be stopped,' Mr Pitt stated.

'Oh dear,' said Mrs Rose.

In May, Canning got up a dinner at the Merchant Taylors' Hall to celebrate Mr Pitt's forty-third birthday. Mr Pitt would not come. He was embarrassed by the notion and tried mildly to discourage it. But a thousand people did come, and many more tried to but couldn't get tickets. The affair ended with the singing of a new song composed by Mr Canning:

And shall we not his memory hold dear,
Whose example with envy all nations behold?
A statesman unbiased by interest or fear;
By power uncorrupted, untainted by gold.
And O' if again the rude whirlwind should rise,
The dawning of peace should fresh darkness deform,
The hopes of the good and the fears of the wise,
Shall turn to the pilot who weathered the storm

Gussie, Jane, Elodie, and Joseph went to London in late May, as Jane and the children made their way to France. They stayed with Gussie's parents in Mayfair. His father was old and frail, but his mother was a kind, sensible woman, only regretting they had not brought her grand-daughter Sophia.

'If we had, you'd have wished her away,' said Jane. 'She won't sleep.'

'She is a spirited child and finds slumber does not come easily,' explained Gussie. 'I recollect your telling me I was the same.'

'It is all too true,' agreed his mother. 'Your nurse and nurse girls took it in turns to sit up half the night with you. My other children were much quieter and not so given to singing and dancing.'

Jane took her children to see Mr Newton, who had helped her so much when Antony died. A young woman showed them in with the unconventional introduction of 'More people!'

'People are my trade,' Newton said, 'but I grow so blind I can no longer recognise them. I am afraid you will have to tell me who you are. I remember you very well. I am glad you have married again and to meet your children. Your new husband is not here?'

'He wished to go to Evensong at Westminster Abbey,' said Jane truthfully. She did not say that Gussie had declared, 'I hear he's a worthy man but I am not enamoured of those gloomy, garrulous evangelists.' She had pointed out forcibly that John Newton was neither gloomy nor garrulous and that Mr Pitt very much admired him.

'I wish I was with him,' said Mr Newton. 'The singing lifts you to a better view of the world.'

The young woman who had shown them in, and whose cap was on back to front, left them abruptly.

'My niece, Eliza,' Newton continued, 'she looks after me, oh so devotedly, but she is subject to depressions and this is one of her bad times when I cannot get through to her and nor can the Lord. Do you stay long in London?'

Jane explained the arrangements.

Newton responded positively to the news, 'You do very well to take the children to their father's country. They will enjoy it. Do you fear danger?'

'Yes,' said Jane, realising for the first time that she did.

'There has been evil in France and I fear it lingers. My head tells me you will be safe enough but my heart says otherwise. If we prove right, remember the class that showed itself closest to God were the country people. You may rely on them, or most of them, and a good curé will always be able to advise you who to trust. You are fortunately young enough to disregard a little discomfort,' Newton explained.

'Mama says you were a slaver,' asked Joseph. 'Is it really true?'

'Is it really polite to ask?' put in Jane.

'No,' answered Elodie, 'but it is interesting.'

'I fear it is all too true,' replied Mr Newton. 'I was very far gone in sin and selfishness. How far, I did not realise until I began to travel back, showing us, as I often preach, that anyone can come back. But I realise now, as I should have done then, the appalling things I did to helpless Africans.'

'They do it to each other, too,' pointed out Jane.

'Very true, but no excuse. You two, Elodie and Joseph, will have the opportunity to fight slavery, and you have the opportunity, as few do, to value both the Catholic and Protestant religions,' Newton said thoughtfully.

'Will you give us your blessing?' asked Joseph.

'Gladly,' Newton said.

When Jane said it was more than time, they went. Mr Newton said, 'Perhaps you will be so good as to see yourselves out. I hope Eliza is sleeping. She sleeps but little at night.'

They agreed the preacher was a wise and fascinating man.

:

Gussie came with them as far as Dover looking more and more like a spaniel whose mistress was packing. The Général announced that he was an excellent sailor. The others didn't know because they hadn't sailed before. Jane looked apprehensively at the white water. It was blue really, but there was a strong breeze, and with all the white horses she seemed only to see silver. The d'Arblays had brought their son Alexander who was Elodie's age, eight, and the children were already firm friends and wildly excited. Jane, as she had expected, was very sick indeed. So was Fanny, but not as badly as Jane. Her maid, Clara, was every bit as bad. The Général had got them a cabin, but it was a sordid scene. The Général disappeared after showing them to their quarters. The children ran in and out and were very good about emptying and washing bowls. They were in no way affected, and when not being helpful, were apparently playing highwaymen all over the ship.

The voyage took over three hours with a very strong headwind, but it seemed longer to the suffering women. The Général installed them in a good hotel in Calais, and Jane and Fanny immediately went to bed. The Général promised to look after the children and took them on a tour of the town, which they enjoyed very much, the more so as their French worked, though some shopkeepers and waiters remarked on their accent.

'It is in fact the accent of Paris,' the Général explained, 'and therefore much the best, but the people here speak in an unendurable northern patois.'

They had a good dinner, but Jane and Fanny did not eat much. The others made up for it, and Elodie, having asked for another strawberry ice cream, received it from a smiling waiter with a polite 'Bon appétit, mademoiselle!' and she exclaimed, 'I like France!'

They agreed an open carriage would be the best in this hot weather, so the efficient Général hired one, complete with driver, and the next morning they were soon bowling along, under the shade of a fringe, admiring the countryside. The driver, a cheerful youth called René, chattered away to the children when he found they spoke

French. After a pause, Joseph said something and Elodie obligingly translated for her mother. 'He said there are very few men working in the fields.' This remark prompted a burst of animated speech from René.

'He says it is true, it is indeed true, all the young men have been taken to fight. They are chasing glory and France is setting the world free, but they do not eat as well as they used to.'

The roads were very good and the Général said he had been told Napoleon had turned his attention to them, and to the canals, and made sure they were both improved.

In Paris, they stayed in a comfortable hotel. Everything was very grand and stylish, though Fanny said it was not very clean. She told them the story of a Frenchman who had escaped to Brighton, ill and shattered by what he had seen. He'd gone to a hotel and woken in the night with a high fever, and the conviction that he was in a French prison and must escape before they took him to be guillotined. He struggled about with a candle, trying to get out, and at last found himself in the kitchen, 'which,' he had said, 'brought him to his senses in an instant, for no French kitchen was ever as clean.'

The Général's friends and relations were delighted to have him back, and they dined out a lot. It was oppressively hot, and when one of the Général's cousins asked them all to come down to the country with him and his wife, they agreed enthusiastically.

Two days before they left Paris, the Général, Fanny, and Jane were asked to a dinner party with the son of one of the Général's old friends. 'He has some job in the government,' explained the Général. 'It must be a good job, for it is a very good address. His father and I were close once, but he drove on like so many, and became a Jacobin, while I remained moderate. He was guillotined for his pains. I will not say it served him right, for it would hardly be a very Christian sentiment, but I restrain myself with difficulty.'

It was a large, sumptuous house, and large, sumptuous party. Jane stayed with the d'Arblays while they drank champagne before dinner. Several men and one couple came up to the Général. He introduced them to one of the men. Fanny's French was slow and painstaking but fairly fluent. Jane kept quiet. A good-looking man claimed her just after dinner was announced. 'I am to take you in,' he said, 'because my

English is of the most elegant. I am overcome by the privilege and I only fear I shall forget my English for the cause that it is so long ago since I have spoken it.'

He turned out to be diplomat called Duvet who had spent a year in London before the war. On her other side, Jane had the Général, so she thought herself very well off and blessed her hostess's tact.

'One will never believe,' said Monsieur Duvet, 'when I declare English women are often most beautiful. But I am sure all who see you tonight will be persuaded of it. Such a complexion!'

'Rather weather-beaten, I'm afraid,' Jane proclaimed.

'But how? Why? You do not betray it,' asked Duvet.

'I ride, hunt, and walk, and take soup to old ladies,' revealed Jane.

Looking a little perplexed, Duvet asked, 'For what purpose? Are you a nun, then?'

'No, I am married to a clergyman,' Jane replied.

'Ma foi. This clergyman, he is here?' Duvet asked expectantly.

'No, he would not desert his parish. But before I married him I was married to a Frenchman who was killed at Quiberon and so I have two half-French children, and thought I should take the opportunity to show them something of their father's country.'

'This émigré, may one ask his name?'

'He was the Marquis de Chavaise,' disclosed Jane.

'Ma foi! This is dangerous, even now. It was better not speak of it. I tell you...' Duvet answered in consternation.

Here, a tall man the other side interrupted them, and said to Jane, 'I am told you know Mr Pitt.'

Jane replied, 'Well, yes. Not to say know perhaps, but my husband was chaplain to a bishop who was Mr Pitt's tutor at Cambridge and is still his friend. I have sometimes been in company with Mr Pitt.'

'I should have sought out this bishop. Two heretical bishops might have dealt well together. How would you describe Mr Pitt?' asked the tall man.

'He's fun,' Jane answered.

'Fun? Sacré bleu! Fun, she says! I went to Mr Pitt with my elegant, fluid plans and what did he do, this so funny young man? He froze me and my plans like a New York winter. Oh, he was the most polite, but one would find more give in a glacier.'

'They tell me he is like that with strangers. He is a very shy man, but with a small party of his friends he is playful, lively, with a gift for fantasy,' Jane tried to explain.

'Give me, I beg, some examples of this gift,' the man asked.

'Well, he had a silly joke with me that I was a mouse and he was an otter, so when I saw him not long since I said, "I am glad to see you have jumped off the terrace of the House of Commons and vanished in a string of bubbles", and he said, "So is Mr Addington".'

The tall man smiled. 'There is a quickness there of a certain. What else?'

'One of the company said that the peace had fallen into Mr Addington's lap and Mr Pitt said, "It is to be hoped he likes a lap peace and scratches its chest and induces it to linger". So a duchess, one of the company, asked, "Is the peace a cat or a dog?" And Mr Pitt said, "I see it is as a golden cocker spaniel – silky and very affectionate, but nervous and apt to vanish in case of unpleasantness".'

'I, too, would wish to pamper this spaniel,' the man declared.

'Yes,' said Jane, 'but I think…'

'What do you think?' said the tall man gently, seeming to almost draw it out of her.

'If you give a man masses and masses of soldiers he's going to play with them,' Jane said philosophically.

The tall man's face was impenetrable. 'Give me, I pray, another example of Mr Pitt's humour.'

Jane told them the story of the bird. There were exclamations of amazement.

'The English are capable of relaxing,' said the Général. 'But, perhaps, because of this, they are also capable of great exertions.'

'I thank you,' said the tall man. 'You give me more of an idea of Mr Pitt's mind.'

The conversation became more general again.

'He approved of you,' said Jane's left-hand neighbour. 'He likes one who stands up to him.'

'Who is he?' enquired Jane.

'Monsieur de Talleyrand,' was the response.

Jane got no more out of her left-hand neighbour except compliments. 'I am sure they all, or nearly all, knew something we don't know,' she said on the way home.

'Are you?' replied the Général. 'I will try to discover it, then. But you were the success of the evening. Monsieur de Périgord was lost in admiration.'

'I thought my neighbour, whose name I never really caught, said he was Talleyrand,' Jane asked.

The Général continued, 'It is much the same. Talleyrand du Périgord, a very old family. Before the revolution we mostly called him Périgord. He was also the Bishop of Autun.'

'How very odd. Did he just stop being a bishop?' Jane enquired thoughtfully.

'You could say that. His heart, I think, was never in it. His family desired it because he had a club foot. He is now Napoleon's Foreign Minister,' the Général continued.

'Lawks! Did he mind what I said about Napoleon?' Jane said more worriedly.

'I suspect he entirely agreed but was far too discreet and ambitious to say so,' the Général alluded.

Fanny, Jane, and the children had been shopping. Much to Fanny's and the shop people's surprise, Jane wouldn't buy anything but one very pretty and fairly cheap scarf. She feared she might need all their money. The children were delighted with a trifle each, a pendant for Elodie, and a picture book for Joseph. Fanny bought some shoes with gilt buckles, a necklace of Venetian glass, another picture book for Alexander, a cravat for the Général, and a grey silk dress for herself.

'No wonder it suits her so well,' thought Jane. 'She's just like a little pouter pigeon.'

'All Paris is talking about you, Jane,' said the Général when they were drinking iced lemonade before dinner, 'and what you said to Talleyrand. Most laugh, but others are more likely to cry, for they think it is all too true. I do not doubt it has got back to Napoleon, by now. If only it returns to his redoubtable mother, she might read him a lecture. She is very shrewd and he listens to her.'

'It's just as well they don't know about me,' said Fanny.

She had been a lady-in-waiting to Queen Charlotte and could have told Talleyrand quite a bit about the King.

'Indeed, my love. I thought that, too. Fortunately, the French are not in the main very interested in the English, or anyone, but themselves. I went to the Duke of Gramont, and he told me in confidence that they have given poor Antoine's lands, or most of them, to Fouché.'

'Heavens!' gasped Fanny.

'Indeed. Had I known I would not have brought Jane and the children. We must consider, but there is more…'

'Who is Fouché?' enquired Jane.

'I forget what silly titles they give him now. I paid no heed. But he is Napoleon's Chief of the Secret Police, and a very dangerous man. You were correct, Jane, when you sensed they all knew something we did not know. It was that. Talleyrand has sent you a note, by way of the Duke. He has not, of course, opened it, nor have I.'

The note had written on it: 'To the fair and eloquent *unknown*'. Jane opened it. It read:

Beautiful know-it-all,

I thank you again for your honest account of Mr Pitt's playfulness and love of peace, which is rare. As your admirer and debtor, I would wish you to know that Fouché has your first husband's lands, and may decide to dispose of all other heirs. Be very careful. Go home soon.
If I can ever serve you, I will do so.

Your devoted servant, who has never met anyone like you and only hopes he may meet you again one day

There was no signature. Jane handed the note to the Général, and then Fanny. 'This is terrible,' said the Général. 'Do you want to go straight back to Calais tomorrow? I can arrange an escort, I am sure.'

Jane replied cautiously, 'No-o, I don't think so. It's just what this man will expect. I think we'd be safer to come on with you to your cousin's house, and then, quite soon, go home quietly by a cross-country route.'

The Général replied, 'As you will. My cousin is old and scholarly and not very well. I think I shall not tell him or his wife. But my younger cousin, if he can get away – he's a soldier – is just the man to consult. He will help us.'

'Is it not rather unscrupulous to accept your cousin's hospitality without warning him we may be dangerous?' wondered Jane.

'I fear it is a little, but I still think it better not to disturb him and hope we never need to. He is subject to sudden heart seizures,' the Général told Jane.

:

They had another pleasant journey in an open carriage. The château was gorgeous. Not so very large, but comfortable and moated, with flourishing, formal gardens. Their hosts, the Comte and Comtesse de Beauvais, welcomed them, the children were sent off to nurseries and their elders sat down to dinner. The Comte de Beauvais, was tall and bent. He spoke good English because he had been in exile in England for fifteen years. His wife was a small, decisive woman, very well dressed and still very good-looking. They were expecting their son Henri anytime now, and they had three more sons who were with the army in Italy. The Général told them what Jane had said to Talleyrand and they both laughed heartily. 'That is indeed the danger,' the Comte laughed. 'But I think his other Counsels, and his talent for administration, and his beautiful wife will restrain Bonaparte in time.'

'He is a very great man,' said the Comtesse, 'but impetuous, like all Corsicans. His ideas are good, but he does not prepare sufficiently. To capture Egypt and then India, excellent, but one must have allies and, above all, one must not annoy the Grand Turk.'

'He should have consulted you, my dear. Do you two intend to stay in France?' said the Comte to the Général and his wife.

'It will depend,' replied the Général, 'on how well my wife likes the country and whether I can secure employment.'

'Then we must hope she is entirely content here and we can find you a pleasant occupation. Do your wife's so celebrated books make money?' asked the Comte.

'A little,' said Fanny, 'but they are not so celebrated as they used to be. When I wrote *Evelina* I was all the crack for a while.'

'I have read it,' declared the Comtesse. 'A good plot: the adventures and misadventures of an innocent young girl in good society.'

'Dr Johnson thought highly of it,' said the Général proudly.

'You knew him?' the Comte asked Fanny eagerly.

'Very well,' she replied.

'You must tell me all about him. For me he is a supreme example of English good sense. Also—'

'Tomorrow,' interrupted the Comtesse. 'She is tired from her journey. Tomorrow, if you sleep well, she shall tell you everything about the so-sensible Doctor.'

They went to bed early and Jane, after the oppressive heat of Paris, slept well in the lovely, breezy bedroom. The next morning they had breakfast, at which their hosts did not appear, and later Jane ran races with her children and Alexander on the grass walks between the yew hedges.

'Brava! What a pretty sight! The mother is victorious!' said a young man coming out just ahead of them through a gap in the hedge.

'I won't be much longer. Are you Henri?' asked Jane.

'I am Henri, and I am enchanted to find a pretty guest waiting for me,' the man replied.

'You won't be when you hear the trouble I'm in,' Jane said.

'He was not so very young,' she thought, 'a bit worn-looking, but trim and impressive in that magnificent uniform.'

'On the contrary, there are few tasks I relish more than helping damsels in distress. The Général has briefed me, and we must consider. Would the children perhaps like it if we all went to the *potager* and ate strawberries and raspberries,' Henri said.

'Yes,' returned Alexander.

'That would be delightful, Monsieur,' exclaimed Elodie.

'You have a very well-mannered daughter. Pretty, too. How old is she?' asked the Comte.

'Eight and her name is Elodie, after an aunt who walked over the mountains to Spain to escape with her family,' Jane informed him.

'Ah, we are a widespread lot, we aristos. We were some of the first to come back. Before that we served with the Austrians, we boys. Here we are. I will pull back the nets for you,' said Henri.

A good time was had, particularly by the children.

'However did you get your beautiful château back?' Jane later asked Henri.

'It was stolen by an associate of Marat, and when the Jacobins fell, my father negotiated with the Embassy in London. We would return and his four sons would serve France in her armies if we could have our château and some of our land back,' he replied.

'I see. Are you the eldest?'

'Alas, no. He is already married with sons, but he is a good fellow and will make room for me, I am sure, unless I marry an heiress with estates of her own.'

'Is it true that the peasants have most of the land now?'

'Most? I do not know. I do not think so. But they got some and that I think is good. Another of the few good things the Revolution did was to free the slaves, but, alas, the Directoire have locked them up again. They say you cannot run the sugar islands without them, and the sugar islands, you must know, are very valuable, very lucrative.'

'We kept taking them off you,' said Jane.

'You did, didn't you?' agreed Henri, 'but now you have given them all back, as is most proper. I think perhaps we had best go in. My parents like to drink and talk a little before their dinner.'

'We shall have no appetite.'

'The children need not eat, if they do not wish. My old nurse is indulgent. But you and I must make pretence.'

After lunch, Henri rode off to a nearby barracks where he had a friend who might be able to provide an escort to the coast for Jane and her children. At lunch, Fanny was able to tell her host a great deal about Dr Johnson. He was enraptured and took notes, declaring he should read a paper on it to the Académie Française. Then Jane, her children, and Alexander swam in the moat in a curious assortment of petticoats and underpants. Their host had said no one would see them there. It was heavenly. The air was full of butterflies and dragonflies, as well as beautiful birds. The water was warm and the air hot. Water lilies grew in the moat and roses poured down the walls of the house. Elodie and Joseph found they could swim a little, and better all the time. Alexander was not so bold but Jane found a shallow place where he could walk, sit down, and splash. Henri was back by dinner, hot, tired and cross. His friend had been away on leave and the other officers had been uncooperative.

'One forgets, living with civilised people,' he said, 'the vulgar prejudices against the English.'

'Considering they've just been fighting us for years and years,' said Jane, 'I wouldn't call it vulgar prejudice. I call it natural enough.'

'Henri is correct, my dear young lady,' said his father. 'Civilized people do not feel so. We are all at the mercy of events and governments, but if we are educated and well-informed, we do not blame our neighbours for what they cannot help.'

'The English are often coarse, stupid, and drunken,' said the Comtesse, 'but at root they are not commonly spiteful, as the French all too often are.'

After dinner they strolled about a bit in the gardens and Henri flirted with Jane.

'I cannot believe you have three children,' he said. 'You look twenty. No seventeen. Your husband is a very lucky man. Does he know it?'

Jane replied happily, 'He finds me a bit wild sometimes. He thinks I hunt too much and languish too little, but otherwise he seems satisfied.'

'I should hope so. I think he neglects you. Otherwise he would be here, guarding you,' Henri suggested.

'He has his duties, although perhaps he sings and acts too much, as I hunt too much. He is quite a conscientious priest, and we both build schools, hospitals, and cottages,' replied Jane.

'My mother, too, indulged in charities, and begins to do so again. She misses the nuns. Tomorrow is Sunday and the Curé is coming. Shall you accompany us to Mass, little heretic?' Henri asked playfully.

'Why not?' Jane agreed. 'My church has no silly law forbidding it. Those irises are really magnificent.'

'As blue as your eyes; one kiss between enemies?' Henri asked.

'I think we would be wiser not to,' Jane retorted.

'I am sure we would be wiser not to, but we shall be old and wise for a long time, God willing. Now we are young,' Henri suggested philosophically.

'Well, fairly young,' Jane reminded him.

'Young and a little in love! Shall we waste it?' Henri continued.

Jane let him kiss her but then pulled away. 'I must go back. What will your parents think?' Jane said.

'My mother will frown and fear you will entrap me. My father will smile and envy me,' Henri replied.

:

That night Jane was blissfully asleep, naked under a linen sheet, when she was woken by a child screaming. She lit a candle, despite the flint and steel seeming very slow to catch, threw on a nightdress, and ran barefoot to Elodie's room. She opened the door and bumped into her daughter, who was still screaming. Putting the candle down on a chest, she hugged her. Elodie stopped screaming and began to sob.

'Joseph?' Jane asked, for Elodie had told Jane yesterday she'd been frightened, and so he'd come and slept with her until it was light. To her immense relief a little voice answered, 'Yes, Mama. I'm in the corner. There was a man.'

Joseph came out of the space between a big wardrobe and the wall.

'A horrid, beastly, ugly man,' sobbed Elodie, 'with a light in his head.'

'He was wearing a hat with a light in it,' corrected Joseph, 'so I said ran and Elodie ran to the door.'

'What happened?' asked Henri, coming in with a naked sword. He was wearing a long cloak, with, Jane fancied, nothing underneath.

They told him, and he said, 'I had two men watching outside. But they'll never catch him. He's a professional and he'll have a horse tethered somewhere. Tell me exactly what happened, Joseph.'

Before he could, the old nurse appeared, fully dressed and coiffed, questioning and exclaiming. By the time Henri had quieted her, the butler arrived, followed by the Comte and the Comtesse in wraps, and two maids in petticoats. Henri sent the servants away with a few words of explanation.

'A robber?' asked his mother, 'but why should a robber climb upstairs?'

'I fear it was an assassin, but I did not want the servants to know. Sit down comfortably, Papa, while I light a few more candles, and then Joseph after Elodie shall tell us exactly what happened.'

'But why should anyone want to kill the children?' asked the Comtesse.

'Fouché has been given their lands,' Jane revealed.

'You knew this, and came here endangering us all?' the Comtesse questioned.

'I wanted to tell you but Henri and the Général said it would be better not to,' Jane explained.

The Comtesse said something in French which it was fortunate that Jane did not understand.

'Mama, I am sorry. I did it for the best. I thought we had more time,' Henri interjected.

'Let the children speak,' ordered the Comte.

Henri agreed, 'Indeed. My father is wise as ever. What happened, Joseph?'

Jospeh began telling the story. 'Elodie's screaming woke me, and I looked and saw a man climbing in through the window with a light in his hat and something that shone in his hand. So I said "Run!" to Elodie and she did but she couldn't get the door open. The man was between me and the door, but a voice in my brain said, "hide in the corner", so I went and hid, and he went up to the bed and hit it, and then he turned round and went out of the window again, and then Mama came in.'

'Thank you, Joseph, a very clear account. This light in the man's hat, was it a candle?' asked Henri.

'No. It sort of shone but I don't think it was fire.'

'Now you, Elodie,' Henri asked, turning to the girl.

Elodie gave her account. 'Something woke me. I think it was a noise, and there was this huge man coming through the window, so I screamed and Joseph said run, so I ran, but I couldn't get the latch up. It needs both hands and I was so frightened I forgot. And then Mama came and the man was gone.'

'Another good, clear report. How I wish I had you two to train my officers! Now, for the rest of the night you will, I think, be best with your mother. I will arrange for a truckle bed for Joseph. You are quite safe now. The man will not come back tonight. The good Lord and your own good wits preserved you.'

'We will dedicate tomorrow's Mass to thanksgiving,' said the Comtesse. 'Are you all right, my love?'

'I am in excellent health, thank you, but I think I will go back to bed now. Alas, for my unhappy country,' Jane replied.

There was a tap on the door and a young man came in, fully dressed. Henri asked him a question and he answered volubly.

'He says he saw the man climbing down and swimming the moat,' Elodie told her mother. 'So he called his friend and they gave chase, and they were just catching up with him when they came to the road. The man had a horse tied there and he jumped on to it and rode off very fast.'

Henri spoke. 'He says it was just as well he didn't catch up because the bad man had a knife. This man says so and he threw it after him and he is sure he hit him. Monsieur le Comte says he did very well.'

The next morning they were all rather tired. The priest came to lunch. He was small and slight, with amazing blue eyes, and a brown face. They spoke in French for his benefit and Jane understood nothing. Once he asked first Elodie and then Joseph a question, and then listened carefully to their answers.

'The clever Father has in mind to arrange to send the children to Boulogne by canal,' Henri told Jane. 'Canal boats are examined, but not nearly so often or carefully as coaches. Then tomorrow, my father and I take you to Boulogne to meet the children, and you go home on a fishing boat.'

'But if our coach will be examined…?' Jane began.

'It will but you impersonate the Comtesse. She has a perfectly hideous bonnet that was fashionable the year before last. It will not become you but to save your life you will perhaps endure it,' Henri reassured Jane.

'Henri, you are impertinent. My bonnet is not perfectly hideous. It is stylish. Above all, it is concealing, which is what is required,' the Comtesse added.

Elodie translated the conversation to the Curé, who chuckled happily afterwards and thanked her.

'Your life is not in danger,' said the Général. 'Even the person whose name we will not speak would think twice before killing a British citizen without provocation.'

'I am enchanted to hear I shall survive my children!' Jane retorted.

In the afternoon, they all slept. Before dinner, the Curé came back. A reliable bargee and his wife were to take the children. He usually took his own children but on this occasion he would leave the two youngest behind with his mother.

'You must not speak English,' Jane told her children.

'No, Mama,' said Elodie.

'I will try very hard to remember,' said Joseph.

'And you must be obedient and helpful,' Jane added.

'I want to go canalling, too,' bawled Alexander. 'Please! Please! Let me go, too!'

Elodie translated for the Curé.

'Why not?' he replied in French. 'If Madame, his mother, does not object.'

'I…no,' said Fanny. 'I never coddle my ram lamb.'

'She is a good mother,' the Général told them. 'Very unselfish.'

'I'll just run and get a night bag for him,' said Fanny and trotted off.

They were sitting in the garden surrounded by scented flowers and singing birds.

The Curé spoke.

'He says,' interrupted Elodie, 'the bargee, whose name is Gaston, is dependable, and his wife, Annette, is dependable and a good cook.'

'Tell him that as I trust him,' said Jane, 'so too I trust this Gaston and Annette.'

The Curé spoke again.

'He says the English courage is, as he has heard, of the most formidable,' Elodie kindly translated again.

Jane replied, 'Tell him we must trust each other and we must trust God.'

Elodie did so, and the Curé nodded eagerly and spoke volubly.

'He says when Joseph heard a voice in his brain – that it was his guardian angel,' Elodie explained.

'Without doubt,' agreed the Comtesse.

'I thought that,' said Jane, 'or perhaps his father's spirit. His father was killed at Quiberon.'

All the French motioned the sign of the cross over themselves.

'How much should I give this bargee?' asked Jane.

'He says he is glad you asked,' said Elodie. 'For Gaston and Annette and their son, Jean, risk their lives. Two gold pieces would seem like a fortune to them.'

Fanny came puffing back. 'Was I not quick? But he won't need much.'

The children kissed their parents. Elodie and Joseph thanked the Comte and Comtesse, and left with the Curé, skipping, and exclaiming around him.

Fanny and Jane looked at one another.

CHAPTER TWENTY-SEVEN

France/Woolsthorpe

The Curé came back again towards the end of dinner, ate some of the strawberries, and told them the children had glided off happily. 'He also says,' translated Henri, 'the whole district is in a ferment of horror and indignation about last night's attempt, and all declare they are not of the party of Fouché. Some of them, of course, are lying.'

'I presume,' said Jane, 'as we worshipped in a barn, that they have stolen your church.'

'Truly,' replied Henri. 'It is now a foundry and the bells are now cannons.'

'I do not feel you are fighting for a true Christian,' Jane confessed.

Henri shrugged. 'I have a long spoon.'

'When I am being seasick, and you are returning from this jaunt, how will you account for the disappearance of your "mother"?' queried Jane.

The men looked at one another in horror.

'Mon dieu!' exclaimed the Comte.

'We never thought of that,' admitted the Général.

'We could find a girl in Boulogne,' suggested Henri. 'Say we needed a maid.'

'Or better,' said the Comte, 'my maid Amélie goes to Boulogne by the stage and comes back with you. We copy her papers, and Jane takes the real ones. They are of a size. It should work.'

She translated rapidly for the Curé who nodded and said something.

'He says he has become, of necessity, good at forgery,' Henri told Jane.

Later that evening, Henri and the romantic garden resumed their attempts at Jane's virtue.

'Who will ever know?' pleaded Henri.

'I will and I like to keep my word,' Jane said.

'I honour you for it, but, as we have discovered, the world is very dangerous and unpleasant. Can we not take a little pleasure among our struggles and our sufferings?' Henri continued.

'You can,' Jane told him. 'It agrees with your nature and nationality, and your trade, but if I did it, I should have much less courage for tomorrow and for the journey.'

'I do not see why. I should have thought the reverse was true. However, I will not plead anymore in case it is true, for I would not risk making your danger greater. If only we had met in London after your husband was killed,' Henri imagined.

'If wishes were horses then beggars would ride. I am going to bed,' Jane replied firmly.

'One more kiss,' asked Henri.

:

The journey was amazingly easy. They were stopped twice, but the soldiers were polite and friendly.

'That is just one of the blessings Bonaparte has brought,' Henri told them as they went on after the second time. 'Before, in the Revolution, the officials were rude, suspicious, and greedy. A man might spend fifty livres and risk his life travelling ten miles. Now, they employ soldiers who are civil and quite satisfied with a small tip, or even none from the poor.'

Boulogne was very busy, but at last they got to the docks and drove along them slowly looking for barges.

'There!' cried Fanny. And there indeed was her son, standing on the roof of the barge, smiling and waving. He was soon joined by his mother and Jane.

Everyone was beaming and trying to describe what a wonderful time they'd had. Gaston, a tough, dark, little man, said they were good children; Annette, buxom and cheerful, said they were little angels. Gaston was reluctant to take the money but Jane insisted. He had already found a fisherman who was willing to take them but he wanted fifty gold coins. It was exorbitant. It was ridiculous! But he said he risked his life. 'I expect I can get him to come down quite a bit,' said Henri, as they walked along the quay. 'How much have you got?'

'Fifty-three,' answered Jane.

'Can you get money soon when you land?' Henri asked further.

'I shouldn't think so. Mr Pitt will lend me some and he's not very far away, if he's at home in Walmer Castle. But we have to get there,' Jane explained.

'I will lend you some money,' Henri said.

'How will I get it back to you?' Jane wondered.

'We'll think of something,' he returned.

The fisherman, Jean, was scrawny, grim, and very weather-beaten. There was a furious argument between him and Henri. Elodie whispered once, 'He says they do not risk their lives for nothing, he and his son.' Finally some sort of bargain was struck and the fisherman's son, Louis, ran to leave the money with his mother.

Jane thought the fishing boat looked poky and smelly. 'We might meet a British ship,' she said hopefully.

'I said that,' agreed Henri, 'and he admitted he often did and sold fish to them.'

Fanny, who was crying, passed some smelling salts into Jane's hand. The Comte said she must be like the dauntless men who sailed to Canada. The Comtesse taught her the French for chamber pot. The Général said he had observed how resourceful she was, and that he did not greatly fear for her. He also offered money but Jane refused it.

Henri gave her a kiss and ten gold coins and, 'a fact to steel you for the sea: we found a slash deep into the bed, both in the children's room and in Joseph's room.'

In no time they were sailing out with the children waving to the disconsolate Alexander. Jean said they must get into the cabin until they were out of sight. The cabin was tiny, with one pallet and two stools, and it smelt fusty. Jane was sure she'd be dreadfully sick if she had to stay long inside.

The sounds of the town faded away; the water sounds grew louder. Elodie peered out of one of the little portholes. 'I can see nothing but sea and rocks. Joseph said, peering out of another, 'I can see a cow.'

'Thank you, thank you Mama, for taking us to France. I really loved it, and the canal was best of all. Gaston let us stop and swim. Annette cooked us a divine omelette, and Phillippe showed us how to dive, in return I taught him some English words.'

'I liked the château best,' said Joseph. 'It was so beautiful and it smelled so good. Shall we go back one day?'

'If Fouché dies or falls from power, certainly. I liked it, too. I was surprised how much I liked it. What is the time?' Jane asked.

Joseph produced his pocket watch, which his stepfather had given him for Christmas last. 'Eight o'clock, and I had not thought it so late. Shall we have some of the food the Comtesse sent?'

'You can,' said Jane, beginning to unpack it. 'I daren't.'

'Are you feeling ill, Mama?' asked Elodie.

'No,' said Jane. 'But I shall.'

In fact the movement was slight and still quite pleasant but the cabin was so stuffy. She longed to go on deck. Half an hour later, Louis said they could, though they must go down again if a boat came close. It was deliciously cool on deck. They sat on a thwart, a seat that ran round both sides.

'Voilà l'Angleterre,' said Louis, pointing to a grey bank on the northern horizon.

'There is England,' translated Elodie.

Jane thought she'd never seen anything so beautiful, but it was still a long way off, and France was still much nearer.

'Ask him when we shall arrive,' she said.

'He says about five tomorrow morning if the wind holds, but it is dropping,' Elodie translated.

Jane was very sorry to hear it in a way, but she supposed it accounted for the fact she felt perfectly well. 'Ask him where we shall arrive.'

He replied, 'not far from Deal.'

Jane slept quite well that night, snuggled up to her children, though Elodie was a bit restless. When she woke it was daylight and England was quite close. To save any embarrassment the fisherman might have felt, Joseph emptied and washed out the chamber pots. For breakfast, they finished the Comtesse's food. Jean simply ran his boat ashore and Louis carried first Jane, then the children, and then the luggage. He said something as he brought Joseph ashore.

'He says we are good children and were no trouble,' Elodie explained.

'Thank him for a most comfortable trip,' Jane asked.

Elodie did this, and Louis nodded and smiled. Jean nodded and almost smiled. Louis pushed the boat out, turned his head round and hopped in. As the sail began to fill he shouted.

'Now we go fishing,' translated Elodie.

There they were, on a lovely, bright morning, standing on an empty beach.

'Thank God we're back,' thought Jane, 'and safe. Well, anyway, safer. We must try and find a hotel,' she said. 'But it may be difficult.'

The first hotel they came to said it was full. The owner, a man, was clearly horrified by the appearance of a woman with two children and very little luggage at six in the morning.

'You see, we've just come from France,' explained Elodie.

'Indeed,' he said coldly. 'We do not cater for tinkers.'

'What's a tinker, Mama?' asked Joseph, as they trailed down the street.

'People who travel about and mend pots,' explained Jane.

The next hotel was smaller, and a middle-aged woman was mopping the floor in the hall. She was kinder and responded more sympathetically to their predicament than the last person. Her name was Mrs Rands. Showing them to an empty room, she brought hot water and then breakfast.

'Shall we try to go to sleep for a bit or try to hire a carriage?' Jane asked the children.

'I think we had best get a carriage,' said Joseph, 'in case Mr Pitt is from home and we have to go.

Jane agreed and Mrs Rands sent the boots to the best livery stable. An open carriage and driver arrived within an hour. They bowled along merrily. Elodie wanted to stop and pick flowers, feed donkeys, and paddle in ponds, but Jane and Joseph refused until it was lunchtime, when they stopped by a stream to eat the food Mrs Rands had packed for them. Their driver, a pleasant, polite, rather shy youth, went on to a pub he knew, but came back before long. Too soon for Elodie, who was looking at butterflies. The wild roses were out, the larks were singing, and they often breathed the sweet scent of hay. They discussed which was more beautiful, England or France. Joseph said you wouldn't see a wild boar in England as he had one early morning at the château. Jane said you wouldn't see a host of rosy, well-dressed children in France. Elodie said they were the same really in many ways, and that the two countries should try harder to be friends.

:

At last, Walmer Castle loomed up, and it looked more imposing and stern as they got closer. They drove into the courtyard and rang the bell. There was a long wait.

'Do we still look like tinkers?' asked Elodie.

At that moment the door was opened by a footman in livery.

'Is Mr Pitt in?' asked Jane.

'He went for a walk, Madam, but I believe…'

'Who is it?' enquired a well-known voice from behind them, that of Mr Pitt who had returned from his walk. 'Is it the little match girl? Is it Meg Merrilies? No, it is Jane, Elodie, and Joseph! What could be better? Have you escaped from France?'

'Yes,' said Elodie. 'A man tried to murder us so we ran away in a canal boat, and then a fishing boat, 'til we got to near Deal this morning, and then we came here.'

'I hope we can stay for a few days 'til Gussie comes and fetches us,' asked Jane.

'Indeed you may and Gussie will arrive expeditiously. He has been moping. Shall I pay the carriage?' asked Pitt.

'No, I will. I've still got nine gold pieces,' Jane proclaimed.

As they went in, Jane declared, 'Gussie can't have been moping much. It's only been twenty days.'

'Ten days too long for him, I do assure you. I met him at the Duchess's rout and he was a lost soul. I felt he refined too much on terrors past, but it seems not. Do you want something to eat? Pitt asked.'

'Yes, please,' said Joseph. 'Could we have bacon and eggs, and cake? There wasn't any in France.'

'Bacon and eggs, and cake, it shall be,' said Mr Pitt.

'What a little pig you are, Joe,' Jane told him.

Pitt carried on, 'There is no one here but Mr Canning, who will be enraptured to have some tonish company. Wilberforce is expected, but late, as usual.'

They had barely sat down to dinner when wheels were heard, and soon in came Mr Wilberforce. 'I cry you mercy,' he said. 'I stayed too long over a petition with an associate in Canterbury. Shall I go away again?'

'You will not. Another cover, if you please. Jane was just beginning to tell us about her adventures with our martial neighbours over the water,' Pitt said.

'Continue then, I beg. A good tale and green peas: what more could anyone want?' Wilberforce said.

'Clean hands?' suggested Mr Pitt, for the interval between the sound of wheels and the appearance of Mr Wilberforce had been very short.

They all exclaimed during the dinner party over Jane's brush with Talleyrand. She showed them the note.

'I fear I cannot even remember the gentleman,' said Mr Pitt. 'If he is a lover of peace, we might have dealt extremely together.'

'You are an iceberg with strangers,' said Mr Wilberforce, 'as he complained. Go on, Jane. What next?'

When she had described the night of the assassin all three of them looked at one another glumly.

'Could he send someone here?' asked Mr Wilberforce.

'He could,' said Mr Canning. 'He'd stand out rather in England. You need to be wary of anyone who makes out they are tremendous royalists and aristocrats, but I don't think there is much danger.'

'I will speak to Addington,' declared Mr Pitt, 'but I do not think there is much danger, either. You must never go to France again, unless Fouché is dead of course.'

'That's what I told the children,' Jane confirmed.

'Only in Shakespeare,' said Mr Pitt, 'do we find heroines as dauntless as our Jane.'

'Indeed! Indeed!' agreed Mr Canning. 'Let us drink to her health.'

He leapt to his feet and drank a toast.

'We must thank a merciful providence for the children's preservation,' said Mr Wilberforce. 'Mr Newton was concerned for you. He will be very interested to hear of your escape.'

'I am sorry to hear that Napoleon is casting cannon,' said Mr Pitt. 'He was, of course, a gunner, and therefore understands the importance of artillery, but it bodes ill. I have sent an express to your husband and look to see him tomorrow.'

'We must persuade him to stay for a s'enight or so,' declared Mr Canning. 'We need Jane to make us laugh.'

'Am I so funny?' asked Jane.

'Hilarious! Your combination of candour and simplicity is unique,' confirmed Canning.

'I must have my mouse,' agreed Mr Pitt, 'but I fear the ecclesiastical cat will carry it away. Your husband confided that he was missing his infant daughter almost as much as you.'

'He does dote on her,' admitted Jane.

Gussie duly arrived next day, complete with carriage. He was infinitely relieved and much affected to see Jane, and could hardly bear to hear what had happened. He wished to whisk them away immediately, but clever Mr Canning persuaded him to stay for a couple of nights by declaring Jane had been quite exhausted, small wonder, and, although she was somewhat restored, she needed more rest.

:

It was wonderful to be back home in Woolsthorpe, though the new cottages were not nearly as far on as they had hoped. Elizabeth was equally concerned about new cottages, and also that young George was going to Eton. Where would they be without his good sense and good temper? The weather broke up in thunder storms. The farmers were pleased at first because the hay was in, and everything needed a drink, but they soon began to fuss about the harvest. Harry came to fetch his daughter and livened things up for a week. He still hadn't got a ship with this peace, and money was getting very tight, what with his half-pay and Emily's extravagance.

Henri wrote and forwarded on the luggage that Jane had left behind. His guarded references sounded as if he'd spoken to Talleyrand about the attempted murder. Talleyrand had been horrified, and had promised to speak to Napoleon, making sure at the same time no other murderers followed them to England. Gussie managed to get a draft and return the money Henri had lent to Jane. Fanny wrote, too. The Général had found work and they were all very comfortable and happy, 'and I repine a little for my country and my family, I am sure it is monstrous ungrateful, the more so as we hope to return for a visit sometime next year.'

In September, Mr Pitt was taken ill, and for a few hours his life was in danger. But his doctor, Farquhar, managed to revive him, and Pitt made his usual fast recovery.

'I do not like these recurring illnesses,' confided George to Elizabeth one night as they lay in bed together.

'Nor do I. We know so slight an amount about the human body,' she agreed.

'We have made but little progress since Roman times. I had hoped that when Mr Pitt was out of office and therefore under less strain he would improve.'

'He does seem to improve when we have a good summer, and then he does too much and has another attack,' Elizabeth said in reply.

'It is all too true. If the improvement occurs again next summer, I will venture to warn him,' George announced.

Jane asked if Elodie and Joseph could come and stay in the Palace, and go to Richard and Camilla's school. They had rather outgrown the Dame School in Long Clawson. Elizabeth agreed gladly. Richard was missing his brother.

Mr Pitt went to Bath and took the waters, and then went to visit his adored mother and nieces at Burton Pynsent. Mr Addington brought in a budget, but this one Mr Pitt did not approve of. Too much money was borrowed and too little paid back.

Young George came home for the Christmas holidays, saying he liked Eton but there was not enough to eat. He seemed to have made as many friends in a term as Ned had in three years. That added up to about a dozen of all sorts, from the son of a doctor in London who had won a scholarship, to a son of the Duke of Grafton. His report was nothing like as laudatory as Ned's always were, but they spoke highly of his French and History.

Harry stayed again for a week when he came to fetch Camilla, who confided, 'He's happier here than he is at home. Mama has too many tea parties and she doesn't like us playing games, whereas here he can play whist and tennis in your court, and hide and seek with us all over the house.'

They had an agreeable Christmas, with Jane, Gussie, and the children coming for a few days. Madame Lebrun's son came, too, having arranged leave from the Austrian service. His English was bad, but he did not let it worry him and therefore improved rapidly. He was fascinated to hear of Jane's adventures in France. 'You tell Talleyrand that Napoleon vill play vit 'is soldiers. Dis I like. Dis I love. You do ver' vell. Vat else you tell eem?'

'Some of Mr Pitt's sayings and doings,' Jane explained.

'Dat vould interest eem. Ee is not bad man. Bien élevé, but vat can ee do vit a Corsican bandit?' said Lebrun's son.

'Not to mention his large and loathsome family,' Madame Lebrun agreed.

'I tell dis story to Archduke Charles. Ee like too much.'

In January, 1803, Jane and Gussie returned to Woolsthorpe, leaving the children with the Pretymans. Madame Lebrun's son, Etienne, went back to the Austrians.

'Eef I get bad vound or reech vife,' he told them before he left, 'I fly back to you, Maman, and dis so comfortable England.'

In February, Mr Pitt had another bad bilious attack cured by the local chemist. And in April, Mr Pitt's mother, Lady Chatham, died and was buried in Westminster Abbey. Pitt was much affected but aware that it was time for her to go. This left her two nieces adrift. Hester Harriot Pitt-Eliot was claimed by her father's family, but no one wanted Lady Hester Stanhope. Her own mother had died when she was four. Her father was a revolutionary idiot. She was now twenty-seven years old and, after her grandmother's funeral, she rushed off to travel in Spain. Everyone knew, though, it was only a temporary solution.

Napoleon invaded Switzerland, and was surprised and displeased when the British were rude about it. He was incapable of understanding, like many before and after him, that, because they believed in the freedom of information, the English didn't attempt to control their journalists and cartoonists.

In May, Napoleon declared war on England again and shut-up all the tourists and merchants he could catch. The Général and Fanny were not imprisoned because the Général had wisely won back his French citizenship, but there could be no more prospect of returning to England for a visit. Harry soon got another ship, which pleased him very much. Jane was having another baby, which did not please her at all as she was very sick again, and would not be able to hunt that winter.

'A lawyer from Grimsby desires to interview me,' said George at dinner one day. 'I am at a loss to conceive for what purpose.'

'I expect he is after money for his worthy charity,' replied Elizabeth. 'You must not give him much. We have a sufficiency of worthy charities of our own.'

'It may be,' speculated Madame Lebrun, 'that he hopes to persuade you to invest money in his manufactuary.'

George replied, 'He hopes in vain if such indeed is the case. I have invited him to stay for a night or two on June the twelfth. I trust that will not inconvenience you.'

'Not in the least. Camilla has had a letter from George. It appears he is enjoying his boating.'

The conversation became domestic. The lawyer, Mr Giles, duly appeared. He was fat, jovial, and explained he was fond of shooting and fishing. Elizabeth had asked Amabel and her husband to entertain him. The little party was a success as Mr Giles turned out to be a well-read man who could discuss books and plays with Amabel and Madame Lebrun.

George had his interview the next morning and emerged before long looking startled.

'Can you remember Mr Tomline, sweetheart?' he asked Elizabeth, who was cutting a burr out of her spaniel's ear. 'Marmaduke Tomline?'

'Why, yes – hold still, Bracken!' she snapped at the dog. Continuing, she returned to the subject., 'the rather shy gentleman who liked birds? He used to come and stay with us some years ago. There, all done! He often asked us to go and visit him in North Lincolnshire, but for one cause or another we never could.'

George replied, 'I think I recollect him. It had rather slipped my mind. It transpires he died last month after a long illness and he has left us the place.'

'The place in North Lincolnshire?' asked Elizabeth.

'That's it. Riby Grove. And there is quite a lot of money, too,' George revealed.

'But why did he leave it to us of all people?' Elizabeth supposed.

'I enquired as to that. It would seem that Mr Tomline had few relatives and found those uncongenial. He found the Palace pleasant and our family amiable. Particularly you, my love, and there I can only commend his taste,' said George.

'We shall be able to get on with the hospital,' Elizabeth realised.

George replied, 'Yes, indeed. I should have wished to go to the funeral, but Mr Giles explained that Mr Tomline specified I was not to be bothered with it. He wished, however, that we should change our names and that of our elder son to Tomline.'

'That would seem to be only common gratitude. It will be a bit odd, though, to have three brothers with two different names,' said Elizabeth, scratching her dog. 'We must go there and see it before long. Perhaps not 'til the holidays so we can take the children. Is Mr Giles staying for dinner?'

'He said not. He wished to get back. But I asked him to act for us and so we will see more of him,' George explained.

Mr Giles appeared with a bag in his hand. 'I have come to take my leave and to thank you for making me so much at home. I already feel sure Mr Tomline chose wisely.'

'You have certainly surprised us,' Elizabeth told him. 'We had thought, perhaps you came to ask for money, for a good cause, and instead you shower us with riches.'

'I am glad to be the bearer of good tidings. I will say farewell now, then, as my carriage awaits.'

:

There were various negotiations to get Mr Pitt back into Government, but he wouldn't have had control, and the King didn't ask him to come, so he declined. He spoke in the House in May, and people said and wrote that it was a fine speech, but Mr Pitt did not look well.

In late June, there was the unusual phenomenon of a letter from Emily. 'You had better keep Camilla,' she wrote. 'We are all partying here and she mislikes it and glumphs about.'

'Is there such a word as "glumphs"?' Elizabeth asked George at the breakfast table.

George replied, 'I should not have thought so. It is, however, descriptive, though I can hardly approve of her sentiments. However, Camilla is no trouble now and is eager to see Riby.'

'When you think how Emily adored that child at first,' said Elizabeth sadly.

Camilla was delighted. 'It is sad that Mama and I find each other dull, but as we do I am better off with you.'

In July, they all went off in three carriages to Riby Grove. Elodie and Joseph begged to be allowed to come, and Jane wrote that, as she could do nothing for them at present but run away to the nearest basin, it seemed a sound plan.

Riby Grove was a plain, tall house, built, it appeared, by Mr Tomline's father fifty years before. Inside it was comfortably furnished, with lots of pictures of birds, and beautiful woodwork. It was, though, shabby, which is what you might expect of the house of an elderly widower. The housekeeper, Mrs Sentence, was always known as "Mother", because she mothered everyone. She was small, round, and elderly, but was a wonderful cook who had trained up Minnie Mat from a terrified cottage girl to her own high standards. Her husband, who had died young in a fall with a horse, had been the groom. One of their sons, Ezekiel, commonly known as Zeke, was the present head groom. Another son, Josiah, known as Joss, was the keeper. Three daughters were married and living nearby, and were willing to come and help when wanted. Mrs Sentence was delighted with the children and soon had all their favourite dishes and pastimes straight.

The country round and about was up and down, and mostly pasture. There were some good woods, though, as George said, slipping into the shoes of his ancestors, 'they need coppicing.'

There were stone walls instead of hedges, and vast tarns instead of ponds.

Madame Lebrun was fully occupied and very content, painting harebells, grass of parnassus, and bog pimpernel. They had a lot of visitors, from the local parson to the Lord Yarborough, who appeared suddenly one morning, having tied his horse to a tree.

'Ought to leave a card or something, I suppose,' he confided to Elizabeth, whom he met in the hall just after Joss, doing butler for now, had let him in. 'Trouble is, I never can remember what. I was passing, so I thought I'd look in.'

'Very kind,' said Elizabeth weakly.

'It's Lord Yarborough, Ma'm,' said Joss in a stage whisper. 'Often comes here.'

'Did in Duke's day. Very fond of poor Duke. You'll be Mrs Pretyman,' Lord Yarborough said.

'Well, I was, until last month, but now I'm trying very hard to get used to being Mrs Tomline,' explained Elizabeth.

'M' wife said the same. Kept signing herself unmarried. Years ago. How do you like it here?' the Lord asked.

'Very well. Everyone's so kind and helpful. Would you like some sherry or Madeira?' asked Elizabeth in reply.

'Rather have some beer, Joss. Glad to see you have not changed much. Your husband writing sermons?' Yarborough enquired.

'No. I fear he has gone fishing with some of the children. Did you know the Tomlines well?' Elizabeth proposed.

'Pretty well. Good sort of woman, but she wasted away with the consumption. Terrible to see. Poor Marmaduke never got over it,' Yarborough revealed.

'So I understand. I recollect him being very happy once over a large collection of cranes,' Elizabeth recalled.

'Ah, he would be. Nothing like a large bird to cheer up Duke.'

Joss returned bearing a glass of beer. 'I took the liberty, m' Lord, to send Zeke to put your horse in a stable. Flies is bad.'

'Quite right. Thought I'd probably find them from home or busy. Ah, that's the stuff for a hot day! Did you put it in the well?'

'Yes, m' Lord. How is her Ladyship?' asked Joss.

Here he was interrupted by Camilla who ran in holding up a large trout on a string of rushes. 'Look what I caught! Tod said – oh, you've got company.'

'Only a neighbour. No call for fuss. Well, done indeed! Should think it's well over a pound,' remarked Lord Yarborough.

'I'll go and weigh it.' She departed as suddenly as she had come.

'Wash! And put on a clean dress!' Elizabeth called after her.

'Like to see 'em enjoying themselves in the holidays,' Yarborough announced.

'Will you stay for dinner?' asked Elizabeth.

'Tempting, but I'd better be off. Expected at home. M' wife's going to call with a card turned down twice or some fiddle-de-dee. You must come over to Brocklesby. Bring the bairns. I've got several, too. Give you goo' day.' And he, like Camilla, departed rapidly, pausing only to call out in the hall, 'My horse, Joss, if you please.'

Elizabeth followed and took slightly more formal leave of him on the doorstep.

They were all sorry when it was time to go. Mother and Joss begged them to come back for the partridge shooting in October. Ned and young George thought it a splendid notion, but their father would not hear of it.

'The pheasants, then, at Christmas,' persisted Joss. 'The woods are full of fat pheasants.'

'An I'll cook 'em for y' with bread sauce,' added Mother.

'We'll have to see,' said Elizabeth firmly.

:

In August, Mr Pitt took Lady Hester Stanhope into his household. The Pretymans were divided as to how well the arrangement would work out. Elizabeth thought it would liven up his houses; George thought it would make them altogether too lively and noisy.

The Warden of the Cinque Ports had been a ceremonial job for some centuries, but it became a front line area in 1803. Mr Pitt was soon a Colonel in the local militia, and spent a lot of time riding about inspecting and drilling the troops. He also purchased nearly two hundred gun boats and saw that they patrolled regularly, for Napoleon was encamped, like an outbreak of plague, at Boulogne. His army, or most of it, was with him. So, too, was a very large quantity of barges. But the major ships which were meant to escort them across the Channel were bottled up in various harbours by the English fleet. Harry, for instance, was going up and down, usually cold and hungry, outside Boulogne.

Jane's ferryman, Jean, was so horrified by the advent of 'The Army of England' that he barricaded and locked his house and garden. He was making quite a lot of money out of them, though.

In November, Jane had another daughter, as expected. The midwife, however, had quite a job stopping the bleeding. 'She says I ought not have to anymore,' Jane told her mother, who had come for a visit.

'How often have I been told that? I know Mrs Potts saved my life. Not once, but twice, so I always send her a Christmas present and write her sometimes. Have you noticed how women never die having a baby in books but they do all the time in real life?' Jane's mother asked.

'I suppose it would be just too grim. Books mostly prefer to concentrate on the drama and fun of courtship. But I've got to have another, damn it, because Gussie wants a son,' Jane explained.

Her mother responded animatedly, 'Oh, darling, don't! We cannot spare you. We really cannot. Think of the children. Did I tell you I sat next to Joseph's headmaster at a dinner party and he said he was a remarkable child, so kind and responsible? He asked if it was true that Joe was really a French marquis.'

'It does seem odd, doesn't it? But it suits him. It's different and romantic. He was so sensible and brave that time in France,' Jane said.

'He would be. He is like his father. But, Jane, you must tell Gussie he can have you or another baby, but not both.'

'Not I. It would upset him terribly. But I must say, it's a bit much to feel sick for eight months and then feel like a wet cloth for another month,' Jane described.

'Women have such a hard life,' sympathised her mother. 'Can you not persuade Gussie to not call that poor little mite Charlotte? It's such a commonplace name.'

'It was his grandmother's, and he adored her, and fancies it might look like her. But I held out for Charlotte Amabel.'

'I'm flattered. Have you heard from your friend, the author, who is trapped in France? Fanny Burney?' asked Amabel.

Jane replied, 'Not since September. She sounded rather sad, and the boy had been ill, though he was rather better now. Her husband's cousin, who we stayed with, writes surprisingly often and I write back through the Vatican, as he told me to. He's in Italy.'

'It is too romantic. He's in love with you, like Romeo and Juliet,' Jane's mother said smiling.

'He thinks he is, certainly, but I expect there are others. He says he will protect me when the French invade.'

'I'm told Lord Vincent says he does not say they cannot come, only that they cannot come by water. That is my comfort. The Navy, and Harry. But if the Navy does not drown most of the French, we shall be in trouble, with our armies all over the place – Corsica, the West Indies, India.'

'I never worry about what may not happen,' said Jane, with the confidence of youth.

Camilla went south with George in late November because her father hoped to get a few weeks' leave while his ship was refitting. The Pretymans, who were mostly now Tomlines, spent the Christmas of 1803 at Riby. The weather was very cold, but there was no snow, and so the journey was quite easy. George regretted being away from Lincoln at Christmas, but the boys begged to go to Riby. It was only for a fortnight, and Mr Giles arranged for him to preach at Grimsby. The Sentences were delighted to see them, and Joss provided some good shooting. Lord and Lady Yarborough gave a party where they ate and drank and talked while the young played hide and seek all over the house.

Zeke had bought them some good horses, so Elizabeth and her children all went hunting with the Brocklesby hounds and enjoyed themselves. Elizabeth rode back, tired, at two o'clock, accompanied by Richard, who'd clearly been very frightened but would not admit it. Ned and George arrived back long after dark, tired, muddy, and ecstatic.

Elodie and Joseph came for a few days, and then their stepfather sent his coach to fetch them home for Christmas. As the cold winter slowly gave way to spring, impatient acceptance of Addington's government slowly gave way to plotting to get Pitt back. Lord Eldon, who was the lawyer Elizabeth had sat next to at Windsor when he was just 'Scot', approached Pitt with messages from the King. Pitt wanted a government of the most effective politicians in this emergency, but most MPs, while perfectly happy to have Charles James Fox, did not want Pitt's high-handed cousin, Lord Grenville. The King, while perfectly happy to have Lord Grenville, did not want Charles James Fox.

CHAPTER TWENTY-EIGHT

Riby

Bread was still very expensive, and the poor were very hungry. George and Elizabeth, now they were rich, were able to be fairly sure no one was hungry in Lincoln, but Mrs Giles told them the children of recently quite rich tradesmen's families were begging from door-to-door in Grimsby. So in March, 1804, they went to Riby. With the help of Mrs Giles, Goodchild, and the local clergy they soon had a soup kitchen up and running. The lines outside it were a hundred yards long, but fortunately one of the local clergy was energetic, though poor, and his wife was vigorous, though cumbered with eight children, and his cook was enthusiastic, though overworked, so they could always get more soup and bread when it ran out before the line of people did. Some of the comments made them realise how much the soup kitchen was needed, and that it had been for years.

'Bless you, Mum. You wouldn't credit the difference that make. Now we're sure of a good dinner. I kin generally git together somat for breakfast and supper.'

'I ain't never tasted meat afore,' a small child told her. ''At's good.'

'Nothin' like soup for warmin' you up and stillin' the hunger pangs,' a young man told Mrs Giles.

'That young man's father was a prosperous tailor,' Mrs Giles told Elizabeth, 'but they went broke in '99. Too many bad debts, and now the poor fellow is a porter in the market. All he could get.'

George and Elizabeth agreed when they were going back to Lincoln that they must look into the food situation in Grantham and Sleaford.

Mr Pitt started making speeches criticising Addington's government. The King refused to consider having Fox in his Cabinet, and Lord Grenville, who'd joined up with Fox the year before, refused to serve without him. Addington soon gave up and resigned. The day he gave the Seals of Office back to the King was also the day Napoleon was confirmed as hereditary Emperor of France.

In May, Pitt was back. He told the King he looked much better now than he'd looked 'when last we met.'

'It's not to be wondered at,' said the King, 'for then I was losing a friend. Now I am regaining one.'

George and Elizabeth were entertaining George's brother John and his wife Anne. Mr Pitt had made John a Precentor of Norwich to please George. Anne was a clever woman but rather a chatterer and tactless with it. John, on the other hand, was a quiet, scholarly, and contented man.

'I apprehend feeding the poor is to feed the wolves who will one day devour you,' Anne announced when she and Elizabeth were walking back from the soup kitchen.

'You mean if they get the vote?' Elizabeth asked.

'To be sure, or if they are against us just as the French invade. I rejoice that you are to have a dinner party tonight, for the constant company of one's inferiors has such a lowering effect,' Anne replied.

'It's hardly a dinner party. Just a gathering of a few old friends,' Elizabeth explained.

'John finds Mrs Andrews congenial as she has read most of his favourite long, boring books. Do you not, on occasion, find Mrs Lebrun a little trying? She is so blunt and outspoken. I should not want to have another woman always in my house,' Anne said.

'No, not in the least. She is very unobtrusive, and, then, she was so very helpful when the children were all ill with the measles,' Elizabeth reassured her.

'You were fortunate not to lose one. Most women do. That is another infliction with the poor. They give us the most dreadful diseases. Doubtless, it is our duty as Christians to preserve them, but I have misgivings as to whether it is wise. George is looking older,' Anne mentioned.

'We all are, but, then, we all are older,' Elizabeth confirmed.

'This constant travelling cannot be good for him. As you get older you need more repose. I am thankful being a bookworm keeps John quiet, though it means I must arrange everything.'

:

In June, George went south again to attend the Lords. He went to stay at Walmer with Mr Pitt, who was enjoying a short break from London and people pestering him. He had to admit, Elizabeth had been right about Lady Hester brightening up Mr Pitt's household. Besides her, there was Mr Canning, Lord Castlereagh, and Granville

Leveson-Gower staying, as well as Brigadier John Moore, who had ridden over from Shorncliffe Barracks in Folkestone where he was defending Kent against those many men and barges over the water. Pitt consulted him a lot over anything martial.

At dinner one night, Granville Leveson-Gower, which was pronounced 'Loosen-Gower', said, 'Russia is the sword that will win the war for us.'

'You've been there, have you not?' asked Lady Hester, admiringly.

Leveson-Gower replied, 'Oh certainly. When my cousin was *en poste* in Moscow he asked for me. Rummy old place, Moscow. They go about in rivières of diamonds, and dance waltzes, while the people are dying of hunger in hovels.'

'Does not the church arrange for distributions of food?' asked George.

'No, that I ever heard of,' he replied.

'Will the French come?' asked Lady Hester.

'I do not expect them anymore,' answered Sir John Moore. 'They have missed their tide. Their opportunity was that day last November when we had thick fog and no wind. I expected them then, and so I had watchers every half mile riding along the coast and the troops in readiness. The Navy could not have stopped them.'

'How well I remember that day,' exclaimed Lady Hester. 'I went for a walk, being unable to sit quiet, and every time a blackbird flew up and cackled I thought it the French. You know how things loom up in a fog.'

'Indeed,' said Mr Canning. 'It is always strange.'

'Well, I heard hooves, as I thought, and saw a regiment of horse advancing on me. Imagine my relief when one of the fiery steeds lowed and it was but Farmer Smith's cows going to be milked.'

They laughed at her and Mr Pitt said, 'One of my young officers confided he was hoping the French would come.'

'The ignorance of youth is only surpassed by its impudence,' said Mr Canning.

'I apprehend it was no more than a desire not to have gone to all that trouble for nothing,' said Granville Leveson-Gower.

'We have risen to the opportunity,' said Lord Castlereagh. 'We have proved worthy of our ancestors, who must have sat in this very room and seen the invincible Armada sail by in all its majestic imperiousness.'

'Prithee, sweet youth,' said Mr Pitt, 'hast thou marked the bright flaming of Master Drake's fireships?'

'Aye have I,' said George, 'and the spitfires of Sir Walter Raleigh's guns withal.'

'It is mighty strange how history repeats itself,' said Lady Hester. 'Do you think people will sit here in a hundred years' time or so and look at the smudge of the French coast, and see their death waiting for them, if it could but come?'

'Seaborne expeditions are notoriously difficult,' pointed out Sir John.

'They tell me you are getting up a new regiment,' said Granville. 'Skirmishers and sharpshooters. If I were not a diplomat I should be tempted. Sounds just the thing for me. Lots of excitement and very little drill.'

'I think to call it the Light Division and for their song I will give them "Over the Hills and Far Away".'

Lady Hester sang it in a powerful pleasing contralto. But she sang the light opera version and not the nursery rhyme:

Were I cast on Greenland's coast
And in my arms embraced my lass,
Warm amidst the eternal frost,
Full soon the six month's night would
pass

She waved a knife and everyone, except Lord Granville and Lord Castlereagh, joined in the chorus.

If with me you'd fondly stray
Over the hills and far away

'How I wish you had brought Elizabeth,' confessed Mr Pitt to George. 'Now my mother and sisters are dead and the Duchess is ill, Elizabeth is the only woman I know, save Hester here, who can keep a quick, dancing conversation.'

'I fear I cannot keep up with a quick dancing conversation,' said Sir John, 'yet I love to hear it.'

'There's Jane,' suggested George.

'Jane is something different,' declared Mr Pitt. 'Jane does not so much dance through good talk as discover a nail and hit it on the head.'

Next morning was a perfect day, and George and Mr Canning dragged Mr Pitt, who wished to write a speech, out for a walk. Hester came, too. Sir John had ridden back to Shorncliffe before breakfast. Lord Castlereagh and Granville did not appear. The farmers were haymaking, and the smell was everywhere. Several men and women greeted Mr Pitt, and one old lady in a white sunbonnet left her rake and came over to ask, 'You'll keep 'em out, won't you, sir?'

'Sir John Moore, who is in charge of the coast, thinks they have missed their tide and will not come now,' George said.

'It ain't for m'self I'm a thinking. I've had m'day, and a good day that was, too, but I got eight grandchildren an' I don't want 'em to have to be French,' the old lady said.

'God forbid,' said Mr Pitt gravely.

'He will forbid,' said George firmly. 'Such wickedness will never prosper.'

The old lady replied, 'I'm glad to hear you say so, sir. An' I 'opes you're right. But I seen wickedness prosper time and agin.'

'So have I,' agreed Lady Hester.

'We must put our trust in God and the Navy,' said Mr Pitt.

'And you, sir,' said the old lady, going back to her rake.

'I hope I am worthy of her trust,' said Mr Pitt as they went on.

'None more so,' said George.

A cloud of butterflies blew in from the sea, beating strongly towards them and then past.

'How glad I am Bonaparte is not a butterfly,' remarked Mr Pitt.

The hedges made a continual cascade of flowers – rose, wild hops, elderflowers, and scabious. A lark was singing, as were some of the haymakers. A farmer came by driving a trap and called out, 'You got 'em on the run, sir. They see you a drilling and they ain't a coming.'

'Let us hope so,' said Pitt.

'They all admire you,' said Hester.

'A poor thing but mine own,' answered her uncle. 'Had I settled in Sussex they would be less confident. I fear I really must return. I shall be uneasy 'til I have at least roughed-out that speech.'

Hester went back with him.

'She's after the wrong man,' said Mr Canning, with his customary abruptness.

'Lady Hester?' asked George.

'Who else?' She's hypnotised by that popinjay, and thinks of Moore as she might her grandfather, a worthy man but antediluvian. She is over-old to think in that missish fashion. His Lordship is a well-looking man, but he's no good to any girl unless she be rich. And, even then, not much good – too pleased with himself. And Moore is one in a million,' Canning explained.

'But would Moore marry her?' asked George.

'I believe he would, with a little encouragement. He is attracted by her liveliness,' said Canning.

They had come to a small harbour busy with fishing boats, boys swimming, nets, the smell of the sea, and far out, a ship in full sail.

'We had best go back,' said Mr Canning, 'or we'll be late for dinner. I could wish we had time to swim. It grows hot.'

'Fortunately, there is a strong sea breeze. Would I be right in conjecturing Mr Pitt finds Lord Castlereagh invaluable?' enquired George.

'You would indeed. It's a good workhorse, loyal and astute. But there is something lacking there which makes him poor company. Lady Hester calls him "his monotonous Lordship". Not even Mr Pitt can make him laugh, but he's certainly useful.'

They walked back uphill, sweating a little. A golden oriole was singing in the hedge and flitting to and fro. It was a pretty black and yellow bird. George thought of how Mr Tomline would have enjoyed it.

'How do you think Mr Pitt is?' he asked.

'Overworked, but he knows how to play, and he sleeps well. I fear there's something amiss in his bowels, has been for many years, and he drinks too much. I know I do, too, but I only drink to excess on occasion; Mr Pitt depends on it. You never drink too much, do you?' Canning asked.

'I find moderation suits my constitution, but in my youth I thought it unbecoming in a priest,' George explained.

'And so it is. Makes them a laughing stock. Sir Walter Farquhar, Mr Pitt's doctor, told him he must have peace and quiet, but Mr Pitt said his country needed him and he would rather prefer to die at the post than to desert it,' Mr Canning explained.

'One can only commend such patriotism while lamenting the likely denouement,' George said.

Canning agreed, 'True. Here we are. Just in time.'

:

That autumn, Mr Pitt sent Lord Granville to Russia. He realised his government was far too flimsy. The wits were saying it was a government of William and Pitt, and joined up again with Mr Addington, who was now entitled Lord Sidmouth, and his followers. The wits were rude about this, too.

'It seems hard,' said Mr Pitt to Wilberforce when they were out walking in Hyde Park one afternoon, 'to mock me for joining up again with Addington, when we have been friends all our lives, as our fathers were before us. Yet no one exclaims upon the liaison between Fox and Lord Grenville, who have been enemies all their lives.'

Wilberforce was still struggling to stop slavery and Pitt was still helping him, though he feared the West Indian interests would be too strong for some time yet. Mr Pitt also worked very hard that autumn trying to reconcile the King and the Prince of Wales.

The Pretyman-Tomlines all went to Riby for Christmas. The children had set their hearts on it, and Camilla wrote asking if she could stay for Christmas. They had had a good day's hunting, but then it turned much colder and they couldn't hunt any more, though the boys still went shooting and Camilla often joined them, fortified by Joss telling her Lord Yarborough was a nailer at shooting. George disapproved, but Elizabeth told him to let the poor girl have some fun while she could.

Madame Lebrun painted the beck – the ferns covered with frost and the hills with little white lines marking a lattice of walls.

They gave a young people's party for New Year's Eve. A fiddler was found, and a man who played the harmonium. The Yarboroughs came over with their two sons and three daughters and stayed for two nights. The Andrews also came over, bringing Jane, Gussie, Elodie, and Joseph, who were staying with them. The Rector's daughter, a quiet, shy, but intelligent twelve year old, came over, but did not stay. Young George was rather taken with her. Camilla didn't mind at all, as she danced incessantly with the eldest Yarborough boy. Elizabeth, though not a great matchmaker, couldn't but feel how wonderful it would be if…

Ned danced with all three Ladies Pelham, the Yarborough daughters, and was very gallant from the full height of his six foot and seventeen years. Elodie was very popular. She danced and listened so well. Richard was rather shy and apt to lurk in corners, but both Camilla and Elodie firmly danced with him.

Elizabeth Andrews was popular, too, being sweet and pretty. Benjamin made them all laugh, while Joseph was always laughing and waiting on everyone. Every room was taken, and both 'Mother' and Joss remarked how champion it was to see the house 'fettled up and thick o' company'. 'Mother' provided an immense quantity of good food, most of which vanished. Lord Yarborough danced with everyone, even Madame Lebrun. George would not dance with anyone. He thought it ungainly in a clergyman. Elizabeth told him he was being stuffy again, and she twice dragged him onto the floor where he swayed and shuffled like performing bear.

Elizabeth was sitting out with Amabel, when Lord Yarborough came and collapsed beside her. 'Whacked,' he said. 'Too old for these capers.'

'This is Mrs Andrews, our Archdeacon's wife,' introduced Elizabeth. 'This is Lord Yarborough. He is a great reader.'

'Wish I was. Only thing if you're ill or old. I do read Shakespeare,' Yarborough answered.

'Yes, you cannot do better,' Amabel told him. 'Which do you prefer – tragedies, comedies, or the histories?'

'Hadn't even thought about it. Tragedies, I s'pose, but they're a bit uncomfortable. I read Milton and Fox, too, and Defoe, and Scott,' elaborated Yarborough.

'But you do not read only modern novels? Or poetry?' asked Amabel.

'Got so little time I read what I enjoy,' Yarborough replied.

Amabel said, 'Very sound, but you miss the adventure of something new. You could perhaps try Hakluyt's *Voyages.*'

'See if I can get it next time I'm in Grimsby,' Yarborough said in response.

'Do you never go to the House of Lords?' asked Elizabeth.

Yarborough answered her, 'Seldom. M' cousin Spencer tells me if they need me. Happy to talk about farming, or forestry, or the North, but it's not often wanted. Meant to ask you. Giles says you run a fuel charity. How do you do that?'

Elizabeth explained to him, 'We have a depot in Lincoln and we shall soon have one in Grimsby. Just a big shed we fill with wood and coal in summer and put a reliable man in charge. Then in winter, the poor can get fuel at half price or, in some cases, for nothing. But they must have a recommendation from a parson, a churchwarden, minister, or doctor, to prevent fraud.'

'How could you do that in the villages?' Yarborough asked.

'Much the same, I should imagine, but with a smaller shed and perhaps a part-time man in charge instead. Say a retired farmer or baker.'

Yarborough replied positively, 'Have to try and start some. Don't like people being cold. Wish you were here more often. My children miss yours. Especially the girls. Don't see much company.'

'Do you not think, my dear,' said Lady Yarborough, appearing beside them, 'it is time we went to bed?'

Yarborough agreed, 'Quite time – long past my bedtime. But I want to dance with m' hostess first and then this kind lady that's been telling me what to read. Give me a spin, Mrs Tomline.'

Everyone was enthusiastic about the party. Lord Yarborough said, 'Can't take these bun fights as a rule, but yours was good. No nonsense. No stiffness. Skip or sit, just as you fancy. Our own food, our own fiddler, squeezer, all just as it ought to be.'

Lady Yarborough said, 'It was all of the most elegant simplicity, Mrs Tomline. And my girls really enjoyed themselves, which delighted me, because, while the boys have so many pleasures, most of them deplorable, cocks fights, mills, dog fights, hunting, fell racing, horse racing, and cricket, the girls have so few.'

The next day, the young all slept late, but, the day being a bright one, Ned, George, Camilla and Elodie, and the two Yarborough boys, all rode that afternoon. Elizabeth, feeling she must have some air, walked in the park with Jane.

'I think I'm having another baby,' said Jane, 'but don't tell anyone, because they'd stop me hunting.'

'I did the same with George. I wanted to go on riding. You must go to Mrs Potts when the time comes,' Elizabeth warned Jane.

'I suppose I must. Mother will certainly think so. And, while the local midwife is perfectly adequate, there is something rather reassuring about Mrs Potts,' agreed Jane.

'There is, indeed. You feel safe with her. I don't know how she does it. She's retired now, but will always take old patients,' Elizabeth said.

'But could your parents cope with me now your mother's in a wheelchair?' asked Jane.

'They'd love it. My mother gets so bored now she can't garden, and my father still adores talking and making his odd jokes. You feel no sickness?' Elizabeth wondered.

'Not a trace, so it's probably a boy, which is good because it's what Gussie so absurdly wants. And then I shall take every care to have no more.'

'Quite right. I so wanted a daughter, but really, as Madame Lebrun told me years ago would happen, Camilla has practically become my daughter.'

'Elodie, too. She dotes on you,' Jane said.

'Elodie dotes on everyone she knows,' Elizabeth smiled. 'She has the happiest nature, and Joseph, too. I am sure he is helping to clear up right now. The servants would not like it if I did anything, beyond taking the odd glass through, but they quite accept Joseph as cook, scullery maid, butler, whatever he will.'

'Everyone accepts Joseph. He tells me all the local gossip,' Jane smirked.

Their feet crunched in a white world which the sun turned to fire as it fled.

Meanwhile, the young were riding back, and realising they were going to be late for dinner and would have to ride in the dark.

'Let's canter,' said Ned.

'Don't be silly,' said George. 'It is much too slippery here. Wait till we can get off the track and back on the unpacked snow.'

'It's all right if you can ride,' said Ned scornfully, and set off.

'How marvellous he looks,' thought an admiring Elodie. 'Trim. Flexible. As if he could do anything. But George is right. He shouldn't be so rash. It is dreadfully slippery.'

She held in her own homeward bound pony with difficulty.

One moment they were moving beautifully, man and horse, the next they were in the air, toppling sideways. They landed with a crash, and the horse scrambled up clumsily and set off for home, stirrups and reins flapping. The boy lay there.

'Are you all right?' called George.

'No. He fell on me and I think I've broken my leg,' said Ned, sitting up.

'There's a farmer up there – one of our own tenants. I'll fetch him and a wagon. Here take this. It's waterproof. Sit on it.'

Lord Worsely tore off his coat and tossed it to his younger brother, and was off. They saw him opening a gate with his whip and then trotting across a big field.

'Can you hold my horse?' the younger Yarborough boy, Tom, asked Camilla.

She wasn't at all sure she could hold George's horse with her own pony fidgeting about, but she resolved to try. Soon, Ned was sitting on the coat. The sun was very red as it sunk.

'Do we get on again?' George asked Tom.

'Better not. They might need us to help lift. Here they come,' Tom answered.

Four horses, including his Lordship's, were to be seen coming rapidly over the field. Before they got to the gate, a wagon pulled out of the farm yard. The farmer, whose name was Ormerod, was a very effective man, and brushed their thanks aside.

'If a man can't do sommat for his landlord, as always treated him right forward, it'd be a rum old go,' he said in the intervals of getting Ned into the wagon, sending one of his sons to fetch Doctor Croft, and a man to tell them at Riby what had happened.

In no time Ned was in the best spare room, and the other five were sitting down to the sumptuous high tea the Ormerods were about to have when Lord Worsely appeared.

Doctor Croft confirmed to them that the leg was broken. 'A simple fracture. I've bandaged it up for now and I'll plaster it tomorrow. At your age you should be walking about with crutches next week and be as good as new in a couple o' months.'

It was arranged that George should stay and share a double bed with his brother, while the other four went off to Riby Grove in a wagon, wearing borrowed sheepskin coats. Ned's horse had arrived safely. It was rather lame but Zeke got it right. Next morning, they sent a coach to fetch Ned home. Elizabeth went, too, to thank the Ormerods. Camilla was to ride her pony home.

Lord Yarborough and his family stopped on their way home to thank the farmer. It was clear this was an immense honour and they were all given cowslip wine, sloe gin, and tipsy cake, besides beer, claret, and port.

'M' son says you wasted no time,' said his Lordship, drinking beer.

'Should hope not,' said Mr Ormerod, also drinking beer.

'We are very grateful to you,' said Elizabeth, drinking cowslip wine.

‘'Twas right,’ said the brisk, plump Mrs Ormerod, drinking cowslip wine, too. ‘I was a' feared the young gentleman would catch his death but the doctor says he’s like to do well.’

‘Our boys have broken five limbs so far,’ said Lady Yarborough, drinking sloe gin. ‘Mostly trees rather than horses.’

‘How’re the sheep?’ asked his Lordship.

‘Gradely. Feed’s short though,’ Mr Ormerod explained.

‘No turnips?’ his Lordship continued.

‘Turnips done well. Little hay and no mangolds,’ Ormerod continued.

Elizabeth saw where Lord Yarborough got his precise speech from. ‘We’re the same,’ he was saying, ‘'an oats is short, too. We’ve too many 'osses.’

‘If you’ve boys, you’ve too many 'osses,’ Mr Ormerod said.

‘They must have some fun,’ objected his wife. ‘They work hard.’

‘Not short o' fun. Short o' sense,’ her husband added.

‘Must be getting on,’ said his Lordship. ‘Daylight’s short, too.’

‘It is an' all. Good to see y',’ Mr Ormerod said.

‘See you at the garden party, I hope,’ said her Ladyship.

‘May be too busy.’

‘Wise man,’ said his Lordship, handing his wife into their coach.

Goodchild drove Elizabeth back, with Ned lying on an old door.

Ned’s leg improved rapidly, and he was able to go home to Lincoln in the middle of January, and to Eton in early February.

Soon after they had got back to Buckden, an express letter from Mr Pitt arrived. George read it in the drawing room but did not comment, or read bits aloud, or pass it on to Elizabeth, all of which was unusual. Elizabeth could not be curious, however, knowing George would tell her in time. It was some time, though. George had a meeting, and then they were never alone all evening. Camilla wished them to look at her new picture, which was really rather good. Richard wished to play chess with his father. Madame Lebrun asked to read them a letter from her son in Vienna. So it wasn’t until they were in bed that she could ask, ‘What was in Mr Pitt’s letter?’

‘He feels – he wants… It appears that the Archbishop of Canterbury has died and there is not unnaturally much speculation about his successor,’ George explained.

'And Mr Pitt wants you,' said Elizabeth, startled, worried, and appalled.

'Well, yes. I do not feel entirely worthy but – I could do much for charity,' George explained.

'Is it entirely in Mr Pitt's gift?' wondered Elizabeth.

'It always has been but there's been some idea recently that perhaps the First Lord of the Treasury ought to consult the Church,' George said.

'I should have thought he most certainly ought to, and the Cabinet, and the King. Have you and Mr Pitt been planning this without a word to me?' Elizabeth asked.

'I did just mention… he seemed all in favour… the Archbishop has been ill for some time but, of course, we were not to know he was so near the end,' George clarified.

'And I was not to know anything because it was none of my business,' Elizabeth said.

'I should perhaps… I did not wish to upset you, but I was perhaps inconsiderate. I must apologise. Would you mind very much?' enquired George.

'I should hate it. I suppose I should become accustomed to it, but… thank God, we'd still have Riby!'

'It is amazing how happy we always are there, is it not?' George proposed.

'Amazing,' agreed Elizabeth, 'and we have only been there four times. We had such a welcome though. The people of the North are very warm-hearted. I really believe, too, that Mr and Mrs Tomline made us welcome, in their place – for a little.'

'If I had read it in a novel, I would have esteemed it rather far-fetched. It was all your doing, my love – your gift for putting people at their ease. Would it not be well employed as an archbishop's wife? I recollect you were far from enthusiastic about being a bishop's wife at the onset,' George reminded her.

'I've grown into it, but a woman needs a home, and this is my home now.'

'And Riby?' queried George.

'And Riby? For holidays. But this is where the boys first walked. This is where Antony was and we were all so happy. Lincoln is the town we've changed. The Wolds are where I ride,' Elizabeth said passionately.

'"One county, and that the most brute and beastly in all my realm," as Henry the Eighth declared when Lincolnshire rebelled. I shall have to go to London,' George proclaimed.

'Now?' Elizabeth questioned.

'As soon as may be. I am to preach in the cathedral, so I must fulfil that, but on Monday. I very much hope you will accompany me,' George pleaded.

'Not I! Travelling in winter is uncomfortable and bad news will keep. Give Mr Pitt my love and send news when you have it,' Elizabeth replied firmly.

'I will not fail to. It is unfortunate that… We so seldom differ,' George said.

'At least one of us should be pleased,' Elizabeth said dryly.

:

Elizabeth's remarks about travelling in winter were borne out by George getting stuck in a snowdrift just short of Stamford. As this was the Great North Road, there were a number of other coaches and carts, most of which had a spade, so the drift was soon cleared. But next day, just beyond Huntingdon, a wheel came off the coach. Goodchild and Tom rode off to fetch a smith while George huddled in the coach, or walked about in the snow, remembering Elizabeth's words.

The Goodchilds came back in half an hour with a very surly smith. He'd refused to turn out in this weather, but Goodchild had persuaded him, Tom being as large as the smith and a noted bare fist fighter.

George stayed two nights in Cambridge to rest thc horses and enjoy the luxury of his old college, Pembroke, after the cold road. The knowledgeable dons – and who more knowledgeable than a worldly don? – took it quite for granted that he was the next Cantuar and hastened to congratulate him, and themselves, for having had a Fellow who now be very influential. George argued, as he had to Elizabeth, that the time was changing and patronage must not be too blatant anymore.

As soon as he came into the hall at Number 10 and saw Mr Pitt's face he knew the plans had gone wrong.

'George,' said Mr Pitt, who usually called him Doctor Tomline, unless they were alone. 'I do not know how to tell you.'

'You do not have to tell me, Billy,' said George, who always called him Mr Pitt. 'I can see it in your face.'

'I am all apologies. I was…'

'Uncle's heart is broken,' said Lady Hester, running downstairs, 'but the jibbing old King just wouldn't have it. He had determined on that holy bore, Manners-Sutton.'

'You should not speak so of a worthy ecclesiastic, Hester,' said Mr Pitt. 'We sinners are hardly in a position to judge saints. Come in to the morning room and take a wet. You must have had a perishing, cold journey, and then bad news at the end of it. Perhaps some tea, some soup?'

'Neither, I thank you, but some of your admirable Madeira would be most welcome,' George replied.

Dundas, now the Lord Melville, was in the morning room reading *The Lay of the Last Minstrel.*

'It's no' right,' he said, looking up and coming straight to the point as usual. 'It is no' like the King to turn things arsey versey. The prelates were aye in th' gift o' th' First Lord. If he starts meddling too we'll be o'er, like the French, before we can say Robespierre.'

'His Majesty has strong views,' said Mr Pitt.

'That's not what ye told him. Ye told him he was an obstinate, obstructive, unreasonable Monarch. I was but passing on m' way to th' library – they've every one of Sir Walter's – when I heard an angry voice. "Rob Roy Mc Gregor!", I thought, "is that no th' King and he in a rage?" An' then I was after hearing Mr Pitt, Mr Pitt as I n'er heard raise his voice afore, and he howling.'

'Why do you swear by obscure and undesirable Scotsmen?' enquired Lady Hester.

'It's from when I first fared political, and that is a wee whiley since. I was hearing meself saying "Good Lord Almighty!" And even "Christ!" "This no do", thought I. It is no' right for an elder o' th' Kirk. So I swore by my countrymen in th' hope they could maybe help me in yon southern Godless waste.'

'My consolation is Elizabeth did not desire it,' said George.

'That will do something to console me, too,' said Mr Pitt. 'She felt the responsibility would be too weighty?'

'She felt she did not want to leave Lincoln now she has made it our home.'

'Very creditable. It takes a woman to make a home,' said Mr Pitt, smiling at Hester.

'Should I change for dinner?' asked George.

'Please yourself,' said the Lady Hester. 'I do not intend to. Only dear Mr Rose, and dread Lord Castlereagh, are to come. We cannot keep his Lordship off.'

'He is perhaps somewhat solitary with his family in Ireland. He may be soporific to you but he is invaluable to me,' Pitt explained.

'Will they come this summer?' Mr Rose asked Mr Pitt at dinner.

Pitt replied animatedly, 'Now or never. The Emperor is not a patient man and he has been hovering on the brink for two years now. But I do not think he will venture, unless some of his ships come up to chase ours, or sink them.'

'I am creditably informed Bonaparte says, "If the Channel were but mine for six hours I would be master of the world,"' pointed out Castlereagh.

'What would we do without the invasion threat? Life would be sadly flat,' declared Hester.

'I am, at present, engaged in a memorandum as to the optimum disposition of Europe when France is finally subdued, and Napoleon banished,' said Mr Pitt.

'But what on earth will you do with it?' asked Hester.

'Alan Breck Stewart! Ye're delving away at that forbye but arranging this country in yeer spare time!' Dundas said.

'With particular reference to ensuring a lasting peace, I presume?' said Mr Rose.

'Indeed. That is the main purpose. I intend to give you all a copy, and a few other people who are likely to be involved. I realise it will not be wanted for some years, and have therefore paid particular attention to the twentieth century, when we will have flying machines and thinking machines, and people will make economies so as to be able to afford a day trip to the moon.'

There were a number of wild suggestions amidst a great deal of laughter.

CHAPTER TWENTY-NINE

London

George had hardly got home and ascertained the position with the new houses and read half-a-dozen of the Paston letters, when he was summoned back to London by a letter from William Wilberforce. He explained a complicated scandal over a report from the Navy Board Inquiry, saying Lord Melville, who had been the First Lord of the Admiralty then, was accused of taking money, and the Commons was going to take a vote on whether to impeach him.

Wilberforce wrote:

> *I may very possibly find myself constrained by my conscience to vote for impeachment and then poor Billy will have no one to confide in. Mr Canning is well enough, and loyal enough, but he is part of the problem and not of its alleviation. It is he who has turned the most part of Billy's mild critics into implacable enemies. Addington described him to me only last week as "obnoxious". He will never give Billy good counsel, the reverse I fear. Castlereagh is also totally loyal and sadly tactless. Hester is a comfort to Billy but she, too, will advise forward policy where there is a pressing need for caution*

George passed the letter to Elizabeth at the breakfast table.

'I could wish we were nearer London,' he said, when she had read it.

'At least there is no snow now. I shall come with you, for it is full time I went to see my parents.'

:

The journey went well. They stayed a night with Jane and Gussie, and then two nights at Burleigh, for George had found himself sitting next to Lord Exeter so often in the Lords they had become friends. Then they stayed at Elton with the Probys. It was more of a progress than a journey, Elizabeth thought.

Everyone was talking about the debate as to whether to impeach Lord Melville, which was to be on the eighth of April. It appeared Lord Melville and his assistant, one Trotter, had taken some money that had really belonged to the Navy and used it themselves, or, at any rate, Trotter had. He'd paid the money back eventually. Lord Exeter felt this wasn't good enough. 'The days of corruption are over,' he said, 'and must be seen to be over.'

Mr Proby took a different line. 'There can be little doubt they needed the money for the secret service, but they can't say so, d'you see? I never can make out why people dislike Melville so. He's a trifle robust, to be sure, but I've always found him a decent, straightforward sort.'

George didn't want to go back to Cambridge so soon after his disappointment, so they went on to Bacton, where George's parents were very pleased to see them, though George's mother remarked wistfully, 'I could wish you had brought one of the boys.'

'But you've got two grandchildren staying already,' Elizabeth commented, reminding her that her younger son John, his wife, Anne, and their children were staying for Easter.

'Yes, but I seldom see your boys, and they're such friendly, forthcoming youngsters, especially George. George is for all the world like Grandfather was when I first knew him,' George's mother said.

'Did you live next door?' asked Elizabeth.

'No, but I had a grandmother living in Bury, so we often went to stay there, and she'd known my George's father, who grew up here, so George was sent to live with her when he was 'prenticed in Bury.'

'And you fell in love with him aged fourteen?' asked Elizabeth.

'I don't think so, but he was kind to me and I liked him and then later…'

'Later…?' Elizabeth said looking puzzled.

'He told me he wanted to marry me in Grandfather's garden, and then he kissed me under the lilacs.'

'Your son George and I went out riding, and he had a fall and cracked a rib, and then I realised…' Elizabeth recalled.

'Ah but that makes a difference when you realise.'

'They all said you were going to be the next Archbishop of Canterbury,' said Anne to John at dinner, 'and then it was our own bishop after all. He's much too old, I think. They all say he's so holy but he never does anything.'

'He preaches a good sermon,' said John, 'and goes on forever, though you clever men all like him because he's always quoting Latin.'

'He does translate it,' George explained.

'I should hope so. He keeps a very poor table. You and George would've done better there,' Anne said.

'And poor George might've done better with the dons than with you,' thought Elizabeth, 'as far as gossip goes.'

There were daffodils everywhere, the sun was out and the birds sang. The meadows at the back were full of lambs. Elizabeth would have liked to stay longer, but George was anxious to get to Mr Pitt.

They arrived at Number 10 on the seventh April, 1805. The debate was the next day, and was so extremely anticipated Mr Pitt had some trouble getting seats in the gallery for them. They dined quietly, only six of them: George and Elizabeth, Mr Pitt, Lady Hester, Mr Canning and the ubiquitous Lord Castlereagh. Clever Hester brought the conversation on to Homer, where Mr Pitt, George, and Lord Castlereagh were all very happy, and diverted their minds from the worrying present.

They all went early to bed.

:

George and Elizabeth took their seats late, by Mr Pitt's advice, and found them occupied. The two men meekly occupying them left, however, apologising and explaining that after standing for two hours they had hoped the chairs were not going to be taken.

Mr Pitt spoke, but not as well as usual, perhaps as well as he could with slight material and a House that was in many cases hostile. He enlarged on the point that the money had been returned. He admitted it should never have been taken, but said it had been customary in those times.

At last, after many speeches for and against, and a few so rambling they could not make out whether they were in favour of Mr Whitbread's motion for impeachment or against, they came to the vote. It was now one in the morning and Elizabeth had been longing for her bed for hours. Still this was very exciting.

'I could not quite make out,' muttered George. 'They went through with such a rush at one point and it is precious close. But I think we have the advantage, only by one or two votes perhaps, but it will serve.'

But when the votes were announced they were two-hundred and sixteen in favour of the impeachment and two-hundred and sixteen against it. A confused, almost frightening noise arose from the floor of the house.

'What happens now?' asked Elizabeth.

'I believe the Speaker has the casting vote, but I do not know what his opinion may be. Indeed, come to think of it, I do not even know what his name may be,' George explained.

Their neighbours, for in the excitement everyone was talking now, told them this hadn't happened for twenty years and then it was over no great matter.

'Some amendment I believe,' said their neighbour, a tall, bald elderly man, who turned out to be a merchant.

The Speaker was consulting somebody. The Speaker was consulting lots of people. The tension grew.

'It was of course improper,' said the merchant, 'but a mere peccadillo when set against his long service and utility to Mr Pitt.'

'That's what I feel,' said Elizabeth. 'It is so ungrateful and ill-natured.'

'As you know, Mr Marble, I cannot agree with you,' said the hatchet-faced woman the other side of the merchant. 'In the past such dishonesty was all too often condoned, but we are, I'm thankful to say, progressing into a better age, where strict, godly, honesty will soon be the norm.'

'You'll have a job to make some of our fellow citizens strict, godly, and honest,' said the merchant cheerfully.

'It even divides couples,' Elizabeth began thinking to herself privately. 'I am glad George and I are quite agreed, except, as he said, over him becoming Archbishop. We usually are, only he gets a bit stuffy sometimes, and I have to talk or laugh him out of it.'

The Speaker suddenly stood up. He lurched a bit and put his hand on a desk to steady himself. The noise died away and stopped. He voted in favour of the motion. The uproar arose again, worse than ever. There was something frightening about it, thought Elizabeth, like the crowd baying when Christians were thrown to the lions. The noise died down a bit and a loud, coarse, over-emphasised upper class voice was heard.

'Let's see how Billy bears it!'

Some of the MPs lunged forward, others linked arms, forming a big circle around Mr Pitt, which he slowly walked out of. Elizabeth and George joined the crowds jostling to get out. Outside, George took Elizabeth's arm and was looking around for a cab, when she stopped dead and stiffened.

'There!' she said and pointed.

Mr Pitt stood by the side of the road wearing his little cocked hat with tears pouring down his cheeks. Elizabeth took him by the arm. 'Where's your coach' she asked.

'Sold,' he replied.

'Oh yes, I forgot. Get us a cab, George.'

It seemed long and cold before George came back with a hackney.

'It is so ungrateful,' said Elizabeth in the cab, returning to the subject Lord Melville's impeachment.

'Ungrateful indeed. For he has worked away from them for twenty years, neglecting his family, his health and his estate,' Pitt said forlornly.

'God will reward him,' said George confidently.

'I do believe it, but what now? Politics has been his life,' Pitt said.

He'll be busy enough defending himself, thought Elizabeth, but it seemed better not to say it, and anyway, they had arrived.

They let Mr Pitt drink one glass of port, and then Elizabeth made sure they all went to bed. The Lady Hester arrived like a whirlwind when they were on the stairs, escorted by her brother Charles, and full of indignation, exclamations, and wild plans. Elizabeth kept telling her, her uncle must go to bed. She agreed and then suggested they leave the ungrateful country to Napoleon and all go to Canada. Pitt was endlessly patient with her. Elizabeth was not.

'For goodness sake let your uncle sleep. Do you want to kill him?' Elizabeth snapped.

Hester unwisely continued, 'Yes, indeed you are in the right of it, Mrs Tomline. He must rest, but it is infamous. There must be something we can do. Suppose—'

Elizabeth and George practically pushed her out of Pitt's bedroom in the end. He looked exhausted. It was three in the morning but still Hester talked.

:

Breakfast the next morning was a late and lugubrious meal. The Lady Hester did not come. Mr Canning did, full of news, gobble, gossip. 'Where were you when you were wanted?' thought Elizabeth. She asked about the speaker who'd cast his vote to impeach Lord Melville and make Mr Pitt's herculean task even more difficult.

'One Abbott,' said Mr Pitt, 'a weak, well-meaning man. I expect Henry Addington had been persuading him. I should doubtless have sent Rose.'

'You cannot think of everything,' said Mr Canning, 'who could have foreseen that nonentity would suddenly become crucial? I blame fifty people but most of all I blame Wilberforce.'

'You must not blame him for following his conscience,' declared Mr Pitt. 'It is what all Christians should do and most do not.'

'He did at least write,' said George, 'summoning us in the hope we should have good fortune to be of some service to you in this difficult time.'

'You were indeed,' asserted Mr Pitt. 'I never was gladder than when Elizabeth took hold of me last night. I have the impression several young men offered to see me home but I felt at that stage a strong desire to be alone.'

'It is outrageous, though,' said Mr Canning, speaking too loud. 'They know perfectly well he spent that money on the secret service. Why don't we say so and tell them not to be so unpatriotic.'

'It would, I fear, cause them more trouble, and bring down the government. We could perhaps dress you up as Saint George in the mummers' play and get you to lecture the House. "See here, gents, d' y' want roast beef and roly poly puddin'? Or do y' want frogs' legs and soufflés? Make up y' minds, cos if y' want frogs y' going th' right way about it. What I sez is God stand up for roly poly puddin'!"'

Elizabeth stayed a week and saw very little of Mr Pitt. He was patiently trying to put together a new cabinet in Britain and a new coalition in Europe. Austria and Russia, were, as always, difficult; Prussia, as always, impossible.

Elizabeth's parents were pleased to see her. It had been over a year. Her mother was very bad now, twisted and wracked with pain. The doctor had prescribed opium which made her very sleepy, but she seemed happy. Elizabeth thought her mother was always happy now, when she was not in pain and thanks to the opium she was usually out of discomfort. She needed more opium every year, and the doctor was beginning to be worried about the amount she took. Elizabeth's father felt keeping her out of pain was much more important than prolonging her life.

Elizabeth and her father went to take Ned and George out at Eton. They stayed two nights with the head English teacher, who had been at the College with Elizabeth's father and remained friends with him ever since. Ned's leg was quite all right again, though he said he felt it a few hours before rain.

'You are now a human barometer,' his grandfather told him. 'We shall have to stand you in the hall.'

His tutor spoke well of Ned's work and said he could, if he wished, become a beak, or a don.

'I think his mind turns more to politics,' said Elizabeth. 'It may be that an acquaintance with Mr Pitt has been an inspiration to him.'

'Perhaps when he is Prime Minister he will bring in universal suffrage,' suggested Ned's grandfather.

'God forbid!' exclaimed his alarmed friend.

'Women, too?' asked Elizabeth.

'Most certainly, women, too,' said her father solemnly. 'They are in general, I find, better judges of men than men are.'

The tutor was less enthusiastic about George – a pleasant boy, and popular, but lazy. He could write a good essay in English but seldom did so. He sang well and was in the choir. It was hard to say what profession he might go into. As it happened Elizabeth found out the next day.

It was a fine Sunday in early May, and they all went to the chapel in the morning. After lunch, the tutor had parents who wished to see him. Ned wanted to finish a Latin poem he was putting in for a prize. Little George, who was a wet bob, asked if his mother and grandfather would like to come for a short trip up river in his boat. His grandfather declined.

'When you get to my age you begin to be a pin after a good nuncheon and your bed becomes a magnet,' he said.

After a long cold spring it had, at last, turned warmer, and everything seemed to be flowering. Yellow iris, gold buttercups, bluebells, may, water crossfoot, honesty, ransoms, lovely purple orchids, Queen Anne's lace and forget-me-nots. The birds were singing, swallows just touched the water, ducks conveyed their ducklings, and a kingfisher came past. So did two of George's friends. They were rather startled, and one of them was pleased to be factious.

'After the girls again, Jarge?' one of them said.

'I had hoped that even in this Gomorrah of gossip I could take my Mama for a spin without ill-bred comments,' George replied.

'Beg your pardon I'm sure, madam. I meant no harm. It's just whenever I see his red head my tongue seems to catch fire,' the friend suggested.

'Dip it in the river,' proposed George.

'Mind he don't upset you!' called back his friend, as they disappeared round the bend.

'I think perhaps I may become a clergyman,' George explained.

'Do you?' was all his mother could think of. If it had been her scholarly older son, or her reserved youngest, she would not have been so astonished, but lazy, pleasure-loving George!

'You remember when I was so ill with the measles?' he said.

'All too well.' It was like a nightmare in her memory.

George began to allude philosophically, 'I thought I heard voices sometimes. One was a kind voice I thought, though I knew it was my guardian angel and it often said, "There's no harm in him". And the other, which was a precise sort of voice, said, "No good, either – lazy and greedy. What use is he? What use will he ever be?" I thought I will be useful. If I live I will be useful.' The kingfisher went past them again, a streak of deep blue as if it was tied to its pink reflection. 'I don't suppose I'll be a holy sort of priest but I mean to be a useful sort of slum-clearance priest, like Papa.'

'We certainly need more useful priests and philanthropists,' Elizabeth agreed.

They went back the next day to find Jane and Gussie had just arrived. Jane was well, but cross.

'Babies are such a bore,' she said. 'Heavens send this is the last.'

'I am of the opinion,' said Gussie, 'you are pleased to disguise your womanly qualities. A stranger might conclude you had no family affections but I am happy to say, I am sensible the case is quite otherwise.'

'The case is I'm standing in the hall and my back hurts,' Jane replied.

'Come on up, then. Your room is all ready,' said Elizabeth.

There was a letter from George saying that Lord Grenville had made an agreement with the Russians. Another of Mr Pitt's coalitions was forming and looked very promising, though the Russians still blew hot and cold and wanted more money. Some of the French ships had escaped and gone to the West Indies. Nelson followed, just missed them, and came back.

Elizabeth was reading aloud to her mother in the shade of a cedar one morning, when she saw Mrs Potts come out of the house.

'I'll just go and ask,' she said. 'How do you think she goes on?' she asked Potts a moment later.

Potts replied, 'Well enough. Why not? She's no age, healthy and active. Mind you, we'll have to watch out for bleeding, same's we did with her mother, but I reckon that'll be all right.'

'You only just saved her mother that last time and there will be no ice in June,' Elizabeth returned worriedly.

Potts consoled her, 'Well, as that happen, I laid by some ice in February. Farmer Clegg got a deep well with a ladder down and cupboards. That may melt but we packed it with wool, and I reckon it'll last 'til July or August, unless that turn hot. There's a girl at the mill may need it, too.'

'You think of everything,' Elizabeth admitted.

'Not now I don't. I forget everything now I'm in m' sixties, but I hope I remember what I most need to. You keeping well?' asked Potts.

'Very well,' Elizabeth replied, smiling.

Potts continued, 'I got to thank you for what you done for Molly. She bin that happy an John going to become a doctor. Well I never heard th' like! Not many of us village folk get a chance like that.'

'He's a good boy. I must go back to my mother,' Elizabeth said.

When she got back she found her mother was asleep.

:

Valentine Augustus was born on the third of June and weighed nine pounds. It was a long labour but there was nothing serious in the way of bleeding and the ice was not needed. Gussie was delighted and told them all about his great-grandfather Valentine, who had been a judge, and his Uncle Valentine, who was a rich and childless man. Jane recovered rapidly and the baby was very greedy and grew fast.

Elizabeth went back to London but she found it very hot, airless, and smelly, and persuaded George to take her home after a few days. There, all was well, and Richard, who was going to Eton in September, had taken over George's habit of putting flowers in her bedroom to welcome her back. Joseph was to go with him to Eton. Madame Lebrun felt that with the last son away from home, she must find another job.

Elizabeth remonstrated with her. 'I should miss you. We have dealt so well together. Could you not stay and become my dame de compagnie? I am sure you write half my letters for me and do the flowers much better than I do, and you notice when we need to redecorate, when I do not.'

'I 'ave discovered I 'ave aptitude to teach. One must use one's talents. I shall be sorry to leave. I 'ave been 'appy in de Palace. But it will be best. Mrs Andrews tells me 'er daughter Jane wishes 'er children to speak good French so I will go there,' Lebrun revealed.

By now, Kate had a son which pleased her and Roly immensely.

They all went to Riby for the summer holidays. Camilla got her mother's permission in a misspelt, reticent scrawl.

'I think she is a little hurt that you do not wish to go home,' explained Elizabeth. 'But when you come out in a year or two we will take a large house in London, and your Mama shall come and stay and meet grand people. She will like that.'

'But I will not. I'd far rather be at Riby, shooting, fishing, and riding, than in stuffy old London, wearing smart uncomfortable clothes and being bored,' Camilla explained.

'We can do both. The season is over quite early in the summer and then we will go to Riby,' Elizabeth said.

The weather was rather unsettled, but they had a wonderful holiday all the same. Lord Yarborough's eldest son had purchased an air balloon and basket, and was now given to wandering about the sky to the terror of horses, chickens, and sheep. Cattle usually continued to concentrate on grass. Ned, George, Richard, Camilla, and John all had a flight. Neither George nor Elizabeth were very happy about it but they yielded to youthful pleas. Fortunately, Lord Worsely had taken himself and his balloon to a friend at Clumber before Jane and Gussie and their children arrived, as it would've led to marital discord, with Jane always being game for anything dangerous, and Gussie always being very fussy about his children's safety.

George, Ned, little George, and Richard all went south in late August. Ned had left Eton and was going to his father's old Pembroke College, Cambridge. Elizabeth stayed on at Buckden, determined not to waste the last of the summer in a town.

Little George happened to be in the hall at Number 10 Downing Street one morning when the knocker went and a footman ushered in a small man in naval uniform, with a black patch and only one arm. George was sure it was Lord Nelson. He bowed and the Admiral returned the bow. Then he was ushered into Pitt's study.

George knew his father was out at a meeting to do with the finances of Westminster Abbey, but he rushed upstairs and fetched his brother Richard, who was packing all the things he meant to take to Eton tomorrow, particularly cakes. They waited in a little room beside the hall with the door open.

'Do you think we really should go out when he comes,' asked Richard. 'Wouldn't it be a bit pushy?'

'I don't think so. They say he likes being admired. He returned my bow,' little George said.

Before very long, they heard voices, discarded their books, and went rather sheepishly out into the hall.

'... And if that happened we would soon bring Bonaparte to his marrow bones,' said one of the voices.

'I know I may rely on you,' said Mr Pitt. 'Ah, these are the Pretyman boys, my Lord. They are the Bishop's sons.'

'Your father made a good fist of it when he tutored Mr Pitt,' said Lord Nelson pleasantly. 'Are you classical scholars like him?'

'My eldest brother's mad on Latin and this one's mad on Greek but I'm just mad on boats, small boats I mean, not like yours.'

'I was always sculling and punting as a small boy, too. You learn a bit about balance. Well I must go. I have much to do before I sail,' the Admiral said in reply.

Mr Pitt escorted him out.

Lord Melville had been questioned at the bar of the house like Warren Hastings before him. Some people wanted him prosecuted and fined, but, on the whole, the fuss was dying down. Rumours began to reach them that Napoleon had left Boulogne after his long wait and marched south with his army. The third coalition was going well: the Austrians had raised two large armies; the Russians were coming, led by their young Tsar. Even the Prussians looked as if they were going to make up their minds at last and join in.

:

In early September, George sent Goodchild back to fetch Elizabeth, who stayed three nights in Cambridge with Ned, who was enjoying himself and delighting the Dons.

London was hot, noisy, and smelly. Mr Pitt was finishing some business about the coalition and now hoped to escape to Walmer in a day or two. He begged George and Elizabeth to come too. The weather was still and sunny, with misty mornings. Elizabeth and Lady Hester swam every day. Mr Pitt was like a schoolboy, home for the holidays. The Cannings were staying too. Mrs Canning was a pretty girl of twenty five, who looked younger, and was rather overcome by such exalted company.

After dinner on the first night, when the ladies had left, Elizabeth got Mrs Canning on to servants, that fertile, often fecund subject with rich ladies.

Before Mrs Canning could answer Hester said, 'Everyone says servants were much better before. They must've been saints and geniuses then, because for my part I find them pretty good and quite invaluable now.'

'It often seems unfair that we have so much and they have so little,' said Mrs Canning.

'I said that when I was your sort of age,' said Elizabeth, 'but then I observed that hard work and scant money often made them cheerful and resourceful, whereas being rich and lazy had a tendency to make the gentry bored and dissatisfied.'

'Certainly most great ladies are as stupid as owls and spiteful as monkeys,' said Hester. 'Why cannot they take up watercolours or something? I should be ashamed to be of so little use or amusement to anyone.'

Elizabeth thought fleetingly of what George had said on the river.

'We do not have much education,' said Mrs Canning, doubtfully.

'Well then educate yourself,' advised Hester. 'We are so fortunate as to be surrounded by good books and good talkers. Shall we be blind and deaf?'

'It is most true,' agreed Elizabeth, 'or if we have money to spare we will find that charity keeps us happily occupied.'

'I never seem to have time or money for charity,' declared Hester, 'and am far from sure the saucy mob do not just take advantage of us.'

'Some of them do of course, or try to, but most of them are very worthy and pathetically grateful to see their children fed and warmed,' Elizabeth argued.

'How the devil do you heat beggar brats?' Hester jibed.

Elizabeth replied, 'I have never attempted it but with the ordinary poor you just obtain a fuel depot in the charge of a reliable man and give out cheap wood and coal.'

'How do you tell a good charity from a bad wasteful charity?' asked Mrs Canning.

'Look about you and inquire. For example your fellow guest Mr Wilberforce is engaged in trying to free the slaves, so he always requires money and assistance,' Elizabeth revealed.

'Mind it does not swallow you alive as it has swallowed him,' said Lady Hester. 'He was used to be an amusing, well-bred man, but now he is a dead bore, who talks of nothing but slave ships and shackles, of all lowering topics.'

'A good parson will always tell you what is most wanted,' Elizabeth told Mrs Canning, 'and will, most probably be running all sorts of clubs and funds, where the need is much greater than the money. Moreover, by discovering a trifle about the more entertaining parts of politics, you may assist your husband greatly, enabling him to talk things over with you and clarify his ideas.'

'There are no entertaining parts of politics,' asserted Lady Hester. 'It is all infinitely tedious and depressing. They tear poor Uncle William apart like vultures. It is a marvel he remains human.'

'I am obliged to you, Mrs Tomline,' said Mrs Canning. 'You have given me much to reflect on. My mama, grandmama, and aunt told me how to go on, as to dress and entertaining and leaving cards, but when Mr Canning is from home I have experienced a certain restlessness and aimlessness that I now recognise as want of purpose.'

After this conversation Mrs Canning talked freely to Elizabeth and guardedly but quite sensibly to everyone else.

The next day, they all drove over to Canterbury, as the Cannings and Sir Arthur Wellesley had not seen the Cathedral. It was cold and raining hard, but clever Goodchild put them down at the side door of the Cathedral, and picked them up an hour later so they didn't get wet. A verger showed them round, and, after half an hour, a breathless Dean appeared, summoned by the verger's messengers. Between them they knew a lot of history, and Elizabeth, who was not so well informed, asked some sensible questions, which produced informative answers from George and the verger, and witty answers from Lady Hester, Mr Pitt, and Mr Canning.

Mr Wilberforce did not come with them as he had letters to write.

CHAPTER THIRTY

Number 10 Downing Street

'What is India like?' Mrs Canning asked Sir Arthur at dinner.

'A large question, Ma'am. One might say perhaps it is like Massachusetts in the last age, with the Puritans, the Jesuits, the Red Indians, the English, and the French all fighting it out, but there the Puritans are Hindus, and the Jesuits are Mussulmen, and the Red Indians are Marathas.'

'Is it not very unhealthy?' Mrs Canning pressed.

Sir Arthur continued, 'There are various diseases certainly, and the hot weather is monstrously uncomfortable, but, in general, if the English would but use liquor moderately and exercise immoderately, instead of, as so often, the other way on, the climate would be found to be perfectly salubrious.'

'You could compare it to arriving on Mars,' suggested Mr Pitt, 'and finding fierce but fascinating Martians. Who could you trust? How soon could you learn the most commodious local language? One would not wish to interfere with their customs, but when they include the sacrifice of small children, I feel it should be discouraged.'

'Do they really do that?' asked Mrs Canning, wide-eyed, and deliciously horrified.

'Alas yes,' said Wilberforce, 'and they encourage widows to be burnt alive on their husband's pyre. I really think our rule, otherwise hard to justify, is God's purpose, because we do at least put a stop to those horrors.'

'So does the better type of Indian,' said Sir Arthur. 'Thing fretted me most after the famines was all those women locked up in hot little houses.'

'Zenanas,' said Mr Pitt. 'You will not modernize the Muslims in a hurry. I am not altogether sorry; the world would be a sad place if we were all the same.'

'The world is a sad place without Boney squinting at us from over the way,' said Lady Hester, suddenly abandoning her conversation about the latest scandal. 'I knew it would be so. This time last year we lived in dread but at least we lived. Do you remember going for a walk the summer before last and that old lady left her haymaking to beg you to preserve her grandchildren, and a flock of butterflies came from France and you said, "I am glad Bonaparte is not a butterfly".'

They laughed, and Sir Arthur said, 'It was a remarkable circumstance, the greatest man in the world, with all his resources, and he could not advance twenty-five miles, in two years.'

'The Navy was in the way,' said Elizabeth.

'What would you have done, sir, had you been in Napoleon's place?' Pitt asked Sir Arthur.

'I think,' said Sir Arthur slowly, 'once I had grasped that my ships would not arrive safely, I would have ventured one foggy, still day, when there was no wind. The barges had oars, I presume, and men to use them?'

'I do not think anyone knows,' said Lady Hester, 'but it is funny you should say that. It is just what Sir John Moore said about one foggy, still day in the year and how he took every possible precaution then.'

'Good soldier, Moore,' said Sir Arthur.

'It is a pity perhaps that Bonaparte did not get to India that time, through Eygpt,' said Mr Pitt. 'He could have fought the Marathas for years, and the rest of the world could have had a little repose.'

'Certainly not very restful, Bonaparte,' said Sir Arthur, 'and now he's off again, helter-skelter, and a huge army at his heels.'

'He is outnumbered,' said Mr Wilberforce.

Sir Arthur added, 'Never worried him. I could wish the Austrians were using their Archduke and not that mollycoddle Mack.'

'You seem precious well informed about the Austrians' arrangements,' said Lady Hester.

'A man should be precious well informed about his trade. Trouble with young monarchs is they think they're heaven-born generals. I don't suppose the Tsar'll be much use,' said Sir Arthur.

'You complain of a want of royalty in the Austrian service and a surplus in the Russian. It is hardly very consistent.'

'Archduke's a soldier. When do you think you'll hear?' Sir Arthur asked Mr Pitt.

'In God's time. I try to compose my mind and think of Herrick, but the pretty veil is inclined to tear,' Pitt answered.

'Should think it might. Riding composes the mind I collect,' Sir Arthur concluded.

'Or at least stupefies it.'

'Uncle, give us your imitation of Mr Grattan's speech,' begged Lady Hester.

'I should imagine Mrs Canning and Mrs Tomline do not require any more on politics or the military,' Pitt stated.

'Oh, but indeed I do,' said Mrs Canning. 'I wish to learn more about politics.'

'And I too should like to hear one of Mr Grattan's fine speeches,' agreed Elizabeth. 'They say he is quite an orator.'

'If you insist,' said Mr Pitt, and then in a slight brogue, began, 'Will y' allow me to lament an old an' dear acquaintance o' mine, th' Irish Parliament. Of that assembly I have a parental recollection. I sat by her cradle, I followed her hearse. In fourteen years she acquired for Ireland what you did not acquire for England in a century – freedom of trade, independence of the legislative, independence of the judges, restoration of the final judicature, repeal of a perpetual mutiny bill, Habeas Corpus Act, Nullum Tempus Act – a great work! You will exceed it and I shall rejoice. I call my countrymen to witness if in that business I compromised the claims of my country, or temporised with the power of England, but if there was one thing which baffled the effort of the patriot and defeated the wisdom of the Senate, it was the folly of the theologian.'

'It is uncanny,' exclaimed Mrs Canning. 'His words! His intonation! His squeaky voice, his hesitations! How do you do it?'

'I do not know,' said Mr Pitt apologetically. 'I seem to have that sort of memory.'

'Was it true?' asked Mrs Canning.

Pitt confirmed, 'Most of it was. I would qualify it by pointing out the legislators may have been remarkably independent, but a number of them were also remarkably corrupt, too.'

'As he well knew,' said Sir Arthur. 'Having to do him justice – often striven against it.'

'I suppose it is quite time the ladies left the room,' said Elizabeth reluctantly.

'As you wish, but we had rather you stayed. We shall be dull dogs without you to ask interesting questions and encourage us to parade our knowledge. After all, we're but a small intimate party and need not observe the formalities,' Pitt expressed.

They stayed. They laughed. Mrs Canning relaxed and told about her journey to Italy with her parents as a child. She was clearly delighted by her success.

Mr Pitt was going soon, to stay with his friend Lord Bathurst in Gloucestershire.

:

The Tomlines went back north gradually. First Eton, where they had the pleasure of watching George, Richard, and Joseph eat. Joseph loved Eton and was, it appeared, very popular with everyone. Richard was rather bobbing along in his wake but both of them were used to that and quite happy about it. Then London, where, as Mr Pitt had described, they stayed in Number 10 and fetched Mr Pitt's portrait from the studio of Mr Gainsborough Dupont. George had desired a picture of Pitt, who was much too hard-pressed to sit for pictures anymore, but out of affection had had two sittings with Gainsborough before the artist was taken ill and died. The artist's nephew, Gainsborough Dupont, who shared a studio with his uncle, had finished it with one more sitting. The picture showed Pitt leaning with a letter in his hand, looking serious, and a little sad but very alert.

They slept for a night each at two quite comfortable inns on the way, and for five nights at Pembroke College in Cambridge. Ned and his instructors were all delighted with his progress among the Greeks and Romans. He was considering embarking on Hebrew or Sanskrit, too, but his parents discouraged it, feeling he was quite scholarly enough. He remained friends with Lord Worsely, who took him about in the balloon from time to time. Only last week they had landed inconveniently in a duck pond near Huntington. One of his Hubbard cousins had looked him up. His Pretyman grandmother had been a Hubbard.

'He's a muff and swat like me,' Ned told his parents. 'So we deal extremely together.'

'You ride well,' said his mother carefully.

'Everyone rides well,' Ned replied.

'Some better than others,' said George, 'and I was always one of the others.'

'You skate well.'

'Suppose I do. I hope we have some ice this winter then.'

Hubbard came to dinner at Pembroke one night, and he and the Tomlines had a lovely time with Hesiod, Homer, and Euripides. Elizabeth was fortunate to be sitting next to the Chaplain, who was civil enough to speak English. Ned had made friends with another freshman, George Gordon, Lord Byron.

'It was an odd start,' Ned told his parents. 'I had just passed him with his monkey on his shoulder and thought what a jolly little beast it looked, when some boys came by halloing after a football and scared the animal up a tree. His Lordship was trying to coax it down. As it chanced, I had a box of sugar plums in my valise, along with some books and a pen. I offered him some of the sugar plums and it answered very well. His Lordship was most grateful and has been friendly ever since. We're very different sorts of men but he writes verses too, so we read our poems to each other. His Latin verses are indifferent, but I really think he has a feel for the music of words in English, and will make a poet if he takes pains.'

Lord Byron, too, came to dinner. He was a good looking youth and spoke well about modern poetry. He was an admirer of William Wordsworth and Elizabeth told how he had stayed with them so long ago.

'Ah, is it so indeed? You must look him up should you get the opportunity. He's a promising poet, though, to my mind, his friend Coleridge is even better. They brought out a book called *Lyrical Ballads*, that is my bible for the present. I'm partial to Crabbe, too. He's not so much of a poet, but he's a prodigious story teller. Then there's a man in my part of the country, Scotland, that has the true attic salt, Robert Burns he's called, and was but a ploughman it appears, but he has all the drama and rhythm of the finest Border Ballads.'

'Perhaps you will translate Horace and Aeschylus into magnificent English verse,' suggested Ned.

'Perhaps you will. It's not quite in my line, I fear. What poetry do you relish the most, Mrs Tomline?' asked the young Byron.

Elizabeth answered enthusiastically, 'Probably the Elizabethans, and the poets a little before and after them: Wyatt, Donne, Herrick, Nashe, Corbet, Jonson, Spencer, and Milton. The ballads, of course, like you, and some of the old songs, too.'

'I am quite of your mind. Poetry must be musical and moving or it is nothing. Do you rhyme yourself?' asked Byron.

'I used to as a girl, but increasing duties and a dread of boring my audience brought it to a close,' answered Mrs Tomline.

'A pity. With your taste you would write well. There is much in the old saying, "practice makes perfect". Ned you must write with your mother and read each other what you have written. And you, my Lord, what poetry do you prefer?' the young man proposed, turning towards George.

'Being a classical scholar, I prefer the classical, in particular the Greek, but I also have a fondness for Shakespeare and Jonson and Milton,' George answered.

'Admirable! My verse is as yet very juvenile and such facility as I have leads me to write too much and revise too little, but I am in hopes more experience in life and love may amend this fault,' Byron responded.

He told them about his home, Newstead Abbey in Nottinghamshire, and his Newfoundland dog, Bo'sun.

'His Lordship was not at all as I expected,' said Elizabeth as they jolted northwards. 'I expected a coxcomb from Ned's description. I found an earnest halfling, old for his years and used to good company, but sincerely fond of poetry.'

'One of the dons told me he sometimes drinks too much, but I think him a suitable friend for Ned, who is inclined to be over-serious. We must hope the religion and good principles we have instilled will protect him from atheism and drunkenness,' George said frowning slightly.

'You think his Lordship is an atheist?' chirped Elizabeth.

'As to that I am quite ignorant but he did not strike me as one who was following his Saviour,' George revealed.

:

It was good to get home, even to a home without sons, but there was a lot that needed deciding, and they could only stay a few weeks because Elizabeth had realised she should spend Christmas with her parents, as her mother was unlikely to be with them much longer. The whole family had really wanted to go to Riby, but Elizabeth explained to the boys about their grandmother.

Jane and Gussie came to stay with the Andrews, bringing Madame Lebrun, and Elodie. The last two stayed at the Palace, as the Andrews had not got much room, and Madame Lebrun wanted to see as much as possible of Elizabeth, while Elodie wanted to see as much as possible of Camilla. Gussie only stayed two nights. He and Jane, for the first time, were not on very good terms. There were two reasons, one temporary and likely to be resolved; one permanent and likely to ruin their marriage. The first was Gussie's total devotion to his baby son. He insisted on bringing him to Lincoln. He resented Jane's weaning him.

'Damn it, I fed the brat for nearly six months,' Jane complained to Elizabeth when they were alone one morning arranging chrysanthemums.

'Do you find him tedious?' Elizabeth asked.

'He's all right, not as taking as Joseph was, but a good, fat, sensible baby. It's Gussie who's tedious about him,' Jane described.

'I'm glad you mentioned Joseph, I've got a letter he sent you. I've so much to remember at the moment I'm forgetting everything. Shall I go and fetch it?' Elizabeth proposed.

'No. Don't bother. It'll keep and I'll remind you. How is the slippery charmer?' Jane asked.

'He seemed very happy. His tutor said he was popular and doing well at work, and Richard just trots after him.'

'Joseph listens to Richard though, about religion and history.'

The second thing that was infuriating Jane, was that Gussie was delving after a Deanery. He was using his aunt, the Duchess of Rutland, as a trowel, and, while not in the least bothered about which Deanery he discovered, was confident he'd find one soon. Jane didn't want to move.

'Why do men have to be so beastly and ambitious?' she demanded after she'd poured out the sad story.

'It is the nature of the beast. George was just the same, although, of course, I was removing from the town to the country, which I better prefer, and you will be moving the other way. Could you not keep a cottage in Woolsthorpe? Just as a hunting base, with three bedrooms and stabling, say?' Elizabeth suggested.

'It's an idea,' Jane replied. 'Then I could keep an eye on the hospital and the new cottages. There, that's done. Anymore?'

'No I thank you,' said Elizabeth glancing at Jane's concoction. At least most of them were the right way round this time. 'Madame Lebrun is doing the dining room. Sit on the sofa 'til I just finish this, and then we could have some coffee, or chocolate if you wish?'

'Chocolate would be delicious,' Jane agreed.

'Good! I enjoy it too. Just pull the bell, would you!' asked Elizabeth.

Amabel had found a copy of Ossian in a bookshop and was intrigued by it.

'There is a strangeness and unearthly, primitive quality that pleases. Yet I know not why, I do not find it entirely convincing as an early legend or history,' she told them at dinner one night.

'Most knowledgeable people are of the opinion the author invented it,' George told her. 'It caused quite a stir some little time ago. The period and the place are not those I am conversant with but I recall a historian, who had studied Erse, telling me that although Ossian was indeed a character in Irish legends, this version did not agree with any of them. There was something, if I do not mistake, about how the Annals of Lismore was the best authority, but the creator of Ossian did not appear to be conversant with it.'

'You do not altogether surprise me,' said Amabel. 'The author would have done better, I concede, to have taken some genuine story as his starting place and then embellished it as he pleased.'

'Is it not strange,' enquired Jane, 'that learned men know so much about the Hebrews, Greeks, and Romans a long time ago, and so little about the more recent history of their own country?'

'The Hebrews, Greeks, and Romans wrote things down,' her father informed her.

'Just so,' said George. 'Moreover, we would not, I am persuaded, claim to know "so much" about the classics or the Scriptures. Something has survived but much has perished.'

'Surely no one would compare the clear minds of the Greeks and Romans and the holiness of the good book with the ravings of bloody-thirsty, superstitious savages?' stated Gussie.

'The Greeks, the Romans, and the Hebrews were a small thing bloodthirsty on occasion,' said the Archdeacon.

'It is an enthralling debate, but I think we had better leave you to it,' said Elizabeth. 'We start early tomorrow, so we must be up betimes and go to bed in good time.'

They were late starting in the end. A letter from Mr Canning delayed them a little, and then Goodchild appeared without the coach. The letter told of a French victory at Ulm. Mack, the Austrian commander, and his army were nearly all dead or captured. Napoleon was installed in the Imperial Palace in Vienna.

Goodchild had discovered the night before that his daughter-in-law, Nell, was having another baby.

'Not a word. No one ever tells me anything,' he said crossly. 'She thought, if you please, it was too soon to tell. Too soon at six months. She made my Tom promise to keep quiet and she planned to go to her mother by th' public stage in February along o' m' wife. February, I ask you! Eight months gone and m' wife far too old to go searching about through the snow.'

'So you want us to take her?' asked Elizabeth.

'If you'd be so good, Madam. She wanter go home to her ma'm. Quite right, too, being as her ma's th' best midwife in th' three kingdoms. But she's nervous like, since they lost that little girl t' th' measles. An as that happen there's only you two, an' Miss Meynell and th' maid, an' me or Tom, so you got plenty room for another.'

'Could you not return for her?' asked George, 'and your wife, too, if you wish?'

'I could. But you'd be without me 'n' th' coach for a month. Maybe two if th' weather turn bad.'

'Much better, take her with us,' said Elizabeth. 'It will be quite like old times and I shall be quite like a grand lady, travelling with two maids. Can she be ready in an hour?'

'I'll see she is,' Goodchild said.

:

When they arrived at Cambridge flags were flying and people were building bonfires.

'What are you celebrating?' Elizabeth asked the porter at Pembroke.

'Bin a big victory at sea, Madam. Cape Trafalgar, wherever that may be, twenty ships of the line taken, but Nelson was killed.'

They had a celebration dinner and several of the dons got drunk. Ned went out celebrating with his friend Lord Byron. They took Camilla. Ned and Camilla's sleepy accounts of the festivities next morning were far from clear, but they involved a bear and the Master of Trinity who made a speech from a cart.

When they arrived at Downing Street, Mr Pitt was from home and the servants didn't know where to put anyone. The Tomlines and Camilla firmly took their usual rooms, and Goodchild told the servants a thing or two about 'coves as don't know their job.'

Mr Pitt, when he returned, endorsed their proceedings and welcomed them warmly.

For dinner there was, besides Mr Pitt and Lady Hester, the Cannings, Mr Rose, Lord Castlereagh, and Sir Arthur Wellesley. Mr Pitt told them he had always been able to sleep before, when a messenger brought news in the middle of the night, whether it was good or bad.

'I was able to return to the realm of Morpheus, but on the seventh, I lay there reflecting on Nelson's life and death, until, at length, I had as well get up and do something needful, though it was three in the morning. Your father was there, I collect?' he asked Camilla.

'Of a certain, but I have not heard,' she replied.

'You would have if Emily wasn't so lazy,' thought Elizabeth. 'I bet she's heard and had plenty of time to write here.'

'I envy you with all my heart,' said Lady Hester, 'to be a daughter to one of Nelson's "Band of Brothers".'

'No news is good news,' said Mr Pitt. 'Bad news travels fast.'

'I must congratulate you on your speech at the Lord Mayor's banquet,' George said to Mr Pitt. 'It read very well, I thought.'

'You might've read it to me,' Elizabeth said crossly.

'I could not remove the fellow's newspaper,' George answered.

'You could have bought one though,' Elizabeth snapped.

'You may, if you will, hear it from the horse's mouth,' said Mr Pitt. 'I do not at all object to making it again.'

'Oh yes please,' she said.

Pitt cleared his throat and began recalling the earlier events. 'An alderman got rather carried away and said I had saved Europe, so I replied, "I thank you for the honour you do me, but Europe is not to be saved by any single man. England has saved herself by her exertions and will, I trust, save Europe by her example".'

'Marvellous,' said Elizabeth. 'May it prove true.'

'I thought it the best, neatest speech I ever heard in my life,' said Sir Arthur, 'even if I shall live to be eighty.'

'I like to picture you, sir, in your eighties, attending on a speech by an as yet unborn statesman in the year 1860, on the lamentable state of Ireland, and finding it trumps my remarks,' Mr Pitt proclaimed.

'We have all given that speech,' said Mr Canning.

'Where do they hold the Lord Mayor's banquet?' asked Mrs Canning.

'The Guildhall.'

'And they don't let in women?' she asked.

'Not they,' said the Lady Hester, 'but everyone tells me it's their loss, and nothing could be more flat.'

'It is possible,' said Mr Rose, 'that if you desire to talk about cotton, women would be an interruption, and few women would wish to talk about cotton for five hours.'

'One day perhaps you'll let us in,' said Lady Hester, 'but when men control nearly all the money, some of them may be very generous, but few would wish to lose control. We need the vote and only a few women have one. We also need, if we can qualify, to be allowed to join the professions.'

'St Paul said—' proclaimed George, with his usual deliberation.

'All sorts of illiberal things. I know, he would, but we have made a little progress, I should hope. What do you think, Uncle?' Hester asked.

'I should wish women to be free, to fulfil themselves, and I have met many of great capacity, but reforms are more likely to take if they go slowly,' Pitt suggested.

'A friend of mine who reads widely,' said Elizabeth, 'told me a woman poet in the seventeenth century wrote, "You refuse us education and then laugh at our stupidity".'

'How true,' said Lady Hester. 'Queen Elizabeth the First was a well-educated woman, so was Lady Jane Grey, but no one gives their daughters such learning in our day.'

'Hard on the children,' said Sir Arthur.

'To have a mother who isn't stupid?' demanded Lady Hester.

'To have a mother who isn't there. Who will care for the children when we have Lady Generals and Lady Governors of the Bank of England?' Sir Arthur went on.

'But ladies do not look after their children,' objected Mrs Canning.

'I was so fortunate as to have two excellent nurses,' said Elizabeth, 'but I am persuaded, when they were out of infancy, my boys saw as much of me as they did of their nurse.'

'But you have an easy way with you that can get through even to the children,' said Lady Hester. 'I am persuaded I would have more in common with a crossing sweeper than a small boy. When my brothers were young I thought them savages.'

'Your stepmother saw to that,' thought Elizabeth. She also thought it was a melancholy spectacle to see Camilla so quiet, though to be sure no one could wonder at it.

'I have written a poem on Trafalgar and must ask you to help me improve it,' said Mrs Canning.

'Tomorrow perhaps,' said Mr Pitt.

The next day, Mr Pitt and George again found themselves alone at breakfast. George asked after Mr Pitt's health. He admitted he was far from well and had pains in his head and stomach.

'My doctor makes little of my headaches and I am sure he is right, for they often come when I am pressed and soon disappear when I have more leisure. But the bilious tendency troubles him and so I have consented to go to Bath in a se'night. I benefited greatly from it on the last occasion I took the waters.'

'I am sure that is wise, and now Britain is no longer besieged you may be a little easier,' George agreed.

'I do not think any English Minister will find much ease while Bonaparte is still at large. Good morning, Hester. I trust you slept well?' Pitt said, as Hester entered.

'Very well, I thank you, Uncle. I always do. After last night's discussions I feel I should ask to join the cabinet,' Lady Hester asked.

'I will make you Minister of War,' Pitt declared.

'That will suit, though, to be sure, I thought Sir Arthur was in the right of it. And if great ladies may readily find housekeepers and nurses, and easily pay them, we can't all be great ladies,' Hester argued.

'And as Mr Pitt so rightly said, the changes had best come gradually,' said Mr Canning, dashing in, followed more slowly by his wife.

'Yes, but where are they? I don't see any?' Hester asked.

'The Anglo-Saxons allowed women to own property,' George told them.

'I have enjoyed lively discussions,' said Mr Canning, 'as to whether, had there been no Norman conquest, England had been happier.'

Elizabeth and Camilla came down at this point. After greetings and enquiries as to what sort of night she had passed, Elizabeth asked Mr Pitt, 'How is Lord Melville? I still think of him as Mr Dundas.'

'In fine fig. He writes regularly from Scotland where I collect he is, "braw and bright now he is'na scunnered with yon southron loons".'

Elizabeth laughed. 'You catch him exactly, bless him! A bit of it I could not follow, but I never doubted his good will.'

'We miss him sadly,' agreed Mr Canning. 'A tiger to work.'

He and Mr Pitt excused themselves, and George headed for his favourite bookshop.

'I cannot thank you enough, Mrs Tomline, for your kindly advice,' said Mrs Canning. 'I lost no time in consulting our parson and he had a hundred admirable suggestions where help was wanted. I chose to do something for Corum's Orphanage, being vastly fond of children. We took a party to Astley's in October, and they so enjoyed it, and this Christmas we intend—'

Here, Goodchild came in carrying an express.

'Beg pardon for interrupting you, but I spied this flung down on a windowsill. They mighter brought it someday and then again they mighter clean forgot it.'

He handed the letter to Camilla.

'Oh thank you, thank you. I've been waiting and waiting…' She tore it open.

'Papa is safe,' she said a minute later. 'He's not even hurt, but he had to go in to Gibraltar because – here you read it!' and she threw it at Elizabeth.

The letter read:

Dear Miss Meynell,

Although we are unacquainted, I take the liberty of writing to tell you your father has not a scratch. His ship, The Prince, played a gallant part in the recent battle and is therefore somewhat shattered, and so he has put in to Gibraltar to refit. I have written to your mother. Your father speaks of you often with great warmth and pride.

In haste.
Your most humble obedient servant,
Thomas Hardy

'I'm so glad,' said Lady Hester.

'How can I get to Portsmouth quickly?' asked Camilla.

'Come to your grandparents' as we planned, and then after the horses have had a good rest, Goodchild will take you on, won't you?' Elizabeth asked.

'That I will,' answered Goodchild.

'Small haste. Captain Hardy says his ship was shattered, so I am sure it will take weeks to repair. You may look for him in February perhaps, but hardly much before.'

'Couldn't we go tomorrow?' asked Camilla.

'No. The Bishop is to preach at Saint Paul's on Sunday,' replied Elizabeth.

'Couldn't I go on the stage coach? With a maid, if you like,' Camilla persevered.

'No, but I am persuaded there is no need.'

'Did you say Captain Hardy?' asked Lady Hester. 'The one whose arms Nelson died in?'

'Yes indeed. He and Papa are such friends. Oh I am so happy! I think I shall eat some toast,' Camilla suddenly enthused.

CHAPTER THIRTY ONE

Putney Heath

They had an uncomfortable drive, the roads being waterlogged, but arrived safely just as the little light there had been, even on that gloomy day, was fading. Elizabeth's mother was particularly pleased to see them.

'What a Christmas we shall have,' she said. 'I only wish Camilla could stay, though I cannot wonder at her particularly wishing to be there to greet the conquering hero.'

A letter from Camilla's father was waiting for her, assuring her of his perfect health.

> *I asked that good fellow Hardy to write to Number 10, in case you were there and, could I but command the commander in chief, Collingwood, to try Cambridge and Codrington to write to Lincoln, I should be tolerably confident of reaching you. To describe the battle is beyond my power, though I will attempt it when we are reunited. "Noisy," is all I can say now. I long to clasp my beautiful daughters and derive much pleasure from thinking that I shall soon.*
>
> *Your devoted, dutiful father,*
>
> *Harry Meynell*

George and Richard arrived next day, hungry but happy, George having hired a chaise complete with driver. Ned didn't come until Christmas Eve, having spent some time at his friend Byron's Newstead Abbey. It sounded like a cross between a poetry factory and a menagerie.

Harry wrote again, this time to his mother-in-law, and from Portsmouth.

'Having seen but little of my wife's esteemed family recently owing to duty's call, I seize the opportunity to pay you a visit. Being a large party and knowing your house is full, we applied to the Reverend Mathers, who, being childless for the present, has kindly invited us all. From his rectory we hope to wait on you often in the future season, but Camilla and I will ride over and discuss what may be most convenient, about eleven o'clock, on the twentieth of December.'

Elizabeth's mother was delighted and excited by the news.

'I've never seen Arethusa since she was a babe,' she said.

'I suppose we may expect Perseus to fly in, too,' said Mr Maltby.

Mrs Potts was very pleased to have Nell back, and thanked Elizabeth fervently for bringing her. Harry and Camilla duly rode over, very happy in each other's company.

It was arranged that all five Meynells should come to dinner on Christmas Day. Fortunately, there was a moon so they could safely travel back in the dark. They all went to church on Christmas Day, except Mrs Maltby, and they all got very wet just going down the church path when they came out.

Emily was too plump now to wear Elizabeth's clothes and looked very matriarchal in the housekeeper's, which put her out of a temper.

Phineas was a tall, skinny, spotty fourteen-year old. He was at Eton now, but he and his cousins had avoided 'becoming acquainted,' although Emily had told him to 'make himself known to his cousins,' and Elizabeth had asked her sons to 'try and discover your cousin, I think he may be lonely.'

So now they all felt guilty and stared at one another glumly. George asked Phineas which house he was in, and a rather halting Etonian conversation followed.

Arethusa was a sharp-eyed, sharp-featured ten-year old. Her hair was corn coloured, as her mother's had been when she was young.

At dinner the Pretyman boys tried to get Harry to talk about Trafalgar but, at first, he was evasive.

'Was it so very bad?' asked Ned.

'A slaughter-house,' explained Harry.

'Were you very sorry for all the dead Spaniards?' asked Arethusa.

'Very. They fought so well. I had believed it a necessary evil to prevent the fleet escorting Bonaparte and his army over the Channel, but now I hear he had decamped before the battle. It was all for nothing,' Harry described.

'He might come back,' pointed out Arethusa.

'He certainly moves very fast,' said Mr Maltby, 'from a military academy to a royal palace in fifteen years.'

'Tell them about the ship you found!' Camilla ordered her father.

'Whacking great Spanish floating castle called the *Santìsima Trinidad,* dismasted and lurching about, like a log in a mill race, didn't seem to have anyone aboard. Union Jack over her side to show she'd struck. So up goes Bob Collett, our second Lieutenant, with a boarding party at his heels. All they found was one shivering Spaniard. All the rest had cleared off or been killed. Blackwood tried to tow her, as we weren't large enough, but her dead weight got too much in the storm that night, so he burnt her.'

'However much we may deplore the losses,' said George, 'it is apparent that we now have command of the sea, and must therefore be in a more secure and hopeful situation.'

'We just ignore Europe for a decade or two,' said Mr Maltby. 'Here be dragons! Trespassers will be prosecuted, but the world is our oyster.'

They thought this over.

'But is the rest of the world much use?' asked George. 'As allies, I mean, and for trade and so on?'

'Probably not,' said his grandfather cheerfully. 'Though India, of course, provides opportunities for cavalry to charge and skirmishers to skirmish. America shows signs of ever increasing prosperity but as they do not like us, it will not benefit us.'

'It is the great joy to me to have all my family about me,' said Mr Maltby, looking round at all the characterful middle-aged faces and all the rosy young faces.

'Well I am sure,' said Emily, 'I would have come sooner, if I could, but what can a lone woman do?'

'Go to parties,' suggested Camilla.

'When you are old and ill,' said Emily tragically, 'you will find your friends are the greatest consolation to you.'

:

On Boxing Day morning, the nurse, who now slept in Mrs Maltby's room, got up at seven as usual after a peaceful night to find her mistress was dead with a happy smile on her face.

George offered to tell Mr Maltby, but Elizabeth felt she should do it herself. She and her father had always understood each other. Mr Maltby was sitting up in bed, wearing a night cap, and reading from a small, leather volume.

'I am glad,' he said simply.

'You feel it was time?' Elizabeth asked.

'More than time. She had so much pain and the opium, even large doses, which worried the doctor, did not really answer anymore. I could wish, however, that she had lived for another se'nights. She was so relishing yours and Emily's visit.'

George and Elizabeth had intended to go back to Lincoln the next week, but now they stayed longer for the funeral. It passed off well. The entire neighbourhood came. They sang 'He Who Would Valiant Be', 'King of Glory, King of Peace,' and 'The Lord Is My Shepherd'. Harry seemed to be everywhere, cheering up everyone.

It was arranged that Mr Maltby should travel back to Lincoln with George and Elizabeth.

'I have long wished to see your palace,' said Mr Maltby. 'It sounded like a cross between a monastery and a nursery.'

'Hardly a nursery,' objected Ned. 'I'm quite grown up now, and even my brothers are older than that.'

'Hardly a monastery,' said George. 'The superstitious practices of the papists have been superseded in this realm of England by the combination of priestly vocation with family life.'

'And one of the results was Nelson,' said Elizabeth, smiling to herself. She always enjoyed her father's talent for annoying people.

'I shall enjoy conversing with your erudite friends the Andrews,' Mr Maltby told Elizabeth.

'Amabel is certainly my friend but I have never got close to her husband, though he is an excellent dean,' Elizabeth stated.

'My dear Elizabeth, I am amazed that you, who in general are skilled at reading characters, did not recognise a very shy man when you met one.'

:

News came that Napoleon had won another battle in a place called Austerlitz against the Austrians and Russians who fell into his trap. It sounded as if Sir Arthur Wellesley's reservations about the Tsar's generalship were justified.

They planned to set off for Lincoln on the fourteenth of January, 1806, taking Ned with them as far as Cambridge. Harry was to escort little George, Phineas, and Richard back to Eton. Camilla was quite happy to go to Portsmouth, as her father was there, and Elizabeth did not feel her school would teach her much more. But on the twelfth a letter arrived from Sir Walter Farquhar, Pitt's doctor, saying he was very ill and…

> *... all his friends are of the same opinion, with which I concur, that you alone can keep him quiet and content. The smallest exertion or excitement will hazard his life. I therefore desire you to come to Mr Pitt's house on Putney Heath with all convenient rapidity. Mr Canning informed me you were to be found at the house of your parents-in-law and gave me its direction. I need hardly say that Mr Pitt is in full agreement with our proposals.*
>
> *Your most humble obedient servant*
>
> *Walter Farquhar*

It was a shock for they had received a letter from Mr Pitt only last week, saying that 'the waters had not answered as well as the last occasion when I resorted to them, but none the less, I believe I am in the way of amendment'.

'You will accompany me, I trust, my love,' asked George.

'I think better not. You will have your hands full. If a woman is wanted Lady Hester will be there. My duty now is to my father and he requires a change of scene. We will take the Goodchilds and leave you Jennings and Papa's rickety, bumpy old coach,' Elizabeth suggested.

'The distance is not great but I shall find it dispiriting without you,' George stated.

'You will suffer from too much company and have to play guard dog,' Elizabeth said.

'Doubtless. But I am lost without my good humoured, infallible wife,' George replied.

'Harriot was used to calling Goodchild "the Infallible".'

Harry and Camilla walked in, having ridden over after breakfast, as they often did.

'Oh poor Mr Pitt!' exclaimed Camilla. 'He is so kind and funny.'

'He is a great man,' said Harry. 'We are fortunate as to have such servants of the state when we need them. I think it will be found that he has saved us at the cost of his own life.'

'You are in the right of it, but I am apprehensive we will be swallowed up in the void he leaves,' said George.

'Perhaps he may yet be saved,' said Elizabeth. 'People say Sir Walter Farquhar is a very good doctor.'

'They have their limits,' said Harry.

Elizabeth asked Goodchild if Tom wanted to stay with his wife.

'Lor' bless y', mum, ain't nothing he can do. You'll send us back for th' Bishop in no time. He'll be here again afore the babe come likely.'

When George arrived, he found Mr Pitt was a skeleton of himself. His eyes were dim and his voice hollow. He was cheerful, and delighted to see George, and even made jokes, but his voice grew hoarse after ten minutes, and faded to a whisper after quarter of an hour.

'I nearly fainted when I saw him,' Lady Hester told George at supper, 'with a stick and a man supporting him on each side. I ran away so he should not have to make the effort of greeting me and bowing.'

George became Mr Pitt's secretary once again, dealing with his correspondence, turning people away. It was very like old times. For some days, only Lord Chatham defeated him, marching in and starting to tell Pitt all about his new house in a loud voice. George tried to hustle him out. One of the doctors, Henry Reynolds, pointed out that Mr Pitt was very weak, and must not be exhausted, but Lord Chatham only said with complete conviction, 'Oh, he won't mind me.' It took Hester to tell him, 'Uncle. Go Away!' before he departed, lamenting the want of conduct to be found in young people nowadays.

Hester's half-brother, Charles, also appeared, but he behaved very differently. He made no attempt to bother his uncle but fetched and carried cheerfully.

On the thirteenth of January, the day being sunny, Pitt asked to go for a drive, and seemed to enjoy it, but later that day, the Lords Hawkesbury and Castlereagh appeared, determined to see Pitt. Sir Walter Farquhar had unfortunately gone away for a day to see another patient. Hester and George held out for a long time, but the Lordlings were so insistent that the lives of the British troops in Germany depended on it. Castlereagh produced a letter Pitt had written to him only a week before.

'I certainly feel a strong desire to see so valuable a body of troops at home but… by bringing them away now, I fear we shall hardly give a fair chance to the good disposition of Russia.'

It seemed it could not be decided without Pitt, and Hester at last agreed to ask him if he felt strong enough to see them. Of course, he said he did. Before they went, Canning appeared, also with urgent business.

The Lords wouldn't stay to dinner but Canning did.

'I think the change since Bath dreadful,' he told them.

'I know,' said Hester. 'It's all up with him, isn't it? I shall never be so happy again.' She pushed her plate away and ran from the room.

'She never will weep in front of anyone,' explained Charles, 'as if we should think the worse of her for it! If only she would let me comfort her a little, but no! I suppose she's too proud. We must endeavour to remember, I think, that no-one's irreplaceable. For Mr Pitt we grieve, but for the country I am inclined to be hopeful.'

'He has been the country these thirty years,' said Canning sombrely.

'Very true and therefore he has laid down good sound foundations for us to build upon,' remarked Charles.

'May we not lament,' said George, 'that there will never again be a Prime Minister so warm hearted, so modest, so entirely human.'

'We may,' agreed Charles, 'but never is a ridiculous word. I am persuaded there will be Prime Ministers of Great Britain with some of those good qualities.'

'But never, I think,' said Mr Canning, 'one in whom all those good qualities are united.'

That night, Pitt told George, putting his hand on his stomach, 'I feel something here that reminds me I never shall recover. Not cold but a general giving way.'

The next day, Sir Walter Farquhar returned, and Pitt confessed he had disobeyed Farquhar's orders and discussed some things.

'When in conversation with persons upon important business,' Mr Pitt told Farquhar, 'I felt suddenly as if I had been cut in two.'

Lord Wellesley visited Pitt that day and sat with him for a quarter of an hour, as advised, talking about old times. As George showed him out, Lord Wellesley said, 'Notwithstanding Mr Pitt's kindness and cheerfulness, I see the hand of death is fixed upon him.'

The ministers feared that they could not carry on the government without Pitt, but no one wanted to discuss it, least of all with Pitt. James Stanhope appeared, to join his brothers and half-sister. At first, George thought him just a paler copy of his brother Charles, but before long he discovered James was a good classical scholar and after that they got on very well.

James and Hester Stanhope, coming back from a short walk on January the nineteenth, found Mr Rose in tears at the end of their road. He said through his sobs, 'I fear there is danger.'

They comforted him as best they could, which was not very well.

That night Mr Pitt ate two soft boiled eggs and kept them down, which made Sir Walter Farquhar a little more hopeful. On Sir Walter's instructions George kept everyone out of Mr Pitt's room, except the Stanhopes.

On the day of the twenty-second of January George felt he should warn Mr Pitt that he was dying. Hester disagreed but Charles said, 'He knows, I think.'

He certainly appeared to be unmoved and merely asked Farquhar, 'How long do you think I might hold out?'

'It may be still possible that you will recover, sir,' said Farquhar.

As George wrote to Elizabeth that night, 'Mr Pitt received this with a half-smile that showed he entertained no such hopes'.

George then offered Mr Pitt communion, but he refused, saying he felt too weak. He agreed, however, to pray with George, only saying first that he had neglected prayer too long to allow him to hope it could be very effective now. He wanted to write a new will, but found he was too weak, so he dictated it to George. Knowing he had little to leave, Pitt said, 'The public may be kind enough to think of me. I have not earned it, I do not mean that – but perhaps in their generosity they may do something.'

He left a thousand guineas to Sir Walter Farquhar, twelve thousand pounds to the people who had subscribed for him in 1801, asked for pensions to be given to his nieces and nephews, and left his papers to his elder brother and to George. Later that evening he said to George, 'I must thank you for your unfailing kindness to me.'

'The obligation is mostly on my behalf,' replied George. 'No man ever had a better, more generous, friend and patron.'

'Well, well. You were the only man who could follow my flights of fancy. Remember me to Elizabeth. It is generous indeed in her to loan you to me so soon after her mother's death.'

Pitt said a warm goodbye to Hester but when she left twice said, 'Where's Hester?' and once, 'Is Hester gone?'

Farquhar gave him some champagne which hurt him as he swallowed it. The Doctor apologised. 'I am truly sorry. I should have known. I hope you will not take it unkind.'

Pitt said, 'I never take anything unkind that is meant for my good.'

:

Later that night, he began to rave, but it was all about England. Sometimes he thought he was in the House of Commons and said, 'Hear! Hear!' and at other times thought he was speaking to a messenger.

He asked about a letter from Lord Harrowby, who was the envoy in Berlin. He asked where the wind was and when he was told exclaimed, 'East! Ah that will do. That will bring him quick.' He moaned a bit and muttered things they could not hear.

'He is dying of old age at forty-six as much as if he had been ninety,' said Farquhar.

'He has worn himself out in the service of his country,' agreed George.

'I do not think he is conscious now or that he will speak again,' Farquhar muttered.

James came in quickly at about half past one in the morning. George was holding Williams Pitt's hand.

Suddenly Pitt spoke, clearly, and urgently, 'Oh my country! How I leave my country!'

Lightning Source UK Ltd.
Milton Keynes UK
UKHW02f1119210118
316557UK00008B/163/P

9 781326 413859